4

SAINTS AND SINNERS

Book Four ~ Darcy and Fitzwilliam

KAREN V. WASYLOWSKI

SAINTS AND SINNERS
DARCY AND FITZWILLIAM, BOOK 4

Printed in the USA.

Cover Design and Interior Format
© The Killion Group Inc.

BOOK LIST

Pride and Prejudice
By Jane Austen

Darcy and Fitzwilliam, Book One
The Pride and Prejudice Family Saga

Sons and Daughters, Book Two
The Pride and Prejudice Family Saga

Wives and Lovers, Book Three
The Pride and Prejudice Family Saga

Saints and Sinners, Book Four
The Pride and Prejudice Family Saga

By Karen V. Wasylowski

All books can be read stand-alone or as a series
Available in both ebook and print form on…
Amazon, Nook, And other sites

For my wonderful husband, Richard
The Saint to my Sinner

"Every Saint has a Past;
And, every Sinner a Future"

~ Oscar Wilde

CHAPTER ONE

1861

LORD RICHARD FITZWILLIAM WAS RESTING near the fireside at his favorite Gentlemen's Club, Brooks, awaiting both tea and the arrival of his cousin Fitzwilliam Darcy, when the muffled bells of St. Paul's Cathedral began to toll. Again. It was a solemn place this cold morning, the men around him uncharacteristically subdued – men he'd supported and opposed in Parliament, men with whom he'd fought, laughed, and worked his entire life. Servants wearing black armbands shuffled around silently, covering mirrors in black cloth, stopping clocks.

Bong. Bong. Bong. He moaned, his hand going up to his throbbing forehead – those damn bells had been clanging for hours. He hadn't heard such a commotion… well, for years. *Not since Princess Charlotte's death in '17.*

Or was it in '23?

Or, was her name Caroline?

Oh, the hell with it.

It was the 15th of December,1861 and His Royal Highness, Prince Albert of Saxe-Coburg and Gotha (Francis Albert Augustus Charles Emmanuel, 26 August 1819 – 14 December 1861), husband and consort of Queen Victoria, was dead.

Puffing on his forbidden pipe, Fitzwilliam stared deeply into the fire. *Well, there you have it. The longer I live the more I realize there is neither rhyme nor reason to life, or death. A man such as Albert – a man given to measured, thoughtful behavior – is gone at forty-two, while I continue to drink, smoke and eat like a newly released galley slave.* Experiencing a sudden and unwelcome swell of emotion, he swiped away a stray tear and cursed the sentimentality that had possessed his *golden* years.

Golden. Ha! That's rich. If these are Golden Years where is my Amanda – taken from me so young? It's damned unfair, I tell you. If only I could see her beautiful, innocent, perfect face once again I'd give her *a tongue lashing for dying on me she'd not soon forget.*

At a nearby table a man sneezed violently and woke himself. "What... what in heaven's name was that fearful noise?" He looked anxiously about the room. "What's happened now?"

"Ghastly business. Someone sent back the turtle soup and Chef killed himself. Yes. Bullet right between the eyes. Awful mess I hear. Eyeball plopped smack into the souffle."

"*My God,* that *is* dreadful! Who'll do afternoon tea now?"

"Prepared it just before he done himself in – a matter of honor, you see."

"Thank heaven for that."

"Pity it woke you from your nap though, Bagshawe."

"No, no, no, no, no. I never nap. In fact, I am of the view that excessive rest is bad for one, Fitzwilliam. Yes. Always best, I say, to keep oneself active physically as well as mentally, encourages a dynamic mind, and..." The man was snoring before his sentence ended.

"Sweet dreams." Fitzwilliam checked his pocket watch for the third time. Darcy would be arriving soon, more than likely finishing up his daily five-mile walk. That couldn't be healthy for someone of their age, could it? It was all Fitzwilliam could do to sit upright at the edge of his bed and piss into a chamber pot when he awoke, let alone walk upright.

Seeing Bagshawe begin to slump Fitz leaned over to straighten his snoring neighbor. The fellow's head hit the table anyway. "Oops. Sorry. Can't say I didn't try. Think I like you better this way, Lionel; at least your snoring's stopped."

What's that? Why am I here you ask? Well, here's the thing. I'm waiting for my cousin, Fitzwilliam Darcy. Excellent fellow – when he isn't preaching at me the way he does, on and on, all the time, 'Why so negative, Richard? You yourself can choose how you feel each day, either joy or sadness, Richard. Try and see the bright side of things, Richard.' Bollocks, to that. All I know is a good man has died, a family has lost its father, and my country has lost its head of state. Although… mourning will probably cancel Christmas festivities this year as well. Hmm. Perhaps there really is a bright side to everything. "Hate to mention it, Bagshawe, but you're beginning to drool a bit."

Truth was, the family feared Fitzwilliam was becoming something of a recluse in his old age. Lonely. Remote. It was even suggested that perhaps he find an unsuspecting widow and remarry; that without feminine companionship he was becoming a grumpy old soul. Well, grumpier than usual.

Rubbish. I'm no grumpier than I was before, and I will beat to death anyone who claims otherwise. Wait, that doesn't sound right. Besides, who could ever consider him lonely? He was bossed about by eleven interfering young people – his own offspring plus the three children of his cousin – and, add to that bothersome mix all those wild grandchildren underfoot. No, he'd grant them he might be irritable at times, even a bit short-tempered (obviously with good reason) but, *never* lonely. In fact, there was no room left for another person in his life. Not one more living soul.

Unless.

Unless he could convince his sons – (*even the priest at this point*) – to present him with a male heir for the family title. By God, that would be one little hellion he'd welcome in a heartbeat…

From out of nowhere a cane smacked his knee. "Ow! Who in hell – Oh, I should have known it was you, Darcy. You've nearly broken my leg!"

"Stuff and nonsense. If your leg could survive a horse falling on it at Waterloo I'm certain it can survive a walking stick."

"I had different legs back then."

"No, they just weren't so fat back then. You've grown soft, admit it. Or don't. Good heavens, look at that face. Should I ask how we are today, Fitz?"

"We are shite, Darcy. And would you please stop smiling."

"I will cease smiling if you cease scowling." Darcy smoothed the jacket of his dark blue *three-piece suit* (the latest in fashion) as he sat, then brushed off his 'creased' trousers (another fashion first). "Your facial expressions will spoil my appetite. Medusa presented a more pleasant aspect."

"Hell to be you then. What are you wearing? You look like a street performer."

"My new suit." He motioned for the waiter to bring him coffee. "Are we done with the clever banter? Good. Because, I have news concerning my daughter, Anne Marie, and her husband, Jamie, and your son, Andrew. The Duke of Sutherland and I met this morning during my walk in the park."

"Never tell me. It *is* war then." Fitzwilliam's blood ran cold at the thought. His son, Andrew, newly appointed Captain of the HMS Orontes in the Royal Navy, was already sailing to Canada due to a threat of imminent war with America.

Tensions had begun in November with the capture by an American naval vessel – the San Jacinto – of a British mail ship that had given passage to a Confederate delegation crossing the Atlantic in search of European support for their side in the war between the states. To the British this seizure of their ship in open waters was a clear violation of international law. And, as luck would have it, Anne Marie and Jamie Durand, Darcy's daughter and her husband, had been visiting relatives in Canada when all transatlantic traffic came to a halt.

"What? No, calm yourself, let me explain. It seems war has been averted. You know that Prince Albert, God rest his soul, had stepped into the negotiations two weeks ago? Well, evidently that action helped turn the tide as they say; his words effectively calming the rhetoric and diffusing the more volatile anger. Sutherland *claims* to have no idea how Palmerston's angry missive meant for the Americans made its way to the Prince first–"

"Good to hear. Darcy, are you having coffee?"

"Fitzwilliam, do you ever hear me out until the end?"

"Yes… sometimes; but, the truth of it is you do go on and on about things and at my age it is sometimes difficult to stay awake throughout. I don't suppose you could just come to the point?"

"Oh, all right. His intervention has been successful. Prince Albert I mean. Sutherland has been assured by the War Office that the worst of the tension is over, and hopefully the blockade is to be lifted soon. My daughter can return home by late January, her children will be over the moon, and Elizabeth and I can have our quiet life returned. Most importantly, your son will not be sailing into war."

"Thank heavens for that. God bless Prince Albert. To think he was so ill during it all and none of us knew."

"Yes. I wonder how many realize what a great loss his passing will be to our country. He was Her Majesty's rock, her strength. She depended upon him for everything, both in their private life and with affairs of state."

"Selfish of me to say this, I know, but I pray Albert's passing will not rescind the truce."

"No, it won't, I'm certain of it. Mr. Lincoln was heard to comment the Americans should fight only one war at a time; and, at present, they're fully occupied."

"A quarrelsome lot, those people – I know, I married one."

"And the luckiest thing that ever happened to you."

"I agree completely. Well, with everyone flooding back into the city for one reason or the other this year you certainly won't be having the big family Christmas in Derbyshire. Such a pity."

"Then why are you grinning?"

"Stomach gas probably."

"Sorry to disappoint but Christmas is my favorite time of year to be with the people I love most in the world, my wife, our children, our grandchildren, your children and grandchildren, our sisters, our nieces and nephews. Even you. We shall merely celebrate on a smaller scale, here in town. The place where we gather doesn't matter, it's the joy of being together that counts."

"Charming. Let me know how you all get on."

"Oh no. Not this year, Fitz. England has lost its Prince, we have been precipitously close to war again with America, my daughter is halfway around the world, her children in my home crying themselves to sleep each night from worry, and your son is commanding a battleship sailing into enemy waters. You are going to celebrate the birth of our Lord Jesus Christ this year or I'll beat you senseless."

Fitzwilliam grunted over the bowl of his pipe. "Well, when you sweet talk me like that, how can I refuse?"

CHAPTER TWO

BY THE THIRD DAY AFTER Prince Albert's passing every mirror and lamp in the nation had been covered, blinds drawn, the city silent. Mourning black was everywhere – ribbons, wreaths, iron fences, doors, even the shining brass plates outside homes were shrouded. Omnibus drivers tied scraps of crepe to their whips.

Seemingly overnight there had emerged a public demand for mugs, plates, cartouches – anything and everything as long as it was emblazoned with Albert's image. Photographic *carte-de-visites* of the Prince – 70,000 in all – were sold within a week of his death.

Then, of course, there was mourning fashion to purchase, *de rigueur* among the socially minded, as well as for their entire household staff. Aristocrats insisted upon being seen dressed in the most elegant costumes created by English couturier, Charles Frederick Worth, from the new world of 'fashion design'.

Special material for these fashions was insisted upon as well – a lucrative bit of snobbery for Jay's London General Mourning Warehouse in Oxford Circus.

And, although Darcy and Fitzwilliam profited tremendously from investments in the textile mills producing those materials, owned jointly by Darcy son-in-law Jamie Durand and his brother Alex, he would gladly give up all those profits – all he had in the world in fact – to have his beloved daughter, Anne Marie, returned safely to him; and, more importantly, to her worried children.

Lost in these thoughts during his morning stroll he failed to notice how the snow flurries were increasing or that the temperature was dropping – it was fast becoming the coldest December in years – or, that a strange carriage was parked on the street before his home.

Darcy's groom saw his master approach and tipped his hat in greeting. "G'day to ye, sir."

"Jeffers, didn't see you. Good day to you as well."

Shoulders hunched against the wind Jeffers hurried forward to open the large iron front gate, freshly painted in black. "Looks like we're in fer it, sir."

"Good heavens, it really is shaping up to be quite a storm, isn't it? You must be freezing, man. Why aren't you inside with a hot chocolate?"

"Didn't want t'leave this fellow alone out 'ere, sir. 'ired cabby. Poor lad's been waitin' for them what's inside 'bout an hour now."

"Oh, I see. Well, this won't do; shelter the cattle in our stable while I see who's visiting. You can take the driver downstairs as well, get you both something warm to eat and drink from cook."

"Thank 'e, sir. That I will, sir."

Who could have shown up now? People Darcy hadn't seen in years were returning to the city either to attend upcoming memorials planned for Prince Albert, or they were concerned by Parliament's threats of war with America. London would certainly be crowded this Christmas holiday; however, there would be no large parties, no private balls, no concerts… so, why were they all gravitating to his house?

Before he even reached the door, the under-butler had it open and Darcy hurried inside. "Ah, thank goodness for the ever-vigilant Brendan."

"Good afternoon, sir." It was not until he spoke that Darcy noticed his aged head butler, Winters, was sitting in the foyer as well. "Sorry that I cannot stand at the moment, sir. No disrespect meant."

Darcy handed his coat, hat and gloves to a footman. "Don't be ridiculous. Winters, what am I going to do with you? Now, listen to me, it is beyond time you allow me to contact a physician about your knees. I know you're not overly fond of the medical profession – no one is – but, they do have their occasional uses."

"I thought we'd give it another week or so, Mr. Darcy, if you do not mind. Perhaps once the damp weather clears?"

"He can barely stand at all, sir."

The under-butler's unsolicited comment was met with a glare from Winters. "That is quite enough from you, child."

"Yes, father – I mean Mr. Winters."

Darcy tried to keep the smile from his face. The 'child' was fifty years old, the father well into his eighties.

"Tell Mr. Darcy about the visitors, boy."

"I was about to…" Brendan closed his eyes in exasperation before he spoke. "Mr. Darcy, you have visitors."

"Yes, I gathered as much when I saw the hired cab out front. If I remember, Mrs. Darcy said something about one of the Welsh Bennet's arriving in town this week, though I don't recall which." At the far end of the hall the door of the drawing room opened and Mrs. Darcy herself peeked out. Even after so many years the sight of her sent a warm thrill through him. Lizzy was his joy. "And, there she is."

With her brightest hostess smile in place she turned to whisper something to whomever was in the room behind her then closed the door. Immediately, her smile vanished; she nearly ran down the hallway to greet him.

"Elizabeth, whatever is the matter?"

"Thank goodness you're here, you will not believe what's happened." She cupped his cheek with her hand. "Heavens, you look dreadful."

"Good to see you too." His initial warmth at seeing her was paling a bit.

"You have dark circles beneath your eyes and are trying to hide them by wearing your spectacles. It is probably because you tossed and turned all night." She lowered her voice to a whisper. "It was like sleeping with a sack full of hedgehogs."

"And, how precisely would you know the feeling of sleeping with hedgehogs, Mrs. Darcy?"

"All those meetings at the War Office, meetings with lawyers, meetings with bankers… you know you work too much."

"And, you know you worry *too much*." To avoid prolonging this on-going discussion regarding his work habits he took her hands in his and kissed them. They were the happiest of couples, lovers and best friends – had been from the first moment they met. Well, to be honest, initially *she* had thought him too proud by far while *he* had experienced unwelcomed lust for a country girl socially far beneath him, and therefore unacceptable. What an idiot he'd been, wasting a single moment away from her for her family's want of a 'proper connection.' Elizabeth Bennet was his one true love; always was, always would be. She had blessed him with three beautiful children and had brought with her the most contented years of his life. Wherever she was, was his home.

Even if she could be aggravating as hell at times.

"You need a proper tea, I shall send downstairs for it straight away. Oh, no, that won't do either. Oh, William! Your note promised you and Richard would be busy all day. You should leave."

"You can be a very confusing woman at times." Darcy rested his fists at his waist. "Did you not just say…? Never mind; I thought you'd want to know about the news from America as soon as possible. Of course, it seems you'd prefer I go."

"Stop! Don't you dare leave now. It is war then. Oh, my poor little girl."

She was so worried about their daughter, so frantic, that he immediately forgot his pique and pulled her into his arms. "No, no, no. Calm yourself, dear. From what I've learned there certainly will be no war and I have been assured we shall be contacted as soon as the sea lanes are open again… unless something unforeseen weighs down the negotiations… which you know is always possible. After all, England *is* still outfitting ships for the Confederacy, although we claim neutrality in America's, ah, conflict – forget I said that out loud. Why, there is every indication Prince Albert's involvement defused the tensions completely! I sincerely doubt there is any cause for alarm… although the Prince's death *may* delay things a bit..."

"William, it is exceedingly bothersome that you attach loopholes onto the end of every assurance. Now, how long is a *bit*?"

"Perhaps till the end of January."

"End of the January! Are they mad? It could be very dangerous to cross the Atlantic if they wait that long! Oh no, no, no! Let me speak with these fools. I'll tell them a thing or two. Yes, all right, I know I'm being *unreasonable* – but, when was a mother ever *reasonable* about her child?"

"Well, certainly not often if you're the norm."

Lizzy's eyes sparkled with love for this man. He was the handsomest in all London – in all the world perhaps – at least to her he was. "Beast. You're little better."

"Absolutely." Darcy nodded in full agreement. "Sutherland promised to contact me the moment he learns the blockade is lifted." *Or not lifted*, he added to himself – better not give voice to another loophole…

"What is it?" She stared at him so intently then that he wondered if she really could read his mind as she sometime claimed. It was unnerving. Marriage, at times, was an exhausting dance.

"Listen to me. America has no more desire than we do for war, Lizzy. They want to end this, and for very practical reasons. They're already at war among themselves. Apologies have been given and accepted; now Westminster merely awaits news of the Trent's return. It's nearly over, sweet. Be patient."

"William, I am the very soul of patience; and, may I remind you it is still considered rude to laugh at your wife."

"Sorry."

"They should mandate mothers and grandmothers govern countries. None of this dawdling would take place, and all children, young and old, would be safer."

"But then none of the nations would be speaking with each other."

"That's a terrible thing to say, especially since it's probably true." Laughing, she kissed his cheek." Did you hear anything of Her Majesty? How is she?"

"Inconsolable. Someone quoted her as saying, 'this is like the flesh being torn from my bones'. Poor, poor woman; and, already rivals are jockeying for power. I only hope someone steps up and takes command soon."

"What of the Prince of Wales?"

"He's not his father, that's for certain. He's not even his mother."

"Somehow this is not helping my nerves, William."

"Sorry. I trust all will pass in time."

"You always say that."

"And, it's never failed. Who are our visitors?"

"Good heavens! I nearly forgot about them." She clutched his arm. "William, I am terribly sorry about this, however you really do need to leave."

"What? Don't be ridiculous. Wait. Good god, it's not Lydia and that new husband of hers, is it?"

"No, they aren't expected until the Spring – unless I can find a suitable excuse to avoid them. Actually..." She glanced over one of her shoulders then the other. "It is Sir Alex Durand. Yes. He was concerned over Anne Marie and Jamie's situation."

"Perfectly understandable. I did write him though. I suppose – wait, why are we out here whispering?" Darcy began to head for the drawing room. "Let me speak with the poor fellow. He must be worried sick to have come all this way."

"Not so fast, sir." Lizzy clutched at his arm. "I wasn't finished. *They* are in there."

"*They?* Who are *they?*"

Lizzy glanced again side to side.

"Lizzy, for heaven's sake just tell me and be done with it."

She leaned in. "*Bridget* is also here. And someone else as well – *their son*."

"Oh. Well, I suppose it may be awkward with Bridget at first, since she was in our employ years ago. Lizzy, surely you aren't still peeved at her for running off with Alex? By the way, did we know they have a child?"

Sir Alex's wife, Bridget, had been nursemaid to the Darcy's granddaughter, Roberta, (now staying in their home while her mother, Darcy's daughter Anne Marie, was being detained in Canada) when she suddenly left their employ and married Sir Alex Durand, the brother of Anne Marie's husband Jamie Durand, changing the former servant relationship into what was now that of sisters-in-law.

It was complicated.

"Yes, we knew they had a child. You sent them a lovely gift."

"How thoughtful of me. Has Anne Marie ever mentioned him?"

"*She's never met him,*" Lizzy added with meaning. "You know very well Anne Marie felt uncomfortable visiting Sir Alex and Bridget at the family estate in Scotland because of her former relationship with Bridget. She felt badly at first, concerned that it might cause a strain between the brothers; but, it never did really. Whenever Jamie would visit Scotland he'd go on his own or with Roberta while Anne Marie remained behind with the other children. And, of course, whenever Alex would come to London for your yearly meetings, he was alone."

"Amazing fellow with what he's been through. How is he?"

Lizzy sighed. "He's aged a great deal since he lost his leg, William." She swallowed around the anxious lump forming in her throat before she went on. "One other thing, William – now, please don't argue with me – they're staying at Claridge's while they're in the city."

"Utter nonsense! Surely you've asked them to remain with us."

"Oh, I was afraid you'd say that, and please, William, *do not offer*. They've taken perfectly suitable rooms with Mr. Claridge; and, under the circumstances, I think it best they remain there. Now, go away."

Darcy was stunned by his wife's comment. After all, Sir Alex Durand was family, or near enough. It would be beyond ill-mannered to not ask them to stay.

"What possible reason could there be for them to remain at a public inn? No, that would be unpardonably rude. I've always liked and admired Sir Alex, his brother is married to our daughter! Besides, he's a business partner of mine as well. Whatever has gotten into you, Lizzy? This isn't like you."

His wife wasn't even listening to him. "Sorry, dearest, what did you say? Was that someone on the front steps? No? Thank heavens, must be the wind. Now listen. I have performed all the niceties, expressed your regrets and told them we will visit them tomorrow. We mustn't delay them, they are about to leave – don't spoil it!"

"Give me one good reason, Mrs. Darcy."

"For what, dear?"

"For their remaining at the Claridge's! I am not in the habit of insulting friends or family by not offering them the comfort of my home. Explain."

"Mr. Darcy, it is not something I care to discuss in public."

"We are not 'in public' though; we are alone in our own home."

Lizzy glanced about at the two butlers nearby, the three footmen… was he serious? "Oh, I do wish you'd listen. Trust me when I say this is neither the time nor the place to explain. It really is best for all concerned that they leave this house as soon as possible. Besides, Matthew and the girls may be returning any minute with this storm brewing."

"Matthew is with the girls? That's very kind of him, Roberta's been so lonely without her mother, and she and Amanda have

such a special friendship… however, I don't see at all what that has to do with the Durand's."

"You will. Matthew and the girls left for the park over an hour ago. To skate. To practice. To practice skating. However, as I said, they may return early with this weather. Why are you staring at me like that? You know all the children are taking lessons."

"I repeat. What has that to do with Sir Alex?"

"Would you just leave?"

"Elizabeth, step away from the door."

"*Please* do not go in there! There isn't time. Oh, dear. Well, I tried to warn you."

"Warn me of what? You make no sense at all."

"Truly? I will in a moment." Her arms crossed in front of her, Lizzy tapped her foot impatiently as her husband reached for the doorknob. She was obviously aggravated, but the Darcy family had long-standing values that were sacred.

"Mrs. Darcy, after all these years I thought you understood me, felt as I do. Family always comes first. Sir Alex and Bridget – despite the fact that at one time she was a nursemaid in our home – are family."

"Mr. Darcy! I like to think I'm not such a snob as all that."

"Nevertheless, I will be offering them our hospitality during their stay, or until Sir Alex secures a permanent residence for them when Commons sits in spring; and, there is nothing you may say that will change my mind. Are we clear on this subject? Have you anything to add?"

"Only that you are a horrible beast, and I tried to warn you."

"Honestly, Elizabeth," Darcy huffed. "There are times when you sorely try my patience!"

He understood her reasoning within moments.

CHAPTER THREE

"PAPA?"

Matthew Fitzwilliam glanced down at the adorable child holding his hand, his beloved daughter, her cheeks rosy from the chill, her eyes bright with joy. He wasn't biased in the slightest – however, Amanda Rose was *the* most beautiful, *the* most loving, *the* most brilliant child ever born. "What is it, my darling?"

Perhaps he was somewhat biased.

"Don't you just adore skating?"

"Only when I'm with you and the little mischief maker over here."

Roberta, the child grasping his other hand, tried to look offended but broke into giggles instead, causing her to suddenly slip and slide on the ice. "Oopsie."

Matthew steadied her quick enough.

"Careful there. Are you all right?" He loved his cousin Anne Marie's daughter nearly as well as his own. A delightful hoyden, she charmed everyone she met, and the weeks during which her mother and stepfather had been away had shown her strength of character as well... comforting her brother and sister, calming her grandparents. She was an amazing little girl.

"Please don't fuss over me, Cousin Matthew. It's terribly embarrassing. Someone might see." She could also be proud as a peacock at times.

"Forgive me, your Grace. However, hundreds of pounds have been invested into your education, and you still say 'Oopsie.' And here Beacon told your step-father you were the most brilliant child in the whole world."

"Miss Bitsy said that? Did she really?" Roberta's eyes were wide with shock. "Well, that was extremely kind of her. Such a pity she had to be let go, I was truly fond of her. She could swing upside down on a trapeze, did you know that?"

"I did not. An admirable quality for any nanny."

"Absolutely. And she brought me the very best of the chocolates and cakes when Mummy and Papa weren't looking, although, um, perhaps that's a secret best kept between ourselves."

"I have absolutely no idea to what you refer."

"You are the best, Cousin Matthew. Thank you. I wouldn't want her to have any more trouble because of me."

"Birdy, whatever do you mean? It wasn't *your* fault Bitsy was let go." Amanda called Roberta by her babyhood alias, Birdy, as did most of the other children. "How were you to know the neighbor's coachman was in her room? You only ran in there to save her."

"I suppose, though I still feel awfully bad. It's just that the way she was screaming I thought something dreadful was happening to her."

"Yes, ahem, well, ladies, perhaps we shouldn't dwell on that. Your grandfather will explain it all to your mother and father when they return."

Yet, Birdy continued on. "He was very fat. And very hairy."

"Why don't we speak of something else?"

"He actually shook the house when he fell out of the bed, then he tripped over his boots. I wonder what…"

"Roberta, where are your spectacles?" Matthew needed to change the subject before the awkward questions began.

"Oh pish. I only use them for reading."

"You know you're to wear them all the time."

"Not all the time, surely."

"Yes, young woman. All the time!"

"Well, that's just silly. Grandpa only wears his when he's tired. Besides, 'all the time' infers nighttime as well. Who wears spectacles to bed?"

"There are the other activities than sleeping..."

"Yes, I realized that when that coachman ran down the stairs wearing only his smalls."

"Roberta! I meant other nighttime activities when you should be wearing your spectacles!"

"Well, I know that *now*! Why, I could hardly see anything at all in that bedroom."

"Why is your face turning all red, Papa?"

"It's the cold. I must be cold. Heavens, I cannot wait for Anne Marie to return," he mumbled.

Already bored with the subject, Roberta tugged on his hand with another question. "Cousin Matthew, do you think Mama and Papa shall be able to ice skate in Canada? I mean, do they have ponds and lakes there?"

"Yes, of course they do. They even have cities and homes and families and schools."

"I am glad. I thought they just had polar bears and forests. Oh!" Leaning forward, she whispered around Matthew to Amanda, losing her footing again slightly with the maneuver. "Mandy! Do show Cousin Matthew what you've been practicing." Matthew's pride and joy, Amanda Rose Fitzwilliam, was Birdy's best friend in all the world, even if Amanda was an *entire* year younger. "She skates brilliantly, Cousin Matthew! Absolutely first-rate."

"What's this?"

"Shush. Birdy, I'm not that comfortable with 'it' yet." Still, as she spoke her father could tell she was eager to show off her new skill. All she needed was a little encouragement, and Birdy was nothing if not her shyer cousin's greatest champion.

"Give it a go, Mandy! You know you're absolutely the finest skater in the class. She really is, Cousin Matthew."

"Then I insist on seeing whatever 'it' is, daughter."

"Well, all right, if you *insist*. Watch me, Papa. Are you watching?"

"Absolutely."

Hesitating only a moment to take a nervous breath, Amanda pushed off, turned around and then began to skate backward for several feet.

"Splendid." Matthew clapped politely. "Bravo, darling."

"No, no!" Exasperated, Roberta rolled her eyes. "That's not 'it'! Even I can do that, and I'm hopeless. Mandy go on!"

Gaining confidence, along with speed, Amanda suddenly executed a very graceful little hop and then a spin in mid-air, only wobbling slightly on her landing. Beaming with success she brushed away the few strands of hair that had come loose from her bonnet, before looking up to see her father's utter amazement – and with that, as with any child, all was perfect in her world.

"Well?" Breathless, she was eager for his praise. "How was I?"

"That was wonderful! Brilliant! I am speechless!" Immediately, she rushed into her father's arms nearly toppling him over.

Roberta applauded wildly. "You were spectacularly spectacular, Mandy, brilliantly brilliant – *oops!*" As her feet slipped out from under her she grabbed for Matthew's arm. "My, oh, my, oh criminy, oopsie times… *No, oh no! (oof)*" She landed right on her bottom.

"Roberta!" Matthew set Amanda down quickly and crouched next to the fallen child. "Don't move, Roberta. Are you all right?"

"Yes, of course I'm all right." Holding onto his shoulders she slowly righted herself. "I asked you not to make such a fuss, Cousin Matt, please. Mandy, you don't think Billy saw me, do you?"

"No. I shouldn't think so."

With his hands on his knees Matthew stared up at his two little girls and began to wonder what was going on.

"I shall die if he saw me. I shall whither and scream. Cousin Matthew stand up, so I can hide behind you."

"What are you both talking about? Who is Billy, and should I be worried? Amanda? Roberta? Hello?"

"Nonsense, Birdy! I told you they wouldn't be here this early in the morning."

"And of whom are we speaking, ladies?" Matthew's paternal instincts were on full alert now.

"Thank heavens my skirt didn't fly over my head as it did last Friday – I would never be able to look Billy in the face. Oh, that sounded funny, didn't it?"

"Now you're being silly. All they saw then was a bit of your ankle, and perhaps some underskirt – Birdy, stop squealing. He's not here."

"Ladies!" demanded Matthew. "Who is Billy!"

Amanda looked up at her father, surprised by his frustrated tone. "Why, Mr. Ayers, Papa." She was helping to straighten Birdie's bonnet.

"Mr. Ayers? Mr. Ayers, your skating instructor? That Mr. Ayers? Since when do you refer to a teacher, a grown gentleman, by his Christian name?" *Bloody hell!*

"We never do, of course – not to his face, at any rate. Only behind his back when we speak with the boys, because that is what they call him. Bill Ayers is the fastest skater in all England. Everyone knows that. There, Birdie, you look splendid once again. You have the most beautiful hair."

"Thank you." Birdie took a deep breath. "I was so hoping we'd see them, but now I'm glad we're too early. Just two days ago he was praising my improvement, remember? I would just hate to disappoint him."

"You could never disappoint him, Birdy. You know you're his favorite."

"All right, that does it. Good heavens. I don't believe this."

Amanda Rose brushed snow from Birdie's bottom as her father's grin turned into a chuckle. "Believe what, Papa?"

Now he could really tease them. "This Mr. Ayers of yours – I suppose he's very young and extremely handsome. Are my two little ones smitten?"

Roberta wrinkled her nose. "With Mr. Ayers? Why would we be? Cousin Matthew, he's very old. Nearly thirty."

"Just a minute! I am thirty-nine."

"Really, Papa?" Amanda patted his arm sympathetically. She looked concerned. "Do you need to sit? You look tired. Doesn't he look tired, Birdy?"

"Amanda Rose Fitzwilliam, I'm not *that* old... oh, never mind. Well, what is his great attraction for you then? I wondered at your sudden interest in skating lessons, since you never mentioned skating before this month."

"Well, Papa," His daughter spoke to him slowly, and it seemed a bit louder than normal now. "For one thing, before this month it wasn't cold enough to skate. It seemed to take forever to get cold this year, remember? We needed to wait for the lake to freeze."

"I have a vague comprehension of the effect of extremely cold weather on water, but thank you for your patience with me, Amanda. Now what is the real reason?"

"Well."

"Well?"

"Well... there are a few boys of our acquaintance who play for the St. James Bandy Club under Mr. Ayers's supervision and training. He was a rather well-known player on the Bury Fen Bandy Club, or something like that, and the boys seem to think him rather amazing. They admire him a great deal."

"So, you're taking these lessons because of boys."

Roberta sighed. Old people were so slow to grasp new ideas. "Of course we are. Lord Fletcher's son, Bradley, belongs to St. James Club, and he's lovely. Bradley, I mean – not Lord Fletcher. He looks like a radish."

"Bradley is quite taken with Birdy, Papa."

"And his friend, Jeffrey Higgins, is mad for Amanda!"

"Oh, he is not, Birdy."

"He ate that awful dead bug on a dare just to impress you, don't deny it."

Matthew stared at them in numbing horror – this could not be happening to his little girls. Was it possible they were old enough to notice boys when they were little more than babies themselves? Why this rush to grow up? There were so few years to the innocence of childhood, why not enjoy them?

There were times he wished he could return to his youth, when his father was untitled and his mother alive; they were poor and happy, all the cousins playing until they fell exhausted on the ground to watch the clouds and dream. He'd had no problems then, no responsibilities, no disappointments…

The smack of heavy snowflakes on his face brought Matthew back to the present. The sky had turned ominously grey. "It looks as if we're in for it, ladies. I'm afraid we'll need to cut short our excursion."

"I wouldn't throw a fuss if we did, Papa; I'm hungry."

"Ooh, yes!" Birdy nodded. "I am as well. Let's hurry back to grandpa's house for cake and hot chocolate, or perhaps those lovely little ham pastries with melted cheese."

"Now you've both gotten me hungry." Matthew looked around for a place to sit. "Let's see… ah, yes. There's a bench where we can unstrap these blades – off you go. Perhaps we can return later in the week if my old bones permit." The two girls scampered quickly up the bank to where Matthew had pointed and plopped down, happy, giggling and bright eyed. It was amazing – they were hardly out of breath and he was sore everywhere on his body.

He really was old.

"This will be a great surprise for grandmama – she wasn't expecting us for another hour at least. The poor thing hates to be alone, but she hides it well claiming delight in finally having the time to sit in quiet solitude and read a book. Today Grandpa is out somewhere with Uncle Fitz, and Deborah and Steven will be napping. I try and follow her around the house all day, you know, to ease her nervousness over mummy. I'm certain she is miserable and lonely this very minute, missing us all horribly. Especially me." Pulling off her mittens Roberta began rubbing her cold hands together. "I am so *hungry*. I hope cook has enough clotted cream and scones, and fresh bread tea sandwiches, and cakes, and biscuits, and fish with sauce, and pudding. She's never run out before, but there's always a first time. It sometimes worries me."

"Good heavens, all that? Haven't you had breakfast?"

"Ha! You're so funny, Cousin Matthew. Miss breakfast; very good. Oh. You're serious. Yes, of course I've had breakfast – actually two – but I'm cold! When I'm cold I become ravenous, and food fends off bone chill. That's what Mama tells Papa. He says neither Mama nor I will ever freeze to death." She turned to Amanda, "What would you like cook to prepare, Mandy?"

"Oh, I suppose a little vegetable broth."

"*Vegetable broth!* You need heartier fare in your diet to survive the winter, missy – more bread, cake and beef – you really do. Especially cake. And ham pies. And puddings and cream."

"Mama doesn't want me to gain more weight. See how full my cheeks are, Birdy."

"You're eight years old. Aren't everyone's cheeks full at eight years old? I look like a squirrel."

"I suppose. But Mama considers eating sweets outside of a holiday to be un-Christian. Wish I could eat anything I like as you do."

"I do eat like a farm animal, don't I?" Roberta sighed.

"I never meant that! You only eat when you're hungry."

"But I'm hungry all the time. Aren't you?"

"Yes, but Mama says eating whenever you're hungry is improper behavior for a lady."

This talk of dieting infuriated Matthew. His Amanda was perfect, she was not to be starved simply because Clarissa obsessed over appearance. *Improper behavior* indeed – by God, that was an absurdity coming from her. Odd how thoughts of one's own sins faded over time, how people would conveniently reimagine their past.

"Amanda give me your foot and I'll remove your skates myself.

The way you two are jabbering away we'll be here all day." He'd need to speak with his wife immediately, the prospect of which he never relished. They rarely spoke, and it was only about the child when they did.

"Yes, Papa."

When he was finished undoing his daughter's skates Birdy stuck her feet out as well. "Could you help me, Cousin Matthew? Please. I can't seem to make out the laces." Without her glasses Birdy was having a difficult time.

He examined the convoluted ties. "That would probably be best, and quicker."

"Thank you." She turned again to Amanda. "Did you know my Mama eats mountains of food and never gains an ounce? She takes after me. I remember before they left for Canada Papa said we may need to hire another cook just to keep up with her appetite. Or, she just may be with child again. Then he said if she *was* with child he'd probably walk into oncoming carriage traffic – are you all right, Cousin Matt?"

Matthew nodded. At first the sounds he was making sounded like laughter but then had quickly turned into a cough. "Yes, Roberta, I am perfectly fine."

The girls resumed their conversation. "Well, *my* Mama never eats breakfast nor has tea but she still gains weight – although, truth be told, I never can tell. It must be true though because she's always needing new gowns. Did your Mama receive *The Englishwoman's Domestic Magazine* this month?"

"Yes. Evidently, bosoms are big this year, very 'in fashion'."

Matthew stopped struggling with the knots on Roberta's skate. What an odd statement. *Were bosoms ever* out *of fashion?* Not to any man he knew. Besides, this discussion of bosoms was startling. Only moments before he'd learned they were stalking little boys and now they were discussing high fashion magazines, sounding like married women. They *were* still babies, weren't they? It would be years until either was old enough to be presented at court, let alone worry about merits of a big bosom – and, then didn't a father's real worries begin! Both were fair and blue eyed, both promising the sort of physical beauty women pray for and men desire, and… damn! That thought was unacceptable. He didn't like that idea, not one bit!

"Amanda, did you bring Mrs. Finnywigg with you today? I'm so glad. We can have a tea party up in the nursery. My Lady Enfield doll is one-year old today."

"What fun. I brought both Finny and my Mary Queen of Scots, and new ribbons for their hair."

Yes, thank heavens, they were still his babies – for a little while longer at least. "Roberta, just how many knots did you tie in this?"

"I was trying to recreate a fir tree."

"If all else fails perhaps we can cut off your foot." He'd been a young suitor long ago, stealing kisses from girls, brushing his hands across bottoms *and* bosoms – accidently, of course, if he could pull it off convincingly. More than once his face had been slapped; but, not often enough to discourage him. *Hell and damnation.* He suddenly felt very anxious that Amanda would be snatched up her first season, married within the next few years, then motherhood; he'd be a grandfather before long. Finally releasing the blade and hooking Roberta's shoe up tight, he finished with a grunt and a pat. Enough of this – the snowfall was quickly becoming a blizzard.

"*Ladies!* Up here – eyes to me. Are you two magpies finished selecting your wedding trousseaus? Excellent. Then I say we should be getting you home to your grandparents, Roberta, before the snow covers us and we disappear on this bench. Please button up your coats, both of you. Amanda, where is your muff?"

"What muff?"

"The one you were wearing five seconds ago."

"I was? Oh. Here it is, Papa."

"Hand me your gloves, please. That's my girl."

His daughter cheerfully stood as her father slipped mittens onto her hands, tied her scarf tight. "I say, Birdie, wasn't it rather nice to have the pond all to ourselves today? I confess that when there are crowds of people I worry about the ice breaking. Some of the skaters are very big. In fact, most of them are *huge*…"

"Where are your skates?"

She looked around.

Dumbfounded for a moment he stared at his daughter. "Your skates, dearest. The ones I just removed from your feet and handed to you."

"I don't know – wait a moment! There they are, behind the

bench. How silly of me." Amanda handed them back to her father to carry. "Mama was right, you know. She doubted there would be many people skating today. Remember when she said that, Birdy?"

"She said most people would consider it improper during this time of 'loss, grief and heavy sorrow' to gad about on skates." Roberta sighed, her gay mood momentarily gone she began to chew on her thumbnail. "We are bad, aren't we? We asked if we shouldn't go, but then she said perhaps propriety could make an exception this one time; and, you know, we were already dressed for it. It really is awful about our Prince Albert passing; I cried for an entire hour I was so sad. We didn't mean to be disrespectful to his memory, Cousin Matthew, we really didn't. Oh, I do wish he hadn't died so near my birthday,"

"But, he didn't, Birdy. He died *three whole days* ago. Didn't he, Papa? So, you see, it wasn't really near your birthday all."

"That's true. Oh, thank goodness! Well, I really don't mean thank goodness that he died..."

"Not to worry." Matthew patted her cheek. "We all love you and know you mean nothing but good, Roberta." The child and her two siblings had spent weeks fearing for their parent's safety, missing them, missing home. Uncles, aunts, cousins and grandparents were making a special effort to bring comfort and joy to these waiting, worrying children.

Everyone except his own wife, apparently. Did she truly consider a harmless day of skating inappropriate? Ridiculous woman. Again, he vowed to have a word with her straight away – if he could find her in that huge mausoleum of a house they shared. What unmitigated gall! What hypocrisy! Not so many years before Clarissa had been famously inappropriate herself, and on a much grander, much more lurid scale. She'd been London's most notorious wild child, as promiscuous as she was lovely.

However, with her bishop father's passing she was now the embodiment of virtue, a pillar of the church, judge and jury for all things socially and morally acceptable. He couldn't stand the sight of her anymore. They rarely argued because they never spoke.

Any discussion between them now usually centered about the daughter they both loved – a love that was, notwithstanding, expressed in completely different ways. Clarissa's parenting style was more traditional and formal, seldom visiting the child more than once daily – for tea – making Clarissa more the glamorous guest than parent.

Not so with Matthew. He preferred his daughter's company to anyone else in the world, doted on her, as his parents had doted on him. He could not remember a time when his mother hadn't hugged him, or praised him, or scolded him, or told him how much he was loved. In fact, both his parents had been almost overwhelming with their attentions, discussing everything, endlessly. No topic was considered taboo, no question unanswered.

It was a way of family life Clarissa just could not fathom, and so the antagonism between Matthew and Clarissa over their child's upbringing was one more open sore. And, of course, bitterness lingered over affairs both had engaged in, especially Matthew's indiscretion, years before…

"All right, ladies, let's get a move on here. Last one to Pemberley House must dance a jig."

Tears suddenly brightened Birdy's eyes and she hugged Matthew tightly.

"What's this?" he asked.

"Nothing. Everything. Only, thank you for surprising me this morning, making today special for me. I don't know what I would have done if not for you and Amanda these past weeks." It was at times like these, moments of gentle sweetness, that she reminded him so of her mother – a cousin more sister to him than not.

"Who are you, and what have you done with Roberta Wentworth Durand, leader of the family hooligans? Here, blow." He held a handkerchief up to her nose.

"Thank you," she blew into it then giggled. "Poor Cousin Matt. I am a trial, aren't I? Ooh Mandy, I've just thought of something wildly important. Will you have plumes in your bonnet for the memorial service? If not, I have extra we can sew on. They're pink. I do love pink against black – very wicked looking."

"Brilliant! We could have our bonnets match, *and* our dollies bonnets if we have enough feathers! Papa, will you be here for the service? You're not going all the way to Windsor for the Prince's funeral, are you?"

"No, pet. That service will be very small and private as the Prince himself wished, with not much pomp nor ceremony. Not even the Queen shall be in attendance."

"What? Oh, the poor lady! Where will she be?"

"From what I hear she's already gone to Osborne, on the Isle of Wight. Now, now, no reason to look sad. Women are rarely in attendance at funerals, especially the fellow's widow. You see, the common belief is that females are much too delicate, frail and weak for such an experience." The girls' look of disbelief was comical. "Yes, I know. Obviously, the women in our family are made of sterner stuff."

"What about the Princesses? Princess Alice and Princess Victoria and Princess Louise?" Roberta, like so many other young girls, adored the Royal Princesses, loved learning about their court balls, their fashions, their day to day lives.

"They've all gone to Osborne as well I supppose. More likely than not only Prince Albert and Prince Arthur will be present."

"It is very sad." Amanda Rose's eyes grew moist. "I feel very badly for the princesses now I think on it." She'd never really contemplated death before, of suddenly never seeing either of her parents ever again, especially her father. No, she could not imagine leaving her father's side a moment longer than necessary, under any circumstances. Just let anyone try and make her.

"Smile, both of you. In a few days it will be Christmas, and Boxing Day, and the Yule Log, and cookies, and presents; and, then … Roberta, where are your mittens?"

"What mittens? Did I have mittens?"

"Yes, of course you had mittens. Wait a moment. Ladies, where in heaven's name are your bonnets? Weren't you just wearing them…?"

CHAPTER FOUR

BRIDGET DURAND FELT HER STOMACH lurch the moment she heard the voice of her former employer, Fitzwilliam Darcy, speaking to his wife outside the door. Years before she had been a servant in his house, how was she to behave with them now? Although she had been raised a gentleman's daughter, her father's early death forced her into service years before she'd met the family, so she'd never felt their social equal, even with her husband's title. The truth was Bridget's composure faltered at the mere thought of her former life in London as the mistress of, to her shame, a married man.

It had been a mistake to return; too many memories would stir up. It was dangerous.

"Sir Alex, Lady Durand, how good to see you."

Standing to her side Bridget's husband was lost in thought, his heart heavy with worry over his brother. He hadn't heard Darcy 's greeting, so she tugged on his sleeve.

"Yes?" Turning away from the fireplace he stumbled a bit when he saw his host. "Mr. Darcy!" Sudden movements were awkward for him – his damn wooden leg never allowed for graceful stride, let alone when he was this tired.

"Sir Alex. Stay there, I shall come to you."

"Nonsense, I'm fine." Alex leaned heavily on his cane as he limped forward. "It's no trouble to walk, really. I'm just a bit stiff at first." He clasped Darcy's outstretched hand warmly. "Oh, it's grand to see you again. Truly grand, sir."

"Please, you must call me William – we are family, after all, not only business partners." He'd seen Sir Alex a handful of times before the fellow's leg had been amputated, but not since. Darcy could not imagine the pain he must have experienced then, experienced still.

"Thank you, William; and, of course, you must call me Alex. You remember my wife, certainly."

Bridget stepped forward, a cautious smile on her lips, and then curtseyed despite all her vows not to show deference. "Mr. Darcy."

"Bridget, how nice to see you again. Please pardon me, I should say Lady Durand. Yes." Was this the reason for Lizzy's fussing? Women! The situation was a bit awkward, surely; but it hardly warranted his wife's rushing their visitors out the door. Being a naturally gracious host, Darcy wanted his guests to feel comfortable. "Scotland must agree with you, Lady Durand. You look lovelier than ever."

"Thank you, sir." Her gaze glued itself to the floor, her lips compressed. Would anyone notice if she backed into the shadows? Silence followed. A clock was heard ticking loudly in the hallway. It was all a bit strained. Yes, indeed it was.

"Well. Very good. Oh, Scotland's a wonderful country. Mrs. Darcy and I traveled there on our wedding trip in eighteen… something… well, years ago. Ahem. Why don't you tell them, dear? Women love to talk about weddings, you know."

"Do we? Shall we pretend you haven't forgotten the year we were married, then?"

"Nonsense. I remember the day like it was yesterday, Elizabeth. It was in… early autumn?"

"Summer, dearest. The fourth of August. Goodness, will you look at the time, William –"

"Lady Durand, your home is in northern Scotland, is it not?" Darcy interrupted his wife deliberately, hoping his pointedly arched brow would convey to Elizabeth how shocked and displeased he was by her rudeness to their guests.

It did not. She arched an even higher brow right back at him.

"Yes, sir." Bridget replied meekly, looking from one host to the other.

More of the ticking clock was enjoyed by all.

"Interesting. Ah. I see. Quite. Near Aberdeen, are you? Very quiet compared to London. You shall miss that calm during Alex's time in Commons. As you must remember, London is a bustling city."

Bridget smoothed out the new crinoline skirts she wore, wishing she felt more at ease. Her clothes were expensive and in the very latest style, yet she felt as if she was still in her black servants' dress and white cap, still a baby's nanny.

"No, sir."

"What's this? Oh, I'm certain you must remember how busy this city can be."

"Oh, aye, I do, yes," her voice faltered a bit, her Scottish brogue more pronounced these days. "I said no, however, to the other statement. I mean your comment about me remaining. My son and I go home once Alex's brother is returned safely, and Alex's household in the city is established."

"Ah. Really? I hadn't known that." Darcy was at a loss for what to say next. He'd never understand the modern attitude toward marriage, the fashion of society couples spending time apart, and this separation promised to be an unusually long one for the couple if she remained in Scotland during the entire session of Parliament. Well, it was none of his business, really. The only marriage that truly interested him was his own. He and Lizzy were never apart, and he genuinely adored his wife, considered her his closest confidante, his life, his reason for living.

Except for now. Now she was annoying the hell out of him. Now she was poking him in the back, pinching his elbow black and blue, making vague *throat clearing* sounds at his every comment. He slid gracefully away from her. Oh, yes, Darcy could be very smooth. "Again, may I say congratulations on attaining your seat in Commons, Alex."

"Aye, Thank you. Though, without your support, William, I dinnae believe I could've defeated m'opponent so easily."

"Untrue. You are the right man for the job." It was then Darcy noticed a pair of small boots fidgeting behind Alex. They belonged to the slender form of a child – however, since the boy's back was to him Darcy could not make out his face. "It appears you already have chosen your assistant; excellent planning. May I ask who this young gentleman is?"

"Oh, aye. This is m'son, Ewan. Here, lad, tear your gaze from that dish of candies and meet a great man."

"Your son? I had no idea. What a pleasure." The moment the

hour and Matthew usually took them for treats after their excursions. Surely, there was time before he and the children returned for a brief word to him from her husband.

Very brief.

"At least have a seat, we'll order tea. No, No, I insist. Afraid it will be a while yet before you are able to leave."

Lizzy's voice dropped an octave. "William."

"Elizabeth. If you would kindly look outside, you'll notice a storm is brewing. I am afraid we shall need to *inform your sister* we'll be arriving late at the very least. Besides, when I arrived, I sent their cattle to our stables for food and shelter, and their driver is downstairs warming up. It will take an hour or so to reassemble them all again – so, we may as well have something to eat."

Elizabeth's face paled, but she relented. What else could she do? "Of course. I shall send word to Jane."

"Now, where were we?" Truth be told Darcy wanted nothing more than to get to know this boy better. He rubbed his hands together. "We'll ring for hot chocolate and tea straight away; and, in the meantime, I can give Alex the latest news of Jamie and Anne Marie."

Alex sighed with relief. "Thank ye so much, if it's not too much trouble; I have been verra concerned. But please, tea is unnecessary, William. We dinnae want to be a bother."

"Nonsense, Alex. No bother at all. First, tell me, how long have you been in town?"

"We arrived three days ago. When I learned of the Prince's death I found it difficult to remain away any longer. Is it true he intervened with some communications two weeks before his passing? Can you tell us what's happened?"

"Well, as you know reaction here to America's capture of the packet ship was utter outrage, and the obligatory 'angry ultimatum' was composed… but, never sent. It turns out that cable mysteriously became lost, then found its way to Windsor and provided the Prince, ill as he was, an opportunity to intervene, emphasizing diplomacy, not war, was the proper road to take. Well, all I can say is thank heaven for cooler minds. Mr. Lyons, the British Ambassador to America, relented, saying that all could be resolved with a simple apology to our government; and, I have been assured that very apology has been received at Whitehall. Hopefully, Jamie and

Anne Marie will be home before the end of January."

"What a relief! Thank ye, William."

"It was no thanks to me, I assure you. I have also been informed Anne's cousin – Lord Fitzwilliam's son, Andrew – is seeing to it she and Jamie sail back aboard his ship, the Orontes, if possible, once the neutrality of the seas is reestablished. Hopefully, all this talk of war will die down very soon."

"You see, Alex." Bridget reached for her husband's hand. "Alex has been so worried I was fearful it would reverse all the fine progress he's made."

"M'wife fusses over me too much." He brought her hand to his lips for a quick kiss. "And I love her all the more for it."

"Indeed, where would any of us be without our wives' practical concern?" Darcy reached for Lizzy's hand but saw she was nervously staring at the clock on the mantel. Then it all became clear; her earlier words coming back to him. *Matthew! Dear lord, Matthew was with the girls. Damn and blast. Perhaps the storm has slowed them down? He probably took them back to his home nearer the park. Yes, that's probably what he would do… because if he arrived and saw this boy…* Lizzy was right. He'd best hurry this visit along.

"Would you like cook to wrap up some candies to take home, Ewan?"

Tea was soon served however, and conversation flowed, initially centering upon the death of Prince Albert. The only event planned as yet was the memorial service to be held at St. Paul's, and Darcy emphasized his hope that Alex and Bridget would join the rest of the family at the church. Then there was talk about how it would be such a sad Christmas this year, and the difficulty of raising children in modern society, and the cost of livestock feed, and the cold winter. Even Elizabeth became caught up in the conversation and began to relax. It seemed to her as if the storm outside had saved them, the silent deep snow protecting the streets from traffic hubbub and barking dogs and vendors' calls. More like than not Matthew and the girls had found shelter somewhere else.

Until…

Suddenly there was a commotion that could be heard even through the closed doors of the parlor, the front doors slamming open by the storm followed by boisterous chatter and children's laughter. There was a bang, a thud, and then squeals as something in the hallway crashed, followed by a deeper male voice demanding decorum even as the fellow himself laughed.

Lizzy touched her husband's arm as he turned to listen. Gradually he was able to make out the words more clearly, realizing too late to whom the male voice belonged. "Is that…?"

Elizabeth nodded. "Would you all excuse me for a moment? No, please don't stand, gentlemen; I won't be but a moment." Darcy watched Lizzy move hastily to the door while the laughter and squeals in the hall grew closer, louder. Then, just as she reached for the knob… the door burst open… and banged her in the forehead.

CHAPTER FIVE

"GRANDMAMA! MY WORD, HOW SPLENDID you look." Birdy engulfed Lizzy in a rib crushing hug. "What's happened to your head?"

"Girls, I wasn't expecting you back so soon." Relief washed over her that Matthew was nowhere to be seen. Evidently, he had just dropped them off and then left. Hopefully. Lizzy closed the door behind them. "Are you… alone?" Better safe than sorry.

"Yes, Granny."

"Thank heavens."

Amanda kissed her cheek in greeting. "Whatever do you mean, Auntie Lizzy?"

"I mean thank heavens you're in from the cold, dear. Sorry your father had to leave however."

"You know my Papa, always working. He rushed off, I forget why."

"I think he may have needed to return home for dry clothes, Mandy. We did push a great deal of snow into his boots."

"And down his collar." Both girls giggled.

"You two are scamps. Well, other than torturing your father I hope you enjoyed yourselves."

"Oh, yes. We had great fun."

"Roberta, Amanda, did you see your 'friends'?" Lizzy knew the girls were madly in love with two or more of the boys who skated at the park.

"No, more's the pity. There was no one around to admire our skills – only park keepers breaking up ice near the edges of the lake for the swans, which was rather sweet, actually, but a bit noisy. Besides, the cold made us very hungry." Roberta gave her grandmother a loud smacking kiss on the cheek. "Oops, was that your foot I just stepped on? It was, wasn't it?"

"Yes, darling; but, not to worry, I have another. And, where are your spectacles?"

"Well… Grandmama, have you seen the snowfall? Green Park looks positively white."

"Answer my question, dear. Where are your spectacles?"

"I, um, have no idea. Possibly lost or stolen. Possibly."

"Imagine my surprise that children's spectacles are high priority for thieves. Now, don't tell tales. Remember, I see and know everything."

"I'd forgotten that. Well, truthfully, Grandmama, I felt it unnecessary to wear them to the park since I only really use them for great distances. Or, not so great distances. Or for reading. Secondly, they make me look *tres* dowdy! And 'C", I really detest them. Ah! There is my favorite Grandpa. My, aren't we looking handsome today – what's this, you have visitors, and here I am chattering away." Roberta squinted as she neared, then recognition took hold. "*Auntie Bridget*!" The gregarious whirlwind immediately launched herself into the arms of her beloved former nursemaid. "Auntie B, I thought you'd *never* come to London. But, this is *merveilleux*! Is Ewan with you? He is? Where? Oxie! There you are you little beastie, how absolutely *merveilleux* to see you!"

Ewan was already on his feet and beaming, buoyed by the sight of his pretty cousin and her friend. At last he had playmates – even if they *were* girls! "Hello, Birdy! Mangling French now, are we? What happened to German?"

"Fertig."

"*Gesundheit.* We thought you'd gone with your Mam and Da to America."

"No, although I do miss them both terribly, someone had to remain to care for Grandma and Grandpapa. But, look at you, you've grown taller. You're taller than I."

"I'm nearly tall as Mama."

"Well, who isn't? I was nearly tall as Auntie B when I was five years old. Where are my manners? This is my cousin, Amanda Rose, Ewan. She is my dearest friend in all the world – aside from you of course. Mandy help me bring two chairs up to the table would you – there's a dear – and, meet my *schrecklich* cousin Ewan and his parents, whom I adore. I call him Oxie sometimes because he was big as an ox when he was born, or so his Papa told me. They're really the only reason he turned out so fine. Ooh, and do you know what? Ewan is absolutely the best skater in Edinburgh, except when I'm there. We must have him join the boys skating club, then we'll have the perfect excuse to join in. *Tarts!* Capital! I'm faint with hunger." Two peach tarts immediately disappeared from the plate. "Oh, these are scrumptious!"

"Extremely happy to meet ye, Mandy. I dinnae know how you stand the company of m'cousin. She exhausts me. Birdie, stop touching all the food; are ye looking for the apple tarts? Afraid I've eaten them all."

"Not to worry. Grandmama, are there – say, wait a moment, I just noticed something! Do you know you look *very* similar to each other? No, not you and my Grandmama, Ewan! You and *Amanda*. I'd never noticed before – well, I'd never seen you both together, had I? You look so very much alike it's truly astonishing! I say, don't you think Mandy and Ewan look alike, Grandmama? Grandpa? Auntie Bridget? Oh, dear. Have I said something wrong? What's happened?"

It was a surprise to see the adults staring in odd directions, each one locked in rigid silence, some pale, others flushed. Birdy was about to apologize for whatever she'd said that had made them all upset, when a scratch on the door was followed by it being swung opened.

Matthew Fitzwilliam leaned into the room. "'Girls, lower your voices to a dull roar, would you? You can be heard all the way to the street. Uncle Wills, might I borrow one or two of your footmen? Beastly storm outside. Seems my carriage wheel is stuck in ..."

He froze in mid-sentence.

It would be years before he could admit he'd been waiting for this moment, hoping, dreaming of seeing her again. Oh, he had gone through the motions of life, visiting gentlemen clubs, midnight dinners with younger and younger women, taking his seat beside his father in the House of Lords, attending the theatre, the opera, the ballet, frequenting museums and parks, enjoying family. He was a powerful and busy man, never left the city for the family estate.

And no one ever questioned why he'd become such a frequent caller at the Darcy home over the years, or at the home of his cousin, Anne Marie – but, deep down, *he* knew. Bridget would visit one day – she was family now – and he would be certain to be nearby when it happened.

The frustrating years of anger and hurt he'd spent in a bottle imagining one scenario after another! He despised her. He obsessed over her. He would humiliate her for certain, he would expose intimate details of lovemaking to her husband, or, seduce her and then expose her to the world.The thought of her pleading for his silence, or his forgiveness, even for a second chance helped him remain sane through the initial years.

However, this red-hot fury eventually played itself out, becoming unsustainable by year six – the rage was hurting only him and, therefore, senseless to continue. So, he relegated her to his past, slipped her neatly into a pocket of his brain where secrets rested and dreams went to die, and he moved on. Until he walked into that room and saw her.

Bridget, the woman who had changed his world. Bridget, the woman he had loathed beyond reason, the woman he would love to his grave. Damn her. She was as beautiful today as the first time he'd seen her, nine years before.

Darcy stood stiffly, saying something Matthew couldn't comprehend. It was a moment before he could even move before turning to close the door behind him. He gave himself time to compose his wits, took a deep breath, and then turned. "Um. Sorry, I had no idea you were entertaining visitors, or I would not have barged in so."

He saw then the compassion in Darcy's eyes, the sympathy – and also, perhaps, a silent plea for restraint. Matthew was reluctant to look away from those eyes. His uncle had always been the rock of their families, the one person they all looked to for common sense, even his father. He just needed another moment to start his heart going again, gain some composure, think…

"Matthew, you remember Sir Alex Durand and his family."

"Yes, of course." The butler silently entered the room behind him and settled a chair beside Darcy then motioned for another servant to bring his lordship a brandy to warm him. No one said a word, everyone just watched, and waited, the clock ticking away. Finally, when the servants had left the room, he acknowledged Alex. "And to what does England owe this tremendous honor?" The cold smile never reached his eyes. "Oh, yes, I'd forgotten. You'll be joining Commons this session."

Lizzy settled a hand on Matthew's back, out of view of the others. He had always been impulsive, hotheaded like his father – still, he was like a son to her, her heart arched for him as a son. The truth was she loved all his brothers and sisters as if they were her very own, and had promised their mother, her dearest friend in the world, that she would watch over them. Was he even aware there was a child? If not, his greatest shock was yet to come.

"Sir Alex and Bridget are in London with regards to his brother Jamie and our Anne Marie. They were concerned, of course."

"Well, they've certainly come to the right place, Uncle Wills. Hope you've been able to put their minds at ease."

"Yes, I believe I have." Darcy walked to the fireplace mantle to retrieve his pipe, his absence exposing a side table where the children sat in silence, their huge eyes watching the adult drama unfold before them. Amanda Rose kept her gaze intently on her father, sensing his tension. Birdy watched her grandmother's eyes moisten with tears for some unknown reason.

His back to the adults, Ewan leaned over and tugged on his father's sleeve. "Papa, are you all right?" It had been a while since he'd seen his father look upset; it brought back bad memories, it frightened him. "Is your leg aching you?" he whispered.

"Ach, no, I'm fine, son." Alex squeezed his boy's hand and smiled reassuringly.

Unconvinced, Ewan quickly looked to his mother for reassurance but found little comfort there, her face even paler than his Papa's. In fact, it was a rarity in his young life to see his mother distressed at all. He gulped back his panic. "Mama? What is it? Is everything all right?"

Bridget pressed a hand to her stomach as the room began to spiral. She had tried to fool herself into believing she was travelling to London with Alex out of her love and concern for him, nothing else; yet, her heart knew otherwise. From the moment she'd heard his voice in the hallway she'd known the truth – her very soul belonged to *him*, and only him. But, how could that still be true? How could she still love him? How? He was arrogant, selfish, cruel; everything Alex was not.

"Mama?"

Hearing her son's voice jolted her; he was speaking but her mind was a jumble.

Birdy broke the silence with what she thought would be a pleasing observation. "Cousin Matthew, you haven't met my Auntie B's son yet, have you? He's a great bowler, and he loves to skate, don't you Ewan?"

"Oh aye. Especially if there's a game of bandy anywhere nearby. I even brought m'goaler's stick with me."

Matthew stepped forward, rested his hand on his daughter's shoulder. So, the bitch had a son, did she? Good for her, may he bring her nothing but heartache the rest of her days. "I had no idea. May I be introduced?"

"Stand up, Oxie and make your bow to my cousin. Here he is, Cousin Matt. Doesn't he look so much like our Amanda?"

When the lad looked up at him and smiled Matthew's world stopped.

My son. As sure as he breathed, he knew. Wild emotions shattered within him, overwhelming him long before they became manageable. Shock, wonder, joy, pain. *Love – Blinding love.* Everything about the boy was familiar, intimate. It was as if a part of himself was staring back.

Tears threatened, he shot a narrowed glance at Bridget. How could they have kept this from him all these years – both Bridget and that bastard cripple beside her? All these years. A son lost to him, all these years. He wanted to kill them both.

Alex cleared his throat. "Lord Fitzwilliam..." he began then stopped when Matthew glared at him, realizing he knew the worst of it now. There was no more hiding. Although he disliked Matthew intensely, Alex felt great compassion at that moment. Perhaps he should have pressed Bridget harder over the years to contact him. A man had a right to know about his own son, after all. It was wrong, all wrong, to learn of his child this way. "Good afternoon," he finally said, feebly, quietly.

"Good afternoon? *Really*?" Matthew spit out, amused in spite of himself. "That's all you have to say to me after – well, shall we say after all these years?"

"I hope you are well."

"Well, that's much more sensible, isn't it?" The fury in Matthew fueled his spite and he smiled kindly. "Never felt better*, old man.* Physical exercise such as skating exhilarates me, as does cricket, tennis, swimming. Oh, do please forgive me; how insensitive. You'll never know that joy again, will you?"

Facing the only rival he'd ever known for his wife's affection, Alex wanted to spit in his face. He had always hated the fellow's arrogance, his contempt – the younger man with the still robust physique, handsome looks… full head of hair. *And with both his legs, the bastard. How can I compete with this?* To hell with him – he had never deserved Bridget, and certainly did not deserve a son like Ewan. "I have been blessed in other areas," he answered gruffly.

"I can see that." Matthew's gaze briefly skimmed over Bridget's body as he tried to convince himself he felt nothing but contempt for her, that any shred of tenderness remaining from their past was destroyed. *A youthful dalliance, that's all it had ever been, nothing more* – her long-ago betrayal evaporated his imagined ardor like steam from a kettle. Then, to have given birth to his flesh and blood but never tell him? He would never forgive her for this. Never. He could not, nor ever would, say it was a pleasure to see her once more. That would give voice to a lie.

It was no pleasure at all.

Bridget wanted to scream. This was not how she'd imagined he would find out about Ewan. So many years had gone by, oceans of tears. In her desperation to see Matthew again she had forgotten how cold he could be, how cruel. He looked at her with hatred in his eyes, and suddenly she felt terrified of the man who had abandoned her in London, before she could tell him she was having his child. Didn't he understand why she'd run off with Alex? Where was his compassion for that? His understanding? Where was his love?

She must not panic, must gain control of herself somehow. She had done nothing of which to be ashamed when she married Alex, except go on with her life, secure a future for their baby. Matthew hadn't thought about her welfare when he'd left her on her own nearly nine years before – alone, ashamed, frightened, pregnant. Why should she care what *he* believed now?

As all this played out across her face her son slipped a hand into hers. "Mama, please sit. You don't look at all well."

She closed her eyes, love chased away her fear. *Ewan.*

Smoothing a hand across his hair she relaxed; as always, his voice calmed her. It was amazing the amount of courage and strength she had gained from being a mother. When all was said and done, her months as Matthew's mistress had given her the greatest gift of her life – *her son.* "No, my darling, I feel fine." For her boy's peace of mind, she even managed to face Matthew. "Lord Fitzwilliam, may I introduce you to…"

Good heavens, she had been about to say, 'our son,' but meaning hers and Alex's, of course. She quickly composed herself and continued, "… *my* son, Ewan. Ewan make your bow to Lord Fitzwilliam, please."

"Yes, Mama." Seeing his mother's features relax again he smiled, then stepped forward and bowed. "Tis an honor to meet you, sir."

His son was glorious – *and it* was *his son*, of that there was no doubt; an added reason to go on living, working, pick oneself up from the ashes that sometimes were life. "Ewan, it is an honor to finally meet you as well. An honor." He glanced briefly at Bridget. "And, that is a fine name – it was my grandfather's."

At that Alex looked up; no wonder she'd insisted upon the name. *Why the secrecy, though, lassie?* Well, at least she had the decency to blush and look away when he stared at her.

"What a fine lad," Matthew continued. "If I may be so bold, may I ask your age?"

"I'm nearly nine. Well, I shall be nine in eight months."

"That old, are you? Very good," Matthew pressed his lips together, fighting off the urge to shout. Nine years. It was all true. "Well, this is certainly well met, Ewan. I hope we see a good deal more of you now that you're in London. But you must become acquainted with my nephews and their friends. They're a wonderful group of boys, some around your age. I shall make certain you meet them all." Bridget's soft intake of breath at that statement wasn't lost on him; he wanted to laugh out loud. Let her try and stop him, please God. He could care less what she thought.

"While he's here we hope he'll join the St. James Bandy Club, Cousin Matthew. He's very good, an excellent goalie..." Birdie backed away from further comment when she saw her beloved Bridget becoming upset.

Matthew noticed it too and it warmed his heart. He hoped her suffering was just beginning. "Really? Why, that's splendid! The very group to whom I was referring. So, you'd like to join in with the lads?"

"I should like that *verra* much, sir. Oh, it would be grand fun, I think."

"It certainly would. I doubt your parents will deny you some entertainment and exercise during your visit, making new friends, meeting family."

Bridget was becoming more uneasy by the moment, her mind racing for rebuttals; however, each time she opened her mouth to object either Matthew would interrupt, or, worse yet, Ewan would laugh happily, too excited to notice.

"Oh, no, sir! I'm certain they'll be pleased. My mum and da have spoken of you, and of your family, often. And, o'course, you are a great favorite of Birdy's – I mean Cousin Roberta."

"Rather surprised your parents mention me to you at all. We were not – that is to say, your *father* and I – were not that well acquainted with each other. Just what have they said?"

"Oh, mummy often talks about the olden days in London, about the Darcy's and the Fitzwilliam's, and about how everyone was so verra kind to her."

As her son spoke Bridget watched Matthew stare intensely at him, drinking in his every word. She could see he already adored the child, and it both thrilled and terrified her. "The *olden* days you say? Around the time of the flood, is that what you mean, young man?" The girls giggled and his son guffawed, both sounds warming his heart.

"Amanda Rose, darling, I see you've met these friends of your *'olden days'* father already, Sir Alex Durand and his wife, Lady Durand."

The child happily ran to her father's side. With angelic features, softly curling golden blonde hair and immense blue eyes, she beamed proudly up at him. "Yes, Papa; and, Lady Durand is as pretty as Birdy told me she was." She turned to Bridget. "Birdy said your home in Scotland is a wonderland, and that you have sheep and goats and mountains and fish leap from the streams." The child's voice was unique, a bit richer than one would expect of a little girl, melodious. She sparkled, innocence shone in her eyes.

Bridget smiled warmly but could have easily wept. "That we do, dear. Aye, she's lovely, Lord Fitzwilliam." She had yearned for a daughter; however, after two dangerous miscarriages reality had taken hold and she'd stopped hoping. There would be no more children for her and Alex – sons or daughters. "You are your father's image."

"*Tres vrai!*" Birdy clapped her hands with delight. "And Ewan's as well – is that not *tre vrai* amazing?"

The room became deathly quiet. Matthew's gaze narrowed. "What do you mean?"

"Well... indeed, Cousin Matthew... that is... sorry. Have I said something wrong, Mandy? Am I being too loud?" she whispered. Amanda looked from one person to another then shrugged, confused as always by the inexplicable tensions that occasionally flowed back and forth between adults.

Matthew cleared his throat then turned to Lizzy, his smile brittle. "Well. I believe I'll wait out the storm here in the bosom of my family. I know you won't mind if I settle my cattle in your stable, Uncle Will, until the snow lifts. Tea anyone?"

CHAPTER SIX

IT HAD BEEN NINE YEARS since a broken-hearted Bridget fled London, her bridegroom and dependent sister in tow. She'd been two months *enceinte* at the time, fear for the future of her unborn child obliging her to abandon her dreams, her hopes, her lover. It had nearly killed her – or at least there were times she prayed for death – but she would gladly do it all again. Nothing came before her child, not even Matthew; no sacrifice was too great. She would banish all memories of the man who had been her life, her other half, her soul mate, and resign herself to a loveless marriage. Stoically she had accepted her martyr's existence…

Imagine her surprise, then, when the years following had turned out to be not only pleasant, but joy filled. Never in her wildest dreams had she expected to fall in love with Alex Durand, the kind man who had rescued her from shame – but, she did. Oh, it might not be the romantic, all-consuming adoration she'd known for Matthew, but it was a dear romance nonetheless, a great friendship, and it had provided her with a loving home.

Bridget wanted for nothing, physically or emotionally, better yet found no burden in being extremely wealthy for once in her life. With tenant farms in the north, breweries in the south, their numerous textile mills around Glasgow, and a large estate near Edinburgh, the family traveled often, with every other year including a tour of the continent, visits to Italy, France and Germany.

In the end, the Darcy's nursery maid had emerged like a swan into Lady Bridget Catriona Durand – privileged, well-heeled and titled. She had forgotten completely about Matthew Fitzwilliam, could not recall the last time she'd even thought of him or the little love nest they'd shared in London.

Or so she'd told herself time and again over the years.

Then why had she eagerly returned to this place now, if she was so happy in Scotland? Certainly her only motivation had been to support Alex as he awaited word of his brother, to comfort him as he had comforted her – saved her, really – so many years before. All had been going according to plan until that meeting at the Darcy's home.

Matthew.

Seeing him – well, it was like being awakened from a deep sleep. All the feelings rushed back to her, all the emotions. The world was shimmering with tension, excitement, passion again. It vibrated.

She felt so ashamed.

Turning from the window, Bridget pressed cool hands to her warm face. Why was she having these thoughts? He was her past, never her present, and certainly not her future; and, she had no intention of rekindling their love affair – that thought never crossed her mind when she'd agreed to come to London.

Possibly.

Probably.

Alone with her feelings she began to pace the room. Ewan and Alex had left to visit Tattersalls and survey the stock there, then planned on visiting the Crystal Palace and Regent's Park. A pity she'd dreaded joining them; but what if someone had recognized her? What if someone knew of her past? Would that cause problems for Ewan? For Alex? She had worked as a servant in two families before the Darcy's, would Ewan be ashamed of his mother if he saw people whisper as she passed, or smirk and laugh behind her back? She shivered and pulled her shawl closer. *Ewan and I must return to Scotland as soon as possible,* she decided. *Best that we both forget this place.*

Yet, tears filled her eyes at the thought. Heaven help her, she really did want to see Matthew once more before she left. No, that wasn't true. Was it? Perhaps just for a moment? Was that asking too much from God? She needed to busy herself, stop these ruminations. Picking up a basket of mending she vowed to forget his coldness toward her at the Darcy's, his sarcasm with Alex. He'd soften only when he would look at Ewan and Bridget cherished that memory. How many thousands of times had she'd imagined their first meeting?

Of course, he'd known immediately it was his son, but had not become cruel with the child as she feared he might. In fact, he'd spoken kindly with the boy, like a favored uncle. It was all that she had ever hoped for… so, why was there a sense of foreboding in her heart?

Much too quiet in these rooms, that was the problem; it was much too quiet. She was edgy, nervous. The man she had known was unpredictable, his moods mercurial at times. He would never do anything to harm his child, would he? He might have revenge on her and Alex, but not at the expense of the child. She returned to her mending, sorry now that she'd not gone with her husband and boy.

This waiting was driving her mad.

At the soft rap on the door Bridget started then laughed at herself for being such a fool. "Come in."

A female member of the hotel staff peeked inside. "Madam?" It was one of the maids who daily cleaned their rooms, brought them meals, changed their sheets.

"Yes, Dora. May I help you?"

"Madam, you have a visitor downstairs. A gentleman what says 'e 'as news for you and Sir Alex."

Bridget tensed immediately. "A visitor? At this early hour?" Who would be calling at ten o'clock in the morning? She wasn't expecting anyone, wasn't dressed to receive guests; besides, she and Alex had become acquainted with very few people in London. Then it struck her – *Could this be news of Jamie and Anne Marie? Mr. Darcy told Alex he would have someone from Whitehall call on us before any information was made public.*

"Does the gentleman appear to be a government official?"

"I dunno, Madame." The young woman glanced over her shoulder before continuing in a whisper, "'e refused to give Mrs. Tenny 'is name; but 'e do look very grand, I must say. Could be Lord of the Admiralty for all and that, 'e certainly acts like it."

Finally! And Alex not at home! Dear Lord, she prayed it was good news for her husband's peace of mind; and, selfishly, for her own so she might leave here quickly and return home. She would send for Alex, now, right away – wait! Unless it was bad news. She prayed it wasn't bad news! Well, they'd deal with that if, and when, the time came.

"My husband is not present, it would be improper for me to welcome the gentleman here. Is there a parlor downstairs available for me to speak with him?"

"No Madame, and 'e insisted that 'e be allowed to deliver 'is news to you straight away. 'e said it was a matter of grave importance – what you might call National Security – and, be quick about it so's 'e could deliver 'is next message."

"He actually said all that?"

"No. But that's what we all thinks. 'e does look like 'e's in a big 'urry. Very somber like."

"Good heavens. It's bad news then, I fear. Very bad."

"That's what Mr. Chappie, thought as well, so 'e sent me up to warn you that gentleman was already comin' up. I am that sorry, madam; but none of us 'ad the nerve to say no. I know it weren't proper and all to bring 'im 'ere to your rooms, what with Sir Alex away; but… well, it do seem very serious, and Mr. Claridge isn't about for any of us to ask what 'e thinks best. 'onestly, ma'am, I'm certain 'e won't mind." Many of the hotel staff knew the Scottish couple were awaiting news from the War Office, as were so many others.

"I suppose you're right." Her heart pounded. "Could you please see him in then and remain? I'll be just a moment – I shall need to put on my shoes and change my cap. Oh, and could someone take a message to my husband immediately? I believe he and our son can be found at the Crystal Palace, or at Regent's Park."

"I'm sure we can find a lad outside to take it for you, ma'am."

"Yes. Yes, that would be very kind of you. Here I'll write it down…" Hastily she scribbled out a note and handed it to the servant.

Matthew gazed about the elegant hotel room, the parlor of a large suite that encompassed a good deal of the top floor. Durand was certainly doing things up grand for his woman – all this must be costing him a pretty penny. Pity she was of a lower class, though, unable to appreciate the finer things. A good tumble in the sheets had made up for her lack of connections, he supposed. And, Bridget certainly had been damn good in the sheets. That thought brought on a hot flash of anger he could not hold back a moment longer, and Matthew kicked a nearby chair cracking the leg. *Damnation, get hold of yourself, man.* He must remain calm, he cautioned himself, his objective paramount. He wanted his son.

Spying a small daguerreotype by the window he walked over, snatched it from the table and pulled back the curtain for better light. Just as he thought. It was *her.* The Bitch. Sitting with his infant son in her arms, her idiot husband behind them looking as smug as if it was *his* son in her lap, his seed that had taken root in her belly. Damn cripple should go to hell. Again, a rage flashed through him. How could she not have told him about this? She would suffer – they'd both suffer – *suffer as I have been suffering without her, every second, every day, every month, every year...*

"Forgive me for keeping you waiting, sir. I am – Matthew!"

Emotions surged through him when he heard her speak his name, heated memories, long suppressed images. Every loving moment between them, every fight, every morning waking with her sleeping in his arms, laughing with her, shouting with her. Pain and ecstasy, both at once. He replaced the picture before he turned and bowed. "Lady Durand."

"Why on earth are you here? Where is the gentleman from the Admiralty?"

"How should I know? Probably at the Admiralty."

"I don't understand. The maid informed me someone from there was wanting to speak with me about my brother-in-law."

"Nothing to do with me. Perhaps she misunderstood, possibly I did mention something along that line. Oh, stop staring at me that way. I could hardly offer her my true identity, could I? Gossip charges through London society like a flaming carriage. Besides, why run the risk of your refusing to see me."

Considering how hard she was trembling he had probably been right. "I don't know what to say to you." Although nine years had passed he still was the most handsome man she'd ever seen, the bits of grey at his temples very striking. How dreadful must she look to him. It was an unfair fact that years wore harder on a woman than a man. Was her figure a bit thicker, her hair dull and lifeless? She suddenly felt matronly and dowdy, foolishly shaking like the last leaf of autumn.

"Instead of looking at me as if I had four heads you could ask after my health. That's a common courtesy – even in Scotland – and, one you neglected to extend at the Darcy's."

"Sorry." She was certain she'd vomit at any moment. "How have you been, Matthew?"

"None of your business. And, I should prefer you address me as Lord Fitzwilliam if you please." There, that told her plainly enough he wanted to conduct this in a calm, detached, sensible manner. Odd then how he was grasping his hands behind his back to avoid reaching for her. He thought he was done with her, yet she still could arouse him, the years detracting nothing from a face and figure that remained those of a Siren. He was gratified when annoyance flashed across her face. He wanted her annoyed.

"Well, *Lord Fitzwilliam,* you should have warned us of your arrival. My husband is not at home to receive you."

"That works out well since I have no desire to be received *by* him."

His narrowed gaze on her was so intent she imagined rivulets of perspiration streaming down her forehead. "I see." She looked about. "Where is the maid I asked to remain?"

"Said she'd be gone only a moment, that she was going to find someone to send a message for you. I told her to do it herself and not return."

"Oh. Then I must insist you leave. It is improper for us to remain alone here."

"Improper? Damn me if you haven't got the cheek. *Lady Durand,* you forget I've seen you *naked.* If I recall correctly, we even danced a waltz completely bare-arsed once. Do you still have that curious mole on the inside of your thigh? And now see how she blushes, pats the moisture from her upper lip with her handkerchief. Must mean you do."

"Matthew! How dare you!"

She looked humiliated – perversely exciting to him. He sat down, crossed his legs and tossed his hat on the table, reached into his pocket for a cigar. "Feel free to make yourself at home, Bridge; take a seat." He clipped the end of his cigar. "Here's the thing. I shall be staying as long as I wish, with or without your consent, unless you desire an anonymous complaint be entered with the authorities against Mr. and Mrs. Claridge."

"What are you talking about?"

"Well, for accommodating shocking and unsuitable behavior involving the wife of a new member of the House of Commons seen entertaining a gentleman who is not her husband, while alone with him in their rooms.

"Believe me, a few words whispered in the right ears and the scandal to the owners, not to mention your husband, would be devastating." He leaned over to light his cigar with the table lantern, took several puffs then rolled it back and forth in his fingers. "These really are delicious. Would you like to try one? Do you remember, years ago, when we were taking a bath together, you insisted I allow you to take a puff on my cigar for the first time, and you began to cough? How we laughed. Later you went on to take another large object into your mouth for the first time as well."

Bridget tried not to show her horror at his words, or her shame. Most importantly she tried not to throw something at his head. Oh, she knew this man – he would be increasingly crude and provoking if he saw it upset her, but she wouldn't break, she would need to take care. "Please, may I at least open the door?"

"No." Glancing about the room, Matthew puffed away. "I must say, well done, you. You've made this drab room look almost homey. Such a perfect little wife." On the mantel he saw another daguerreotype, this one of Bridget staring adoringly at Alex, immediately setting his blood to boil. He wanted to hit something, put his cigar out on that likeness. Instead, he cleared his throat. "Sir Alex appears very *laird* of the manor in that one. I notice he's seated while you stand, though. Tell me," he tapped his ashes onto the floor. "Are *all* the activities of a healthy, vigorous man difficult for him?"

Her humiliation was beginning to give way to rage – but, she bit her tongue. She needed to steel herself against lashing back, keep in mind that Matthew came from a large and powerful family that could easily destroy her little one. "May I ask after your wife, Lady Fitzwilliam?"

"Clarissa? Completely unhinged, a lunatic. Or a changed woman, reborn. Take your pick. Most of the time the old tart is holier than the Archbishop of Canterbury – who is her actual godfather, by the way. Fortunately for me that particular metamorphosis occurred after our daughter's birth, and not before. Poor thing had a rather bad time of it, apparently, clamped her legs shut, and willed her 'Virgin's Flower' to mend. Probably succeeded, too."

"Get out! I refuse to listen to you any longer. You are being deliberately vulgar and disgusting."

"My, how delicate you've become. Seems my wife isn't the only sinner turned saint." It was satisfying to see Bridget's temper enflamed, even though Matthew knew in hurting her he would be hurting himself much worse, they were still one after all. Ah well, that would come later when he was alone – it was the present that concerned him. He stood and began to stroll about the room before turning to face her. "Shall I tell you a very funny story?"

"Yes. Please. Especially if that will speed your departure."

"How rude." He almost laughed. "You do realize you said that out loud, don't you?"

"Did I? Imagine my embarrassment. Excuse my bad manners." What time was it? Her husband said their excursion would take at least an hour then they would visit a shop for sweets. She glanced at the clock, suddenly remembering the note sending for him. Could this morning become worse? Evidently, yes.

"Where have they gone, by the way?"

"Who?"

"Queen Victoria and her dogs. Whom do you think – the boy and your husband, of course."

"Not that it is any of your concern, but they have gone to Tattersalls, and to the park."

"Tattersalls *and* a walk in the park? Good God, whatever is Durand trying to prove? That he is normal, that he can function as well as any man? The fact that you haven't a house filled with children already tells me he is incapable of fu–"

Bridget jumped to her feet. "How dare you!"

"Temper, temper, Lady Durand. By the way, I should be quiet if I were you – hotels are notorious for employing servants with large ears." He grinned in satisfaction when her mouth clamped shut. "Finally, something to silence you. After all, how often did you regale *me* with tales of my cousin Anne Marie and her then suitor, James Durand, when you were employed at the Darcy home, trusted by them?"

Perhaps if she fainted, he would leave. Doubtful. She would probably awaken covered in cigar ash. Hopefully her husband would not receive her note and Ewan would find something interesting to occupy them a while longer. One thing was certain, Matthew was in a vicious mood; she really needed to end this before they returned. "Tell me what you have to say and be done with it."

"All in good time, all in good time. First, I must tell you my humorous story."

"I am in no mood for a story."

"You believe I care – how quaint. Well, this story concerns something that happened to a married friend of mine many years ago. Poor fellow thought he was madly in love with an unsuitable young woman. Lived for her. Trusted her. Nothing would have come of it, obviously; she was a common thing, socially far beneath him. Truth be told she wasn't much better than a tart. Oh, I see I'm upsetting you. Again, pity. To continue, one day my friend finally left his wife, told her he was going to divorce her, even though doing so would bring scandal upon both their families. He then hurried out into the night to be with his great love; and, do you know what he found?"

Her head ached, her eyes burned with tears – *please God, help me to not cry, not in front of this man.*

"Have you no curiosity? No? Well, I shall tell you anyway. She'd run off with another. He wasn't even a whole man – rather more half man, half invalid. And, if that wasn't insult enough, she chose the one fellow he despised. They even sold the house my friend had settled upon her. Made a decent profit from it too."

"Matthew." Bridget rasped, unable to speak another word for several moments. "Matthew, please leave this place. I beg you."

"Go on, you say? Yes, happy to oblige." Taking a seat again he pretended to ponder. "Where was I? Oh yes… Well, what was my friend to do? Intellectually he knew that one woman is much like another in the dark, so he returned home, and in a brief, drunken union with the missus, he created a child. A gift from God that saved his sanity, not to mention his life. So, you see, the moral of the story is this – if you've been cuckolded by a heartless little bitch, do not fret; in the end it may actually turn out to have been a blessing."

Bridget was trembling. Damn him and damn his lies. Her rage was quickly turning into fury. "It was the best outcome for them both then," she hissed.

"Don't spit, dear. You may want to wipe your mouth there a bit, on the side." Pulling his pocket watch out he checked the hour. "Well, haven't much time left for this delightful visit, so I'd best arrive at the true reason for my visit. I have come to speak about the boy."

Bridget's chin rose a notch. "I think not, Matthew."

"Then think again."

"You have no reason to discuss *my* son."

"*Your* son? God, the gall of the woman. You mean *our* son?"

She jumped up from her seat, nearly tipping over her chair. "You should leave, Matthew."

Unlike her he rose calmly, but then grabbed her arm, surprising her and yanking her to him. "You bitch! Not until you explain to me how you could have given birth to my son – *My Son* – and, not inform me!" His voice grew louder and angrier, all attempts at calm abandoned. His words choked him. "You filthy little whore. How could you do this to me? I loved you, I worshipped you. Did you and Durand have a good laugh at my ignorance? I suppose he was incapable of fathering a child so you two thought you could–"

"Stop it!" Bridget slapped his face. "You bastard!"

"Not me, woman – but, the boy, well that's another subject."

"No, not a bastard! He is legitimate, he has a father. You think you know everything, do you? You're a sanctimonious prig, that's what you are. The great Lord Fitzwilliam, so outraged! Where were you nine years ago? When I sent you messages, tried to see you, begged to see you – and then that vile servant of yours did your dirty work for you, turning me away, humiliating me. Oh yes! He made it painfully clear I was not to contact you again, that you were uninterested in seeing me. Common he called me, and common I was.

"You discarded me like trash, forcing me to fend for myself and my child. *My* child. You say I stole *your* house from you – but, had you not, months before, told me to use the house as my own, that I had the right to sell it if ever needed? Well, I did need it! What else did I have? I was alone with no position in the world, penniless, an unmarried woman carrying a married lover's child, and responsible for a blind sister! What was I supposed to do, Matthew? How was I to carry on?"

"Oh, you have a way of turning a knife in a man with your lies, don't you? You never once wrote to me! Besides, you could have waited for me! Trusted me! I told you I would return; but, with the first man who offered you money you were gone. I've known courtesans with more loyalty."

"Wait? Are you mad? You *are* mad. I would need to wait for your father-in-law to die, Matthew, so you could petition for a divorce since you had often informed me you could never petition while the pompous fool was alive – am I correct? He would have disowned his wayward daughter, your wife, if you were to divorce her during his lifetime, isn't that what you told me? It would leave *her* destitute, and you were unwilling to support her forever. Money was your concern, not me! How long did her father, the great bishop, live then, Matthew? *Five years*, Matthew... five years! I was large as a barn by five months.

"And, as for Alex being just any man for me to snatch, you lie again. Alex was a student of my father's, a dear family friend, a decent man, and he loved me! Was that so wrong? He was willing to make an honest woman of me, Matthew – to take me, my sister, and *my* baby, and give us a home, safety and security. But, most of all, he was willing to give another man's son his name, eliminating forever the child's disgrace at being base born.

"Let me tell you there is not one day that goes by that I regret marrying Alex Durand! And you, why you should thank him on your knees for being the loving father to your son that you could never have been!"

"Be quiet!" Matthew raised a fist as if to strike her but then stopped short. "For the love of God, be quiet!" Pacing the room, he willed himself not to grab a chair to crash against the wall. Slowly though, eventually, his blood calmed, a semblance of reason returned. Raking a hand through his hair he took a deep breath. "All right. Perhaps we were both wrong. Perhaps we could have both handled things differently. None of that matters now. All that matters now is the boy. What was between us is over, that is for certain; but the tangible result certainly exists. Damn you – do not turn away from me. Look at me! I don't give a shite for you or your cripple; but you can no longer deny me my son. I *will* be in his life from this moment forward."

"How? No, that's impossible. Ewan and I are leaving London as soon as Jamie and Anne Marie have returned."

"Think again, Bridget! Oh, *you* may leave if that is your wish, return to Scotland – go on to hell for all I care. However, the boy remains. From this moment on you will afford me complete and unfettered access to *my* child."

"That's not possible. Ewan has his tutors, classes, friends to whom he shall wish to return."

"You're not hearing me, Bridget! You will either bring his tutors here or find new ones for him in London, but my son will remain." She began backing away from him toward a closed door, seeking escape. He grabbed her by her arms. "Come back here! Look at me. Do I look like a man who has doubts? From this moment forward he will be raised here, in London, he will live in London."

"No, no, no. We have made plans for him, for his future in Scotland. He is already scheduled to attend the University of Glasgow when the time comes. All has been arranged."

"Then it can be unarranged. *My* son shall enter Harrow when he is twelve, as his father did – his real father – and his grandfather before him; then he'll go on to Oxford. My cousins' children are already in attendance at Harrow and will take him into their circle. Their friends shall be his friends. He will become a Fitzwilliam in deed, if not in name."

"I don't have to listen to this! I'm going home immediately, and so will my son."

"The hell he will!"

"How could I allow such a thing, Matthew? How would I live without him?" Her voice began to crack with sobs. "You can't seriously wish to do this, tear him from his home, his mother. Please, Matthew. Besides, everyone will know then, everyone will see… your family will see the truth."

"My family will welcome him with open arms. As for everyone else, they will *see* exactly what my family *tells* them they see."

"You can't do this to him, you cannot risk exposing him to the censure of the world as a bastard."

"Have you learned nothing? We are speaking of the aristocracy, Bridget; nearly everyone I know has uncertain bloodlines. Why, there are a dozen men of my closest acquaintance who show not the remotest resemblance to their fathers; yet, they are accepted as gentlemen, eagerly courted in the highest circles – because of the power of their families. My family has that type of power, Bridget.

Ewan will be the same."

"It would kill your father!"

"That old man is strong as an oak. He's been through this before with another of my brothers, another bastard child. We're a randy group."

"I won't listen to any more of this." She turned to run from the room. "Show yourself out!"

"I can and will destroy your husband."

"What?" Her heart began pounding so fast and loud he must hear it. "How? You wouldn't."

"I can squash him slowly and painfully. I'll have him frozen out at Parliament, shunned. And, then you know, he and I still have that fight over *you* to finish. Actually, I don't even need to fight him. I can just whisper in his ear, details that would drive any husband mad. I know what makes you lose control, Bridget, so many intimate places to lick..."

"No! Please, I beg you. He's not a well man. His health has been poorly since the leg was taken. Please."

She stopped at the sound of a stairway door closing below and with it the familiar voice of her son chattering away as he made his way up the stairs to their floor. Bridget grabbed Matthew's arm. "You wouldn't really hurt Alex, would you?" He wrenched his arm away.

"Matthew, please!" In terrified silence she listened to Ewan's laughter. "All right, all right – I agree, I shall find a way," she whispered, panicking. "But, promise to not expose my lie to Ewan, my shame. Please, I beg you. They are so fond of each other, Matthew. Ewan loves his father – this would break his heart."

That statement alone broke Matthew's. "You have voiced the only reason I would never reveal the truth to the boy. We are agreed then. My son remains in the city, you will not refuse him my presence, nor from association with my family?"

"Yes. Yes, I agree. Hush. Ewan, Alex," she called out. We have a guest." The door to their rooms opened – however, only Ewan stepped inside, the hotel porter beside him.

"Thank you, Tom, for bringing me upstairs, but it was unnecessary. I was all right. Papa worries too much."

"Can't be too careful these days, Master Ewan. Besides, I like your Da..." The porter quickly felt the tension in the room, saw the elegant gentleman with his back turned, staring out the window. "Oh. 'Scuse me, ma'am. I was unawares that you had a visitor. I'll be goin' now." He began backing away, a knowing smile on his lips, then closed the door behind him.

"Lord Fitzwilliam is here, Ewan. You met at…"

"Mr. Darcy's house. Aye, o'course, I remember. Good morning to ye, sir; verra nice to see you again.'

"Good morning." Matthew's heart swelled with pride. "Very nice to see you as well, Ewan. Very nice."

"You're Mandy's father. Papa and I have just been with her and Birdy. Mama, is there any food lying about?"

Matthew smiled politely as if he were speaking with any other child in the world, any other stranger. No one could tell that a fist had grabbed hold of his heart and was squeezing it dry. How was it possible? How could he already be in love with this boy, a person unknown to him a week before? "Ewan." His eyes felt moist suddenly. "You say you were just with my daughter?"

"Aye! She's verra nice, and we had such fun! Papa and I accidently met Lord and Lady Penrod in the park. Well, truthfully, it wasna really an accident. Birdie told me they'd be there today so I steered Papa in that direction."

"Ewan, you didn't!"

"Sorry, Mummy. Papa didn't mind, really, when I told him. He and Lord Penrod get on well – they were there watching the Thursday morning skating lesson and I was able to join them on the ice. It was jolly. Especially when several skaters, the lads, asked me t'join them. Poor Birdy was upset they asked me and not her. Lassies can be silly. She was looking at the lads so much she fell. Often."

Matthew chuckled. The boy was wonderful; so clever and personable.

"You should not have –" Bridget's comment was cut short by Matthew.

"If you please, madam, the lad and I are speaking." She'd soon learn, this was his time now and for the foreseeable future. "Did you know that Lady Penrod is the former Alice Darcy, daughter of Mr. Darcy? Yes, she's sister to your Aunt Anne Marie; *and,* Lord Harry Penrod, is *my* brother – well step-brother, but a true brother in every important sense of the word. The Darcy's and Fitzwilliam's are a closely-knit group – too closely at times, but to be a part of it is wonderful. And a bit confusing."

Ewan nodded, his eyes still sparkling from his day, his cheeks rosy. "Yes, Miss Alice explained it all to me, or tried to, while Sir Harry teased her. They were funny, and quite nice to Papa." Ewan leaned forward to whisper, "I think she's *awfully* bonnie."

"They're wonderful people, you're right about that. I often say Harry is the best of us Fitzwilliam boys. And, as for Alice being bonnie, I wouldn't be a good judge. She and Anne Marie were more sisters than cousins – the two of them tormented me the entire time we were growing up. Yes, we indeed are a large group of cousins and brothers and sisters – the Fitzwilliam mob some have called us, always into mischief, always having such fun together." Matthew hesitated, as if an idea had just come to him. Bridget tensed. She could sense him plotting something. "Well, you must know the feeling, have the same fun with your own brothers and sisters, your cousins."

Ewan shrugged and began fidgeting with a delicate knickknack on the table. "Not really. I havna brothers nor sisters – and, no cousins at all other than Birdy, and she's only visited occasionally."

"What of the village children?"

There was wistfulness in Ewan's eyes. He sighed. "The village is far, and the tenant children are all older than I. Besides, we travel so often I ne'er get close to anyone."

"Ewan, I doubt Lord Fitzwilliam is interested in our life up north." What sort of seed was he planting in her young son's mind?

"On the contrary, Lady Durand. I find this fascinating; and, frankly, rather sad. A young boy needs activities, sports, socializing with other children. Stability. Ewan, do you have no one with whom to play? Why, I would have gone mad without my childhood cohorts, my brothers and sisters, my cousins. It must be very lonely for you. A simple answer might be boarding school, you know, while your *parents* travel. Is that something you might consider?"

NO! Oh, no. Oh, no. Oh, no. "Ewan, I should like to speak with Lord Fitzwilliam alone, please."

Ewan, however, was mesmerized that such an important man, an adult outside of his family, appeared interested in what he had to say, didn't sense his mother's growing concern.

"My parents are protective of me, they dinnae want me to leave, and I do love them for it; but, perhaps it's different in England? I'm to wait another eight years for university to leave home. What do you think about it all, sir?"

"That is quite enough, Ewan!"

"Have I said something wrong, Mama?

"No, of course you haven't, Ewan. It's just that we don't wish to keep Lord Fitzwilliam. I'm certain he has an important appointment somewhere." Bridget glanced nervously at Matthew, but he made no move to leave.

Instead, he smiled. "Nothing that can't wait."

"Oh, Mama, I nearly forgot! Downstairs, when Papa asked Tommy to see me up, he said I should tell you he's had word to meet with someone important at the Admiralty, and that he may be home late."

Bridget pushed her son's hair back from his forehead. "Well, hopefully it is good news about your uncle. Shall I ring for your tea now? You said you were famished, and you have lessons to finish before supper."

"Oh, yes! I *am* ravenous! What about Papa, though; he was hungry as well. Should we not wait, have tea with him?"

She felt weepy suddenly, proud. "I'm certain he won't mind, dearest." Her little boy was always so thoughtful of others that she found it difficult to not pull him into her arms and kiss him senseless, however he was growing up and hated to be 'babied' in front of others, so she just rubbed his arm. "Now, why not go to your room and wash-up."

"Yes, Mama."

Such a little gentleman, such a good boy. She turned a haughty face to Matthew. *I raised him. He's my son, not yours, and he is absolutely perfect, even without the exalted Fitzwilliam connections.*

"Mama? Did y'hear me?"

"Pardon? Sorry, I was daydreaming. What did you say?"

"Mandy and Birdy said next week their families, the cousins, uncles, friend –

well, everyone – will be meeting at St. James Park since the family usually plays bandy – that's what they call *shinty* here – at Mr. Darcy's home in Derbyshire when they're there for Christmas – however, since they're all in London this year instead, they'll be having a family game in town –"

"Ewan, please take a breath."

"Yes, Mama, so, we were wondering, well, if I'm still here and waiting for Uncle Jamie next week, Birdy and I were wondering if I could join in with them. Birdy said its great fun. And, she said I was as good a goalie as her cousin Will Darcy, and he's all grown-up and going to Oxford, and –"

Bridget had been blindsided. "Heavens, no!" Her tone unfairly harsh with panic. She cleared her dry throat.

"But, Mama, why?"

"The decision is entirely your father's to make, and he is too upset at the moment to be bothered with this nonsense."

"Papa won't mind, you know he won't; and, he loves watching me play *shinty*."

"Be that as it may, I seriously doubt you'd be able to join in with the Fitzwilliam family –"

"But…"

"Ewan, quiet! Even if we do remain longer than this week, you are already far behind in schoolwork. We shall need to find tutors for you, and who knows how long that may take. There would be no time for bandy, or any other games for that matter. Your schoolwork must come first."

"Lady Durand, perhaps I can be of assistance with that. Both my sister Kathy and my cousin Alice spend enough time in the city to employ several excellent tutors here. I'm certain they can suggest names to you. Perhaps Ewan can even join in with their boys for classes. They are all of the same age, or thereabouts."

"Oh, thank you, sir! Did y'hear that, Mama? That's capital!" Ewan grabbed her hand in his excitement.

Unable to look her son in the eye she turned away. "I don't believe it would be wise."

"Mama why? Please!"

"Yes, Lady Durand, why ever not? Are you concerned there will be too many children involved in the classroom? I can assure you that there are only three other children, four at most. I know boys can be a bit boisterous at times, but they are good children, all of them. When I was Ewan's age, we enjoyed most the classes where we were all taught together – brothers and cousins. We had great fun and even learned a good deal."

Ewan nodded vigorously – so eager for friends, so lonely for the company of other children, that it nearly broke her heart. His gaze darted from one adult to the other. "Oh Mama, doesn't that sound wonderful?"

"Ewan, I… I simply don't know what to say. Playing bandy with older children could be dangerous, you could be hurt… we may not even be here much longer. No, I believe we should wait for your father, hear what the news is from the Admiralty first."

"Or, perhaps the *news* from the Admiralty was nothing more than a distraction of some sort, possibly a misunderstanding; or, a jest."

She realized the truth then. Matthew had known all along where Alex and Ewan were for the morning because he'd been to one to send Alex that message – a ruse to ensure he would not be disturbed when confronting her. He probably stopped the maid from delivering her message to Alex as well. Furious, she turned on him, desperately wanting to scream. "I do not appreciate my husband being inconvenienced for a *jest*."

Matthew ignored her to concentrate solely on Ewan. "The family cousins will be thrilled with your joining them. Every Christmas we struggle to come up with enough experienced players, you would be helping us out tremendously. You're a good skater, I hear."

"Father says I'm an excellent midfielder too, although I *dinnae* get to play often as I'd like."

Matthew nodded. *And your* step-father's *a useless cripple.* "That is a shame. Well, I can see you're strong. How much do you weigh?"

"Stop this!"

Ewan jumped at Bridget's sudden outburst. "Mummy, what's happened? Are ye angry?"

"No, Ewan, not with you; never with you. However, Lord Fitzwilliam is taking too much for granted!"

"Lady Durand. I meant no offence and if I have overstepped my bounds, forgive me. My only thought was that you would wish your son to enjoy his stay here, no? My nephews and their friends are home from school, all are from excellent families, I can assure you; and, you certainly cannot expect the boy to stay locked up in a room when there's all of London to see. Never fear, he will be welcomed into our family with open arms. As if he were one of our own.

"Let me see, there will be private family gatherings Christmas Day of course; however, the family is going on a sleighride immediately *after* Christmas, and there shall be a huge skating party coming up in January before the aristocracy return to their estates and the boys leave for school – which is another reason Amanda and Birdy are so single minded in their lessons. Lady Durand, I am certain Ewan would enjoy all of that."

"Oh, Mama, doesn't it sound grand? May I? Please? We really shouldna leave. It will be months and months 'til we see Papa again if we return home now."

"You are leaving, Lady Durand? I had no idea. I know it is none of my concern; however, wouldn't London be a very lonely place for your husband without you and the boy? And you mentioned his health is just returning – why in the world would you abandon him?"

"I am not abandoning him, sir! I would never abandon him on his own. He will have his brother and sister-in-law here, and it will be for only a few months. We can visit him later, perhaps."

"Mummy, is that true? Is Papa still sick? Oh, no; I shouldna want to leave Papa now. I would worry about him. And the Darcy's and the Fitzwilliam's are nearly family, you know; and, the cousins must be fun if they're anything like Birdy and Amanda. Oh, please, Mama, please, may we stay!"

"We would be intruding, Ewan."

"Nonsense." Matthew brushed a nonexistent fleck from his sleeve. "Not in the least. We should love for him to join us."

"I was speaking with my son!"

"Sorry, just trying to help."

"Well, you're not. Now, Ewan, we shall say no more on this subject until I discuss it with your father."

"But, ye know he'll do anything you say, he always does!"

"Your schoolwork, Ewan!"

"Mama, I can study with the others, Lord Fitzwilliam said I could! I *dinnae ken* – I mean, I *do not understand* why you're being so mean about this. Birdy says–"

"Enough. This is neither the time nor place, Ewan. Now go to your room and wash for tea."

"But –"

"I said we will discuss this later! Go to your room!"

"All right," the boy groused. "But, may I say this is grossly unfair. I *dinnae* – I mean I *do not* understand you at all, Mama, I really don't! Good bye to ye, sir. Please, make my good-byes to Amanda and everyone else for me since I shall probably never be allowed outside ever again, at least until I am very old and dead. No one ever listens to what I want; I never have any fun…" And he continued grumbling under his breath as he stomped off to his room, slamming the door behind him.

"You are despicable."

"Whatever do you mean?"

"You did that deliberately!"

"Yes, of course I did. I told you, Bridget, despite your duplicity I *will* have my son, I'll never give him up – you'd best accustom yourself." Matthew strolled to the door, self-satisfied with her distress. "I am pleased with him Bridget; very pleased. He has spirit! And quite the temper, just like his father."

"Don't you dare say another word against Alex!" Bridget hissed, nearly in tears. "He is the kindest, dearest, most decent man I have ever met!"

"That may very well be; however, I wasn't referring to *Alex*. Good day. Now don't forget about the skating party after Boxing Day. You and the boy can sit with me."

Matthew moved swiftly down the staircase and out into the cold, feeling better now than when he'd entered. If all went well perhaps his son would be living nearby, even attending Harrow in a few years. Matthew could visit him as often as he liked then; and, best of all, he'd be out from under the influence of that cripple, damn him.

Kathy and George's son, James, had just been enrolled in boarding school – in fact, that was all the lad spoken of these days, and most especially playing on the cricket team as his father and grandfathers had, years before. The lads could attend together; James was such a charismatic boy, strong and robust like Ewan. Matthew considered that for a moment and began to chuckle. And wasn't Alice and Harry's lad, Bill, in his final year at Harrow – as was George and Kathy's son Benedict, another excellent young man. He would introduce them all to Ewan quickly as possible, begin setting the wheels in motion. Throw in Oxford student Will Fitzwilliam – the undisputed leader of the Darcy and Fitzwilliam cousins – and, Ewan would be screaming to remain in London forever.

And, if Ewan remained in London, possibly so would Bridget.

Why should I care?

He closed his eyes. Because he wanted her.

The stupid woman still had a grip on his heart, sent his blood pulsing; she was desirable as ever, damned if she wasn't. Fire and Frost – he had missed those ice shards and sparks between them, aching arousals, explosive completions. The intense feelings between them were still there, the passion undeniable. She may not like him, but she desired him yet.

Soon, Bridget, soon…

Bridget watched from her window above as Matthew left, heard the doorman's unctuous words of farewell, watched as others stood back, staring in awe at someone so obviously above them in station, gaping at his huge black carriage pulled by four magnificent Fresian horses, gaping at the liveried footmen. She heard the cheering as gold coins were tossed out to the children. How could she fight such a man? How could she resist him? She should have let him know about Ewan long before, but the dislike between her husband and Matthew frightened her. Alex was so good, so kind. She loved Alex with all her heart; but… not in the way she had loved Matthew; the way she still loved Matthew. Therein lay the real reason for her silence these years, the true problem. She prayed nothing bad was going to come from all this.

From his room Ewan watched the impressive gentleman leave, giggling because it really was so comical to see everyone dart about and fall over themselves. But it was the man himself who fascinated. Why did he feel so drawn to Amanda's father, and to Amanda herself for that matter? She didn't appeal to him the way pretty Birdie did – something he'd rather have his tongue ripped out than admit. If only he could have spoken with Lord Fitzwilliam longer.

"Ewan," he heard his mother call. "Would you like hot chocolate?"

"Oh, yes, Mama," he replied, then returned to the wash basin to dry his hands and face.

CHAPTER SEVEN

DARCY WAS GREETED WARMLY AT the door of White's Gentleman's Club, his coat, hat and gloves taken by none other than the establishment's manager himself. "It is very good to see you this afternoon, Mr. Darcy. If you will follow me, Lord Fitzwilliam is awaiting you in the coffee room."

"You seem in a good mood today, Royce. Is Lord Clarendon arrived, then?"

"Who? Oh. No, sir, not as yet. *However...*" a smug grin spread across the manager's face. He cleared his throat. "We do have a most distinguished nobleman from the Continent visiting with us today. He is, at this very moment, seated with Lord Fitzwilliam – an incredibly illustrious gentleman. The visitor I mean."

The establishment's administrator glanced about to ensure others were listening as they walked through the room. "The Duke of *Aliaga y Castellot* – a *Grande de Espana* no less. A Royal Duke of the Spanish Court. I doubt Brooks could best that. *And,* one has it on good authority that his grace is a direct descendant of none other than *Queen Isabella and King Ferdinand.*"

"My goodness. Right here at Whites? Fancy that."

"Yes. Quite an honor."

"And you have allowed him to be seated with Lord Fitzwilliam?"

Darcy saw terror dawn in the man's eyes. "Perhaps we should hurry." Having by now reached the door to the coffee room Royce smoothed his hair, straightened his cuffs and surreptitiously checked his breath. He opened the door for Darcy to enter then stopped just inside doorway when they heard inhuman shrieks.

A dozen or so terrified men stood among tables and chairs to the far left, while on the far right a tall, dark, and distinguished nobleman was repeatedly smacking Lord Fitzwilliam's head with an antique magnifying glass.

"Stop hitting me you damnable Spaniard!" Fitz made several unsuccessful attempts to grab the handle. *"Are you insane? Give me that!"*

"*Sapo! Que te folle un pez,*" the *Grande de Espana* shouted in return, turning at the sound of Darcy's burst of laughter. *"Guillermo!* How do you put up with this *pendejo* all these years?" Just in time he saw the cup of coffee Fitzwilliam was about to toss at him, and he jumped back. *"Bastardo!* You are most fortunate that I moved out of the way before you poured that vile liquid on me. If you had ruined these ivory buttons, I would have taken you to court." Milagros brushed imaginary smudges from his sleeve.

"You look as preposterous as Darcy."

"This, my ignorant friend, is my yachting club jacket. Impressive, no?"

"No. And when did you begin wearing bowler hats? Makes you look like a pimple." Fitzwilliam dug out his pipe and began searching in his pockets for his tobacco pouch. He was thrilled to see his old friend again, even if their banter terrified the surrounding tables.

Dr. Anthony Milagros, now the distinguished *Duke of Aliaga y Castellot,* had been family physician to the Fitzwilliam and Darcy families for many years, having met them through Richard Fitzwilliam's late wife, Amanda; and had, over time, become accepted as family. In some ways his life had mirrored Richard Fitzwilliam's. Both had fallen out of favor with their fathers over life choices made as young men, and both had eventually inherited their family titles through the death of an older brother. It was an outcome neither of them wanted – Anthony had cherished his work as a doctor, and Richard had enjoyed overseeing the Board of Ordnance. However, it was also an outcome neither could refuse.

Milagros snatched the pipe from Fitz and handed it to Darcy. "Enough! Now sit still."

However, that was an impossibility for Fitz. "What in the world is the matter with your hand? Why does it shake like that?"

"I am old. How would you prefer it to shake?"

"I would prefer it not shake at all when you're poking in my ear like this. Ow! Bloody hell, that hurt!"

"Nonsense, I didn't feel a thing. Aha! There is the cause of your hearing problem."

"Well? What is it?"

"Someone fetch me a long hook, perhaps a chisel and hammer..."

"Anthony!"

It was sometime later, the chaos in the room settled down, when Darcy, Fitzwilliam and Milagros could sit at their favorite table, begin manly gossip, smoke their pipes, and enjoy afternoon tea.

"I half expected you to run screaming from the room, Fitz. Did you really believe I would shove a hook in your ear?"

"I knew all along you weren't serious – you weren't, were you? See. By the way, I feel dreadful about that unfortunate palsy remark I made to you."

"Oh, you do not."

"Not really, no. Ah, the food has arrived at last. Pass me those sandwiches, would you, Anthony? Dear me, there goes that hand again, you'd best pass me the entire tray. Wouldn't want the food to go flying about. Thank you."

Darcy snatched the cucumber sandwich dish from Fitz before he took them all. "You're looking very well, Anthony."

"I know, isn't it marvelous. I see appreciative glances wherever I go."

"You certain it isn't whenever you leave?"

Anthony sat back, stared at Fitz in total silence. Curious, Fitzwilliam looked up from his mince pie. "Whatever have I said now?"

With a huff, Anthony turned his attention to Darcy once again. "You look splendid as well, Guillermo; you never seem to age."

"It's in one's heritage – my father always appeared years younger than he was. And, of course, I try to eat sensibly, walk briskly each day, limit my smoking and drinking."

"As a physician I often notice that an excessively overweight man rarely sees old age. Speaking of which, Fitzwilliam, you've written your will I hope?"

"Pardon me? I should call you out for that. I'm not fat."

"As compared to what? Your chubby arms can barely lift high enough to reach the table. By the way Darcy, I love the cut of your coat. You must give me the name of your tailor."

Richard motioned a servant over. "Yes, sir."

"Ask someone to bring me a shovel, please."

"That was delicious. Now for a good pipe and coffee." Darcy dabbed his mouth with his napkin and pushed his plate away, motioning for the waiter. "So, Anthony, I assume the responsibilities of your title give you little time for medicine these days."

"Unfortunate, but true. However, I do find time to work on various medical boards, try to keep up on the latest innovations."

"Good for you. You'll need to revisit your old hospital then. I'm certain you've heard that Florence Nightingale has opened a school for nursing there, first of its kind."

"Yes, isn't she marvelous? I definitely am planning to visit as I am interested in introducing her procedures to the medical community in my city. She was very helpful in Crimea, saved so many lives. Her methods are remarkable."

Richard motioned for more brandy to be poured. "When did you arrive in London?"

"Only this morning. Tomorrow I shall be taking the earliest train available to Windsor for the funeral; but, naturally, I could not resist stopping *en route* to enjoy a long visit with Elizabeth and Darcy, and all my beloved friends here in London. Unfortunately, you were here today as well."

Fitz cupped his ear. "What was that?"

Laughing, Anthony blew a smoke ring into the air.

"And, I suppose you insist on supping at my home this evening?"

"But of course, Richard. Your Mrs. Nash is an excellent cook."

Darcy leaned back in his chair. "You will be returning to London after the funeral, will you not, so you can join Elizabeth and the family for dinner at Pemberley House as well?"

"I should be delighted. Your cook is even better than his."

Fitzwilliam sighed. "In that case you'd better remain at my house over Christmas. The grandchildren enjoy your visits for some profound reason."

"Meg and Beth have already invited me – we correspond regularly. Do try and keep up. Ah, marvelous, look's who's arrived!"

"Is this a private party?"

Darcy turned to see his son George, along with Fitzwilliam's sons Mark and Luke, striding toward them. "Gentlemen, well met. Come and join us."

"Good day, everyone." Mark squeezed his father's shoulder then shook hands with Darcy. "My god, but it is wonderful to see you, Uncle Tony; it's been too long. Meg and Beth told us you were visiting so we came here straight away. I hear you are on your way to The Funeral?"

"*Si,* I'm on the first train out in the morning."

Luke joined his brother in greeting Anthony, then motioned at his father's tobacco pouch. "You are not to smoke as much as you do, you know that."

"I rarely smoke these days, only after the occasional meal."

"Give it here."

Fitzwilliam grunted then tossed the pouch to him. Luke was another of his bossy children Fitz wished would marry instead of monitoring his every move. There was little chance of that though. Women adored Luke – too many women. At this rate he'd never have an heir.

"Stop grumbling, Papa. You smoke too damn much, you know you do, your doctors know you do – we all know you do. You need a keeper." He filled his own pipe with his father's tobacco then settled back in his chair. "By the way, where is Matthew? I expected he would meet us here. Mark, are you 'sensing' anything?"

Fitzwilliam's twin sons Matthew and Mark possessed an intuitive bond that both amused and amazed their family. Playing to that, Mark pressed his fingers against his closed eyes and meditated for a moment. "Yes, yes. I see it all now. He will be here within five minutes."

"Bollocks. I suppose you know what he's wearing as well," Luke snorted out a laugh as he puffed away on his pipe. "You two are always pulling this trick on us."

"Doubting Thomas, are we? All right, give me a moment and I'll tell you… the vision is getting clearer now… he wears a black dress-coat with full collar rolling low, white vest, neck-tie looped loosely with a – pearl…no, I tell a lie, a *ruby* stickpin, and black doeskin trousers."

Luke stopped puffing, intrigued despite his common sense. "Are you trying to tell us you sense that through your other worldly linking with Matthew?"

"Don't be an idiot. I saw him about an hour ago when he told me he'd meet us. And, there he is – Matthew, over here." Mark was already moving a chair beside him for his brother's use.

"Who allowed this riff raff inside? They must be lowering the requirements for membership. Luke, move your foot. Hello, Uncle Wills, George. Uncle Tony! Now our impressive table location is understandable. Father, don't you dare light that cigar. Luke, you were supposed to watch him today."

"I took his tobacco pouch, didn't I? Sneaky old man has more pockets than Fagin."

Oftentimes, Fitzwilliam was so proud of his sons that the emotion embarrassed him. Today it felt more like aggravation. "My little nest of vipers. We should have sold this lot to gypsies when we had the chance, Darcy."

Luke snatched the cigar away. "Don't be silly, Papa. You know you would have had to pay them to take us."

A few hours later, after the two fathers had left, Anthony and the younger men were left to finish off the last of the brandy and cigars. "Matthew, would your coachman be available to drive me to the train station tomorrow morning? I hate to put your father out any more than I am."

"Of course, Uncle Tony. I'll send him by around eight, shall I? Good. Mark, pass me a cigar. Are we playing cards this evening?"

"What in the world? I have told you twice already today that we've cancelled cards this evening."

"Pardon? Oh, yes, of course. My mind… I must be more tired than I thought."

"Is there something bothering you?"

"No, of course not. You worry too much." Wanting to quickly change the subject, he turned to Anthony. "So, you're off to the funeral tomorrow. Did you know the Prince well?"

"I've met him at a few court functions. Actually, the only reason my presence is required is to assist an old friend of mine, Albert's cousin, the Duc de Nemours. He has been quite ill this year but is determined to attend. From what he tells me this will be a very simple affair, just as Albert wished."

"I read in *The Times* all of Windsor is shuttered down, the chapel covered in black. Well, it's just as bad here, I cannot remember a bleaker Christmas. No theater, no ballet, no carolers – although, now that I think on it that one's a mercy. When Papa tries to join in, singers weep, dogs howl, cats screech. George, I hope your father is still having Boxing Day at Pemberley House."

"Absolutely. Mother is removing the black crepe and sneaking decorations around the house whenever old Winters isn't looking." George accepted a cup of coffee from the waiter. "Why do you ask?"

"My Amanda is convinced there'll be no Father Christmas this year, or any of the usual celebrations. I just want to reassure her that life does go on. By the way, the girls and I met Alex Durand and his son at your father's house the other day. The man is in town awaiting word of his brother and your sister. Will they be invited to the family holiday activities, do you think? It would be a shame for the lad to be excluded."

George glanced up, his surprise evident. "Kathy and I were speaking of this just today. You won't mind then?"

"Mind? Of course not." Matthew coolly stirred his cup of coffee. "I have nothing against the child. Yes, I know, I know – I had that awful brawl with his father, but that was ages ago. All forgotten now. In fact, I was thinking – Will is home from Oxford for the holidays. Perhaps he could take the boy under his wing, make him feel part of the family? I'd hate for the lad to suffer because of my prior misdeeds."

"Who are you and what have you done with my cousin?"

"Very funny, George. Imagine how I'm laughing inside."

"Truth is, I haven't met the son as yet, didn't even know he existed until father told me. Odd that Anne Marie never mentioned him. Still, he's here now and part of the family. And, that's an excellent idea about Will, too, I'll mention it to him."

Anthony smiled, patted Matthew's arm. "So, after all these years you've decided to make peace with the fellow. Good for you, *hijo*."

"It's only right since I was clearly in the wrong. I'll have you know I've already visited with the family. Well, my God, will you look at your faces. George, stop staring at me as if I had two heads,

I'm not a monster. I like to think my temper has been tamed by age."

"That's news to me." Luke scoffed. "You're usually the most consistently irritated person I know."

"Damn you, Luke. That's a hell of a thing to say."

"You see? Can't even take a ribbing. It's not my fault if you act the temperamental diva at times."

"I do not, you ass. I'll have you all know we had a damn pleasant visit. In fact, when his parents were out of the room the boy confided to me his desire to attend school at Harrow. He said his parents had tried several times while in town to secure at least an appointment, but with the Prince's death… well, evidently, they now are hoping to speak with the administration after the new year. It is all very hush hush – not to leave this table. The family would be mortified if it were known they've been unsuccessful; but, they have hopes. Perhaps with our family's long history at the school father could call in a few favors." Matthew felt his brother Mark's gaze on him.

He could never fool Mark.

Even George scowled. "This news is a surprise to me. Father said the boy's mother made it very plain they'd be returning to Scotland as soon as possible. In fact, he was amazed Bridget came to London at all."

"Really?" Matthew cleared his throat. "Well, as I said, they wish this kept secret since they've been unsuccessful in their attempts. One thing for certain, Ewan – that's his name, Ewan – is desperately lonely. I mentioned the boys and their ice games and he nearly burst out of his skin with excitement. George, perhaps you could invite him to join them. When are we scheduled to begin, by the way?"

"A few days after Christmas. And, I do believe we're short on numbers, so another warm body will be most welcome. Is it too much to hope he's a good defender? How old is he?"

Matthew felt the glow of fatherly pride. "Eight; however, he's a big lad for his age, looks very strong."

"Eight? That's awfully young. We'll make certain he doesn't face off against the older lads. Oh, and Kathy wanted me to ask about the family pew numbers. You and Clarissa are both attending at St. Paul's for the Prince's service?"

"Clarissa, my Clarissa, not delight the *ton* with her expansive mourning wardrobe? Please be sensible. She's been in a frenzy of buying for days now, even purchased a complete mourning wardrobe for *me*. Wishful thinking on her part – unless she's preparing me for my own funeral."

CHAPTER EIGHT

THE FUNERAL OF PRINCE ALBERT. [From the London Times, Dec. 23]

During Monday's funeral, sermons were preached at all the principal churches on the loss the British nation has sustained in the removal by death of the Prince Consort of England. *With little of the pomp and pageantry of a State ceremonial, but with every outward mark of respect, and with all the solemnity which befitted his high station and his public virtues, the mortal remains of the husband of our Queen were interred in the last resting place of England's sovereigns — the Chapel Royal of St. George's, Windsor. By the express desire of his Royal Highness the funeral was of the plainest and most private character; but in the chapel, to do honor to his obsequies, were assembled all the chiefest men of the State, and throughout England, by every sign of sorrow and mourning, the nation manifested its sense of the loss it has sustained. Windsor itself wore an aspect of the most profound gloom. Every shop was closed and every blind drawn down. The streets were silent and almost deserted, and all who appeared abroad were dressed in the deepest mourning. The great bell of* Windsor Castle *changed out its doleful sound at intervals from an early hour, and minute bells were tolled also at St. John's Church. At the parish church of Clewer and at St. John's there were services in the morning and afternoon, and the day was observed throughout the royal borough in the strictest manner. The weather was in character with the occasion, a chill, damp sir, with a dull, leaden sky above, increased the gloom which hung over all.*

Mark Fitzwilliam downed his whiskey in one gulp then set the glass down hard on the pub table. As he searched his vest for a pocket watch he turned to his brother and belched. "Pardon. Oh, good god, Matthew, you look as if you've just crawled out of the bottle. I better not look half as bad."

"Much. Worse."

"Splendid. And I have only two hours til I'm due at Bunny's house. We should have returned to Papa's after the service, instead of sneaking out to drink, Matthew. Matthew?" Mark pulled his brother's head up by his hair. "Hello?"

"Stop shouting." Gasping back bile, Matthew leaned back in his chair to stare at the ceiling. "There's something stuck up there. Looks like beef."

"Well, at least your eyes are open. Do you remember when we left the memorial at St. Paul's – supposedly because you had something vastly important to tell me, but the subject of which we have not, as yet, discussed?"

"Too many words for me to comprehend right at this moment. Ask me again in a week."

"Half-past one in the afternoon, Monday, that's when. We've been in this filthy pit for nearly eighteen hours and all we've done is drink." Mark looked around him. "Why is this hovel even open? Any respectable tavern has their doors closed out of respect for the Prince."

Matthew rested his chin on his fist and attempted to get his brother into focus. "The telling word in your statement was 'respectable' I do believe."

"Have you ever been here before?"

"Once, years ago, when it was owned by an older couple. Simple people. Nice. Had some teeth missing, but all in all they were relatively pleasant. George, Charles and I had snuck away from university, desperate to locate 'accommodating' women nearby willing to accept our money. Yes, I know, we were pigs; don't glower at me like that – we were also very young and very stupid and very eager to lose our virginity. Speaking of women, wasn't there one on my lap? When did she leave?"

"Around three this morning, just after the brawl."

"What brawl?"

"Unimportant. We avoided it."

"And, just why did the love of my life leave?"

"A *paying* customer required servicing."

"There you have it. The devil is always in the details."

"Well, as entertaining as this has been, Matt – even that pissing contest you lost during the early evening to the two sailors – I do need to be on my way."

"Now? But we haven't spoken yet."

"And whose fault is that? I told you over and over I needed to be at Bunny's house today by eleven, one at the very latest. We're taking the train to that new station in Hampstead, visiting her relatives there. In Hampstead, not the train station. Won't be returning until after Boxing Day at the earliest."

"Bunny? You mean Lucille Armitage? You were in earnest? You're actually going to propose to her?"

"Yes. Matthew, try and pay attention to me for once. And, I am having one of mama's rings sized for her but it wasn't ready yesterday, so Luke is picking it up instead. He'll be taking the train out tomorrow and meeting me."

"I don't understand. There's no need for marriage. Lucille Armitage is a wealthy widow… you're rich as Croesus in your own right and she's the majority shareholder in the largest shipping business in Britain. Just take her to bed and enjoy yourselves. Or, have you already?"

"Have I what, taken her to bed? None of your goddamn business."

"That's a yes then. Listen to the voice of experience. After all these years why not wait a while longer before you propose, until next year sometime, the Spring perhaps. Or 1870."

"No putting this off again – I only thank heaven I don't need to speak with her father first. Don't look at me like that, she's been expecting a proposal for the past year, Matt. She's a nice woman. It's a good family. We get on very well."

"Very true."

"And?"

"And, you don't love her."

"What has that to do with anything?"

"Well… I forget. Besides, why are you rushing into this?"

"How bloody drunk are you? You know she and I have been courting for a very long time. Besides, I'm nearly forty years old."

"We're twins, remember? I was there when you were born. In fact, I'm two minutes older."

"And by the look of you now those must have been two very rough minutes. The thing is, you have Amanda Rose, you have a child, something of yourself that will live on after you die. All I have are stone buildings and monuments to dead poets I've designed. Look, I'm tired of being alone. I want children. I want a home."

"Children are bloody wonderful, I'll give you that. But I warn you, it is hell to be leg shackled for life to someone you despise."

"Clarissa was *your* grand mistake, not mine; in fact, if I remember rightly, I told you not to marry the woman."

"Yes, you did. So, I am returning the favor. Do as I say, not as I do." Matthew began to slump forward in his chair.

"Be a good fellow and turn your head away; your breath could kill a horse. As I said, we're forty years old, Matthew, and I've never believed in some sort of grand love waiting out there for me, you know that. I'm a mathematician. Logical. I am not given to whims. Bunny's a good match, pretty, she laughs at my stories. I doubt she loves me either, really, but we enjoy each other's company, our families are known to each other."

"Father's pushing you into this, isn't he?"

"Isn't he always? It's time though, he's right for once. I just hope the wedding fuss is over quickly. Beckman wants to consult with me about a new train station he's designing, are there are several monuments to Prince Albert already being discussed." As he spoke Mark finally located his pocket watch and clicked it open. "Bloody hell, look at the time! I need to leave now so I can at least change my smalls and have a wash-up at home. Are you ready?"

"The spirit is willing – but… I forget the rest. Let's have another bottle."

"Matthew, get up. I'm not leaving you here alone."

"Then don't leave. You there, bring us another."

Mark waved off the burly man from behind the bar. "Absolutely not. Go away. Never come back here again."

"But I haven't told you... wait a moment; sit. Please. I really do have something we need to discuss."

Mark hesitated, anxious with his brother's sudden seriousness. In fact, Matthew had been acting oddly since they'd met their father and Uncle Wills at Whites' days before. "Listen to me, whatever is wrong, whatever demons are torturing you, put them to rest. Go home. I'll see you in a few days and we'll have a good talk. A sober talk."

"Home? What home? Have no home. One more drink, Mark, just one more."

"No and wipe your mouth." Mark handed him a handkerchief. "You've lip rouge all over. Damnation, Matthew, put your arm down – I didn't give you that to summon the barman again. That does it, we're leaving." A sudden grip on his arm stopped Mark rising from his chair and he looked down at his brother's rather green face. "Good lord, you're not going to be sick all over me, are you?"

"No. Maybe. Before I do though I really must tell you something."

"So you've been stating all night long only to drink more whiskey instead. Sorry, Matt, it is too late now; I haven't the time. As I said, we'll talk in a few days."

Abruptly Matthew released the grip on his brother's arm and ran his hands through his hair. "All right. Here it is. Papa has his male heir. There, I've said it, aloud. An illegimitgate… an ullematimate… a bastard child. What's happened to my tongue?"

"Pardon me?" Mark turned his brother to face him. "Of course, father has an heir, he has five sons. He's lousy with heirs, and all quite legitimate."

"No, mean now there's a child heir, following generation heir. Except the boy cannot inherit, cause he's a bastard."

Mark sat back down with a thud. "Just a moment. Has Luke gotten a child on a woman? Is that why you and he were snarling at each other?"

"Oh lord, him too? I had *no* idea! By heavens, we are a hopeless family, aren't we."

"Matthew, I am *asking* you about Luke, not *telling* you. Now, try to concentrate – look me in the eye – that's it – did Luke get a woman with child?"

"Not of which I'm aware… of, no. Besides, we always snarl at each other. That's how we express our – oh grand, now I'm hiccupping – brotherly love." He tried holding his breath for a moment to stop the hiccups then stood to look around for a water pitcher.

"Here's a glass of water, Matthew. Turn the other way, I'm behind you. Now, drink this upside down like Mama used to have us do… that's it. Better? Good. Now, tell me what the fuck is going on. Which of our brothers is the idiot? Is it Andrew? Never tell me it's Teddie! Father Ted takes his vow of celibacy seriously; besides, he knows Papa would kill him."

"No. No. No. Not Andrew. Not Ted. Not Luke." For the first time in his life Matthew appeared to be nervous. He tossed back the rest of his whiskey.

"Say something, damn you!"

"It's me, Mark. Or should I say it's I? Sounds ridiculous both ways."

"I beg your pardon?"

"I've a son, Mark. A son. He's beautiful, even if he does look so much like Papa that I want to salute him. Just like Papa. I could not believe it when I saw him, but it's true. And, he has our chin, you know, poor lil bastard boy. Adorable. Slight indentation in the middle of his chin. Just like my beautiful Amanda's. Just like mine. Just like yours. Just like Mama's."

"Nonsense. Do you even realize what you're saying, or is this some drunken fantasy?"

"No fantasy, no; and, yes, I do unner… understand what I'm saying. I've a son. Alex Durand's boy. Ewan. That's my child. Mine and Bridge's. My boy."

Tears began to fill Matthew's eyes, all his bravado gone. Years before he had fought Alex Durand over her, shocking everyone and causing his close friendship with George Darcy to cool for months. His marriage had nearly ended because of that woman. Then she was gone overnight, running off with none other than – Alex Durand.

After glancing about the room Mark put his hand on his brother's shoulder. True or not, this was unwise to discuss openly in a tavern. "We cannot talk here."

"Why? There's no one here but you and I… me… I… and that revolting barkeep, no offence, sir. Besides, he's too far away to hear anything, aren't you? See, he agrees. You do believe me, don't you? You 'member I kept Bridge in that house years ago; she and her nasty sister; and… and, you knew she and I were lovers, didn't you?"

"Yes, of course I remember."

"Well. There you go." Matthew poked Mark's chest for emphasis. "The bitch gave birth to *my son* and never told me. Never knew. No. There should be a law against that, right? Her cripple, Durand, has raised *my* son, instead of me. Durand watched him grow, 'stead of me." Matthew grew more and more incoherent the more upset he became. "I need someone – anyone – to know about m'son – if something were t'happen to me *someone must know*. You believe me. You do believe me, right?"

"Yes, of course I do, calm down and lower your voice! Is that what this night has been all about; why we had to come out here to bloody Whitechapel of all places, to this rat hole for a drink, instead of enjoying the comforts of home, or better yet, White's? Damn me. So, you believe Bridget gave birth to your son with no one in the family suspecting? Would not Anne Marie have said something? She *is* married to the woman's brother-in-law, correct? Would she not have said something by now?"

"Never did. Visit them, I mean. Maybe she never knew, either. Maybe no one told her. Sneaky Scots. It was only Jamie who went up there all the years, alone or with Birdy so she could visit with Bridget. Always thought that was odd. He knew though, Jamie did, the bastard. He knew. Deal with him when they're home."

"Then perhaps you should forget all this until you can speak with Jamie."

"Why? You still don't believe me! Bridget as much as admitted it to me!"

"So that was the true reason you visited them."

"Not them – *her*. I sent Durand on a wild goose chase so I could meet with her alone. Told her I bloody well will have my son with me, whether she likes it or not. I threatened her – well, him actually. The cripple. Told her I'd ruin his career, and when she looked so smug about that, I told her I have things I could tell her *husband*, intimacies she and I did together, enjoyed immensely. They'd break him, Mark. They would destroy any man. I should love to see that."

"Be serious, Matthew. I know you would never do that."

"No, probably not – but, she doesn't! Bloody hell, Mark, he's my son. I want to know him. I don't want Durand to be the man he looks up to – it should be me."

"It sounds like you're more interested in revenge on Durand than gaining a son."

"Whose side are you on?"

"On your side, of course. Always your side. Always." Mark tightened his grip on Matthew's shoulder. "Listen to me, you may, however, be jumping to some very dangerous conclusions here, voicing them out loud in a public place."

"Thank you so very much for nothing! You know, I was afraid to tell you, afraid of your ridicule." Matthew shrugged off his brother's hand. "Damn it, you're one person I hoped would stand with me, Mark!"

"All right, all right. Fact is, I do believe you. Damn it, this is dangerous. What exactly did she say?"

"Bitch told me she had no choice but to marry Durand nine years ago, because she was carrying a child. And before you say anything – yes, I am certain boy's mine and not Durand's! My god, you only have to see him once to know the truth of it. She claims she wrote to me for help but that I ignored her letters. Mark, there were no letters; never. No. Never received any letters from her. What does *that* tell you? Tells me she's a liar, natural born. I know she was never with Durand while we were together. No! She couldn't have been. She was mine, damn it. Mine." He backed into a chair and stumbled, then righted himself.

Mark sighed. "Say no more about this for now, please. For your sake, for Bridget's sake, and most important of all, for that boy's sake – keep quiet."

"I have my rights."

"No, you do not. Matt, be reasonable. You have no recourse that would not harm the child, ruin his life."

"It will be all right, Mark; you'll see." Suddenly feeling ill again, Matthew turned from his brother and began to search for a pail as he headed for the door. "I have a plan, I know what I'm about. And, I shall have my boy with me, one way or the other. The bitch'll protest, but I'm convinced that after a while she'll come to realize she was always mine, still is…"

Dear God. Mark stopped listening at that point. There it was, plain as day. Matthew foolishly, madly, blindly, loved that one woman still, and probably always would. "Bollocks. You're hopeless, Matthew."

"Ha! And don't I know it! (hiccup) You do realize, Marky, that you are my dearest friend. Love you like a brother."

"You're not going to kiss me, are you?"

"Jus' a little one? All right, all right, I won't. There's one thing more. I must ask a flavor of you. I mean a favor."

"I'll do whatever you wish, just put on your hat. Wherever is Deacon with that ridiculous carriage of yours? Oh, there he is." Before Mark could signal for him the driver was already turning the coach around and heading their way.

"Where did I put that thing?" Matthew patted his coat then reached into his vest and pulled out an envelope. "Here." He drunkenly presented it with both hands, as if it were sacred. "Would you deliver this to her for me?"

"To whom? Bridget?"

"No, Mark, the Duke of Kent. Yes, Bridget."

"No need to be snippy. What's in this, might I ask? I'll not be party to any revenge on the woman, Matt. You'll regret it tomorrow and hate me for agreeing to it."

"This has nothing to do with revenge."

"Well, what is it then?'

"Fifty-thousand pounds."

Mark nearly fainted. "*Are you insane!* Fifty - thous... You're drunk! Put that away." He looked around, greatly relieved to see the street completely empty.

"Are you refusing me? How often do I ask favors of you, Mark?"

"Almost daily. Why do you think I travel so often?"

"Listen to me, this is important. It's for m'boy. If something were to happen to me, if I should die–"

"Never say that, Matt."

"Never know what could happen. None of us expected Mama to die, did we? None of us are immoral, excuse me, immortal And, I am not asking Bridget to reveal anything to him, nor to anyone else; but, I need to know I've contributed *something* to his life other than some long ago bed romp. Please, do this. Would myself, but doubt she'd admit me again. Not that I would blame her. She was a wee bit upset with me when I left. Besides, she always liked you better than she liked me – well, everyone does, don't they? Funny, she was the only person outside of family who could tell us apart, did you know that? Please, Mark?"

Mark struggled against the impulse to either kick his brother in the ass or hug him in pity. God, what misery it must be to love someone this much. "Very well – but, really, you idiot! Of all the damn places you choose to hand this to me, it had to be here in one of the worst areas of the city." Mark checked once again for anyone watching before he took the parcel.

"Wanted to be certain no one we knew would be around to see us."

"Well, you've certainly done that." Mark stared at the package before slipping it into his coat. "Do you know – aside from your fearsome temper – this is your worst flaw."

"My penmanship?""

"No, idiot. It's your rashness. Practically in your dotage and you still rarely consider consequences." He disliked carrying so much blunt on his person; but, better him than his drunken brother.

"Tell me everything she says. Hope she's impressed by the amount."

"You know, there are times when I fear for your sanity."

Matthew nodded. "If I had a pound for every person who's told me that – but, enough of that… so, you'll do it then?"

"Yes, of course I will, but it will have to wait until my return, all right? You know I'd do anything for you, short of murder."

"That's my brother! Remember when I talked you into straddling Magdalen Bell Tower at Oxford – *au naturale*? Won us forty pounds each."

"Actually, I received one hundred pounds for that, I only *gave* you forty."

"So, you see, this is not much to ask really."

"Don't push your luck. What's wrong? Blast, are you going to be ill?"

"Yes, planning on it."

The coachman had reached them by now, jumped down from his perch and opened the carriage door. "Help me here, Deacon, would you? Good thing you were waiting nearby. I feared you'd gone to visit a pub yourself for the night."The two men began to push Matthew into the small, sporting carriage. "I wouldn't have blamed you if you had."

"Not 'ardly, sir. Not leavin' a beauty like this out for some dragsman. Besides, I'm accustomed to no sleep. Was on either middle or mornin' watch for over ten years in Royal Navy; prefer the solitude. And, I'm big enough so no one dare test me. You know 'ow that is, sir, being a big 'un yerself. Night crawlers don't bother us much."

"Excellent point and true enough – watch his head there – ooh. Bloody hell. Sorry Matt, that'll leave a mark. For heaven's sake, how many legs does he have?"

"'e is looking a bit green, sir, don't you think?"

"Definitely. Now, back to what you were saying, my brother and I both learned long ago to never let our guard down merely because we were bigger than the ruffians; there's no excuse for carelessness. Where are his arms?"

"Oh, My God! Have I lost my arms?"

"Shut up, Matthew and pull your knees up... or something. Tell me again why you insisted on using this ridiculous looking contraption?"

"Wanted to show it to you, rides like the wind when I drive, but Deacon was needed, because knew we'd be the worse for wear – at least I am."

"Was the interior this small on the way here? Oh, well. Don't suppose you could move over a little? Matthew? Has he passed out?"

"Ssh! Tryin' to sleep."

"Next time you suggest us both driving in this oversized pram I'll shove the entire carriage up your arse. What do you think about that, hmmm? Don't bother answering, I don't care really. Is all of him inside, Deacon – any odd bits dangling? Excellent. I'll need to sit on the floor on the way home, although it'll be extremely uncomfortable. Drop me off first, if you would, then you can bring Lord High and Mighty Fitzwilliam to his house and personally hand him over to that awful valet of his. Tell him my instructions are he have cook prepare a proper meal and – Matthew! Oh, sweet Jesu, no!"

The sounds and scents of retching filled the morning air – as well as the floor of the carriage. "And there goes the only place left to sit! Thank you so very much, you imbecile."

"What smells so awful – oops, think I'm going to be sick again..."

"Aim away from me!" Mark jumped back, covering his nose with his handkerchief. "That truly is disgusting. Hard to believe all that came from inside you since we haven't eaten in hours. Although… I do believe I see bits of a chicken wing there. At least I think it's chicken…"

"How'll you get 'ome, sir? You can't sit in there, and there's no room up by me. It's only a single seat. Perhaps, if you can drive this rig, I could walk, see if I can find a horse tram anywheres."

"Drive this? I'd be sick myself if I'm anywhere near this carriage now; my stomach's not much better than his. Not to worry, Deacon, you go on, and thank you for offering. I shall walk until I see a cab to hail."

"A cab? 'ere? Oh, I don't know about that, sir. Not many in these parts. Best thing would be to 'ead west if you're goin' to walk. Cabbies begin appearin' about six blocks that direction. And, remember, stay in busy areas."

"Will do, Deacon." Laughing, Mark turned to the left and began to walk. "You take care now."

"'Scuse me, sir."

"Yes."

"That's wrong way."

"Are you certain? Oh, yes, I suppose it is."

"You sure you'll be all right?"

"Absolutely. Probably." Mark looked around. "Damn, at one time I knew this city like the back of my hand, certainly it will all come back to me."

Matthew groaned from somewhere in the carriage. "You'll be at Uncle Wills' on Boxing (hiccup) Day, then?"

"No."

"Good. Come to the house… tomorrow for Christmas Eve… we'll have a sip of brandy."

"Matthew, listen to me and try to focus on what I am saying. I'll be with Bunny's family. Besides, the way you look you'll *sleep* till Boxing Day."

Matthew's obscene hand gesture out the window was his only reply to that. "Can't believe you're going to ask Miss Bunny to marry you. Trouble and strife… take a wife…"

"A Happy Christmas to Amanda. And, Matt, remember, I love you, brother."

Why had he suddenly blurted out that last bit? Sentimentality was seldom uttered between the two.

"Course you do. *You* best be careful. You're the baby of the two of us and my responsibility."

"Idiot." Mark then turned to the driver. "Drive him straight home."

"That I will, sir. That I will. And, if I can be so bold, sir – in keepin' with our previous words – eyes open, sir."

"Yes, yes. Not to worry, Deacon. Off with you now."

As the carriage disappeared around a corner Mark rubbed his whiskered cheek. Now what to do? If he was seriously considering proposing to Bunny (and, he still had his doubts, ring or no ring) he'd better have a wash and shave before meeting her – true, she was generally affable, but every woman had limits. Well, nothing for it but to start off and pray for a passing acquaintance to give him a lift, or perhaps there'd be an inn along the way where he could sink into a nice hot tub. *Now which way did Deacon say was West again?* Ah yes; he turned up his collar, hunched his shoulders against the cold, and headed… west?

Inside, the innkeeper who had been surreptitiously watching the wealthy coves for hours grunted at the sight of the expensive coach stopping for them. 'Twin' marks like these might be considered 'good luck', a profitable omen. And those two, dressed to the nines like they was – why, coulda been big money in this for one of 'is regulars, he'd bet his sorry life on it. Missed opportunity, that's what this was. After all, there'd be no reason for gents like those to be slummin' unless they was up to no good, was there? Could 'ave 'em followed, mebbe… but 'e'd 'ave to tread careful like; didn't want no coppers comin' round again. Nah, they was leavin', wasn't worth the risk.

That was when he saw something that took his breath away.

Did I just see one of them toffs slip a package t'other? 'e did! Bless my soul. That is very interestin'. Very interestin' indeed. Looks like bloke what received package is upset t'other even had that thing on 'im, let alone givin' it to 'im in broad daylight an' all. And now they's gettin' away. No! I tell a lie, only one is leavin' in carriage. Will you look at that! Bloody 'ell, the gent what 'as the parcel is walkin'.

Running hands through his sparse hair the tavern owner laughed out loud with glee. *This 'ere be a rare stroke o'luck!* "Charlie! Monkey

Mike! Get over 'ere." He motioned to two nasty looking fellows in the shadows, a pair he employed specifically for bug hunting – robbing and cheating the drunks that stumbled out the door. The men strolled over, ready as always to make an easy killing.

"M'boys, got a special job 'ere. It'll need a bit o'finesse, if you catch my meanin'. Involves gentry." Resting arms across his henchmen's shoulders, he grinned broadly. "But, if I be right, we may make us a quite a score this very day."

Charlie's smile was more a curl of his lip. "Do we kill 'im as well?"

"Cor, never said any such a thing, did I? Perish the thought. 'owever… we don't want loose ends neither, do we?"

CHAPTER NINE

MARK WALKED ON, LOST IN thought, unable to concentrate on anything other than what his brother had confided to him. Matthew *must* be wrong – at least Mark prayed he was. News like this would break their father's heart if he ever found out. Oh, the old man might drive the family crazy – often he was worse to deal with than the children – but, his family adored him. On the other hand, his desire for securing the family title through to another generation was becoming a bone of contention between his sons and him. It had become an obsession with the old man. A loud obsession. Oh, how often had he shouted at them that he needed this settled so that he could join his wife? To think that, after all the wait and worry, there might finally be an heir, but one who would never be able to succeed him.

And, what of the gossip. *Well, the family has weathered those storms before, that was certain. Hadn't he and Matthew been born into the world a suspicious two months prematurely? What about Harry's daughter of whom no one spoke? The Fitzwilliam's are a powerful family* Mark mused; *important enough in this town to often have been given a blind eye for certain indiscretions.* Odd that his father had sired so many sons, yet none of them had produced a legitimate male heir yet.

Hearing a shout in the distance Mark stopped and looked around… Where in hell was he? He searched for the name of the road on which he was walking, or the name of the street that crossed it, and when he identified both he cursed a blue streak – he'd been walking in the wrong direction! Blast and damn, wasted time that's all it was! Now he really would be late, and Lucille would behave distant; and, worse than that, hurt. Ah, Lucille. *Am I doing the right thing there?*

Perhaps Matthew was right; perhaps he *should* wait for true love to find him. The thing was friends he knew who had been madly in love when they married soon fell out of love with their wives, or had their hearts broken by them, and then found mistresses. Look at all the misery Matthew had experienced with his wife, Clarissa, before he found love with *his* mistress.

Of course, that hadn't ended up happily either.

Much more efficient this way. Forget about love – that was a fool's game. Better to marry properly and settle. Bunny was a good companion, perfectly adequate in bed; and, that was enough for him. Certainly it was.

Meanwhile, he still was a bit uncertain of his location. Bah. All he needed was to turn down the next street, and then circle back to something familiar. When he felt the first drops of sleet he sighed. *Wonderful. I shall completely ignore the fact that it's begun to rain; been through worse.* A chest cough would follow in two days, that was certain. Perfect. Sublime. He supposed Bunny would give him the old hairy eye again for tracking wet shoes through her immaculate drawing room… *I'd better rethink this proposal business.*

Well, it was all Matthew's damn fault, arriving in that ridiculously expensive racing carriage, a man his age – rather, *their* age. Going through a second childhood, that what was happening to him. Then again, he'd always been rash, impetuous, had never considered consequences. *If we had taken the older, more sensible carriage I could at least have ridden up top with the driver* – a reflection that was useless to him now, however. Now he was hungry, tired, cold and wet.

And lost.

Ghastly inconvenient, this; and, now the goddamn sleet is turning to snow, the temperature colder! Shite weather. Shite area. Shite… shite! He pulled his collar up and trudged on, not once concerned that he was walking alone in a deserted back area of warehouses. He was broad shouldered, muscular, taller than most men; Deacon had the right of it – even rowdy fellows avoided him, and those that hadn't still regretted their decision.

Besides there was no one else around.

Turning yet another corner he was relieved to finally recognize something – a shipping office with whom he was familiar. That was more like it, now he was getting his bearings! Pulling the scarf up over his mouth and ears he trudged on, his mother's admonitions from years before coming to mind. Always wear gloves and hat in inclement weather, button your coat, refrain from jumping in puddles, take care selecting companions, pay attention in strange surroundings, and most importantly, always wear clean smalls. He chuckled and groaned. *Heaven help me if you caught a whiff of me now! Sorry, Mama.* Come to think on it, heaven help him if Bunny did. Oh well, he would need to bathe at her house. Better yet, time permitting, they could bathe together. Very efficient, that...

The first blow came hard and swift from behind, knocking him nearly unconscious to the ground. He struggled to his knees, disoriented, confused. He touched the back of his head feeling a sticky wetness there, but never called for help, never had a chance to even look up. The second blow struck his head again, the third his legs. He thought he heard men laugh when the true beating began.

With blood dripping down his face and blinding him, blood running into his mouth and ears, covering his hands, he tried to crawl away under the steady, vicious, pummeling of fists and boots before finally collapsing.

His last thought before darkness was amazement at how he'd never known anyone was behind him, sound muffled more and more by the driving snow. Every sound but the birds chirping overhead that is. Lovely, they were. Sweet... until gradually there was silence.

CHAPTER TEN

WHEN HARRY PENROD SAW HIS step-brother Luke at the ice pond's edge, he skated toward him and called out, "Is everyone here do you know?" Having just finished a turn around the area of the skating area reserved that morning for the children's bandy game, he was still uneasy about the strange weather they'd been experiencing, with the temperatures freezing at times, then warming, then sleet and snow, then sunshine.

Luke, sitting on a bench lacing his skates to his boots, didn't seem to hear him – or, more likely, was hung over – so Harry raced forward, sliding to a stop sideways, sending shaved ice and snow right into his brother's face. "Damn it, Harry!"

"No cursing, Uncle Luke," Will Darcy, George's son and goal tender for one of the teams, smoothly skated past. "Little ears, remember." He laughed at his uncle's glower then sped off.

"I'm getting too old for this, Harry." Luke wobbled a bit at first but soon found his footing. "I'm exhausted already. How long are we playing? I've a train to catch at one o'clock."

"We'll play fifteen-minute half's, that's all. The younger ones lose attention for much longer, and the old folks such as you tire easily."

"Don't you worry about me. I plan to fall over after about five minutes and sit with the women for the rest."

"Impressive. That's longer than your usual duration. Afterwards the boys are racing for around an hour, competing for trophies, but you needn't stay for that. Where are you off to that's so important?"

"Mark is meeting me at the train station in Hampstead; bringing him Mama's ring."

"Oh, that's right. I'd forgotten. That's rather a long ride just to deliver a ring. Awfully nice of you."

"I'm a new man, haven't you heard? Maturing like cheese. Besides, Mark generously paid for my ticket there, as well as for my return trip. You remember my school friend, Parker Stewart? He's accompanying me, loves riding the trains nearly as much as I do. We're looking into investing with a group of American entrepreneurs forming now that their Congress passed the Pacific Railroad Act, laying rails westward from Omaha and eastward from Sacramento. You know, eventually trains will allow one to travel from Boston all the way to San Francisco."

"You'll be heading our American Fitzwilliam branch yet. So, tell me who isn't here?"

"Matthew asked if we could wait for Ewan Durand, said he would be arriving in a few moments. You know, Matthew's acting very strangely today, more than usually wound up. Don't think he's pleased about Mark's upcoming betrothal. I say, he's awfully young for this, isn't he?"

"Mark? Hardly, he's nearly forty years."

"No, you idiot, the Durand child, he's only eight years old. Most of the younger players are at least ten."

"Suppose the lad is a bit young but I've watched him, he's solid, strong, and tall for his age. We'll keep an eye on him nonetheless."

Luke leaned in to whisper. "Is it true the boy looks just like, um, Papa?"

Harry was the oldest of the boys, the one they took their cues from still, even as adults. "Why do you ask?"

"No reason."

"Who's been speaking with you?"

"Your wife, actually. Alice heard it from her maid who happens to be stepping out with Mrs. Lamb's son – you know her, she's been pastry cook for the Darcy family for years, knows everything. Young Ewan personally thanked her for her excellent scones. That is to say the cook was thanked, not the maid… or Alice."

"Yes, Luke, I was able to follow that all on my own."

"The maid said the cook burst into tears, took him into her arms and nearly hugged him to death. The boy I mean, not…"

"Please finish this."

"Yes, all right. Kept giving the youngster kisses and pinching his cheeks. Poor lad was likely traumatized. The woman is bosomy, nearly seventy and smells heavily of butter."

"Listen, we keep this all between ourselves, Luke. No one will question anything if we stand together."

"That goes without saying. One question."

"Yes."

"Keep *what* within the family. I still don't know anything."

"Good. Another thing, Papa will be here soon. Watch him, steer him away from the boy if you can. I doubt if he'll notice the child in this crowd since the old man's too vain to wear his glasses; but, still…"

"Still, it is Papa. One never knows what will happen. Whatever it is."

"That was an Homeric day, warriors facing off against a sworn enemy. 24 December, 1842; I remember as if it were yesterday." Fitzwilliam stood before several exhausted little ones with his hands clasped behind his back, his feet braced. Some of the children yawned, others wondered out loud when he would hand out the candy canes and chocolate caramels he had promised them.

Darcy, sitting to the side, raised his hand. "It was 27 December, 1850, Fitzwilliam."

"Exactly what I said, Darcy. Quite right. We fought the mighty Bury Fen bandy players on that day. There had been a misunderstanding and two teams arrived for the match - Swavesey with Over, and our Chatteris team. Mr. Meadows of Bury Fen chose Chatteris to play, of course. It was a battle for the ages."

"We lost, Fitz."

"Indeed. We were slaughtered. A blind duck heading north for the winter." Fitzwilliam gazed up into the heavens. "I found it impossible to stop any of their points, even when I hid the goal markers under rocks."

A boy in the front began scratching his head. "Is that quite legal, sir?"

"Not in the least. And, may I say it was very unsportsmanlike for you to point that fact out."

Then a little blonde angel who'd been staring in a trancelike state at her nails tugged on Fitzwilliam's sleeve. "Are you nearly finished? May we have our sweeties now? You promised."

Fitzwilliam sighed and opened a bag. Immediately he was swarmed by shrieking children before they all ran off with their bounty.

"No one can charm children like you can, Fitz."

"It's a gift, Darcy."

Harry walked up carrying a chair. "Sit, Papa, be quiet and behave yourself. Please try to stay out of trouble for one hour, that's all I ask. One hour."

"Certainly, son. You know, I could polish the kit for the boys; makes the ball slide like lightening across the ice."

Harry counted to ten. "That is against the rules, Papa."

"Your point being…?"

"Good heavens, you're impossible. All right, everyone on the ice and let's begin."

As the morning progressed, Matthew watched the children's game from the sidelines, like any other father bursting with pride. His boy was playing defender, the same position Matthew had played as a lad. Young as Ewan was, he had strength, grit and determination, a born athlete. He was magnificent, holding his own against older boys who had been playing together for years, gaining respect and friendships. Everyone seemed to like him. The lad was honorable, absolutely nothing like the cripple raising him.

Speaking of whom, Durand was also standing at the edge of the ice, shouting his encouragement to everyone, but most especially to Ewan, and the lad beamed with each and every cheer. Try as he might he couldn't fault Durand for that – if his son was happy, Matthew was content.

"Cousin Matthew?" Birdy fussed with the bow on her bonnet then raised her arms to him. "Please pick me up so I can watch the play."

"Why, Roberta? There's no one standing in your way." He knew she wanted to be noticed by the boys; he had her number now.

"Of course *I* can see them, but they cannot see *me.* Please?"

"Me too, Papa. Hold me up after Birdy." He hoped that, unlike Roberta, his daughter's glow was from the excitement of the competition and the cheers only, the exhilaration of players shooting passed on the ice.

"Oh, all right. Up you go, Roberta. There, can you *see* better?"

"I suppose."

"The ice is the other way, dear."

"Thank you."

"Can you see him, Birdy? Can you see Jeffrey?" There it was again, while hugging a doll his little girl asking about a boy. Damn. He would cling to his daughter forever if he could, keep her forever; but, the natural transition of life stopped for no man – nor, for any eight-year-old girl.

"No, sorry Manda. I can't see anything, it's all a blur. Oh wait – I do see Bradley! Bradley, here I am!" She shouted and waved as an embarrassed boy skated past. "Do I look all right, Cousin Matthew?"

"You look beautiful. Not to belabor a point, but you would see him better if you wore your spectacles."

Roberta smiled sadly. "I couldn't wear my spectacles, Cousin Matthew."

"Bradley doesn't approve?"

She shook her head, quite serious now. "I want him to think I'm pretty."

"Roberta Durand, you are not only pretty, but you are beautiful, inside and out. He would be fortunate to have any of your attention. You are a diamond."

She kissed his cheek and beamed. The fact that she too was holding a dolly while professing affection for a boy made him sigh, knowing both his girls were entering an age between childhood and young adult, between need and independence. Oh, how he remembered the dramatics of his sisters back then. Why, he wondered, did it seem girls found their footing earlier than boys? It was bound to be confusing for all concerned.

"Oh, look at how fast Ewan can skate, Birdy!" cried Amanda.

"Where is he? Oh, I wish I could see him. Ewan! Look here, wave at me so I know which one you are!"

The boy heard his cousin and was distracted for a moment, long enough for a larger boy to skate into him and knock him down.

Matthew quickly set Birdy on the ground and was about to run to the ice but damn if the cripple wasn't there before him somehow, calling out to Ewan – and, there was Ewan laughing and waving, assuring him he was fine, telling his 'father' not to worry. *Durand you bastard! I pray the ice cracks beneath your feet.*

Matthew would remember his vicious thoughts a few weeks later, and weep.

CHAPTER ELEVEN

FAINT VOICES FLOATED PAST, UNPLEASANT smells, sounds of doors opening and closing. Footsteps. Snores. Moans. The black fog was lifting, though his eyes were still too heavy to open. *Warm. I'm so bloody warm, burning up… why do I ache so badly… fucking bastards… must fight back… mustn't sleep…*

As Mark thrashed about, a woman's voice tried to sooth him; a wet cloth wiped his cheek and forehead, his arms and chest, the momentary cooling a relief. The gentle words she spoke to him, the reassuring words, brought comfort. She sounded kind, gentle. He kissed her hand, relaxed.

Then he drifted off into the fog again.

Her clean scent woke him. He needed to open his eyes, damn it, but he was too weak still. If he could just catch her hand, hold onto her, he would be all right; then the dark pit could never retake him… *wait… don't leave.*

Too late – how he knew for certain she had left his side he couldn't tell, but her presence was gone, a bond broken. Then he sensed a threat approaching – something was happening. Voices raised in anger, shouting, tension… danger was nearing… danger was everywhere… *she* could be in danger…

Damn it, wake up! Open your goddamn eyes.

Pain! It was as if someone was slicing his arms open. *Fucking bastards! Let go of me… weaker… life draining away…*

A touch of liquid on his lips slowly roused him. "Just one more swallow of medicine – that's very good, Bob. Are your eyes fluttering? Oh, those lashes. You have lashes any woman would envy – not certain you'd actually find that flattering, however." A feminine hand stroked his cheek. "I shall need to shave you soon. Mustn't have your family find you looking so disreputable." Whoever she was she had a voice like warm honey. He reached out to hold her. "You *are* getting better," she chuckled as she pressed his hands back to his chest.

Better? Better than what? My damn head hurts like blazes; everything hurts.

She was so near now he could feel the warmth of her body. Was he in heaven? Well, either heaven was absolutely wonderful, or this was the best damn dream of his life. He turned toward the warmth, the scent, the woman. "Am I dead?"

"What? Bless you, no."

"This isn't heaven, then?"

"Far from it."

He sighed. "That's a mercy, I'd hate to spend eternity in this much pain. Just a moment – I am awake and you're still here." His swollen eyes opened to thin slits.

"Yes. I am. And look at you, smiling! You had us worried during the night, Bob. Oops, there go your lids once again. Can you please try to open them for me, dearest, just a little? Is it difficult? Here, I'll wipe them again with a moist cloth, remove the crustiness… there, that's much better, Ah! At long last I am able to see their color, a regal blue."

She came into focus gradually, full lips, wide almond shaped eyes the color of silver, long black lashes, creamy skin, outrageous dimples. Her mass of golden auburn hair tucked loosely beneath a starched white cap seemed to form a halo around her face. "This must be heaven, because you look like an angel."

"Nonsense," she protested, her shy smile revealing the pleasure she found in his statement. "I have been called many names in this ward – Clarkey, My Dear Woman, Miss Too Mouthy By Far, – however, 'angel' is a first, and not at all warranted." Her presence warmed his chilled bones like nothing else. "You are very handsome when you , you know." She swiped away tears with the back of her hand. "Heavens. I am a silly goose. Sorry."

"You mustn't cry for me, angel."

"No, I'm not crying. Yes, well, a little. I thought we'd lost you last evening; your fever was rather high."

"Tears of happiness then... whatever is wrong with my voice? I sound like a frog."

She laughed a little. "A dry throat I suspect. Would you care for another sip of water?"

He nodded, agreeing more from the need to feel her near him, the desire to rest his cheek against her soft bosom as he sipped – rather than actual thirst. *A moment ago I thought I was dead, and now I'm trying to push my head between her breasts.* The water did taste bloody refreshing though. She gave him only a few sips at first, then a few more. "Thank you, that's better."

"How are you feeling?"

"Horrendous. Sore. Drained. Take your pick. What happened to me?"

"No one knows, except that you were found badly beaten and somehow surviving a great deal of blood loss."

"I... I don't remember anything. Where am I?"

"You are at St. Thomas Hospital."

"About as far from heaven as one can be then."

She laughed and nodded. "Definitely. A voluntary hospital that serves the poor is not anything akin to a celestial cloud."

"I must be poor then."

"No idea. You had, literally, nothing when you were found. We rather hoped you could tell us more when you awoke."

"Oh. Haven't a clue. How long have I been here?"

"Twenty-six hours and twenty minutes."

"Twenty-six hours? Impossible." A sudden coughing fit racked his body, making him gasp in pain because of his damaged ribs.

"Here, another sip of water. Slowly. I'm afraid it's true about both the twenty-six hours and having no money. We've no idea how long you were lying unconscious on the street before you were found."

"Bloody hell. Excuse my language." She gave him a few more sips of water.

"Quite all right, you've earned the privilege. Mustn't let Matron hear you cursing, though. She'll wash your mouth out with soap. Now, can you tell me your name so that we may contact your family?" It was completely wrong of her, but she prayed he hadn't a wife somewhere waiting for him, or children frightened for their father.

"My name? My name. I have no idea. Family? I don't even know if I have a family."

"Well, you received several blows to your head, lost a great deal of blood. Your memory should return as you recover; and, recover you shall, if I have anything to say about it!"

"Wasn't there any identification in my clothes? Something. Anything."

"No." Her face pinked up; she cleared her throat. "Actually, when you were found you'd already been, um, relieved of your clothing. Perhaps you were robbed."

"Well, here's hoping. I'd hate to think I make it a habit to walk around buck naked – cruel vision to inflict on livestock." Her surprised laughter was adorable. She covered her mouth and looked about, her eyes twinkling. Oh, those rosy cheeks gladdened his heart, stirred him. But, bloody hell, he had no strength in him to follow through.

"Weak as a damn kitten," he griped.

"Not surprising with all the blood you've lost. Be that as it may, that is nothing for *you* to worry about. Thankfully your fever is much lower now."

"What are these marks on my arms? They hurt like the very devil."

"Yes, well, the physician making rounds last evening, Mr. Bridges, has a fondness for bleeding patients, unfortunately. I was away having my supper when he arrived, earlier than usual. Perhaps being Christmas Eve he was in a hurry and therefore never read my notes because I had written everything down on your chart, including a very precise account of your excessive blood loss. He was nearly finished before the Ward Watcher could locate me."

She and the doctor had had a dreadful row the night before, exacerbating an already poor relationship between them. In addition to Mr. Bridge's usual abrasive manner, he was furious with her for rebuffing his flirtations the week before. Many physicians believed nurses to be loose women with little medical knowledge.

But Martha Clarke was a trained Nightingale nurse, professional from head to toe. "Gross neglect of duty is what it was. He makes me quite angry. I shall just have to be more vigilant from now on. I shall watch you like a hawk."

He smiled. "You're a regular spitfire when you get angry, aren't you?"

"Yes, I believe I am!" She brightened up in surprise. "That's another first for me."

"Your eyes are growing misty again, we can't have that."

"My eyes are not misty in the least," she sniffled.

"Thank you for helping me."

"It's been my pleasure." She wasn't usually so emotional, but this patient was different, and she had no idea why, only that she'd felt a deep connection with him from the start.

She is very pretty, he thought; delicate and feminine. It was damned humiliating to be so weak in front of her. "Dreadfully awkward being helpless like this. If I can just rest for a bit I should be able to care for myself. Don't like you having to worry about me any longer." He squeezed her hand. "What I'm trying to say is although I love having you here and holding my hand, I feel quite unmanned. I should be *your* guardian, not the other way round."

"Well, until you can at least urinate on your own, we'd better leave the protecting to me." Seeing his eyes open wide at that comment she pinked up again. "Sorry. Nurses tend to be blunt about bodily functions. I mean I don't mind at all looking after you. I mean…" Smoothing a hand over his brow she smiled. "Sad to say but caring for you has made this one of the most blessed Christmas's I've had in quite a while."

"Good." Her touch was soothing. "Christmas? Is today Christmas?"

She continued to run her fingers through his hair. "Yes it is, Bob Cratchit."

"Is that my name, I wonder?"

"I very much doubt it."

"Christmas Day, I'll be damned."

"It is, in fact, four o'clock on Christmas Day. Hasn't been such a good Christmas for you though, has it?" She enjoyed touching his hair – too much perhaps. "Would you like some broth?"

He brought her hand up to his mouth and kissed it. "Not now, angel. I truly am rather tired…" He was fast asleep before the last word ended.

The ward watcher came quietly up behind her and patted her shoulder. "Poor lad looked better yesterday, even unconscious as he was. Ah well, you should borrow a page from him and rest now, Sister. You look exhausted, standing guard by his side for hours like you have. Mind, I don't blame you one whit! After that madman bled him last evening, I feared Bob here wouldn't survive at all. What was Bridges thinking?"

"He wasn't, that is his main problem – the bleeding itself was too excessive as well, never mind the fact that the patient had already lost a good deal of blood. I sometimes believe physicians should be compensated to be on staff, instead of voluntary. They're too independent, too eager to use the poor as experiments for their wealthy clientele."

"That's the truth; however, best not say that out loud. Anyway, at least this one survived a Bridges Bleeding, some don't. Be thankful."

"Oh, I am. As long as he does not bleed him again."

"A second bleeding? Heaven forbid." The woman crossed herself. "Well, I should make my rounds. You go on up to your room and sleep, Sister. Boxing Day tomorrow, always a busy day, that."

She nodded, but after the ward attendant left Martha remained, pulling a nearby screen around the foot of his bed so she could sit without being observed. Having nursed him for hours on end she felt a possessiveness for the fellow, nothing else. All right, perhaps there was an unfamiliar desire to know him better, even a physical attraction. How long since she'd had a man in her life, felt a man's touch? Years. Since her husband's passing.

Her attraction to him was perfectly logical. Why, without the bruises, the scruff, the… alcoholic odor… any woman would consider him handsome, well-spoken, respectful. All right, enough of this. Evidently, she was more tired than she thought, as well as suddenly love-starved. Whatever it was, this emotion certainly could not be true affection. She knew nothing about the man, and he claimed to remember nothing. That did not mean, however, that a wife or sweetheart wasn't out there, somewhere.

How depressing.

She felt his forehead. Thank the good lord the fever wasn't

returning. No, she couldn't agree with Mr. Bridges that this man was a common drunk, or a destitute. True, his skin was darkened by sun as any cutpurse's might; but she had listened to his mutterings for several hours. Nothing he had said was off putting, or even remotely illicit. Resting her chin on her hand she continued to stare at him. *More likely he was a sea captain who had been set upon, or a builder perhaps – a man who spent a good deal of time outdoors working.* He had been well cared for, that was certain. His nails were clean and shaped, his teeth good, his heart strong, his body muscular. She sighed, he had *someone* around to fuss over him.

Her eyes stung at that thought. Good heavens what was the matter with her! Surely, all she needed was a short nap and she'd feel much better. After tucking the sheet in around him she closed her eyes, wearier than ever before in her life. Was it just yesterday morning, on Christmas Eve, when her life had turned upside down? It had been snowing that day, and cold …

Martha Clarke eyed a comfy looking chair, unoccupied in a corner of her ward, and determined a moment's rest was in order before picking up pen to update patient charts. The afternoon meal had been distributed without one volatile incident; those in her care – the destitute, the drunkards, the mentally ill – all quiet and grateful to be inside now the winter snows had begun.

Besides, the loss of their Prince had closed most of the taverns in the city. It was Christmas Eve, 1861, just another work day at St. Thomas' Voluntary Hospital. Until…

A scream in the distance stopped her heart cold. "Whatever was that, Matron?"

"Oh dear. And here I was just thinking how nice and quiet it has been." Sighing, the Ward Matron hurried to one of the tall windows facing the street. "Nothing unusual I can see."

Matron Sheady, head of the new Nightingale nursing staff at St. Thomas Hospital, had been planning on spending Christmas visiting her ailing brother, her first visit with him in years, and possibly her last as well. She would be leaving in a few hours, as long as nothing dire happened in the meantime. Another scream filled the air.

"Gracious. Shall I go out and see what's causing the ruckus?"

"Certainly not. Wouldn't do to send a young woman into a crowd of intoxicated revelers. Where's Young Charlie? Ah, there he is – Charles, rouse yourself and come here please." Matron motioned over a young boy napping in the corner. "Go outside, would you, there's a good lad. See if you can shoo whomever it is away. Be careful, mind you. If you sense they're ruffians come back inside immediately."

"Yes, ma'am. Know just what to do. I can chase 'em across to Guy's 'ospital."

"No, Charlie, that is not what I meant –. Oh bother." The boy had scurried out the door before an exasperated Matron could stop him. "Sister Clarke, see to your patient, please, before he discharges a lung. And stop chuckling."

"Yes, Matron." Martha was still smiling as she approached the coughing man. "Shall I bring you another pillow, Mr. Hobbs?" The poor dear had been suffering from chilblain and chin cough for several days. "You may be able to rest easier with your head elevated."

He spit into a bowl. "Lord luv ye, lass, but I'm just after clearin' m'pipes. Besides, best not get accustomed to that sort o' luxury."

Nearby a man broke wind, causing those around him to groan and swear. Martha turned away, trying hard not to gasp for breath herself. "Oh, dear, Mr. Kingston. I sense your stomach is bothering you."

"Not no more, Sister. Not no more."

"T'would be merciful if someone opened window," called out a voice from another bed. "What in bloody 'ell did ye eat, Ralph?"

"We'll be findin' out in a minute, mebbe."

Suddenly, more screams and shouts erupted from the hospital courtyard terrifying everyone and Young Charlie burst into the room, panting with excitement. He leaned over to catch his breath.

"Good gracious!" Matron hurried to the boy. "Are you all right?"

"Yeh, o'course Matron; though I nearly copped a mouse just now, it's fair collie shangles downstairs."

Sheady stared at the lad for a moment before turning to Martha. "Was that even English?"

"Well, yes, a version of it – appears Charlie very nearly received a blackened eye. Apparently, there's a row brewing downstairs."

"Yes, ma'am. Dead gent coppers just brung to mortuary tweren't dead at all! Sat straight up on slab. Scared the bloomin' trousers off old Flynn!"

"Here, drink this and catch your breath." Martha handed him a glass of water.

"What in the world are you saying, Charlie? Dead man, come to life?" Matron plopped onto a chair in front of him and pushed the hair from his eyes. "Ridiculous."

"Matron, saw 'im meself, din' I? Naked as the day 'e was born too, blood all over 'is 'ead, and black and blue everywhere else."

"Oh, the poor man. Was he in an accident?"

"It's a odd sort 'o accident what strips a man o'is skivvies. Nah, 'e was probably on the ran-tan, fell in w'bad uns, and got 'imself a good slatin'."

Again, matron turned to Martha for clarification.

"He was possibly inebriated and then severely beaten."

"Ah. Tell me, Charlie, have the perpetrators been apprehended by the constabulary?"

The boy blinked several times at his beloved Matron Sheady then looked to Martha with the same quizzical brow.

"Did the beaks catch the ones who did the slating?"

"Oh. No, they be dead as well. I gather these two blokes tried t'back slang it, trippin' up when they stopped to fight over a sort o' packet. Heard they kept screamin' and hollerin' at each other, grabbin' it all back an' forth and such, runnin' – got a big crowd followin' 'em by this time. And, don't ye know, *they was both gingers* – that's always trouble! Look it up. Well, what do ye think 'appened next Matron?"

"I still haven't a clue what happened before. Why don't you recite the entire episode to Sister Clarke and I shall try and garner the pertinent information from her."

"Hmm?"

Martha put her hand on his shoulder. "Tell me, and I'll explain it to Matron."

"Aye. Where was I? Oh, yeah – there were a right batty fang over the bundle, whole crowd cheerin' 'em on to off each other, a proper fifteen puzzle, when whole kit goes flyin' into river – pinched clothes, boots, coat – includin' very packet what they was fightin' over. Well, that done it - 'ole crowd starts jumpin' into river then, everyone fightin' for one thing or t'other! Them bloody robbers was so mad, what d'ye think! Drew knives and ended up killin' each other!"

"Good heavens. I imagine whatever it is you just said was horrific."

"Oh, yeah. They was both rat bags, but didn' deserve to be dead meat. Anyways, ends up wif one stabbed in stomach and t'other with 'is throat sliced."

"The sad plight of the penurious."

"If that be gingers, then yeah."

"One moment, please, Charlie. Now, what exactly is a ginger, Sister Clarke?"

"Someone with reddish colored hair, Matron."

"Oh."

"I got more. Once them peelers scatter crowd they sends for a dead wagon. Turns out there was one already around, 'ad picked up a bloke nearby – lots 'o action tonight, I'm thinkin' – so coppers toss the gingers atop 'im."

"Your verbiage is horrendous."

"Sorry. Swear I washed my face just this mornin', Matron."

"Please go on, Charlie."

"Yes, ma'am. The bloke what was already in the dead wagon 'ad been found in nearby stairwell, naked as a babe, an' it turns out – wait for it – 'e's got an 'andful of ginger 'air clutched in 'is paw, so coppers figure two dead 'uns 'ad a fallin' out with naked one, beat 'im up and stole everythin' from 'im, includin' the clothes off his back."

"Does the naked gentleman have ginger hair?"

"Nowhere I could see, Matron. Both top an' tallywags was thick brown."

"Oh, dear."

"Like a bloomin' forest…"

"I do have the idea now, Charlie, please go on."

"Yes, ma'am, after a mo, wagon driver 'ears a groan from *the dead pile*! Yeah! Scared the shite – excuse me, matron, that was a… sneeze – scared the driver somfin' fierce. 'e jumps off wagon and runs screamin' mad as hops smack back to them peelers. T'was then they bundled up poor bloke and brung 'im straight 'ere. Poor ol' Flynn knew nofin an' walked in just as the bloke sat up when coppers settle 'im on table, all covered like 'e was dead. Sister, can

I 'ave me tea now?"

"Pardon? Oh, yes, of course."

Other patients had by now approached the boy, excitedly speaking at once and asking questions. "What in the world are you all doing?" Matron clapped her hands. "Back to your beds!" Motioning for Martha to follow she then headed for the door. "Sister Kelly, please remain here with the patients. We shall return as soon as possible."

"But, Matron, I'm finished with my shift."

She waved away the young nursing trainee. "Yes, and I am supposed to be leaving for my brother's home. I do realize you are off duty, Kelly; however, if you wish to succeed in your chosen profession, if you wish to be a Nightingale nurse, you will always place your patient's well-being before your own. Sister Clarke, follow me. Charlie, you lead the way."

CHAPTER TWELVE

IT TOOK TIME FOR THE two women to properly clean the beaten man of all the dirt and blood, wash and dress his wounds, then bundle him with blankets to warm him. With no physician attending Christmas Eve, and several nurses absent to visit family, the available staff was minimal.

"Well, that took the starch from me, I am exhausted. Thank you, Sister Clarke, for your customary excellent assistance."

"Yes, Matron." Martha gently touched the injured man's hand. It was always sad to see lost souls brought into the hospital, but for some reason the very strong looking fellows like this one seemed particularly vulnerable. Both men in her life – her late father and her late husband – had been proud but slight of build, short, forever attempting to prove their manhood. This one would never have that need.

"Amazing how difficult it is to kill someone," Matron glanced up briefly from making notations on his chart.

"I beg your pardon, ma'am?"

"Well, look at this fellow. Beaten and left for dead as he was, half frozen – yet the life spark remained. He could have bled out or died of the cold; many others would have. His size helped, of course, he's young and healthy. Interesting. Pity he was naked as a gibbon though. If he had presented with clothing, we could have determined into which rank of society he belonged."

Matron was always so blunt in her assessments that it might have surprised another; however, Martha understood her. Both had been nurses in Crimea, both were soldier's widows, both had seen worse in war. Caring for slaughtered bodies tended to immune one after a while; little could shock delicate sensibilities after two months ankle deep in mud and blood and sawed-off body parts. To remain strong enough to be of some use was difficult if one became involved or cared too much. Martha had kept her sanity by regarding patients more as puzzles to be solved, not people.

So why did she want to weep now? Why fret about this one man in particular? As Martha continued to stare, his torso shamefully exposed, his face cut and swollen, his body broken… it all threatened to overwhelm her. She felt an unfamiliar pull, an uncharacteristic longing to care for the *man*, not the patient. That realization alone stopped her cold.

Good heavens. Was she physically attracted? Impossible. A patient? Never. Yet with each look, each touch, the sense of familiarity intensified, the attachment deepened. It was inappropriate to say the least. She was a nurse, for goodness sake, and a God-fearing Christian woman. She knew better than to allow personal feelings interfere, overpower. And still she found she was growing more and more anxious for him. "Will he be all right, Matron?" Her heart beat quickly, waiting for a response.

"Pardon? Oh, well, he shall survive his wounds if he's allowed to regain his strength, rest. However, there lies the problem. Bridges is scheduled for rounds today, and he is forever lamenting on the fact that we inadvertently admit the indigent when we take in fellows such as this. In fact, he would have us adhere to our weekly Tuesday admissions of the poor alone and refuse accident or assault victims entirely, leave them to die in the streets. He's a beast – and, a pathetic excuse for a physician. No, dealing with that man is invariably unpleasant. I should very much like to avoid all the fuss this once. Very sad. I have an uneasy feeling for this one."

"Yes, I do as well." Fear quickened Martha's heart. "We don't actually know this fellow is indigent though, do we? I can't believe Mr. Bridges would toss him out. Would he?"

"I have no idea. I've given up second guessing the man. One thing in our patient's favor is his body – it could never be viewed as one of a destitute. This fellow was well cared for, someone took pride in his wellbeing. In fact, he is a truly beautiful specimen – large shoulders, well-formed chest, calves and arms, clean and trimmed nails, excellent teeth... do you not agree?"

Martha blushed. "I hadn't noticed."

"Sister, either you are blind, lying, or being uncharacteristically coy."

Of course, she *had* noticed the masculine beauty beneath all the bruising, which made her blush all the more.

"You are red as a radish, dear." Matron checked her pinned watch and noted the time. "My meaning was purely clinical. Drunkards and street men are not known to care for their health, their nails, or their teeth. Our friend here keeps himself very fit." She patted Martha's hand. "You must learn to be more observant, Sister Clarke – or, at least, less transparent. Now, if you have everything in hand I shall go to my room and put up my feet for a while before I leave. You know when I was your age long hospital hours never bothered – but now, my knees ache something fierce after a mere half day, my back, my shoulder. It's dreadful to get old."

"You are not old, Matron. Merely well-seasoned."

"Like mutton."

"Off with you now. I'll finish up here then have him situated within my ward."

"Very good. I may not see you before I leave for my holiday, so Happy Christmas to you, dear. Try and not kill anyone before I return."

"Yes, ma'am. Happy Christmas to you as well."

Her immediate supervisor gone now, Martha was finally alone with her odd patient. *What is it about this man that moves me so? Nonsense; put it from your mind, Martha.* Thank heaven for the cold! It had been the cold that saved him, slowing his heart rate, preventing him from completely bleeding out while he lay in that basement well. Martha had seen this happen before, during the war in Crimea. Soldiers brought in half frozen from the field would sometimes live to tell the tale because of it, while men with lesser wounds would die of infection.

"Sister?" Old Charlie, the orderly, stood in the doorway with his gurney, waiting for her instructions. "Are you ready, Sister?"

She motioned him forward. "Thank you, Mr. Gregson. Yes, we're quite ready."

CHAPTER THIRTEEN

AFTER WAKING FROM HER NAP at Bob Cratchit's bedside Martha quietly began her usual rounds through the ward, always keeping her gaze on him, reassuring herself that he was breathing easier, appeared comfortable. When at last she was finished she came to him again. All was quiet.

"I wonder who you truly are," she whispered while adjusting his covers when, with a start, she realized his swollen eyes were open and he was watching her. (Yes, his eyes were definitely, beautifully, blue.)

Moments passed before he spoke, his voice still rough and gravelly. "Hello, again. How long have I been asleep?"

"Around two hours."

"You look done in," He coughed weakly.

"Always something a girl loves to hear. Would you like a sip of water?" She cupped the back of his head gently to raise it, then let him drink slowly.

"Thank you, madam." His voice was clearer now.

"How are you feeling?"

He took a fortifying breath to speak. "Like I was spit out of a donkey's mouth."

Martha brushed the hair from his brow realizing another fever was beginning. Well, it *was* evening, fevers tended to rise in the evening; besides, that could be a good thing if controlled, a detriment to possible infection. She checked his pulse, listened to his heart – both steady, but still too weak for her liking.

"Have you told me your name?"

"My name is Sister Clarke."

"Your first name?"

"That would be inappropriate."

"Inappropriate Clarke? What were your parents thinking? Ah, good, you're smiling. You stayed near me while I slept. Thank you."

A warm feeling simmered in her heart at his words. "It is no more than my duty. I have assigned myself as your nurse tonight and possibly through tomorrow if we are still short of staff. Now, more importantly, how is your memory? Have we recollected our name?" She was certain with the fever controlled and with more sleep, the previous day's events would start to return to him.

"*Our* name? Do we share the same one – how bizarre."

"Honestly, I do believe you're being willfully contrary."

"Yes, I am. Sorry."

"You should be. We need to find out who you are. Do you remember anything?"

"No." He shook his head, mildly frustrated. "I just can't seem to recall. Bloody nuisance."

Martha didn't like the sound of that. Perhaps his head wounds had been worse than they initially thought. His color remained too pale, even if his spirit was strong. She'd stay close during the night, let the watcher supervise the rest of the ward. "I suppose we shouldn't be surprised; after all, you've had quite an experience." As quietly as possible she pulled her chair closer to the bed.

"Actually, I do remember flashes of things. Snow… the sky… birds… someone kicking me."

"Well, that's a good start – except for the kicking bit. All right, enough of this. Time for you to have the bone broth I've had cook prepare. This will build up your blood." She turned and called out for Old Charlie to fetch the broth.

"Sounds disgusting."

"Yes it is, I'm afraid." She could not resist running her hand through his hair again. "But it will help you to gain strength, and that's all that matters."

"Bring me my soup then; and, keep doing that with my hair as well, please."

"I'll think about it." *As if anyone could stop me.*

"I believe that is the worst thing I've ever eaten in my entire life. Of course, I don't remember eating anything else." In the end, she'd had to feed him the last few spoonful's. He was looking absolutely drained.

"You've never had my bread pudding."

"Bad as that, is it?"

"Yes. I'm an awful cook. My late husband remarked that when I prepared a meal it was like the miracle of the loaves and fishes."

"What does that mean?"

"My dishes could be passed around a crowd and return intact, with other samples of my culinary attempts thrown in on top."

"You poor darling."

"Enough about me. It appears the laudanum is finally taking hold. Try and sleep now."

"I'd rather speak with you. I've never enjoyed myself so much."

"How would you know?"

"Harpy. Stay with me again, Inappropriate?"

"I'd like nothing better." She took his hand in hers and gave it a gentle squeeze. "I'll remain until you're snoring louder than your neighbor, Mr. Hobbs." She turned to Mr. Hobbs. "That all right with you, Clive?"

"Makes me no nevermind, lord love ye. Long as you don't try and cook for us..."

"That's quite enough from you." It warmed her to see Bob smiling up at her, his gaze frankly admiring. "Is something wrong? Is my face smudged?"

He shook his head, his eyelids growing heavy. "You're pretty. Have you been an angel very long?" He yawned but fought off sleep. "I mean a nurse... you been a nurse very long?"

"Nearly ten years."

"... born in London?"

"No. My father was serving in the Army when I was born."

"Really? Where? Who is he?"

"Was. He was General Sir Charles James Napier."

"Napier? Command... in India."

"Yes, see you're beginning to remember things. I spent my childhood there."

"A gentleman's daughter. Why aren't you at dancing at court balls... with some duke or other?"

It took a moment to answer. She rarely spoke about her family. "Well, you see I left that life behind when I married a soldier against my father's wishes. My father never approved of women following the drum, so naturally being very young and full of myself I did just that. My husband and he never got on."

"Where is he…your husband?"

"He was killed in the Crimea."

"Forgive… didn't know."

"No reason you should, and nothing to forgive. That was over eight years ago now."

"Hope… family softened." Mark tightened his hold on her hand and struggled to remain speaking with her as long as possible.

"No. Unfortunately, my father passed before we could reconcile; then my mother remarried and moved to Germany and her new husband forbade her to speak with me. You see, I had compounded my horrendous behavior by training to become a nurse – to be useful to my husband, support him."

"A true rebel, independent… I like that." He laughed, a deep rumbling she found very appealing, the sound doing something to her emotions, sending her bloodstream thrumming as if a thousand bees were buzzing through it; or, on second thought a thoracotomy was being performed by sawing through the midshaft of both clavicles and cutting through the ribs of both hemi thoraces.

On third thought, perhaps she should refrain from reading quite so many anatomy books.

"Sister Clarke? Why did you cease speaking?" He brought her hand to his lips to kiss, just as his own eyes were closing.

"Yes, well. Afraid my ramblings are keeping you awake. I should be quiet."

"No… love your voice… just need rest. Can't seem to fix a thought to my head… You know, your hands are soft as doves… so pretty… could watch you for hours, and hours, and…"

"Evidently not." Martha smiled as he drifted off.

It was past nine in the evening and Martha was just returning from using the facilities when she saw the night watch scurrying toward her in a panic. "I think you'd better come."

When she spied Old Charlie wringing his hands beside the

screen surrounding her patient's bed, she began to run. "What's happened?"

"Sister, how dare you abandon your duties!"

Mr. Bridges' angry question, and the unexpected sight of him with her patient, stopped Martha dead in her tracks. He was quickly scanning through the notes she'd written about Bob's progress, shaking his head all the while. With a grunt he then tossed the chart aside.

"I wasn't expecting you at this time of night, sir."

"Evidently. And how does that answer my question?"

"I stepped away for a moment to use the facilities."

"Don't be vulgar. I see our drunkard is still with us. Why has he not been shown the door?"

"He is still very weak. This gentleman was the victim of an attack, sir."

"Gentleman? Really, Sister."

"I do believe so. As you can see his nails are clean, and physically –"

"What I see is a disgusting lurker who received just what he deserved – a good thrashing. Probably was caught stealing from his betters. Why, look at him! The brute is still passed out from drink."

"Not in the least, sir, I administered laudanum to him, so that he *could* sleep. And there is no reason to believe the man a drunkard, or a lurker. Or a thief! If you'd look at his teeth –"

"Check his nails? Look at his teeth?" Bridges laughed derisively. "I am examining a patient not purchasing cattle, madam; or, do you even know the difference? You Nightingale nurses believe yourselves so superior. Do you even realize he is feverish?"

"Of course I do, sir. I was about to prepare a cup of basil leaves and ginger for him."

"Nonsense. I will not have our supplies, or your services, wasted on a ruffian."

"But there are no other duties for me to perform at this time, and the night nurse will tell me if any of my other patients are in distress. It would be no hardship for me."

"I wonder about that as well. Is it not rather unseemly for you to be hovering around a male patient at all hours?"

"I was not hovering. First you claim I am abandoning my duties and then you accuse me of hovering!"

"Keep a civil tongue in your mouth. Are you challenging me, madam? May I remind you I am on the board of this teaching hospital, I shall decide what is to be done. Well, since he remains here, perhaps he can be of some use. It's an interesting case, if I must say so – surviving out in the cold as he did. Yes, quite. In the interests of science we need to discover how and why he survived at all. How much blood loss is too much for a fellow this size, that's what we need to learn from this one. The bleeding yesterday seems to have done him no harm. I believe I will remove an equal amount now, and every twelve hours. That shall test his endurance."

"Bleed him again?"

"My heavens, do you have a hearing problem?"

Stupefied by what he was planning, she shook her head no. "Excellent, glad to know that. All right, let's hurry on with this, I haven't time to dawdle. My wife is expecting me at a family gathering in one hour."

The man she thought of as Bob had lost so much blood already, surely another bleeding, and another after that, would kill him. But, what could she do, the doctor was already in an ugly mood for any number of previous disagreements between them – personal and professional – that it wouldn't do to antagonize. Still, she needed to stall him somehow, invent one obstacle after another if need be, until it was too late for him to remain any longer...

An hour later Martha slumped into a chair and breathed a sigh of relief, her hands shaking. She had managed to delay and frustrate Bridges long enough to avoid the bleeding – although at what future price? The doctor was furious with her when he stormed out; she'd made a true foe this night. Mr. Bridges might be an incompetent fool, but he was also a very influential one.

CHAPTER FOURTEEN

"WERE YOU ALWAYS BEAUTIFUL?"

Mark's voice startled her from her early morning work of folding towels by his bedside. She had brought a table and a basket of freshly laundered items to the side of his bed, unwilling to leave him alone for long. "Was I always beautiful?" She grinned, happy to have him awake again. "Now, how could one answer such a question without sounding conceited?"

"You've every right to be. I'll tell you how I picture you as a child – I see you as a wisp of a thing, a little hoyden, laughing and playing and free, a bundle of happy sunshine."

"In fact, I was quite chubby and, yes, a hoyden. My father always said I was a born she-devil, an *ek jangalee bachchesent* in Hindi, sent by *Shasti*, the goddess of children, to drive him insane. Good morning, Bob. How long have you been awake?"

"Not long, Inappropriate. I've been watching you work. Do you never rest?"

"No. I don't seem to need very much." She put a hand to his forehead, relieved it was finally cool. "Your fever has left. How are your injuries? Do your legs and arms feel painful?"

"Check for yourself."

"Don't be sassy."

"All right, fair enough. Truthfully, everything hurts like the devil."

"See, was that so difficult? I'll give you a bit of laudanum after you eat."

"No. No more laudanum. Makes my mind muddled, and I'm

muddled enough, thank you. Besides, it's considered unmanly for a fellow to surrender to pain. We smile through our tears, grit our teeth."

"Pity men don't give birth then. Raise your head a bit and I can adjust your pillow."

Mark laughed outright, warmth in his eyes. She was breathtaking up close, and she smelled wonderfully – of soap and freshly washed hair and even the starch in her crisp uniform was pleasant. She was everything he thought perfect in a woman, witty, smart, compassionate; and, with a face and figure of a goddess. "Where have you been all my life?"

"Covered that in Chapter One, remember? The majority of my life was spent in India and the Crimea. We still are undecided about yourself, however. Look at the time. Let me run into the kitchen quickly, more than likely cook is firing up the ovens for breakfast. You must be at least a little hungry by now."

"Extremely – but, first finish what you're doing. It's restful to watch you."

"Tedious more like."

"Inny, there isn't a man breathing who doesn't enjoy watching a pretty girl walk about."

"Inny?"

"Short for Inappropriate. I think we've made great enough strides in our friendship for me to call you Inny."

She knew speaking might be tiring for him, but without him near, without the sound of his voice, she would feel desperately alone. Without his presence she would be lost. She hated to think of his leaving. "Thank you, Bob. You're very sweet, and very kind. Well, now, how about those memories? How are we faring on that front?"

"Clouds seem to be thinning. In fact, I have had one vivid memory return to me where I am watching my father – I believe it was my father – reading to me from a storybook, and he was wearing a uniform of some sort. Beautiful thing, good deal of gold braid and brass buttons."

"Aha, so you're a soldier's brat as well, are you?"

"Perhaps. He looked to be a giant of a man. I remember, too, that first we all gathered around him, then scrambled on top of him… it was great fun…"

"You said 'we'. Do you remember anything else?"

"I did say 'we', didn't I? Well, there was one odd thing, a mirror sitting beside me on the floor and I'm leaning on it, and we're laughing and talking."

"A twin perhaps?"

"Yes, yes I think you're right." He rubbed a hand over his eyes. "Blast. There's so much just at the surface, waiting to burst open. Why can't I remember?" He was growing agitated, anxious, so she covered his hand with her own.

"Perhaps it's best you relax, allow the memories to come back on their own."

"Inny?" He interlaced his fingers with hers.

"Martha."

"Excuse me?"

"Martha. My name is Martha." She smiled, warmed by the look on his face. His heated gaze seemed to mirror her own feelings at that moment, an affinity for a stranger now dearer to her than anyone else before in her life. "What did you wish to say to me, Bob?"

"When will I eat?"

"Ha!" She blurted out, amused by her own folly. Had she thought he was about to profess undying love? Propose? Poor man was merely hungry.

"Again?" she sighed dramatically. "The fact is our cook has taken a shine to you and is preparing something special for Boxing Day, but that is for later. Here. While I go down to the kitchen you finish this warm, fresh bread. She makes the most wonderful cakes as well. What is it?"

"Warm bread. I remember someone – my *mother* I'm sure of it – at the hearth oven, and hot fresh bread. All of us would be standing around her, waiting with jam pots. Poor dear rarely got a loaf to the table before we attacked."

"'Us' again. It seems you have a large family."

At that moment a door to the ward banged open and two men, struggling to bring in a small tree without waking the patients, were shushing each other, crashing about, disturbing tables, catching bottles in mid fall. Apparently, they were still celebrating from the night before.

"Gentlemen, please be quiet."

"Wot's that? Ah. 'appy Christmas, Sister," one whispered very loudly.

"And a Happy Christmas to you. What have you there, Mr. Banks?"

"Beg pardon?"

"What are you hiding behind your back – and very poorly, I might add."

"Wot? Oh, this? This 'ere's a tree. Found it in street. Thought it'd be a fittin' tribute to our late prince."

The sniffling man beside him blew his nose and nodded. "Lord love 'im."

"Mr. Banks. Aren't you late for work?"

"Yes, ma'am."

"Also, do you expect me to believe you found this tree in the street, with berry garland and candles already tied to the branches?" It was comical to watch the cook's assistant and his brother look at each other, and then her, as they attempted to think up some logical response. In their current inebriated state, however, all either finally managed was a grin.

"We thought it be nice to 'ave a bit of cheer for our bare-arsed, beaten fella there – 'e's a celebrity o'sorts, comin' back from dead an' all; and, for our sad 'olidays so to speak." After wiping his nose with his sleeve Banks held the tree up as if it were a plucked goose ready for the oven. "Point o'fact, we found two o'these beauties layin' about near unlocked windows. And, no one caught us neither."

"You are impossible, Mr. Banks."

"That's what me missus says as well. Can we stash it – I mean, can we put this one up in 'ere, Sister?"

She scowled at them for only a moment and then laughed. "I think that would be lovely."

Stumbling, tripping, trying but failing to hold back their laughter, the brothers set about propping the badly mangled tree up in the corner of the room. "That's a beauty, that's what that is. Wait, nearly forgot. Found this as well, Sister." The fellow pulled a mass of mistletoe from his pocket. "Thought we'd put some o'these up outside nurses' rooms, and at other, what you might call, strategic places in 'ospital. Here ye go." With a flourishing bow he handed Martha a sprig. "Now 'ow's about you give this poor young chap a kiss?"

"Mr. Banks! You should be beaten with sticks."

"Me old lady says that too. Well, best report to the kitchens, Neddy. Sister Clarke, beaten bare-arsed fella, felicitations of the season to ye." He winked at them both. "Don't do nuffin I wouldn't do!" Laughing at the blush spreading up her cheeks Mr. Banks then flung his arm around Neddy and they both stumbled out the door.

"My goodness," she muttered to herself, fanning her face with her hands. "Those two are dreadful."

"I thought they made great sense."

"Yes. Well." Martha came to her feet immediately. She began to putter about, trying desperately not to look at him, placing her folded towels on a nearby shelf and studying bottles of medicine in a cabinet with great intensity. "My goodness it is nearly five in the morning. I should bring this dish to the kitchen. Cook usually needs all the plates at hand for breakfast."

"Come here first, please. I have something I wish to say to you."

Martha hesitated before turning. "Yes, all right, I'm here. What was it you wished to tell me?"

"Could you come a bit closer?"

She approached slowly, her hands clutched behind her back.

"I should like a kiss."

"Pardon me?"

"I know you heard me."

"Yes. I mean no. No, no, no. Ridiculous. That's just not done." Martha knew she must try and sound more forceful, less breathless, hide the desire that at that very moment was drying her mouth to dust. She certainly should. Yes indeed. That he tempted her at all was merely concern for a very battered, vulnerable man.

At the very least she should explain how common it was for a patient to form an attachment with their nurse, then clarify the hospital policy forbidding fraternizing with someone to whom she was providing medical assistance.

She should.

But, she didn't.

She just couldn't.

"Lick those pink lips one more time and I'll go raving mad. You know, it sounds to me as if everyone is sleeping, no one would be the wiser. Come closer, hold that mistletoe aloft, and kiss me. Just this once. It is Christmastime, after all."

Even as she came forward, she was shaking her head no, then scowling as she settled slowly on the edge of his bed, fiddling with the mistletoe in her hand. Her mind was a muddle. She had never betrayed her oath before. Never. But, neither had she felt so alone in the world, or so lost – or desired a man as she desired this one. It was a pull of nature that made no sense to her.

After all, gynecological doctor William Acton's 'Functions and Disorders of the Reproductive Organs, in Childhood, Youth, Adult Age, and Advanced Life, Considered in the Physiological, Social, and Moral Relations', stated that the majority of women (happily for them) are not very much troubled by sexual feeling of any kind.

So, then what in the world is my *difficulty? I must be devoid of all morality, completely flawed. A wanton. Why else should I want nothing more than to crawl into bed with Bob Cratchit?*

Whatever would Charles Dickens say?

She attempted to study him objectively, his bruised face, his swollen lip, his bloodied eye. He was still the handsomest man she'd ever seen. "You are a sight only a mother could love you know." Nervously she placed the mistletoe beside his head and leaned down to press a chaste kiss on his cheek. At the feel of his skin, however, a charge shot straight through her, tingling her heart, heating her stomach, burning her skin. She found herself staring into those dark blue eyes… then at his lips…

Lips so close she could feel his warm breath.

Initially, Mark had resigned himself to that disappointing peck on his cheek; but when he saw her staring at his lips her desire was plain. He cupped the back of her head and pulled her mouth to his. Tender at first, the kiss soon gave way to passion and desire. His tongue swept and suckled hers, their heads angled, the kiss deepened, and Martha was absolutely lost. Her arms enfolded him as kiss gave way to kiss, and then again and again. His hand began to fondle her breasts, kneaded them gently while she moaned… until the clanking of a cart coming down the hall broke the spell. Struggling with her own passions she pushed away from Mark. It was the hardest thing she'd ever done.

"I believe my fever has returned for good," he mumbled, his

hand reaching for her again.

"No. I… I must see to the other patients. Breakfast will be here soon, there's so much to do."

"You'll come back?"

Martha pretended not to hear. Over the years other patients had formed attachments to her, their joy at being alive after a traumatic illness or accident mistaken for true affection. It rarely lasted and was easily transferred from one nurse to another. She had never remotely returned these feelings before, certainly her heart had never been threatened. This man could be married, could have a family – the very idea made her gasp for breath.

"Have I offended you with my forwardness? I'll behave from now on, I swear."

"Yes. I am afraid I must insist you do." Did she even want him to behave? No. Definitely not. And that, in a nutshell, was her problem. She straightened her cap, patted her hair. "Truthfully, though, I blame myself for this, not you; this was terribly unprofessional of me. No, please, allow me to speak. I am very disappointed with myself," she had to stop for a breath, tears were so close. "I have dedicated my life to the nursing profession, to elevating it to a respectable standard. However, I seem to have no common sense around you." Another fortifying breath secured her resolve. "If this should ever happen again, I must ask another nurse to take over your care."

Mark had felt her passion equal to his but kept that observation to himself. He could see how upset she was, how hurt. She was a soldier's daughter as he was a soldier's son. No matter the circumstances, you understood what was deemed right and wrong in a soldier's house. "No need. I promise to conduct myself as a gentleman. And, one more thing, Sister."

She turned around too quickly, felt her knees buckle at the sight of his beautiful smile. "Forgive me for this, but I can't remember ever knowing such a wonderful Christmas before."

"How is our patient this Boxing Day, Martha?" Sister Kelly stood beside her friend, placing a hand on her shoulder.

"He slept well thanks to a small dose of laudanum I slipped into his tea."

"Are you all right?"

"Yes, yes. Why would I not be all right?"

"Oh, I don't know. You seem to have grown quite fond him. You were at his side all day yesterday."

"Don't be ridiculous, he's my patient. I know nothing about the man."

"Oh. Well. Sorry, Martha. I meant no offense. Um, has he remembered anything?"

"A little; his memory seems to be coming back slowly. He believes he has a very large family."

"What sort of large family? Brothers and sisters? Wives and children?"

"Neither wife nor child have come to mind yet."

"Well, that is surprising," her friend enthused. "Such a fine-looking man, I was certain some fancy woman would have snatched him up long ago."

Martha fought back a rush of jealousy. "Sister Kelly, might I remind you that we do not engage in flights of speculation, or gossip, here."

"Ha! That's news to me."

"If I may be allowed to continue, I believe his father was, or is, a soldier, serving at the same time as my father. I shall contact the War Office, inquire if anyone has reported a son missing."

"You know you need not go so far out of your way as that, he'll be gone before you know it. Was Bleedin' Bridges attending last evening?"

"Annie!" Martha almost laughed out loud. The woman meant well but she had so much yet to learn regarding hospital politics. "You mustn't call him that. Yes, he was here; however, he was already late for a gathering and I stalled him to such an extent that he had no time for one of his horrid procedures, saints be praised. Oh, but Annie, he was furious with me."

"You *are* a brave one."

"Foolhardy is more accurate. The truth of it is he was livid. I could be dismissed with a bad character and then no other hospital will have me. Hopefully, the yule season will soften his heart – if he has one – and good cheer will keep him occupied long enough for our patient to regain strength."

"I think he has his eye on you, and not as a nurse. Martha, you be careful. He's a dark one."

"Annie Kelly, you are being deliberately provocative." Her friend was beginning to annoy. "The man is beaten, bruised, feeling alone and vulnerable. It must be very frightening to have no memory of your past. He's merely reaching for someone, seeking kindness..."

Grinning, Sister Kelly searched Martha's face with real interest now. "I was speaking of Mr. Bridges."

"Oh." She turned a bright pink. "Of course you were. I see. I can't think what came over me."

"Are you certain about that?"

"Yes!"

"All right, all right, don't get on your high horse again. Well, Martha, forgive me for saying it, but if you don't wish to frighten this fellow to death when he awakens you'd better get hold of yourself, you look positively hideous. Have you had any sleep at all? Have you eaten at least?"

"You are sweet to be concerned, if not continuously insulting." Martha patted the hand resting on her shoulder. "I've napped, was able to enjoy a bowl of soup and some boiled chicken last evening with Mr. Cratchit here, took time to wash my face and hands, of course." She smiled wistfully. "You were right about one thing – I do rather like him. Bob and I spoke often yesterday, and then again last evening. Made the time very enjoyable. I sincerely believe he's a good man." She thrilled at the memory of their kiss. "If he continues improving, he should be well enough to leave soon." It was wrong of her to wish he'd stay, of course – it was the man himself she dreaded leaving, not a patient.

"I knew I saw a sparkle in your eye."

"That is probably spittle. Mr. Hobbs had another coughing fit only moments ago."

"Lovely. Why is there a burnt tree in the corner?"

"A gift from Father Christmas caught fire."

"I see. Evidently, he does not approve of charity hospitals. Did he bring the mistletoe as well?"

Martha nearly leapt from her chair. "What? Why do you ask?"

"Sister Clarke, the weed is hanging everywhere and there are two very inebriated cooks wearing it in their waistbands." After a moment of stern silence both women burst into laughter.

"Well, that's a lovely sound."

"Ah, your Romeo is awake and calling for you."

But Martha didn't hear her friend's comment. She was already hurrying to his side.

CHAPTER FIFTEEN

THE GEORGE DARCY FAMILY ARRIVED for Boxing Day late as usual and handed over their coats, hats and boots to Mr. Winters and his son, both greeting them at the door –one seated, one standing. Most of the house's servants had this day off to spend with family, but not the Winters. The Darcy's had been their family for as long as memory.

"A happy Christmas to you, Messrs. Winters."

"And to you and yours, Mr. George. Thank you most heartily for the kind gifts from you and Mrs. Kathy."

Kathy gave the old fellow a kiss on his cheek. "I knitted yours myself. Does it fit you?"

Winters' cleared his throat. "Yes, madam. I am certain it does."

"You have no idea what it is, do you, Winters?"

"Don't be silly, George. Of course, Mr. Winters knows a sweater when he sees one. It's called a 'Cardigan', Mr. Winters, after the Earl of Cardigan. Isn't that precious? He wore one just like this at the Battle of Balaclava. I thought it rather patriotic."

"Absolutely, madam." Every year young Mr. George's wife knit something especially for him, always a mystery, but always with love. "I shall wear it this evening when my boy and I sit down to supper with Mrs. Timms."

"Just don't trip on the hem, Winters. I told Miss Kathy you weren't seven foot tall, but I doubt she believed me."

"Shush, George. Mr. Winters, You and Aunt Elizabeth have outdone yourself this year with decorations." Kathy loved the Darcy's home for Christmas. The hallway sparkled with candles and decorated evergreen boughs wrapped around the bannisters leading upstairs; in fact, holly, candles and bright ribbons and bowls of sweets were everywhere.

At that moment Alice, George's sister, peaked around the door of the dining room at the end of the hall and waved. She cupped her hand to her mouth and shouted. "You've arrived too late. We've eaten everything." The Darcy's home was alive with good cheer – relatives stopping by after services with gifts, uncles, cousins, brothers, sisters, all contributing gossip, and laughter equally. "No family arguments have begun yet, so you haven't missed any fun."

"Sorry we're late," George called back, "but Catholic masses are endless." He knew his wife would scowl at that remark; and, she did. "Well, they are."

"And you needn't have spoken with Father Dubin for three quarters of an hour afterward either."

"It was worth it. He knows amusing tales, a few of them rather naughty."

"Do not lie, George Darcy. I distinctly heard you asking about the leak in the church roof. How much will that cost us?"

"Saving your eternal soul is worth the price."

"Must be very expensive then. And what of yours?"

"My what?"

"Eternal soul."

"I was rather counting on you sneaking me in through a back door."

"We'll see." Laughing, she kissed his cheek then turned to the huge hall mirror and sighed at her appearance. "Look at me, George. I hate 'bonnet hair' – looks as if a squirrel's nested up there."

Alice had already scampered past her brother and his wife, ignoring them completely, to throw her arms around her giggling nieces and nephews. "I dearly love you little monkeys." She straightened up and turned to her old friend. "I'm sure your hair looks fine, Kath. Turn around and look at me – *good heavens.* Well, let's see what we can salvage. Happy Christmas, Georgie."

"Happy Christmas, Al." George kissed his sister's forehead before she began to rearrange his wife's hair. After all, with over thirty odd years of friendship the girls knew what they were about with fashion, who looked best wearing what, and how to hide the rest.

"Georgie, wait until you hear, Papa says he has a great surprise of some sort upstairs for the entire family, but most especially for Uncle Fitz. We've been waiting forever for him to arrive – oh, sorry Kath, was that your scalp?"

"Am I bleeding?"

"Not that much."

"Alice, I do wish you would pay attention to what you're doing before you randomly stick hairpins in my head. Heaven only knows what a mess you've made… oh, never mind, I look marvelous again. Thank you."

"May I take this off, mummy?"

Kathy crouched down beside her little boy sitting on the floor, struggling with his woolen Bolero jacket. "No, Henry. You leave your jacket on."

"But it's scratchy."

"Mummy doesn't care, you look very handsome. All right, you may remove the jacket after everyone's seen it. Wait." She stood and spun around. "Henry, where is your shoe? Cooper, could you please find Henry's shoe. Again. And however did he get dirt on his blouse?"

The children's nanny grumbled under her breath as she led the boy to a chair in the hallway and Kathy turned to shout at her raucous children. "Benedict, James, Louisa listen to me. If anyone falls or breaks a limb, I swear I shall leave you where you lie to rot and decay. Are you listening to me?"

The children were too excited to mind though. When Alice held up her hand for attention, they stopped mid-shriek. "Gifts, treats and games are up the stairs and to the left. Off with you."

With a hurrah they were off again, racing past their mother and father and charging up the stairs. Kathy stared after them. "Is there a room there where we can lock them all and throw away the key?"

"Sadly no."

"Bother. Happy Christmas, Al."

"The same to you, Beef. You're late."

"Henry needed to use the facilities."

"I do not understand why –" Alice stopped the moment she saw her favorite nephew home from university.

"Auntie Al, Happy Christmas." Will Darcy hugged her warmly,

kissing the top of her head.

"I've missed you, you irritatingly young person!"

"Feels like I've been gone for years, I persevered like a true Darcy though. Done with the worst of the homesickness by now, hopefully."

"Don't let him fool you, Alice. The moment he met his roommate's sisters he was pleased as punch. Both pretty little things, baking him cakes and sending him gifts stuffed with little love notes…"

"Mother."

"Stop teasing the boy, Kathy." George slipped his hand around his wife's waist and beamed at his son, the first-born grandchild of Fitzwilliam Darcy and Richard Fitzwilliam. "It has nothing to do with women. No. He loves university because he's brilliant, that's all, just like his father; loving every moment, he is – never saw anyone take to leaving home with such unbridled joy. Rather ungrateful wretch, actually. Kathy, I think we should be insulted. That's it, I'm writing him out of the will."

Will Darcy shook his head. Parents could be so embarrassing.

"Ignore them, Will, we all do. I say, you must be tallest in the family now." Even stretching up on tip-toe Alice was at least a foot shorter than her nephew.

"That's what I keep saying, although Grandpa Fitz still insists he's taller. He says that even as I tower above him and pat his head."

"That sounds like the old troublemaker. Oh! By the way, George, did you bring the Christmas crackers?"

"Yes, of course. I had the coachman bring them round to the back. Now, are we finished with the hallway greetings; I want food." George turned and quickly made his way to the dining room, Will, Alice and Kathy following close behind, all arm in arm.

"Happy Christmas, everyone!" George called out cheerfully, returning each friendly greeting with a wave of his hand. "Sorry we're late – you know, Catholic mass and all." At that a few of his more devoted Church of England relatives appeared to suddenly be smelling cabbage.

"Yes, well… ah, Mr. and Mrs. Gardiner, how wonderful to see you; Aunt Kitty you've left me some pudding I hope. I'm teasing you, truly I am… unless there are no jam tarts and then I shall wrestle you to the ground for those crumbs… good to see you Uncle Charles, Auntie Jane! Oh, I say, I'm so glad you could make it this year. And my beautiful Bingley cousins as well – lovely to see you all. Miss Charlotte, Reverend Collins! I had no idea you would be here, grand top coat you have there, sir. By the way, where are the plates – ah, good. You know, I think it may be about to snow again out there... *Yikes*!" He started in terror when he turned to see his cousin Matthew's glowering wife just behind him.

"Heavens. Clarissa. Don't know what came over me; forgive me for screaming like that." His first impulse – to bolt from the room – was impossible when staring into that fierce countenance. "Happy Christmas?"

"Our prince is dead, and our dear Lord will be tortured and killed within four months of today. What, in that, is there to console me?"

In view of her statement it was a struggle for George to provide an appropriate answer. "Well." He cleared his throat. "It only happens once a year – I mean our Lord's death, not the prince's…"

Clarissa's narrowed eyes turned to slits.

"It's an argument you cannot win, George; believe me I've tried for years. Move on." Matthew nudged at his cousin's back to encourage him forward in the buffet line. "The true reason for her irritability are her new mourning bloomers. Isn't that right, my dear? Chafe you, do they? Self-flagellation, the gift that keeps on giving for the holidays."

Conversation quieted as those in the room strained to hear the husband and wife's angry words. Their arguments were legendary at times.

Clarissa slammed her plate down. "I am not the one who will burn in hell for all eternity."

"I sincerely hope not since I will be there."

Standing between the two of them George stared at the ceiling. "Do you know what?" He set his plate down and nervously wiped his hands on a napkin. "I do believe I should say hello to mother and father before I eat; I should search them out. Anyone know where they are? Anyone? Probably in hiding from all this Boxing Day gaiety. Never you mind, my boy and I shall go look for ourselves. Will? Where did he go? Will, you rat, wait for me!"

"Coward." Alice hissed as her brother hurried from the room. By then the marital battle had called a cease fire, the show was momentarily over, and the conversation of the others slowly had begun to pick up exactly where it had stopped. She turned to her cousin, Kathy. "I love Christmas – there's always at least one ripping good fight. By the way, why did you need to return home to use the facilities?"

Kathy blinked once or twice, trying to recall from where that particular comment had come. "Do you mean for Baby Henry?"

"No, I mean for your husband. Yes, of course I mean for Baby Henry. Are you aware my parents have installed indoor plumbing? They're kind people; I'm almost certain they'd allow your family limited access. Fully functional, modern, up to date and everything – the facilities I mean, not the parents." As she spoke her son, eight-year-old Bennet Penrod, his faced smeared in red, tugged, at her skirt.

"What is it, my darling sprig? Oh my. Have you been mortally wounded?"

"I shouldn't think so." He licked his finger. "Jam. Mummy, I've eaten as much as I am able to down here. May I go upstairs and play pirates with the cousins?"

"All right but try not to wreak too much havoc – remember, we may be inheriting this place one day. And, please tell those other barbarians that the next child to run past me with sticky fingers will be locked in the Darcy dungeon!"

Kathy spun out of the way just in time as another child raced through. "The longer I live, the more I believe Aunt Catherine was right. Children should be seen and not heard until well after they're married off. How are the kippers? Kindly move your foot, Matthew."

"Certainly not. You can't just barge in front of people."

"Says who? Listen to me, brother. It is Boxing Day, I am a mother; I've been awake since four in the blessed morning. I can do and say whatever I wish at this point. Now, excuse me I was speaking with our irritating cousin. What were we discussing, Alice? Oh, yes, of course, about the use of the Darcy facilities. I do realize Uncle Will and Auntie Eliza have all the modern conveniences here. The problem is with Baby Henry – he cannot wee unless he's home."

Clarissa, still hovering nearby, was not pleased by that comment. "Must we be subjected every holiday to discussion of your children's bodily functions?"

"Pardon? Oh, you're still here, Clarissa? What hateful thing do you have to say about my children this time?"

Turning his back to the approaching gale force battle Matthew tapped on Alice's shoulder. "Have you heard from Mark? I thought we'd hear from him by now."

"Sh! You're making me miss the argument!"

"Alice!"

"Oh, all right. I haven't spoken with Mark in a week at the least. Just a moment there missy! Kathy, stop taking all the scones! Mummie, Kathy Fitzwilliam is taking all the scones!"

"I am not! Auntie Eliza, She's fibbing! Besides there are strawberry ones left! My word, Alice, you are such a baby. You always were a baby. Baby, baby, baby…"

"Be quiet for once in your lives! Have either of you heard from Mark?" Matthew never could remember a conversation with his female sisters and cousins when a subject was discussed beginning to end without diverting somewhere else, and at the top of their lungs. It was all making him unreasonably anxious; and, it didn't help that children were chasing barking dogs through the dining room and out again.

"Mark? Let me think. Wasn't Mark going to visit with Bunny Armitage's aunt and uncle. Do you think he'll ever propose to her? Father certainly would be pleased. Said she had hips for breeding, or something revolting like that."

"Didn't you know," Alice slapped Kathy's hand away from the remaining pudding they both wanted. "Mark was going there with Bunny specifically *to* propose. Kathy! Leave a bit of the pudding for others, please!"

"Never mind, take it all, it doesn't look that appetizing anyway – wait, what did you just say?"

"Mark is finally proposing to Bunny. In fact, Luke was going to meet Mark there and bring one of Auntie Amanda's rings to present to her. I just this morning sent a note to Bunny at her home asking her to contact me as soon as they return. I was thinking we'd have their betrothal dinner at Penrod Place."

"Are you serious? Matthew, were you aware Mark was proposing to Bunny now? He never said anything to me. Why am I always last to know these things? Matthew, take these, I don't believe I like their color."

Matthew scraped the sweetbreads from her plate to his. "Because you can't keep a secret to save your soul, that's why; and, evidently neither can Alice!" He was as anxious as he'd ever been in his life, but for what reason? Mark had been gone before, occasionally for months at a time. Now he was snapping at his sister and cousin. If only he could remember what Mark had told him before they separated at that awful Inn. Something about returning in a few days, or next day. It was all a muddle. He was about to apologize to them both when a terrible racket from the street silenced them all.

"*'Good King Wants His Applesauce at the Feast This Evening...'*" The voice bellowing off key from outside the Darcy's house, confusing the lyrics of Good King Wenceslaus, was instantly recognizable.

"Papa's here."

CHAPTER SIXTEEN

A BLAST OF COLD AIR AND snow ushered Richard Fitzwilliam, his spinster daughters, Meg and Beth, and an exhausted looking Doctor Anthony Milagros, through the Darcy's front door.

"Good heavens," Darcy called out as he made his way down the stairs. "For one dreadful moment I thought a pig was being slaughtered on my doorstep."

"That's rather rude of you. Are you insinuating I was a tad off key? Hello, daughter. Did you hear what Darcy just said? I should call him out for that."

Kathy hugged her father tightly. "Actually Papa, Uncle Wills was being kind." Standing back from him a little she patted his stomach. "You're getting fat."

"I prefer to think on it as softened muscle, there to protect me should I fall victim to a sudden stumble."

"You could survive a leap from Big Ben with that." She turned to embrace her younger sisters Beth and Meg with equal exuberance. "Hello my beautiful baby sisters. Happy Christmas." Then she turned to Dr. Milagros who opened his arms. "Tio Anthony."

"Katherine, *querida, estás guapísima.* Just lovely. Your Papa says you are with child *again,* yes?" When she nodded, he kissed her cheek, his eyes moist with tears. "So like your dearest Mama. She could become *enceinte* from a sneeze."

"Anthony." Darcy shook his old friend's hand. "Happy Christmas. I hope for London's sake Fitz hasn't been singing all the way here."

"No idea. I wear my earplugs. My advice to you – burn Georgiana's old pianoforte before he begins to sing Wagner. You know, Fitzwilliam, it would not go unappreciated if you learned another verse of 'Holly and the Ivy'. You are driving me mad with that song."

"There are no other verses."

"Someone be kind enough to kill me now then, please."

Darcy patted his shoulder. "Once he begins eating we'll all feel safer. Now, if you'll join the others in the dining room, Tony, I have a very special surprise awaiting upstairs for my cousin. Fitz, if you'd follow me, please."

Fitzwilliam gave Darcy a wink. "Of course. Well, that sounds promising. Tony, take Meg and Beth with you, poor things must be famished, haven't eaten in minutes. Wait..." He patted his coat pockets. "Where in bloody hell is my tobacco? Girls?"

"How should we know?"

"Because one of you is always hiding it from me. All right, hand it over. Now!"

"Worse than a child." Meg pulled a small velvet bag from her reticule. "Promise me you'll not smoke all the time."

"Certainly not. Promise I mean. Now go. Go! You children are too bossy by far these days." After a small tug of war with his daughter he took the bag from her. "Why are you all still standing here? Darcy has a surprise for me, not you."

Beth kissed her father then turned to Milagros. "Have you read the Lunacy Act of 1845, Uncle Tony? We suspect Papa figures prominently in the research for that."

"Go!"

Laughing, both girls then turned on their heels and headed down the hallway arm in arm, followed closely by Kathy and the good doctor.

"Thought they'd never leave. Clever thinking, Darcy, saying you had a surprise. Now, what have you handy for a parched old man? Something to warm the spirit, work out the knots and stimulate the mind."

"Tea, coffee, hot chocolate?"

"Not at all amusing."

"All right, a bit of mulled wine it is then."

"Or whiskey! Lead the way. I'll go anywhere for a drink, you know that."

The two men headed up the stairs and went directly to the library when Darcy stopped and rapped on the door before opening. "Is someone else here?" Fitzwilliam grumbled. "Oh, damn me, Darcy, I just wanted a moment alone to smoke, have a drink," His gaze swept the room, looking for any unwanted relative lurking about, until he saw a tall man standing before the fireplace. His heart sprang up into his throat. *It couldn't be.*

"Teddy?"

The young priest spun around. "There you are! Happy Christmas, Papa."

The family spent the next several hours fussing over their own Father Edward Fitzwilliam. Once word of his return spread downstairs both families had come running, whooping and shouting with excitement. Wassail punch flowed freely, his favorite minced pies, biscuits, sweets and dishes were prepared and brought up by long-standing family servants who had yet to leave for the day, or had returned early, greeting the youngest Fitzwilliam with joyful tears. Questions about his health, his travels, his mission house in China, Chinese culture, Chinese people, were never ending.

Fitzwilliam heard little of it, content merely to settle back in his chair and observe. There could be nothing more gratifying, he mused, than for a parent to see his children all safe and healthy. He nudged Darcy. "How in the world did you keep our Teddy's visit a secret?"

"That was simple enough. I had no idea he was coming. He just showed up on our doorstep this morning, knowing full well we would be gathering here this year for Christmas instead of Pemberley and wanting to surprise you." Darcy settled on the arm of Lizzy's chair. "And may I say, Father Ted, that you look remarkably fit." He pointedly eyed the priest's emerging belly. "Eating well, are we?"

"As you remember I am much like my father in that regard, Uncle Wills – never met a meal I didn't like. They feed me constantly."

Fitzwilliam chuckled between puffs on his pipe. "Sounds all right, I must say. I shall have to visit. Have you made many converts, son?"

"Not many, Papa; however, they are too polite to interrupt so I continue to proselytize. Enough about me. Uncle Wills I'm glad to see you've adopted the German custom of holiday trees and decorations. Father, why don't you decorate as well? It's very jolly."

"Oh, he has, Father Ted." Elizabeth selected a chocolate from a plate at her side. "The Fitzwilliam home today looks like a page from Illustrated London News, tree and all."

"Well, the girls pester me – you know, it's for them." Meg and Beth rolled their eyes at this, knowing he was the biggest child of all. "You'll see tonight."

"Speaking of the girls, what grand news to hear Anne Marie will be returning." He patted Roberta's head as the children played in the center of the room before him. "I cannot believe this little one is so grown up."

"I do remember you, you know." Roberta beamed.

"Impossible. You were too little when I left."

"I was amazingly precocious."

"You were a terror – always pulling off your shoes and throwing them out the window."

"Yes! I remember that too. Oh, Mama will be so happy you're home."

"Well, not forever, but now I want to get to know all my new nieces and nephews, reacquaint myself with Will Darcy the Second over there, and have time with my family, my sisters, my cousins, my brothers… by the way, Kath, where are the others?"

"Other what?"

"Brothers. Mark and Luke. I am anxious to see them both."

George lifted his youngest child onto his lap. "By Jove, I'd completely forgotten about them with the excitement of having you home, Ted."

Kathy fanned herself. "Well, I have surprising news for you, husband. Apparently, the reason for Mark escorting Bunny Armitage to her relatives' home in Hampstead is – wait until you hear this – he has arranged for Luke to meet them there… *with one of my Mama's rings*!" When he did not react as she'd hoped, she explained. "He is proposing, silly. To Bunny. He may be doing just that at this exact moment. Proposing marriage. Why are you smiling?"

George patted her hand. "Kathy, we all know that." She looked about the room and everyone nodded. Even Birdy and Amanda

Rose stopped eating chocolates long enough to confirm Mark had said the same to them.

"I don't believe you. You mean you all knew Mark was planning to propose and no one told me?"

"Mark wished to keep it secret. Telling you is like announcing it from the window at Buckingham Palace."

"Now that you mention it," Elizabeth replaced her teacup on the saucer. "Luke visited us here yesterday morning; said he'd paid a king's ransom to the jeweler and was off to the depot to deliver the ring to Mark. Luke promised to return and tell us what happened, but he never did."

Kathy was still glaring at her husband. "I do not believe I've ever been so insulted in my life. Even the children knew?"

"Only the ones old enough to walk." George popped a candy into his mouth.

"Never mind about that now." The anxious feeling Matthew had been trying to ignore was turning into real concern. He began to pace to the windows and back, his stomach tied in knots. "Something is very wrong," he mumbled. "I can feel it."

"Oh gracious." Smoothing the tight bun on back of her head Clarissa sighed. "Not this drivel again, Matthew."

"It is not drivel to me, wife."

"Speak plainly you two," demanded Fitzwilliam.

A long-suffering sigh escaped her. "Matthew and Mark believe they are privy to each other's thoughts, feel what each other is feeling – merely because they are twins. Is that not the most ridiculous thing you've ever heard?"

"Not really." Beth took her sister Meg's hand in hers. "We understand that feeling as twins ourselves, do we not, sister?"

"Actually, Beth, you are a complete mystery to me at times. I mean really! Insisting we wear identical dresses and matching flowers in our hair? We looked like a music hall performance."

"Oh my goodness, that was one time! Seven years ago! So sorry if I offended–"

"Enough." Darcy's quiet works stopped the bickering at once, except for Clarissa, who had not yet noticed the rising tension.

"It's ridiculous. They oftentimes play a game when Mark visits, writing something down on a piece of paper – a color, or an object – and, if the other can guess what's written, they take a drink. By morning they are stupidly intoxicated, their papers a series of crossed out and mismatched words. It is most disgusting."

Matthew exploded. "Will you be quiet! Mark is in trouble, I know he is. Something is very wrong."

It was at that moment Luke strolled into the room. "Happy Christmas, everyone; sorry I'm late. Uncle Wills, Auntie Eliza, the house looks wonderful, but no one is downstairs. It looks as if the party ended early this year." He glanced around. "Teddy! Damn me, when in blazes did you arrive? Come here." As he embraced his brother, Luke noticed everyone staring at him. Throwing an arm around Teddy's shoulder he looked about and sighed. "All right, all right; what is it? What have I done now?"

"Where is Mark?" Matthew feared in his heart that Luke had no answer.

"Mark? Have no idea. I never heard from him."

"You were to take the train and meet him, were you not?"

"Yes. Why are you glaring at *me*? See here, we took the train to the Hampstead as Mark requested, believing he'd meet us there; however, I never saw him. He was not at the station when I arrived, I waited, and since I had no idea where in Hampstead they were visiting we just took the returning train."

"Weren't you at all curious?"

"Well, knowing Mark I merely surmised he'd changed his mind. Wouldn't be the first time with those two."

"Where have you been all this time then?"

"What is this? Not that it's any of your business, Matthew, but I proceeded on to Jeff Malboro's for cards, and other recreational activities – did excellently well too, thank you very much! What in the world is the matter? Has no one heard from Mark?"

Fitzwilliam felt a pain begin in his chest as fear began to take hold. "I'm certain everything is fine. No need to worry needlessly."

"Madam?" The butler entered with a note for Alice. After she read the first lines her face paled.

"What is it?" her husband asked in alarm.

"You read it, Harry, please. It is a response from Bunny Armitage to my note this morning."

Harry nodded, then read. "Dearest Alice, I thank you for your warm wishes and the kind offer of your home for an engagement dinner. Unfortunately, Mark has again disappointed by failing to appear at our home to escort my parents and myself to the house party of our relatives, as he had promised. This thoughtlessness left me no recourse but to cancel my visit with my grandfather and his new wife, whom I abhor. The new wife, not my grandfather. You can imagine my humiliation. I have been accustomed to his casual treatment of me – he often forgets appointments, his work claiming any attentions not reserved for his family...but, I can no longer approve this behavior. It is with great regret that I shall no longer be entertaining thoughts of wedded bliss with Mark Fitzwilliam, hence eliminating the need for an engagement dinner entirely. Yours sincerely."

Harry offered the note to Darcy then hurried to Fitzwilliam's side, concerned by the stricken look on his step-father's face.

"What could she mean? Where is our darling brother?" Meg and Beth spoke at the same time, immediately taking hold of each other's hands.

As everyone looked around, alarm growing by the moment, Darcy cleared his throat. "I do not recall Mark ever being unkind before. Ever. Something truly is wrong."

"Merciful heaven. He could be unconscious. He could be bleeding in the street, or worse. We have to search for him. He could be lying in one of those awful hospitals. He could be..." Kathy's voice trailed off before she finished her thought.

"Nonsense. You are all such alarmists! Although–" Clarissa tapped a finger on her chin. "But it's too bizarre to even consider."

Before Matthew could start shouting Lizzy turned the woman around to face her. "What are you saying, Clarissa?"

"Well, while representing the Church of England Temperance Society in memory of our dearly departed Prince Albert, Lady Stanton, Lady Belling and I did visit several hospitals during the country's mourning period."

"And..." encouraged Lizzy.

"And, I thought... for a brief moment... a drunkard in one of them looked similar to your Mark. But the idea is absurd, of course."

Matthew approached her slowly. "And you are telling me this now, knowing how uneasy I've been?"

"I suggest you not take that tone with me, Matthew. It was only a momentary thought, I find it very difficult to differentiate among the lower classes."

Matthew controlled his anger for once. "Where was this?"

"Oh really, how could you even think that a member of this family would be lying in some filthy hospital? The very idea is ridiculous." She grimaced as Matthew grabbed her arm. "Stop that, you're hurting me!"

"Forgive me, dearest. Now, think, which hospital was it?"

"Matthew," Father Ted cautioned. "Calm yourself."

"I certainly can't remember right this moment. It could have been Guy's Hospital, or St. Thomas, or The Royal Free Hospital, or St. Mary's – now, let go of my arm!"

Matthew released her so suddenly she fell back into her chair and was ready to immediately jump back onto her feet and scratch his eyes out. However, by that time the room was in an uproar with Matthew, Luke, George, Harry, Darcy and Anthony Milagros all shouting at once.

CHAPTER SEVENTEEN

"NOT A TRACE OF THE good doctor today. Must be very busy with his fancy, Harley Street clientele. How is our handsome fellow?"

Abstracted, Martha looked up briefly from mixing a medicinal draught. "Mr. Bridges?"

Annie Kelly snorted out a laugh. "Not hardly, I refer to our patient here. My doesn't he look improved! I'd tuck my shoes under his bed anytime."

"You are a terrible sinner."

"No. Actually, I am an excellent sinner. Would you like some hot buttered bread and tea?"

"Yes, that sounds wonderful."

Mark reached out his hand. "I would slay a dragon for a cup of coffee."

"Oho, never tell me you are awake!" Annie Kelly covered her face. "Now I'm ever so embarrassed." Her voice trailed off when she peeked and saw the two people before her seemed to have eyes only for each other. "I said, I am ever so… never mind. Shall I go ahead and get the tea and coffee then? Martha? Martha, I seem to have amputated my hand, shall I stick it back on?"

"Whatever you think best." Martha's eyes sparkled with joy. A grinning Sister Kelly walked from the room, shaking her head.

"You've had a nice rest. How are you feeling?"

"Another douse of laudanum? You really must stop. My brain is all cotton fuzz."

"All right, I promise you no more laudanum, besides your color is better, your pain seems more manageable now – is it?"

"Absolutely."

"Ah. Then I do believe you're well on your way to recovery." She sounded very professional to herself, not at all regretful.

"I wish you hadn't allowed me to sleep so long, I was enjoying our talks."

"Do you even remember what they were about?"

"No. I merely know I was listening to you and enjoying myself. Did you mean what you said?"

"About what?"

"You find me handsome, and you'd tuck your shoes under my bed any time."

"Sister Kelly is the one with the sinful shoes. But…" Feeling her loneliness for him already, she took his hand in hers and kissed it. "I should not say this, but if I were to tuck my shoes under any man's bed, it would be yours."

His eyelids lowered with desire. "I want more than your shoes in my bed… Damn me, that didn't sound as romantic as I'd hoped."

She smiled at him. "I understand."

"Do you? I don't believe you really do. Allow me to speak plainly, my angel. I am in love with you."

She stared at him for a long while. "Nonsense, we don't even know each other. Please don't say such things. You may have a wife, children."

"It doesn't matter. Heaven forgive *me* but, I can't stay away from you." Cupping the back of her head he urged her lips down to his, slowly tasting them, nibbling until her mouth parted. She moaned with pleasure. It was heaven. She'd never felt such a desire for a man, such need.

Her head angled for deeper, more urgent kisses. "This isn't right," she whimpered against his lips.

"Bloody hell it isn't," he was becoming more aggressive, more insistent. His hand began to roam, fondle and caress her breast, her hip…

"Sister Clarke! Have you lost your senses!"

Martha jumped to her feet, light headed and dizzy, her heart pounding. "Mister Bridges!" She looked about herself, still in a daze of lust. Over twenty-four hours without sleep, along with constant worry about this patient, had clouded her reason. *Again.*

Still there seemed nothing she could do to keep herself from loving this man.

"And you also appear to be intoxicated!"

"Certainly not."

Mark wondered who could be speaking so rudely to the woman he loved. "What is it, Martha? Who is that?" His memory was slowly returning and with it the inherent entitlement of a member of a rich and powerful family. Mark was incensed. Only a brigand would dare speak to any lady in this manner, and only someone with a death wish dare speak like that to *his* lady!

"Quiet, you filthy animal! Sister Clarke, I shall be reporting this dissolute behavior to your betters. Just look at your appearance, your clothes disheveled, your hair coming undone. You are a disgrace, a very poor specimen indeed of both your gender and your profession, and may I add validating the generally accepted opinion that nursing is but a step up from a whore! I shall make it my business to see that you never work in this hospital again! Get out of my sight!"

"How *dare* you… speak in *such* a … give me a moment, here!" Mark had pushed himself into a sitting position and was having difficulty breathing, already exhausted from the exertion.

Martha spun around and pressed her hand to his chest. "You will tear your stitches, please lie down, Bob."

"You have the nerve to turn your back on me, Clarke? Wait until I discuss your behavior with the governors of this hospital. I can assure you that no decent person would think to work with you again! I hope you are listening to me, I hope you realize the severity of your base actions."

However, she had stopped listening the moment she saw the physician motion for an orderly to bring over a table where he set down a large bowl and several odd looking knives.

"You cannot think to bleed him again, not so soon after the last time."

"How dare you tell me what I can or cannot do! Such insolence is not to be borne. I want you out of this hospital, immediately. Sister Kelly, I order you to come here at once and secure the patient's arm."

Annie Kelly's employment, as others of the hospital staff, was at the whim of the hospital board. She would never stand up to the men in authority no matter what insults she spoke outside of their hearing. What could Martha do? Her patient was only recently regaining strength, he was still vulnerable, weak. No, this would not do! This man was her patient, her responsibility to protect any way possible.

Besides that, she loved him.

"Do not dare touch this man."

"What did you say?"

Martha braced herself before her patient's bed.

"Pardon me. Martha, be so good as to move aside." Mark summoned all his strength to rise again, swinging his legs over the other side of the bed only to become immediately light headed. *Bugger.* Panting and worn, he looked down. His bandages were beginning to come undone, blood seeping through.

"Oh, no! Do you see what you've done? You've opened your stitches. Oh, please lay still." Martha turned back again to confront Bridges. "You heard what I said. You will not bleed him, sir. Not again. That is something I will not allow!"

Mr. Bridges took a step back. *"How dare you!"*

"Who in blazes is this fool? Allow me to handle this, if you will." Mark reached for her, thinking to pull her around to the other side of the bed with him, protect her from that angry voice with the blurry face, bring her to safety. "Do you know who I am, sir?" he croaked. *And bloody hell, if you do, tell me. I'd love to know.*

"Oh, Bob, drink this and hush." She shoved an empty glass into Mark's hand then spun back around to face Bridges. "I repeat, I am afraid I cannot allow you to bleed my patient." Martha's hands curled into small fists at her sides, she raised her chin. "If you approach this man, you approach at your own risk." Her heart was beating so wildly she was surprised her apron bodice wasn't jumping.

"Damn your patient, and damn you!" The physician shook with rage. "And to think I wasted my valuable attentions on you!"

By now, Mark was relatively upright and had finally steadied himself. "Listen to me you bastard. How dare you speak to her in that – oops. Hello. Anyone. I really must insist someone help me here!" Mark looked frantically around as his legs gave way and he began to sink to the floor, hitting his head again on the bed before he checked himself.

"False alarm. I'm all right. Please don't concern yourselves." He was unaware that no one was paying attention though, he could see nothing – blood was streaming down his face. Stitches across his eyes and scalp had given way; in fact, wounds that had been previously healing were now ripping open and seeping blood everywhere, a gory sight. "*I say, you – wherever the hell you are – stop shouting at her!*"

"I'm all right, hush, now. He doesn't frighten me." Without taking her gaze from Bridges she reached behind herself to push Mark back into the bed, all the while trying to appear confident and calm before her enemy. Their enemy.

However, as much as she patted the bed behind her, she couldn't find her patient, and it was too late now to turn around and search for him. If she had, she might have noticed the horrified onlookers peeking around the back of the curtain. *Sweet mother of God I am doomed, Bridge's is going to have me taken out and shot*; at the very least she was certain to be sacked by morning.

"Yes, by all means, speak with my superiors; and, I shall as well. I shall tell them how you jeopardize patients' lives daily with your experiments. You use your excessive bleeding of the indigent to test theories of care, that if successful, you then employ on the wealthy! Unfortunately, if you are unsuccessful, your patients – along with your mistakes – are *buried!*"

"Bleedin' 'ell," muttered someone as other patients began to grumble.

"See here," Mr. Bridges was becoming anxious with this talk. "You obviously know nothing about this. It is what comes from treating *nurses* as if they were on an equal footing with *doctors*! Your kind are severely ill-trained regarding the necessity of balancing the humors within the body – blood, phlegm, yellow bile and black bile. And that, my ignorant miss, is only achieved by blood-letting! Now, step out of my way!"

Unfortunately, Martha reacted instinctively when Bridges began to strong arm his way past her, sticking out her foot and causing the physician to stagger forward into a cart of instruments and fall to the floor.

"Oh, dear. I am so very sorry, sir." Martha felt terrible. She'd not meant to hurt the man, but when he sat up with an overturned bowl his head onlookers howled with laughter. Furious and humiliated, Bridges attempted to regain his footing several times, his arms and legs flailing about like windmills, while Martha tried to assist.

"Take your hands from me!" he shrieked as he finally stood. "You did that deliberately!"

"No! Well, yes, but it was unconsciously done, a stupid, mindless reaction. You're not injured, are you?"

When she saw his toupee was now crooked it was too much for her, and she began to giggle herself. "Oh, dear. No truly. I didn't realize you would actually fall."

"Or even 'ow far a little fella like 'im could fly," shouted out one of the others causing everyone to laugh louder.

Everyone but the proud physician; Bridges was beyond livid. He grabbed her wrist, twisted her arm behind her. *"I shall show you what it means to cross me, bitch!"* he hissed, back-handing her brutally across the face. Her head snapped to the side and she flew backward, first hitting the already upset instrument cart edge – bowls and water and knives sent flying in all directions – then slamming into a nearby cabinet with a crash.

Everyone was frozen in silent shock seeing the blood ooze from the side of her head, her face turned away, her limbs limp. No one could believe what had happened. When someone near her body nudged it with his foot, she rolled over… her eyes open but unseeing. "Shite, I think she's dead."

That was when all hell really broke loose.

"*NO! You bloody bastard! I'll kill you for this!*" Mark had finally struggled forward, an immense, horrific, monstrous sight, blood seeping down his face from reopened wounds, blood and bandages trailing the floor behind him, blood saturating his legs and arms.

He looked like a nightmare come to life.

Mr. Bridges began to scream. He shrank back in terror as Mark lurched forward, step by halting step, a massive form of revulsion, his inhuman growls of pain, emotional as well as physical, eliciting scream after scream from the terrified physician, as closer and closer the bloody form staggered, step by agonizing step until…

Arms reaching out for the doctor, Mark stopped.

His eyeballs rolled up into their sockets.

He began to sway, round and round, back and forth.

Someone screamed, "he's going down – get out of the way!"

And, like the mighty oak, Mark fell – taking with him tables, chairs, the screen, and one incoherently raving physician.

CHAPTER EIGHTEEN

THE HOSPITAL ADMINISTRATOR HAD WALKED out for a moment when Anthony Milagros took the opportunity to ransack his desk, his fear of being caught making him jump back when he suddenly heard the screams. "*Madre de dios!* What was that?"

This was their second visit to this hospital in twenty-four hours. The entire family had spread out across the city, searching hospitals and infirmaries for Mark, even the jails, everyone mad with worry.

Luke put his hand up for silence.

"Was that even human?" asked George.

"No. That was Mark's voice. Listen."

"Mark?" George walked to the window and looked out. "Don't be ridiculous. Sounded more like a cat fight going on down the street. Let me close this."

"It was Mark. Damn it, George, don't look at me like that! I know my brother's voice! I heard him! Dear Lord, that was my brother!"

Although Luke was frozen to the spot by the horror of it, George was not – he reached the door first, yanking it open. "That's good enough for me. Come on, Luke!"

"Yes. *Yes!*" A shaken Luke charged past him with both George and Anthony close on his heels.

The scene greeting them outside the office was chaos. People running, crying, orderlies charging toward the back of the hospital and up the stairs. There were shouts and shrieks, and by the time George, Luke and Anthony arrived, a mob had formed shouting out wagers.

"Get him off me!" Beneath a huge and bare bottomed patient, a terrified man was sobbing like a baby as nearby two orderlies were carrying away a lifeless female body.

"What the hell happened here?" Anthony shouted at a terrified looking nurse, but instead of answering him she turned and ran out.

"George! Uncle Tony!" Luke pushed his way to the prone figure. "Come here! It is him! That's Mark!"

"How can you tell when he's faced down?" asked George

"I'd recognize that hairy arse anywhere. George, help me." Both men pushed through the crowed then slowly lifted up the unconscious figure, between them carrying it back to the bed, and laying it down gently… face up.

"I'll be damned!" George brushed Mark's hair back from bleeding stitches. "How in hell did you recognize him by his backside?"

"It's farted in my face enough times. Uncle Tony, come quickly!"

"I'm here, Luke. Behind you. Move to the side, let me see him."

"Mark! Mark, wake up! Are you all right? Is he alive? My God, what have they done to him? Who did this?" Luke demanded to the room in general. "Come forward you bastard!"

"Luke stop shouting – I want to listen to his heart." Tony pressed his ear to Mark's chest. "Thank the lord, his heart sounds strong. I need soap and water."

George, assisting the whimpering physician to his feet, hissed in the man's ear. "If you've done this to my cousin, I shall beat you to death with my bare hands!" That was all Bridges needed to hear. The physician began screaming in terror once again.

"Silence!" Anthony barked. "Someone, bring me a lantern so I can examine this fellow." With no staff around to help, a patient hobbled over with soap and water while another brought a lantern. "Thank you both, now please be good enough to return to your beds. Please, everyone, return to your beds before someone else is injured." Anthony began washing his hands at the nearby basin. "Why is there no staff? Who is in charge here?"

"Sister Clarke, your worship." The man who had brought over the lantern mumbled in awe to the Spanish nobleman.

"Well, where is she!"

"She was kilt, we think. On the other 'and, Amos was one who looked at 'er, and 'e's blind as a lamppost. O'course, 'e kicked 'er by accident like and she never moved. So, it's a quandry."

"Luke, George find out who is in charge here. Bedlam was better supervised."

"George, you go. I want to stay with Mark."

George nodded and rushed off.

After a few moments of examination Anthony finally began to relax. "Well, I do not believe Mark's injuries are as bad as they look at the moment. Stitches over his eyes have broken, he'll have a scar here. And see here, he had been beaten as well; badly beaten. It appears he has heavy bruising on his chest, stomach, legs. Someone please bring me fresh warm, soapy water, needle and thread. George, you're back. What did you discover?"

"I found the administrator, he'll be here in a moment. He had no idea where the nurses are however."

One of the patients in a nearby bed slowly raised his hand.

"Yes, yes," snapped Anthony. "Speak."

"Sister Kelly and orderlies took Sister Clarke away and they was cryin'. Whatever 'appened must 'ave been bloody awful, I'd say, what with all the shoutin' and then that fella there risin' from 'is bed like a demon from 'ell, takin' down screen an' all – 'All' bein' Mr. Bridges I mean. Actually, t'were bloody wonderful, now I think on it. 'e stayed down long enough for me to win a hat."

"It was hell!" Shrieked Bridges as he backed away. "That heathen attacked me like a wild beast!"

"What did you call my brother?" Luke lunged for the man as George lunged for Luke.

"Luke! Get hold of yourself, man! Nothing can be gained by flying off the handle."

"Yes. Yes, you're right, George. Of course. Don't know what came over me there."

"You must promise not to kill anyone."

"Oh, for God's sake, I'm not a bloody idiot! I am fine! I'm fine. All that is important now is seeing to Mark. It's just… I'm just… I mean, look at him. Dear God, I can't believe he suffered like this." Luke's voice broke and he turned away.

"I understand." George patted his cousin's shoulder in comfort. "Mustn't give way to despair, or bitterness though. Remember, revenge never did anyone any good. Stiff upper and all that."

"You're right of course, George. Thank you."

George then calmly turned to the doctor, grabbed him by his coat lapels and began screaming in his face. *"I promised I'd beat the life from you, you son of a bitch, and so I shall! How dare you! Do you know who that man is? He's no heathen off the streets! That is my cousin, a finer man than you could ever hope to be!"*

"Help." Doctor Bridges gulped as Luke pried George's fingers loose. "Bloody hell, I could have done that just as easily as you!"

"Yes, I know, but I wanted to."

His wits slowly returning now Bridges noted the wealth and standing of the two younger men arguing over which would beat him to death, observed the very elegant older nobleman tending to the patient he had assumed was a drunkard, and finally began to realize he may have made a huge mistake.

"Forgive my error, dear sirs; kind sirs. I had no idea. No one said anything to me, I swear it! In fact, this is the first I've seen of the man, being Christmas and all. I was just so very frustrated. It was the nurse's fault, you see – honestly it was! I was very angry that she hadn't informed me of his presence, or the severity of his wounds; and, when I tried to assist him, she interfered. Yes. That *woman* was impeding patient care. I merely moved her from my path, an action which your cousin evidently misconstrued. That was when he leapt from the bed, probably in *my* defense now that I think on it. Yes, I'm certain of it. Exemplary fellow."

The hospital administrator came running into the ward then and Bridges turned on him, all righteous indignation now. "Do you see what one of your nurses has done? I insist you sack that woman immediately. She nearly killed my patient!"

"Just a mo, guvnor..."

"Be quiet, all of you! Why are you here? Get back to your beds. Now!" Bridges began to smooth back his hair and straighten his clothing. "Such disloyalty! Such treachery! Mr. Hastings, it is your responsibility as Hospital Administrator to have this woman arrested, or at the very least, dismissed. In fact, I really must insist upon it. She put a patient's life in jeopardy and attacked me!"

"If I may interrupt." Anthony was uninterested in this hospital squabble. He needed to notify Fitzwilliam that they had finally found his son, make certain his godson was stable, and then return Mark to his family as quickly as possible. "I shall be writing a note which I would like you to have delivered immediately to Lord Richard Fitzwilliam at a Mr. Darcy's home across from St. James Square; however, it is to be handed to Mr. Darcy personally, not Lord Fitzwilliam. When he learned his son was missing the man began having chest pains and I gave him a sleeping draught. He may still be resting."

"Pardon me." Bridges' eye began to twitch. "Whom did you say"

"Mr. Fitzwilliam Darcy at Pemberley House, the note will be regarding Lord Richard Fitzwilliam."

"Mr. Darcy? Lord Fitzwilliam? No. No, you must be mistaken."

"I assure you Mr. Bridges, I am not. Sister, there you are. Would you bring me another basin of clean, warm water so that I may tend to these wounds? Thank you. I would also like you to assist me with my examination if you will. My eyes are not as good as they once were."

"You cannot be serious."

"Sir, I am seventy years old, of course I am serious."

"No, I mean about the identity of this man's father. You cannot believe this vagrant is any relation to Lord Richard Fitzwilliam, can you?

"El imbecil!" Anthony had had enough. "This *vagrant* as you call him is the Honourable Mark Fitzwilliam, son of Earl Fitzwilliam of Somerton. If I were you I should do everything in my power to assist in tending to his wounds, then move him into an area that is away from any possibility of infection, provide him with a clean nightshirt – the one he is wearing is little more than a rag – and, discover why your patient was found bleeding on the floor in the midst of a brawl!

"And, believe me, I should do all that before you face his father!"

Within hours two carriages pulled up before the hospital along with an enclosed cart that had been well cushioned and prepared to transport a prone, injured man – because, by God, Fitzwilliam was taking his son home! "Ah. Here they are," Waiting outside the doors of St. Thomas Hospital George motioned to a waiting orderly, slipping a coin into the lad's hand. "Please be good enough to go inside and inform Doctor Milagros and my cousin that Himself has arrived." He then hurried down the hospital steps to greet them.

Matthew jumped from carriage before it even came to a complete stop. "How is he?" he called out to George as he ran, the other men still assisting Fitzwilliam and Darcy down the carriage steps, everyone yelling insults and orders at each other that went completely ignored.

Matthew turned and shouted, "Quiet! I can't hear what the devil he's saying! Repeat what you just said, George!"

"Calm yourself. I said Uncle Tony has been monitoring Mark, say's his heartbeat is remarkably strong and there is no fever. However, Matt, prepare yourself – he looks awfully bad. Seems he was worked over by a couple of toughs."

Matthew swallowed. "Do we know who did this?"

"Yes."

"Good. Then I shall kill them."

"Evidently you are too late for that. I'll explain inside. The main thing now is he *will* survive the injuries. It might have been worse; but, frankly, not by much. I was hoping Uncle Fitz would wait at home."

"You can't be serious. I had to sit on him to keep him from galloping over here on horseback."

"Well you had better prepare him for quite a sight. Mark is bruised head to toe."

Matthew wanted to vomit. This was completely his fault, drunkenly handing Mark a thick packet of money, in plain sight of any thief or cutpurse wandering past or lurking in the shadows. *What was I thinking, to have placed such a burden on my brother? To have placed him in such peril? Well, that's it, isn't it? I was thinking only of myself, my wounded pride. And because of me he could have been killed.* "Is Luke with Mark?"

"Yes. Neither of us has left his side since the boy went to fetch you. Quiet, here comes your father now. Uncle Fitz, I really wish you would have stayed home. You look awful." George could see the exhaustion, the anxiety there – however, the old man was as tough as iron, ready and able to tear apart the entire hospital to reach his child.

"Out of my way both of you; do not even attempt to stop me!" Fitzwilliam pushed through, entering the hospital with a roar. *"Where is my son!"*

"Uncle Fitz, just a moment. The Hospital Administrator asked to speak with you as soon as you arrived."

"I don't give a shite what he wants. I am not seeing anyone until I've seen Mark. Damn it, George, where is he?" Fitzwilliam's lungs heaved, straining for breath.

"Are you determined to kill yourself, you fool!" Darcy turned to Harry. "Take him to the administrator's office and make certain he calms himself. Fitzwilliam, you will wait there until we've seen Mark and are able to evaluate the situation."

"Who in bloody hell do you think you are, Darcy – my mother? I warn you, Harold, get your hands off me. Where is my boy? I want to see my son, and I want to see him now! You! Yes, you – stop gaping at me and bring me to my son! *Now, goddamn it! Where are you going! Stop running or I'll shoot!"*

"You're behaving like a madman!" Darcy was the only one who ever dared speak to Fitzwilliam that way. "It's no use. George, you had better take Fitz up to Mark before we're all tossed out; I'll find whoever's in charge here."

Throwing off everyone's hands Fitzwilliam was already storming off, barging his way through a set of swinging doors, forging forward as George kept attempting to grab his arm. "Make certain you tell them, Darcy, that I shall be taking my boy home with me, and that I demand to be provided with all notes, all reports of my son's condition from the moment he was found until now," Fitzwilliam shouted over his shoulder. "And, I want the name of the physician who cared for him! George will you stop yanking on my sleeve! What is it?"

"You're heading for the women's ward! Mark is upstairs."

"Oh. Why didn't you say so?"

"This way, everyone," George began jogging up the opposite stairway, taking the steps two at a time. Hastings rushed up the stairs behind them.

"This is such an honor, to have you in our humble hospital – what I mean is, well certainly not under these terrible circumstances. We've moved your son into a more private area – less chance there of him coming in contact with disease, don't you know." The poor fellow had thought to impress Fitz with this statement, but it only terrified him more.

"Disease! My son has been exposed to disease! Who in bloody

hell are you?"

"I am the Hospital Administrator, your lordship. I met a Mr. Darcy downstairs – such an elegant, distinguished gentleman – and, he said..."

"The hell with that! What was your meaning before? Why are those nurses weeping? Has my son been exposed to disease? Listen to me – if he's been further harmed in any way I'll have this blasted hospital burnt to the ground! I'll do it myself."

"No, no, your lordship, there was very little disease near him! None, I mean. No, of course not; nothing like that. The nurses are young, high strung. They often burst into tears over nothing. Not that death is nothing mind you. The hospital enjoys a relatively low death rate these days. Oh dear, what I mean is the Nightingale nurses are very good, constantly cleaning; everything is... here we are sir, right in here." But before Hastings could reach for the door handle Fitz had shoved him out of the way and opened the door himself.

CHAPTER NINETEEN

ANTHONY LEAPT FROM HIS CHAIR the moment Fitzwilliam entered the room. Throwing his arms around his old friend he began to weep. "Be brave, *viejo.*"

Fitzwilliam began to gasp, his face crumbled. "No. Oh, merciful God. It is as I feared then. My beautiful boy is dead?"

"What in hell are you talking about?" Anthony pushed him away. "*Who said Mark was dead?*"

"You mean he is alive?"

"Well if he's not dead, what else would he be?"

"Milagros, you idiot! You just took ten years from my life with your histrionics!"

"Pudrete en el infierno!" Sniffling, Anthony dabbed an elaborate handkerchief across his eyes. "*Mierda!* Now look what you've made me do, you *pendejo* – this is silk, you know! It's ruined."

"Just tell me my son is alive, Spaniard!"

Anthony blew his nose and stuffed the handkerchief back into his pocket. "Of course, he is alive; look for yourself – but, be prepared. He's been badly beaten."

"I'm a veteran of the Peninsular War, of Waterloo, Milagros! I've seen horrors you could not even begin to..." Although he believed he was prepared for the sight of his child's beaten body, he was not. When the screen was pulled away Fitzwilliam's first look at his son nearly drove him to his knees.

Darcy was there immediately and caught his arm, while Luke supported him from the other side. "Steady on, old man. Someone bring a chair."

"Dear God. Look at my boy," Fitzwilliam whispered. "Look what they've done to my boy."

The requested chair materialized immediately and a shaken Fitzwilliam sat beside Mark, took hold of his hand and kissed it. Darcy turned to Anthony. "What is his prognosis, Tony?"

"Much finer than he looks, fortunately. His heart and his pulse are remarkably strong. I am told he suffered with a fever which is gone now. Despite his appearance I believe he was well cared for; and, I doubt any of these bruises were inflicted here." It was then Anthony noticed that Matthew, standing silently behind his father for support, was struggling to suppress his own emotions. "Matthew, I am certain he shall experience a full recovery."

Matthew gave a short nod, cleared his throat. "We shall be taking my brother home with us tonight. Will you see that he is ready to be moved, Uncle Tony?"

These boys were like family to him, Matthew so like his father in all the worst ways, his temper always at the ready, his insistence on controlling every situation whether for good or ill, his absolute certainty he knew best. "I should prefer we wait a while; however, we may move him if that is truly your wish. Have you brought a suitable carriage?"

"It is outside the front doors, judge for yourself. However, suitable or not my son is coming home, even if I must carry him. He'll not lie here another moment!"

"If I find the carriage acceptable, I shall send two orderlies up with a stretcher. Have you blankets and hot bricks to keep him warm? Good. I shall meet you all downstairs then. George, can you come with me?"

After they left, Bridges and Hastings came to the door with all documents and reports in hand. "I've that information you requested, your lordship," said Hastings. "Although, I really cannot permit them to be removed from the hospital premises."

Fitzwilliam motioned for Father Ted. "Son, would you take those papers down to Anthony, have him look them over. Place them somewhere safe in the carriage."

"Of course, Papa."

"You must not have heard me, your lordship. You cannot…"

Fitzwilliam turned to Mr. Hastings. "Listen to me well, sir. I am removing my son from here immediately and taking those records with me."

"Very unwise." Bridges stopped speaking the moment Fitzwilliam's eyes met his. A cold chill ran down his spine. *Damn me, that creature really is his son.*

"You? I don't give a shite for what you think, sir. From what I've gathered you believed him to be some drunkard and therefore unworthy of medical care. It that true?"

"Not I, your lordship!"

"Really? Was I being lied to then, by my own family?"

"Well, you see, they weren't here to witness what truly happened – oh, it's all a terrible misunderstanding. I have been plagued by a certain nurse who consistently impeded my attempts at care. I had already complained to Mr. Hastings about her high-handed interference before this. A consequence of the new Nightingale School of Nursing here is that the hospital has given these women more and more authority. The publicity has gone to their heads – they believe they know more than physicians who have spent years in medical training. It's outrageous."

"Mr. Bridges, you forget yourself!" Hastings was furious; if this version was spread about it could end their nursing program and set the hospital back years.

"Where is this woman? If this is true. I shall want a word with her immediately." Fitzwilliam rose slowly, the look in his eyes telling – he wanted blood. "Anything short of prison will not be tolerated, believe me."

Hastings could feel beads of sweat forming on his forehead. "I am afraid she suffered some injury when she attacked Mr. Bridges. I was informed that they may have been, um, fatal."

"What did he say?" Darcy couldn't believe his ears.

"She's probably dead." George replied.

CHAPTER TWENTY

THROUGHOUT THE FOLLOWING TWO WEEKS Mark improved quickly, despite the loving care and devotion of his sisters. He had little memory of what happened to him between the moment Matthew's carriage drove away from the tavern and before he awoke to the shouts of his brother Luke and his cousin, George. He agonized over the many days missing from his life, over his dreams of a lovely woman with soft lips and a gentle touch, of kisses and whispers. In fact, if it wasn't for the obvious physical remnants of his severe beating, his bruised head and eye, his sprains, breaks and multiple stitches, he would have thought his family was playing an elaborate joke on him.

Fitzwilliam rapped cautiously on the door to his son's bedroom then stepped inside. "How are we this afternoon?" He looked first to his frazzled looking daughter, Kathy, then to his equally frazzled looking son.

"Well, we finished our soup *finally,* although that was quite a struggle, I can tell you. I prepared it myself, you know, from one of Mama's old receipts. It took me hours." She smoothed her mussed hair back into its tight bun. "Interesting aside, Papa… soup – in fact, most food preparation – is evidently much more difficult to concoct than I had originally imagined. Sad to say I may have mixed up a few ingredients; and, a few others – well, I had no idea what they were actually."

"Understandable. Mark, how are you feeling?"

"Like a laboratory experiment gone very wrong."

"What is that on your face?"

"Ham."

Kathy *tsked* and shook her head. "He squirmed about so very much you see."

"Nah, not really. I spit it out at her."

She turned to her brother. "YOU'VE A BIT OF HAM IN YOUR MOUSTACHE." After picking large food chunks from his face, Kathy dabbed at the additional liquid remnants on his nightshirt arms, in his ear… "Such a scamp. He managed to sling a bit on me as well – oh! How rude of me, Papa. Would you like a bit of my soup, there seems to be a great deal left over."

Behind her, Mark vigorously shook his head and made slicing motions across his throat. He finished up with grabbing his neck as if he was choking.

"Ah. Perhaps later, thank you, dearest." Fitz brushed a noodle from her shoulder then moved to the opposite side of the bed. "Does his color look high to you?"

"I can hear you both, you know. I'm not deaf."

"YOU MUSN'T SPEAK."

Although talking was painful due to his bruised and bandaged jaw, he was capable of providing a rude hand gesture behind her back as response. Kathy place the soiled cloth atop a heaping pile of other soiled cloths on a side table. Apparently, tea hadn't been well received either.

"I believe his color was better when I first arrived today, yes. I wonder if that's the reason he's been so combative. Could it be his fever has returned?" She turned to her brother and smiled kindly. "I FEAR YOU MAY HAVE A FEVER!"

"God in heaven, stop shouting at me, Kath. You know full well the doctor left just an hour ago and assured you I had no fever."

"Do you see what I mean? HERE, LET ME FEEL YOUR FOREHEAD." However, each time she tried to place a hand on his head he slapped it away, turning his head this way and that, back and forth. As a last resort, he tried to bite her. "Very sad. He is obviously delirious."

Mark clutched his father's arm, lifted the patch that covered his healing eye. "Take her away. I beg you. Every time she speaks to me she shouts as if I'm passing on, until I truly will kill myself. And the food! It's not Mama's receipt. It's evil. And, she keeps snatching pillows from beneath me to fluff them then yanks my head up to put them back. I tell you she's insane, father, a menace!"

Kathy heard none of this. She had been preparing medicine at a side table returning with a glass of some vile concoction of her own devise, meaning to pour the liquid directly down his throat… but missing completely when he jerked his chin down, resulting in the oily liquid spreading all over his face.

"This is so much easier with five-year-olds."

That was the last straw. Mark snatched the glass from her hand. "Kathy, go home. Go to your children, your husband. They need you. You are being too kind to me, too attentive!"

"NEVER FEAR. THERE IS NOTHING THAT WOULD COMPEL ME TO ABANDON YOU IN THIS, YOUR HOUR OF NEED, DEAREST BROTHER."

"I have to piss."

Kathy blinked several times. "Well, will you look at the time! My goodness, didn't realize it was that late. Father, I'm afraid I shall have to leave you to it." She began collecting her things, slapped her bonnet on her head and pulled on gloves. "Shall I send up a footman, then?"

Both Fitzwilliam and Mark responded together. "Please."

"Love you both."

When the door closed behind her Mark ran a hand through his hair. "I really am an ungrateful wretch, aren't I?"

"I'll not argue."

"That's a first."

Fitzwilliam eased himself into a nearby chair. "She is only trying to help, Mark. Kathy was beside herself with fear when we couldn't find you. We all were."

"You're right. I know, you're right. I'm sorry, father; truly I am. I don't know what's the matter with me. I feel… empty, as if I've lost my closest friend. Something is wrong, somewhere. If only I could remember all that happened."

"You will in time. If you recall, they said you had no memory of who you were when you were in the hospital as well."

"I didn't? Damn. I don't remember that either." Mark rubbed his good eye until it ached. "I recollect walking down that street one moment, then opening my eyes to see Luke and George lifting me from the floor."

"Good thing you have the standard Fitzwilliam hard head."

"Absolutely. I do remember now Matthew had given me a parcel of money. I suppose that was the reason for the attack? Were the fellows ever found?"

Found after they'd killed each other. Best not tell him that. "Ah. Well, seems they had a falling out which ended badly. The parcel itself went into the river along with all your clothes; none of it found as yet. The police have been searching the Thames for two weeks and I hear they have been dragging any number of people from there recently, only to have them turn around and jump back in. Oh well, the money was probably carried away with the current. Matthew feels badly about the whole thing – thinks it's his fault."

"It *is* my fault." Matthew stood at the open door to his brother's room. "I acted rashly as usual. How are you, Mark?"

"I'll survive, or so I have been informed – but, it would speed things up if our sisters could be kept out."

"We'll do our best. Right now you should get some rest." Just then there was a knock on the door and sisters Beth and Meg swooped in with footmen in tow, one carrying a tub and another carrying a scuttle of coal. Several more followed quickly with buckets of water.

"What's all this?"

"Kathy said Mark was in need of the… thingy… so we brought Sanders up to assist, and we have a tub in which Mark can bathe afterward, and coal to build a fire beneath it. We thought we could put the tub in the fireplace, directly atop the flames…"

"Like soup. Good lord." Matthew closed his eyes in frustration. "For one thing, Uncle Tony said not to wet his bandages. Remember? You were both standing there, sobbing and wailing when he explained Mark's care to us before he left. Another thing, you are both forbidden to touch the fireplace ever again – last week you nearly burned the house down."

"Well, we didn't, did we? So there." Beth pointed to a corner of the rug. "You see, all we need do is cut off that little piece there… and, there… and no one will remember such a tiny mishap at all."

"Out."

"Papa, say something. Are you going to allow Matthew to speak so rudely to us? We're only trying to help our dear Mark."

"Yes, I know my darlings, and I love you both for that. However, in the interest of *my* peace and quiet, and sanity, I believe we shall need another solution."

"But the fire didn't last that long, Papa," sulked Meg.

Beth nodded vigorously. "Indeed. We've done much worse."

CHAPTER TWENTY-ONE

"MAY I HELP YOU?" THE Fitzwilliam butler, Drake, opened the door to a simply clad young woman standing on the front steps, struggling to remain upright as a swirling snow and a wild wind battered.

"I was given this address." She had to speak loudly to be heard over the wail of the wind, her hand pressing her bonnet down.

"I see. Well, you cannot enter here, girl. Service entrance is round the back. Go speak with Mrs. Tubbs. Do you have experience in the kitchen?"

"No."

"Oh dear. Then you had better speak with Mrs. Cardew, the head housekeeper, she always needs someone."

"Pardon me, there seems to be a misapprehension, sir. I should actually like to have a word with…" she glanced at the slip of paper in her hand and gulped, "…with the Honorable Mark Fitzwilliam. If I may."

"I beg your pardon?" Drake's eyes fairly popped from their sockets.

"This is the home of Lord Richard Fitzwilliam, is it not?"

"Yes, it is."

"Well, I was sent by… the hospital." With her free hand Martha crossed her fingers behind her back. It wasn't a very big lie – she had been to the hospital to beg for her job back when fate took a hand.

An hour earlier, Matron Sheady and Martha, longtime nursing co-workers, had sat down to discuss all that occurred during the older woman's absence. The Matron, after inquiring about Martha's hospital recovery from the knock on her head, explained – in all astonishment – that the patient they believed to be have been a drunken sailor was, in fact, the son of this very angry, very powerful, earl, the entire incident having turned into a frightful political mess.

Therefore, for the sake of the hospital, and the future of the Nursing School, they were being forced to dismiss Martha without character. Matron further explained that she was aware the entire incident had not really been Martha's fault; however, if she remained on the hospital staff police would need to be informed, reports written, and, heavens, what a disaster that would be with the nursing school only two years old. It was all very unfortunate, but their hands were tied, the political climate being what it was. There really was nothing more she could do.

Tories were in power.

"In fact," Matron Sheady complained, "Your dismissal could not have come at a more inconvenient time. I have before me a request from the very same Earl Fitzwilliam *for nursing assistance at his home;* can you believe it? First, he threatens to burn us down for incompetence, then he requests our help. The cheek of the upper classes!

"Well, the Board of Directors is insistent we do whatever we can to oblige him, even knowing it will leave us with two fewer nurses now. So, you see Sister Clarke, we are all suffering, in our own way. I do sympathize with you, I truly do." What was unspoken between them was the knowledge that no other hospital would consider hiring the very capable nurse for the foreseeable future, if ever.

"What am I to do? How shall I support myself? Where will I live?" Now that her recovery was complete, and since she was no longer employed there, she would be required to vacate her room in the nurses' quarters as soon as possible. "Do you know of anywhere I might find employment? Please, Matron, help me."

"Actually, there is one place; but, I daresay with your experience and knowledge it would not be to your liking."

"Yes, it will; may I know of it?"

"Well," the woman cleared her throat. "I have heard from one of our Board members that there is dire need for dependable kitchen help at the County Asylum. It might only be for a few months, a year at most, until the unfortunate 'incident' is forgotten. Then I may revisit your employ with the board; after all, you are a most excellent nurse, we do hate to lose you."

Incident? Martha had intervened to save a man's life and was struck by the doctor for her 'impudence' as he called it. She might have lost her own life if not for her mass of hair softening the blow. Martha blanched at the position offered. "May I please be provided with at least an introductory letter from the hospital? Please. Could you ask Mr. Hastings again?"

That was highly unlikely, Matron reflected, seeing as the fellow was still hiding in his office after the dressing down he'd received from Fitzwilliam. Still, the woman really was an exceptional nurse and had always acted in the best interests of her patients. "Wait here for a moment and I'll have a word with him."

So, she waited, nervously. Moments turned into minutes feeling like hours… and then, suddenly, a wicked idea came to Martha. After verifying that the hallway was empty, she ran around Matron's desk, snatched up the letter from Lord Fitzwilliam and slipped it into her reticule. Her heart was pounding when Matron returned moments later with a rather disappointing note to provide any future employer.

Well, it didn't matter now what he wrote. When they found out what she was about to do, no hospital, even the asylum, would hire her ever again.

Drake was momentarily stunned. "I don't believe he expected someone so quickly. Won't you come in and wait for a moment?"

"Yes. Thank you." She had found him. Somewhere in this house lay her Bob Cratchit – actually, now he was her Mark Fitzwilliam. She loved repeating the name Mark Fitzwilliam. Even if she only had one minute with him it would be enough. She needed to see him again, hear his voice. She wondered if he would feel the same now for her as he had at the hospital, feared he could now regret their kisses, wondered if he even thought about them half as much as she. "I believe the hospital is eager to return to his lordship's good graces."

"I shouldn't wonder." Drake looked over his shoulder then whispered. "His lordship can be quite startling when he's up in arms."

"I hear he terrified everyone."

"And with good reason, I must say. Poor Master Mark. I shall tell his lordship you've arrived."

"His lordship? Can I not just go up and see Master Mark?"

"No, of course not. I am certain his lordship will wish to speak with you first. What is your name, please?"

"My name?"

Drake tilted his head and waited. Of course, she'd have to give them a name. Hopefully, the Earl had never asked for it during the confrontation at the hospital, had never even seen her because she'd been knocked out cold and removed from the scene before his arrival. No, she doubted he had bothered with particulars at all once they believed she was dead. Besides, she only had a little while until the hospital actually did send someone. She sighed and took a chance. "Annie Kelly."

"Drake, what is bothering Alfred?"

"I beg pardon, sir."

"My dog here, Alfred; he won't eat."

"Ah. I doubt he likes Brussel sprouts very well, your lordship."

Fitzwilliam grunted. "I don't suppose you would care for these? No. Never hurts to ask. If only my daughters would cease including them in every goddamn meal sent to me. By the way, Drake, you don't happen to know where they've hidden my brandy, do you?"

"Yes, sir. However, I am not at liberty to inform you that it is in the base of the hand painted, Swedish Mora clock your lordship brought back from Copenhagen in 1813."

"The one with the naked woman etched on the inside panel?"

"I was unaware we had more than one Swedish Mora clock, your lordship."

"We don't. I just love remembering… the… naked… woman. Ah, there is that lovely bottle! Thank you, Drake; you may yet receive that increase in pay for which you've been waiting so patiently all these years." He poured himself a glass. As he took his first sip he noticed Drake hadn't moved. "You've not left."

"No, indeed, sir."

"You see what a keen observer I am of my surroundings? So, did you wish to speak with me about something else?"

"Yes, your lordship. The woman you requested from the hospital has arrived."

"Oh, I seriously doubt that, Drake. I only sent the request a few hours ago."

"I am all astonishment, sir."

"Bloody hell. Sometimes I believe I actually impress you, Drake. You weren't aware I was this important, were you? All right, then. Why don't you send her up and we'll have ourselves a little chin wag. One never knows – perhaps *she* likes Brussel sprouts."

CHAPTER TWENTY-TWO

IT WAS SILENT AS A tomb in the foyer once the echoes of Drake's footfalls slowly faded away. She was mad to have come here, she should leave. She really should. If she left now no one would be any the wiser; and, perhaps she could still secure a position at another hospital in a few months. When she turned to leave however, she remembered she had given them Annie's name. Good heavens, why on earth had she done that? Now Annie might be blamed. Obviously, she hadn't thought this through enough.

Or, at all. *Oh, what difference does it make? Matron will realize Annie's not at fault. She'll know immediately who stole the note and will be furious with me. Why do I act so rashly with this man?*

She began to pace as she waited, noticing furniture collected from a dizzying array of periods. Tudor sideboards and tables stood beside Queen Anne and Georgian cabinets, Egyptian urns, golden French plates and draperies, Russian silver. There were Italian masters, a Rembrandt, a Vermeer, and, oddly enough, a huge portrait of George Washington over the fireplace. Across the wall hung an imposing array of ancestral portraits and Medieval tapestries. Gracious. It brought back memories of her own father's eclectic collections from Scandinavia, England, the orient and India – a soldier's journey. It also brought to mind his rejection of her and her husband, the loss of that life of privilege she had once known...

"Madam."

Martha jumped, clutching a hand to her chest. She hadn't heard the butler's return.

"If you would follow me. His lordship will see you now."

"Currently his sisters and cousins are tending to him, or his brothers run in and out with the delicacy of a herd of bison. I fear if it is allowed to continue as is, someone will perish."

Her face went pale, her eyes anxious. "Is your son that ill?" The woman's fear that his son might truly be in dire peril was obvious, which Fitzwilliam found odd.

"No. No, *he's* splendid. My fear is he'll kill the others. Perhaps I should clarify that remark. His relatives are driving him mad. It would help us tremendously if you would take over his daily care, provide whatever assistance you can."

"I shall do my best, sir." He could see her immediate and intense relief. There was something off about the entire situation – she arrived much too quickly and without the letter of introduction he had requested from the hospital; and, she was studiously avoiding looking him in the eye. Very suspicious indeed, but he'd sort her out. He had too many children to be fooled by any youngster for very long. Besides, she didn't appear to mean Mark any harm, only wished to meet him… and, she was awfully pretty – might do the boy some good, spice up his day.

Besides, he had already sent a footman to the hospital to confirm her identity. He just needed to stall her a bit.

"Miss Kelly, might I ask, were you acquainted with the nurse responsible for my boy's abhorrent treatment? I gather she was involved in some sort of physical altercation with one of the doctors and that she may have severely injured herself from a fall which is a pity since I planned to have her punished for her base incompetence."

Hearing the lie that she had mistreated Mark offended Martha, however she was also terrified the hospital's fear of this man might land her in prison. She would need to say something to throw him off her scent. "You speak of Martha Clarke. Wonderful nurse, compassionate woman; unfortunately, she passed away recently, injuries incurred from her fall. Tragic. I never knew her myself."

"Really?" Fitzwilliam narrowed his eyes. "This entire episode is so bizarre. Surprised the hospital never told me. Are you quite certain she died?"

"Absolutely."

"Pardon me, madam, but if you are unacquainted with this woman, how do you know for certain she's dead?"

Martha's mind blanked out for only a moment. "I attended her burial."

"Ah. Yes, well, that would do it." Fitzwilliam tapped out his pipe, all the while watching the young woman intently. "I say, before we go up, I don't suppose you'd want any Brussel's sprouts? No... don't really blame you. Well, why don't I take you up to meet Mark now."

Martha followed the older gentleman while several large and small dogs bounded past. They made their way down a hallway, then across the gallery overlooking the front entranceway, up a beautiful flight of stairs then turning down another, shorter hallway until they reached a set of large double doors at the end. "This was once our boys' wing, oh this was many years ago when all the children were home. Of course, it feels like they're still here. They never fully leave, do they; keep returning over and over and over – well, that's another story entirely.

"The girls occupied the hallway opposite. We called this floor of the house 'the barracks' then, most of it is closed off now. Mark maintains a bedroom with his own library and sitting room here, as well as having a flat of rooms in Kensington." As the Earl spoke, he rapped loudly on the door. "Mark, are you decent?"

"Come in, father. I'm bathed, shaved and completely pissed out."

Fitzwilliam opened the door and peaked inside, "mind your words. I've a young lady with me."

Mark groaned. "It had better not be Alice, Kathy, or the Mary's. I'd rather lose my leg than have any of them change this bandage again."

Fitzwilliam turned to Martha. "He's not usually so irritable. Please wait here. I'll come for you when Mark is ready."

She nodded and took a seat outside the door, her heart pounding, she wanted to laugh and cry at once. His voice! It was his voice! She wondered what he would say to her when they met again, prayed he would not stare at her in some love-sick daze but only motion her forward. She pressed her hand to her cheeks. Hopefully he would not attempt a kiss in front of his father.

But what if he now thought her wanton after their embraces at the hospital? That would be horrible! She was a decent woman. Nothing was her fault! Perhaps she had been vulnerable, lonely because of the holiday – no, she needed to be honest with herself, there was something between them and had been from the first. Some mysterious bond, an impulsiveness that had overtaken their good sense.

The moment she heard Mark speak again she jumped up and, unable to control herself a moment longer, pressed her ear to the door.

"What have the girls done now?"

"What haven't they done? Alice came to visit and sat on my foot, I awoke to find the Mary's saying a rosary over my head as if I were entombed. The boys are no better, roughhousing around me, telling me horror stories about amputations; thank goodness for my nieces and nephews. Only sensible ones in the family. Oh, by the way, do you know if I've received a reply from Lucille?"

Mark knew marriage was not in the cards for the couple and never would be but unfortunately, when Bunny had heard of his accident, she had taken for granted all was back to normal and had written him that very thing in a long letter. After all, she'd said, they'd been great friends forever and would both dearly miss their energetic lovemaking (he'd not read that part to his father).

But something had changed for Mark – what it was he hadn't a clue. He no longer desired a lifetime with a woman he'd never love. There was something better waiting for him. Somewhere. He merely had to get out there and find it, wherever it was. "I want this wedding business settled as quickly as possible. She's been very patient with me."

"Give it time, Mark; you only just returned her letter. Besides, let there be no more talk of weddings until after your brother Andrew, and Anne Marie and Jamie, arrive back from Canada next week. There is just so much turmoil my heart can handle."

"Deceitful old punter. You're strong as an ox."

"True. How's your arm?"

"Well, pretty awful. Kathy was supposed to help me with the exercises, but she talks so much about the children we never get anything done. And Luke and Andrew are too rough. And the Mary's keep crying and feeling my forehead. When is the physical trainer going to start? When is that Bath chair we ordered arriving?"

"Always in such a rush, what is your hurry?"

"I have no idea. Suppose I feel helpless here, useless."

"The trainer will begin on Thursday, and the chair will be here later today."

"Thank God for that."

"I have a surprise for you."

"Dear God, whenever you say that it sends chills down my spine."

"Such ingratitude. I'll have you know I've engaged a private nurse to care for you. Hopefully, that will reduce the bickering going on here, as well as some of these small house fires…"

"A nurse?" Something sparked to life within him, an ember of memory.

"Her name is Kelly. Something Kelly. Or Keeley something. Do you remember her?"

"No. Yes, perhaps." Why was his heart beginning to race? Some memory about shoes? "Bring her in, I'd like to speak with her. I have so many questions. Where are my slippers?"

"Stop! Don't you dare try and get up! Whatever is the matter with you today? You wait right where you are, and I'll call her in."

However, when Fitzwilliam opened the door he found the sitting room empty. "Madam? Bloody hell, now what," he muttered. Walking out to the hallway he saw the nurse running away. "Wait!" he called to her just as she reached the stairs. "Madam! What in blazes is going on here?"

Martha turned to him, tears streaming down her face. Her greatest fear had been confirmed – Mark belonged to another woman.

"Miss Kelly? Wait!"

"Pardon me, Lord Fitzwilliam." She struggled to compose herself. "I am terribly sorry, sir. However, I don't believe I shall be able to care for your son after all. Do forgive me."

"No, I do not forgive you! Whatever is the matter? Hold on there!"

She was down the stairs and out the door before Fitzwilliam even reached the top landing.

"Well, I'll be damned."

He returned to his son's room, irritated beyond belief. "Of all the idiotic things – the woman bolted! Queer as duck's breath. She ran down the stairs and out the door… now, what's the matter with you? You look pale as the sheets."

Mark was sitting up in bed. "Who was that?"

"I told you already – a Miss Kelly something."

"I heard her speak to you just now, her voice was familiar. More memories are coming back to me now about the attack, the robbery. The beating. Great Scott! I was lying beneath dead bodies for a while."

"What are you talking about?"

"Damn me! I was in a corpse wagon… I think. Then, when I woke up, I was in a bed, in the hospital." He closed his eyes. "I was staring into the eyes of a beautiful woman."

"Must have been hit on the head harder than we thought."

"No, she was real." Mark struggled with the bedsheets, thinking to go after the nurse somehow. "I think she was, at any rate. Christmas Day, I remember I had her in my arms and we were kissing passionately."

"You what!"

"Did I say that? Then I must have. Yes. I did. I remember. We must stop Miss Kelly, bring her back here; she must know the woman I mean. I want you to meet her, and the family to meet her. I want to court her properly, you know, buy her flowers…"

"Slow down, boy! Mark, I've not seen you like this before."

"Why in hell am I trapped in this bed, damnit! I don't want to lose that woman and if you won't stop Miss Kelly for me then get out of my way, I'll go myself." He struggled with his father but was still too weak to move him aside.

"You cannot stand, your leg is healing! Whatever this woman was to you –"

"Is! She's the woman I love, that's who she is."

"Love? All right, that's enough. There's something strange going on here. If she isn't this Kelly woman then who is she? What is her name?"

"Oh, damn it to hell! I'm not certain. Her name flits through my mind before I can catch it. Wait! Martha! Martha Cloak? That was it. No. Martha Clarke. Her father was someone very important in the army, in India. She was raised there, I think. She's a widow…

What is it? You know something. Tell me. Why did you just go all pale?"

Fitzwilliam ran his hands through his mane of white hair. "Let me speak with someone at the hospital first. I'll send one of the footmen with a note."

"No! Tell me now. What is it? What do you know?"

"My dear, dear boy." Fitz sat on the edge of his son's bed and took his hand. "This woman who just ran out, Mrs. Kelly or whoever she was, informed me that your Martha Clarke… is dead."

CHAPTER TWENTY-THREE

IT WAS A GLORIOUS MORNING at the old Woolwich Naval dockyards when the HMS Orontes appeared on the horizon. Dozens of people who had been impatiently awaiting their loved ones for days heard the harbor master's shout and a cheer rang out. The crowds swelled, and with it the excitement, the chattering, laughter and tears – both anxious and happy.

It was a full quarter hour later when the magnificent ship, one of the Duncan class of 101-gun two-decker steam battleships, was within docking range and began lowering her sails in preparation. With the assistance of the very latest binoculars Darcy could make out the figure of Richard's son, Captain Andrew Fitzwilliam, standing on the upper deck as his second in command shouted out his orders to the crew.

"Do you see Andrew on the foredeck, Elizabeth? He looks quite distinguished, don't you think? Elizabeth? Elizabeth, what are you looking for? Are you crying?"

"Of course I am not crying. I merely needed my handkerchief to wipe my eyes. It's in this reticule somewhere." She sniffled once or twice.

"Here, love." Darcy took his own out and dabbed at her tears. "I feel exactly the same way, Lizzy. Our daughter and son-in-law are home, our nephew is safe. And, I love you." Then Darcy brought her flush up against his side, nuzzling and kissing her neck.

"Mr. Darcy!"

"Stop grinning and blow your nose, then have a look. You'll see Andrew clearly, and perhaps Anne." He handed her his binoculars.

"It's gone! The ship is gone! I don't see anything!"

"You're looking in the wrong direction. Here let me help you."

"I am perfectly capable of doing this myself. Now, where is that ship?"

Darcy stood behind her and began to adjust the lens. "If I may… turn the dial to focus… that's right. And, don't drop them! I shall have you know these were created by an Italian optician, Ignazio Porro, and are very expensive."

"I don't give a fig if he's a Greek named Plato… Oh, I see him! It's Andrew, it really is! Andrew! Hello! Oh, how elegant he looks."

"That's what I thought as well. Hard to believe he's Fitz's son at all."

"Oh hush!" Slowly and deliberately she began to search the ship's rail until she spied her daughter and son-in-law just as they came on deck. *"William! William, I can see her! It's Anne! Anne! Anne Marie!"* she shouted out to her daughter in her excitement and waved her handkerchief above her head, even though the ship was still too far and the crowd noise was deafening. She turned to Darcy. "You will never guess who I saw! It's Anne Marie!"

"So I heard. You were screaming your head off."

"Oh, I was not. How you do exaggerate." She kissed his cheek and then motioned to her other daughter, calling out, "Alice, come and see through these! They're wonderful! It's Anne!"

"Elizabeth, perhaps we could have Alex take a look for a moment… and could you take the strap off my neck before you offer these to anyone else? You're choking me!"

"Sorry, dear. Alex, you must see your brother."

As the passengers on the ship came closer into view the crowd began to surge forward, cheering and talking and waving whatever they had at hand. "Thank you, Mrs. Darcy. After your daughter though." He limped forward and leaned on a lamppost.

"No, I insist."

"You'd better take advantage now, Alex. It could be a few minutes before my wife and daughter stop squealing. I say though, I know it's none of my concern, but shouldn't you be seated?"

"Thank you." Alex took the binoculars from Lizzy. "William, I am much too excited to sit. By Jove, but that is a magnificent ship. Andrew Fitzwilliam has done well for himself."

"Youngest Captain in the Mediterranean fleet," Darcy announced proudly. "He always did go his own way. Fitzwilliam pretended to be livid when he joined the navy. Fitz was a Colonel under Wellington at Waterloo you know. Never tires of talking about his renegade son, the Captain of the Fleet."

Meanwhile, Alice had arrived beside her parents and was hopping up and down with excitement. "Alex, may I see?"

"Of course! They are standing near the rear of the ship – it's starting to turn now so look quickly."

"Thank you! Oh! I see her! That's my sister! Oh, doesn't she look beautiful!" She offered the binoculars to her brother. "Here, George, see how beautiful Anne Marie looks. These are amazing, it's as if they are a few feet in front of you!"

"No thank you. I have my own spyglass, Alice."

"Where is it?"

"I can't get it away from my wife. Let me have a look, Kath."

Kathy swatted her husband's hand away. "I wish that ship would hurry, I'm freezing. You know, George, I don't think this glass is as good as your father's binoculars. I can barely make out Andrew."

"Imagine how awful I feel about that. Kathy, I have an idea. Why don't you return to the Inn and keep Harry company, and the Mary's, and the children? They have that lovely private room, and hot cocoa and cakes, and…"

She pushed his hand away again. "Will you stop trying to take these from me, George! Borrow Luke's, or Father Ted's. Such a shame Papa and Matthew were unable to come along; but someone had to stay with Mark, I suppose. No one else wants to any longer, he's become so unpleasant to be around."

As George wrestled Luke now for his spyglass, he let out a hoot of laughter at his wife's comment. "He is unpleasant because you spilled boiling hot porridge on his foot."

"Well, you kick at a dish and that is what happens. Not my fault. Besides, I truly don't believe that is the reason for his… sullenness. It's not like him to behave this way, Mark was never bitter or sharp tempered before – that was Matthew. And, he's working much too hard with that physical trainer person. He's working himself to death! None of it makes sense. Perhaps he's remembering things now, and I'm certain they are quite unpleasant memories, poor dear. I'll make him a trifle, or a blancmange tonight."

"Hasn't he suffered enough?" Alice commented as she handed

the binoculars back to Alex.

"I heard that!"

George whispered in Kathy's ear. "Don't say a word of what I am going to tell you. Promise? All right. When I spoke with him this morning, he mentioned something regarding the nurse who had been injured just before Uncle Tony, Luke and I found Mark on the floor at St. Thomas's. Mark apparently had been very fond of her. Very fond. He said because of him she'd been involved in an altercation with that physician and fell, hitting her head. The fall eventually killed her, Kath. Remember, don't mention I told you this to Mark, he asked me to keep it between us."

"Oh, George, that's terrible."

He nodded. "About the woman?"

"No, that you can't keep a secret to save your soul. You're as bad as I am."

"You're not at all amusing, Kathy. Anyway, Mark is devastated. As I said, he was very fond of the woman. Very, very fond, if you get my drift."

"Are you saying he was fond of her?"

George rolled his eyes. "Kathy, this isn't funny. I think he was in love with her."

"Oh, George!" It took a moment for Kathy to realize he wasn't teasing. "Oh, no."

Suddenly, Lizzy Darcy screamed with delight and turned to her husband. "William! Anne Marie saw me and returned my wave! Isn't that wonderful? Alex, did you see your brother waving?"

"I did indeed, ma'am. And I also noticed he's gained weight. What in the world do they feed them in America?"

Within the hour the Orontes was being pulled slowly into harbor by the huge rotating capstans onboard. Dozens of men strained at the horizontal wheel, slowly rewinding cables the size of a man's fist, until the ship was close enough that ropes could be thrown to the waiting dock workers. Once the vessel was secure in its mooring the bosun's shrill whistle called the ship's company to attention.

After receiving the salute of his crew, and after giving final instructions to his second in command, Captain Andrew Fitzwilliam tucked Anne Marie's hand under his arm and lead all passengers down the gangplank to greet their waiting families.

The Darcy, Durand and Fitzwilliam families were whole once again.

CHAPTER TWENTY-FOUR

THE REUNION ON THE DOCK was both joyous and tearful. The moment Anne Marie reached her parent's arms she wept like a child while Jamie and his brother stared awkwardly at each other, albeit briefly, before joining in a fierce hug.

Father Ted and Luke, proud to bursting over their brother, Captain Andrew, were boisterous and loud as ever, slapping him on the back and admiring his glorious uniform. Within moments the families had all individually greeted and hugged Andrew, Anne Marie and Jamie, then, after an instant of quiet, it all began again. Anne finally put up her hands in surrender.

"Not another hug or word until I see my children!"

By this time Darcy had already begun instructing the servants to load the Durand's luggage into the awaiting carts, so arm-in-arm Kathy, Lizzy and Alice steered their beloved Anne Marie toward the nearby Inn.

"Do you think mummy will have become very old looking? Perhaps I won't recognize her." Anne Marie's young son, Steven, chewed on his lower lip as he peered through the window in the direction of the distant dock.

Beside him sat Deborah, Anne Marie's youngest, playing with her doll. "I should always know mummy and papa. Even if they were away for a hundred million thousand years I should know them."

"Of course, you both would. Besides, she's only been away three months, Steven." Bridget smoothed his hair from his face and smiled. "I'm certain she'll look just the same as when she left."

"Truly?" The boy's forehead rested on the cold window, his breath causing a condensation where he was tracing hearts. "It seems much longer. It seems like she's been gone for ages."

"Poor angel. Now, why don't you sit at the table and have your cocoa and biscuits?"

"No, thank you," he answered politely. "Mummy will want to see me in the window, watching for her." He then returned his gaze to the road leading up from the dockyard.

Meanwhile, on the other side of the large room Harry Penrod watched his step-sisters, Mary Beth and Mary Margaret, pace the room, both anxiously awaiting their brother Andrew and cousin Anne Marie's arrival. Twins to the bone they did everything together, even worry. "I really wish you would both sit, you're making *me* apprehensive."

"But Harold," Mary Beth hugged her arms around herself and sighed. "The ship was due hours ago. What if something has happened? Good heavens, what if it was wrecked on some distant shore, or during a horrific storm at sea? Wasn't there a cargo ship lost just last month?" One by one the stunned faces of Anne Marie's children turned toward her. "Ah. Did I say that out loud? What I meant was..."

Birdy turned to her cousin Will. "Is that true? There was a ship wrecked?" Little Deborah slid from the bench and ran into her sister's arms. They clung to each other tightly.

"Birdy, Mummy can't swim," whispered Deborah. "I was going to teach her as soon as I learned."

"Mummy and Papa's ship has wrecked?" gasped Steven.

"No! No. I never said that. Not really. We don't actually know anything for certain yet, do we?"

Mary Margaret pinched her sister's elbow hard enough to elicit a yelp. "Be quiet," she hissed.

Harry quickly swept Deborah and Steven onto his lap. "Listen to me. No one can know the exact moment a ship will arrive. It all depends on so many things – the wind, the currents... but arrive it will. We must be patient. Remember, Uncle Andrew is the ship's captain, and he would never allow anything to happen to his beloved cousin, Anne, or your Papa." Then he turned and glared at his sisters. "And we must only speak of happy things, mustn't we?" he said pointedly.

"Of course! Happy thoughts only. My goodness, there is almost certain to be one or two survivors – ow!" Another angry pinch from Mary Margaret silenced Mary Beth for good.

"Aunt Meg and Aunt Beth," Will Darcy fought off a grin, "Why don't we discuss the skating party next week?" He turned to Ewan. "You will attend, I hope? It will be great fun. Uncle Matthew said you're a fine skater, and you play bandy. We can have a family match – only if you're on my side though. What position?"

"Forward."

"Excellent. A strong forward is always welcomed on my team."

"Did you know my father played with a group in Canada when he lived there years ago? They refer to it sometimes as Ice Hockey. He knows everything about the game."

"Do you think he'd be willing to referee if we do have a match next week? My Uncle Mark usually is referee – he's very smart and funny and never loses his temper – but he's not back on his feet yet. It would be nice to have someone who actually knows the game step in – otherwise my Grandpa Fitz will insist on being referee and he makes up his own rules."

"I can surely ask him. I'm certain he'll be very happy to help out. Mama, Mama, did you hear? There's to be a skating party next week and Will has asked me to be on his team for bandy, and they'd like Papa to referee. Doesn't that sound wonderful?"

Bridget stared at her boy, not knowing how to answer truthfully without hurting him. Luckily, Ewan was immediately distracted when Will Darcy continued. "By the way, Uncle Matthew tells me you'll be attending Harrow which is wonderful news. I say, if you're able to come to bandy practice tomorrow you'll meet several of my Harrovian friends and their younger brothers; and, of course you've met my cousins who'll be going there as well. By the time you enter school there you'll know everyone."

Bridget wanted to weep. How could she ever win against this family? They had London in their pockets, the world was their tomorrow. Well, it would be a few years before Ewan left for boarding school, a good deal could happen by then. However, when she saw how eager he was, how hopeful he looked… well, how could she disappoint him? How would she say no in the end?

"They're here!" squealed Steven. "I just saw Papa and he looks fat! And Mummy is laughing!" He pounded on the glass window, "Mummy! Mummy! Birdy, Debbie – Mummy and Papa are home! Come and see!"

Everyone rushed to the windows, and as Ewan ran past his mother he called over his shoulder, "You will remember to ask Papa, won't you?" He was such a wonderful child, so loving. She had no defense against him.

"Of course I will, Ewan. I'm certain he'll be very pleased."

The laughter and chatter outside the Inn grew louder and louder still, until the door to their private room flew open. "Where are my beautiful babies?" wept Anne Marie.

"We should start heading out," Darcy announced two hours later – after everyone had feasted on the Inn's excellent luncheon. "We have a rather long ride ahead of us before we reach our overnight accommodations. I would like to set out very early tomorrow, arrive in the city no later than tomorrow evening, Fitz is anxiously awaiting the sight of Andrew and our Anne Marie. And, you as well, Jamie."

"Certainly." Everyone laughed at Jamie's grunt of understanding.

They all began milling about then, finding their cloaks and gloves and discussing who would travel with whom, and in which carriage. In the hubbub, Anne Marie approached Bridget.

"Bridget," she said softly. "It is so wonderful to see you again. Might we have a word alone?"

Bridget hesitated at first but then nodded, sending her husband and son off with the others, promising to be along straight away.

"First, let me say that I harbor no ill will toward you for leaving suddenly nine years ago. We are sisters-in-law now. I should like us to be friends."

"Thank you, Mrs. Durand."

"You must call me Anne Marie. Please."

"Of course." Bridget swallowed. "Anne Marie."

An awkward silence followed until a tearful Anne Marie suddenly pulled Bridget into a tight hug, "I understand now what happened, why you felt it necessary to run off with Alex. I do understand," she whispered in her ear.

Bridget's face flushed red and she pushed back from the embrace. "I have no idea to what you refer."

"I see him in Ewan, you know. I see Matthew. It all makes sense now – the animosity between my cousin and Alex, your sudden departure from my house, your impetuous marriage. Poor thing, you had no other choice in the end, did you? I know that now."

"Stop, please." Bridget's eyes flashed with anger. "I had better leave. My husband will be waiting for me."

"All I ask is that you be careful of your actions from this point on. Marriage is sacred. Vows are sacred. Alex is a wonderful man, he's become like a second brother to me. He's a loving father to Ewan, a devoted husband to you, and one of the most noble men I've ever been privileged to meet. Do not hurt him, I beg of you."

Humiliated by the truth, Bridget pushed Anne Marie from her path, crying as she stormed out, "You overstep your bounds, Mrs. Durand. You overstep decency."

CHAPTER TWENTY-FIVE

WEARY OF LISTENING TO HER son's excited chatter, Bridget slipped quietly from the room. After his afternoon skating practices with the Darcy and Fitzwilliam grandchildren it had been a non-ending litany of that wonderful family, of their athletic prowess, of their scholastic abilities, in other words, her worst nightmare – she was losing her son to this overwhelming family, to their power and their fame. Matthew was at the center of it all, she told herself, manipulating their lives for his own amusement.

Or, perhaps he was simply *her* center, and that was the real problem…

The door to their bedroom at the Claridges' Inn opened and her husband entered. "Are you ready to leave?"

"Yes. No. Must I go to this skating party?"

After a moment's hesitation Alex closed the door. He ran a hand through his hair. "It is entirely your decision, Bridget. However, Ewan is excited for you to see him play; it would be..."

"Cruel not to. Yes, I know."

"It's a children's party, Bridget; Ewan's become friends with several of them. He cares about these people." Using his cane to steady himself he moved slowly to sit beside her on the bed. "Truth is he is enjoying himself and the children have taken to him whole heartedly. Why, when some fool at the skating pond ridiculed his occasional Scottish phrases the cousins – girls included – all lined up on either side of Ewan, as if they were daring anyone else to say another word against him. I confess it brought tears to my eyes.

It was heartwarming."

She nodded her understanding but still worried. "Was *he* there?" Alex knew she meant Matthew. Would they ever be rid of that man?

"Yes."

"Was he awful to you?"

"Not in the least. He ignored me at first, then progressed to aloof but polite when Harry and Alice insisted I sit with them to watch the children skate. He doesn't bother me, dearest. I can tolerate anything for Ewan's sake, and you must admit the boy has been happier these past days, now that he has other children with whom to play. I tell you what, if it is that distressful you needn't come. I'll say you have a headache, or it's your woman's time. You know no man would ever question that."

Grinning, she took his hand and kissed it. "Somehow I can't see you explaining about *my Monthly Visitor*. No, I'll just need to learn how to deal with this somehow. Especially since Ewan and I will be remaining in London for much longer than we anticipated."

"You're remaining?" Pleased and surprised, he hugged her, kissed her forehead. "You'll no be leavin' me then, *a thasgaidh,* here in this heathen land o'hades, all on me own?"

"Yer aff yer haid, mon, if y'imagine I'd leave y'alone w'these Sassenach women."

Matthew and his wife arrived for the children's skating party, their morning spent together in stony silence. Amanda Rose, along with the other children, had spent overnight at the house of his brother Harry and all were squealing and laughing with delight. In fact, the pond teemed with skaters, young and old, the weather bright and sunny, the temperature warm for a January day.

"How utterly appalling." Clarissa wished to convey that she was attending under protest and continued her icy glare even as the carriage door was opened and the footman helped her descend the steps.

"She speaks!"

"These people should still be in mourning – well, except for *your* family, of course. They always are contrary."

Matthew ignored her as Alice and Harry approached hand in

hand to greet them.

"You're late, Matthew, but we've saved some cocoa and sandwiches for you both. Hello, Clarissa." Harry kissed her cheek lightly.

"I hope my daughter is not among those shrieking children."

"Of course she is," Alice bristled. "No, I take that back, we have her locked beneath the butler's pantry at home reading the bible."

As always, battle lines were being drawn and Harry stepped in between them. "Amanda is playing with the others and having a wonderful time. Although where they all get the energy this morning is a mystery; there was little sleep last night, I can tell you. They were playing pranks on one another until Alice finally put a stop to it at around nine in the evening."

"Huh! A fine example being set for these children, I must say."

"Move aside, Harold, please." Alice stepped around her husband, raised herself to her full height – which was still several inches shorter than Clarissa – and jutted out her chin. "What is your meaning, Clarissa? They were asleep by quarter past nine. They all had plenty of rest."

"Ridiculous frivolity. I say they should continue to be mourning their prince, a simple matter of respect which is so foreign to certain people."

"*I say* our wonderful prince would never demand an entire empire be run to ground just to appease attention seeking hypocrites. We should be able to get on with our lives; children should be allowed some sort of enjoyment."

"Enough, the both of you are tiresome." Matthew turned away from the women to speak with his brother. The disagreements between his family and his wife were never ending. "Sorry I missed the games. How did young Ewan perform?"

"Brilliantly. He was the hero of the hour. The lad is a natural athlete."

Matthew beamed. "Excellent. Is everyone here?"

"Yes – well, everyone except Mark, of course. I was there to visit yesterday, and his mood seemed much the same. I've never known him to be so detached."

"I know, he's even keeping things from me. I don't like it."

"Evidently Bunny is by his side again. Is the wedding back on schedule? I heard he was considering leaving for America with

Ted."

"That's what she claims. No idea what's going on. Frankly, I think he's insane to want to marry at all; still, I'd rather that than have him so far away."

"Why are those children screaming?" Clarissa was always uncomfortable around children, preferred it when they were silent, or better yet, completely absent.

"They are enjoying themselves, Clarissa. You remember childhood, do you not? I realize it was years and years and years ago, but..."

"Matthew, be serious for once. The weather has been unpredictable, cold one day, warm another. I insist Amanda Rose stop that foolishness. I really have a bad feeling about this. Matthew? Are you listening to me? Tell her to come in off the ice."

"No! It's a beautiful day and the children are happy. Must you spoil everything?" He turned to Harry again. "Is Papa judging the ice races? Good, he'll make certain the little ones win then. I see Beth and Meg warming themselves by a delicious looking fire and a servant pouring out hot toddies. You aren't coming, are you, Clarissa?"

"Certainly not."

"Thank heaven." Matthew pointed to his brother Ted, sitting and laughing with Darcy and Elizabeth. "You should visit with Father Ted. He was mentioning just yesterday that he wanted to discuss theology and you're just the person to knock that idea out of his head."

Clarissa's gaze zeroed on the priest before she hurried down the path toward that happy group. Alice slapped her cousin's shoulder.

"Ow! Why ever did you do that?"

"Because you are a positively awful brother."

"Father Ted's profession is to be kind; takes the load off the rest of us."

"Go and speak with your father; and, while you're there, make certain you ask God's forgiveness for that last remark."

CHAPTER TWENTY-SIX

"MATTHEW, COME JOIN ME." HIS father's call from a bench that had been pulled to the edge of the skating pond was a welcome diversion. The Fitzwilliam butler and a footman were standing beside him making snowballs for the old man to throw as children dodged past, squealing and laughing. "Help me with this! I'm to give them each a half-crown if I miss, and I'm a terrible shot."

The moment she saw her father Amanda Rose skated over (ducking a feeble toss by her grandfather) and hobbled across thick snow on her skates. "Papa, I thought you'd *never* get here!" She threw her arms around his waist and, as ever, lifted Matthew's spirits to the heavens.

"Hello, Dodger," he whispered in her ear.

"Hello, Fagan," she replied. He kissed the top of her head, held her close. "Are you being careful? I see you're under attack here."

"Grandpa Fitz hasn't hit me once! Do you know, at times I think he deliberately misses?"

Fitzwilliam was clearly insulted. "Is that a fact? I shall have you know young lady that I put the *ruth* in ruthless, the *brute* in brutal, the *heart* in heartless! I show no mercy." As she rolled her eyes at that remark, Fitz tossed snow on her.

Laughing, Matthew brushed the flakes from his daughter's hair. "Your mother is concerned about all the roughhousing on the ice. She said to tell you –"

"Hello, sir. It's very good to see you again."

Skating up to the edge of the pond was Ewan Durand, stopping beside the bench and allowing Fitzwilliam to hit him in the leg with a snowball. "You're taking all the fun out of this!" Fitz complained. "At least give me the illusion of resistance." Matthew stilled. The sight of grandfather and grandson together had knocked the wind from him.

"Come here and sit beside me, Ewan." He turned to Matthew. "Earlier he was telling me all about the Highlands. Did you know he can play the bagpipe, Matthew? Seems excessively cruel to me."

"But, not verra well, sir," Ewan laughed. "Sometimes I just wheeze. My Papa is brilliant at it, though."

As Fitzwilliam ruffled the boy's hair he caught his son's eye, kept it, willing Matthew to remain calm. It was then that Matthew knew his father was aware of who the child's father really was. "Is that right?"

"Oh, aye. He piped us a lovely tune on New Year's Day. Everyone at the Inn applauded him."

It was silly, but Matthew felt like weeping as he watched the two. The old man and the young boy before him looking like opposite ends of a lifespan, the ascendance of youth to the decline of age. Only a fool wouldn't notice the resemblance.

"I say, Ewan… is your mother with you today?" He heard his father's intake of breath, saw the disapproval in his eyes.

"Aye. Although I dinnae – do not see her now. I believe she said she was chilled and wanted to walk, mentioned visiting somewhere nearby she frequented years ago when she lived here, before she married Papa."

He looked away and grinned. There was a bench nearby in the park where they often had met years before, when she was the nanny, a pretty Scottish lassie with a figure to make a man's mouth water. It was at that bench where they had fallen in love with each other.

"Come on, Ewan. Shall we race to the end of the pond and back?" Amanda squealed when the boy grabbed her hand and the two children skated away.

Matthew turned to his father. "Sorry you had to find out this way."

Fitzwilliam grunted, never taking his gaze from his grandson. "Find out what? That you've been in love with another man's wife for years; or, that while I prayed you and that silly wife of yours would finally produce a male heir, you had a son I would never be able to acknowledge?"

Matthew bristled. Leave it to his father to make him look too closely at himself. "Yes. That pretty much sums it up."

"Son, I knew already about both. I suspected as much when she ran off with Durand. You remember I told you I had gone to have a word with her? Interesting aside, did you know that after seeing your mother through almost a dozen pregnancies I often can recognize an *enceinte* woman?"

"And, thanks to her and that bastard I had no knowledge of my own son, damn her." Matthew looked down at his fisted hands willing them to relax. "Sorry to have disappointed you."

"What nonsense is this? You sired that wonderful boy out there, Matthew. It's enough for me to have seen him, spoken with him. I couldn't be more pleased that he is alive in the world; we even have him in the family, if distantly. However, if you refer to leaving your lover alone and *enceinte,* then I am the wrong person with whom you should be remorseful."

"That is damn unfair, father! I had no idea she was carrying my child. I only found out a few weeks ago, when I met them at Uncle Wills house. I was devastated."

"I can well imagine. What about this Harrow business, your wanting me to intervene there – is this the reason for encouraging his attendance?"

"Yes, of course it is. I want to know him; I need him near me, not in the wilds of Scotland! I've missed too much of his life already."

Sighing, Fitzwilliam scratched at his whiskers. "I'm too bloody old to go through this again."

"Again?"

"You believe you're the first to father a child on the wrong side of the blanket? That's almost a national pastime for the upper classes. You're not even the first in our family."

"Good God, do I have yet another revolting brother running wild through London?"

"Are you insane? Aunt Catherine would have killed me, never mind your mother."

"*Well?*"

"It's not my story to tell."

"I cannot accept that."

"It's bloody sad to be you then. I have been sworn to secrecy. Let me speak with the other party, see if they'll tell you themselves, or if they give their permission for me to speak. No use to look at me like that, I keep my confidences, especially my children's."

Matthew relaxed. "You must mean Harry and his illegitimate daughter, then. Father, everyone knows about that."

"Who told you?!"

Matthew grinned evilly. "You did, just now."

"I'll be damned." Fitzwilliam shook his head. "Your mother said all men were hopeless at keeping secrets – obviously she was right."

"Well, don't feel badly, it was actually Harry himself who told me years ago. Looks as if mother was right all along. She certainly was beautiful, inside and out. You two were made for each other – opposites attract."

"I won't argue with you there." Fitzwilliam laughed. "You know, the longer I live the more I am convinced a person's happiness depends mainly upon the mate they choose for life – their other half if you will."

"My *other half*'s existence means little to me, outside of our begetting Amanda."

"Matthew, don't lie to yourself. Clarissa was never your other half, was she? The woman from Scotland has your heart and always will."

"You're growing dotty, old man. I despise her and her pathetic excuse for a husband. And, I shall thank you for never speaking of this again. I mean no offense, Father, but that area of my life is none of your concern."

"Listen to me, *Boyo,* you are still my child, and that makes *everything* regarding you *my* concern until one of us dies, and more than likely well after that! You and Durand will somehow learn to live with this situation or you'll both answer to me. Leave his wife alone! Do not cuckold that man, I'll not stand for it."

"Father, you go too far!"

"I put you on notice. Oh, it's not for my sake, nor for your sake, nor for his or hers – this is for *my grandson's sake*!"

CHAPTER TWENTY-SEVEN

THERE SHE WAS, ALONE ON 'their' bench in the park, the one where they'd often met 'by accident' years before. There was no power on earth that could have kept him from her, no matter what his father demanded. How dare the old fool lecture him! What did he know about it; it was none of his business, *any of it*, and it would be a cold day in hell before he'd speak with the bastard again, father or no! Matthew would have his son, and he would have the woman too, heaven be damned. She still wanted him, he still wanted her. And Matthew always got what he wanted.

Very big talk. So, why couldn't he make himself move now? Perhaps he just wanted to watch her for a while, drink in her presence like a thirsty man dying for want of water. Obsessed? Yes, he supposed he was, but not by choice.

As he had stormed away from his father at the ice pond he'd spotted Durand and watched him, loathing in his heart. Look at him, he thought to himself, laughing and smug… well, not for long. He followed him as he left the company of the Darcy's, as he hobbled down to the pond's edge, smiled as Ewan called to him.

"Father, watch me," the boy shouted with joy.

Damn him to hell. Matthew feared the intense hatred he felt for Durand, the blind jealousy. What did it matter if his father had the right of it. Yes, he wanted to cuckold that cripple and in his own bed too. He was almost eager to break up that family, take back what was rightfully his.

Destroy the man.

So, while the skaters whizzed about and everyone else was otherwise occupied, Matthew had walked away, following the path he knew would lead to her

Bridget was bundled against the cold, her gloved hands clutching an old, worn book to her chest. She admired the promise of Spring before her with a smile, the sunlight dazzlingly bright, the trees empty and barren now, but with new buds stirring within, giving her hope. Oh, the memories she could conjure from this spot. So much joy. The first time she'd met Matthew, the first time they sat together and talked, the first time he'd held her hand, their first kiss. She swiped a tear from her cheek.

"I hope that tear was for me."

She jumped from her seat and spun around.

He felt calmer now, seeing her in such distress. Yes, her feelings were as tumultuous as his own, no matter how hard she fought against them. "You look surprised to see me, dear." He strolled around the bench, amused by her confusion, and sat. "You're not going to pretend you haven't been waiting for me to come along, are you?"

"Of course I haven't!"

"No? Pity." He patted the space beside him. "Come and sit with me – like old times. You needn't look down the road, no one noticed my leaving the skating pond and coming here… all too busy laughing and making merry. Interesting aside, I saw your husband go to the pond's edge. Gad, you don't think he's going to try to skate, do you? I wouldn't want to miss that for the world."

Her face flushed with anger, her fists clenched. Why did he always have this effect on her? Why did he always end with cruelty? She hated Matthew more than anyone else on earth at times – but, God help her, she also loved him to the point of madness. Even his bitterness, which she understood, and his selfishness and arrogance, which she sometimes shared… more's the pity.

"Oh, stop sputtering. I was only teasing."

"No. No, you were not. You say vile, hurtful things deliberately." She sat as far away as possible from him and stared forward.

"I know. I do, don't I? Sorry. I seem to enjoy upsetting you, oddly enough. I'm a sick bastard, what can I say? Well, enough about me. You're looking more beautiful than ever, Bridget. I like what you've done with your hair, and your figure is just as luscious as I remember. The Highland kilts must jump around you like rabbits to a hole. Probably think Alex is your father, what? Does he beat them off with his cane?"

"Enough! I can take no more of you!" She stood too quickly, dropping what she was holding in her hands.

"Aha. What have we here?" The book had landed by his boot so he snatched it up before she could. "Not so fast, lassie. What are we reading these days? Poetry? I remember you always did have a syrupy, romantic streak..." He stopped speaking suddenly. For a moment, all was quiet.

"Give that back to me. Now, Matthew." If she didn't leave soon she'd burst into tears.

Matthew stared at the cover, turned the book over. "This is the book I gave you."

"Yes. Please may I have it back."

"I would have thought you'd thrown this away ages ago." His mind spun, emotions stirring more than he cared to admit. The book of poems by Robert Burns was one his mother had given him as he went off to Oxford, a memento more precious to him than diamonds, and he had given it to Bridget out of his love for her years before.

Opening the cover, he read the well-remembered inscription out loud. "*With all my love.*" There was a sudden lump in his throat. "Well, damnation, I'd forgotten I'd given you this." That was a lie. He'd thought about it every day, for years. "Why ever did you keep this?"

She stared at the trees, spoke so softly he barely heard her. "It was all I had left of you, besides our son. I placed it in Ewan's crib when he was first born and there it remained until he was given a child's bed, and then I sewed it into the cotton mattress of that. No one else ever knew. You see, I wanted you to be near him, somehow." Slowly she sat back down on the bench, sighing at all they had missed together. "Oh, Matthew, he was a beautiful baby, and so good – and, now he's a wonderful boy. He wants to see the world and experience everything. And he laughs all the time, no matter what problem he's faced with – he can be a little devil at times, yet he could charm the stars from the sky."

"Sounds an awful lot like my father."

"Must be. It certainly wasn't mine. My papa rarely ventured outside a library. But not our boy, Matthew. He is always searching for adventures." Swiping away the tears she studied the snowy horizon rather than look into Matthew's eyes, dark and brooding now, heavy with wants that were beyond her ability to give. She took a deep breath. "Alex has decided that if Ewan wishes to come here, to attend school here, we'll not stand in his way."

Matthew's jaw clenched. "My, that's awfully big of him."

"Matthew, please, I don't wish to fight with you anymore. Forgive me for doing what I had to do at the time. Forgive me for everything."

His heart nearly broke when he saw tears stream down her cheeks. She was his life, always was and always would be. "Forgive you? *Never.* I love you too much for that." He pulled her to him, his mouth covering hers, demanding and needy. When his tongue swept across hers she was his again, body and soul, lost to a love out of her control. Her arms wrapped around his neck and she kissed him back, tasting both their tears.

"You're mine," he whispered, his forehead touching hers before their lips met again, the kiss even deeper, his hands sliding into her hair. Bridget thought she would die from love....

It was then that they heard the first screams.

CHAPTER TWENTY-EIGHT

IN THE BLINK OF AN eye the world had gone mad. Shrieks and cries and children's screams filled the air as people began running toward the skating pond. There were shouts for help, for ropes, for tree branches – people pushed and shoved at each other, they yelled out names, they shouted for God. The pond icemen, the skating club members, park keepers, spectators all were in full panic. Matthew and Bridget reached the crest just in time to see a large chunk of ice give way.

The screams somehow intensified.

Men and women rushed onto the ice to their children, their loved ones, their friends, only to scramble back in terror as more and more cracks formed under the added weight. Matthew heard Darcy's shouts above the din, pleading with people to stay back; few seemed to listen. He saw his father down on his knees, his hands outstretched to someone in the icy water. He was screaming.

Someone ran past and Matthew attempted to grab his arm, nearly getting clobbered when the hysterical man took a swing at him and tore off in another direction. He grabbed for another man stumbling past. "How many have fallen in?" he shouted over the din.

"My God! The ice! They're drowning! Let go of me, I must find my wife." And with that, the man raced off.

Terror stopped Matthew's heart cold.

Amanda.

The realization struck Bridget at the same moment. She pulled away from Matthew and began running, "*Alex! Ewan! Oh, dear*

Jesus!"

He pulled her back, turned her around to face him. "Alex was speaking with Uncle Wills before I left."

"No! You said Alex walked down to the skaters!" She covered her mouth with her hands and looked around wildly. "*My boy!*" she was hysterical. "*Where is my boy?*"

Matthew shook her. "Get hold of yourself. Stay away from the pond, darling – you'll be trampled there – go, seek out my uncle. I'll find my brothers and we'll look for them both."

He then began running down the hill, pushing people from his path – all the time shouting, "*Amanda! Alex! Ewan!*" He scanned the crowd for them, searching, searching. "Stop, Clarissa!" He shouted when he caught sight of his wife running onto the ice. He ran to her. "Clarissa!" She slipped, falling under the mob as it pushed and trampled across her hands and legs. He strong armed his way through, shoving people aside, pulling her up and into his arms. She was wailing and crying so hard she made no sense.

"Have you seen her?" he shouted. "Clarissa, answer me! Where is Amanda?"

"Out there!" She pointed to where people were trying to reach those struggling in the water. "She's there! Our baby's fallen into the water!"

Matthew immediately began running along the icy bank through the crowds, the police whistles and screams deafening. Men were ripping branches from trees, finding ropes and throwing them into the water, anything for rescuers or victims to grab onto – there must have been twenty people bobbing in the freezing water, men, women and children, their heavy clothing pulling them down.

Then he saw Harry, Luke and his cousin George, all reaching into the water, grabbing hold of friends and strangers alike. Nephews and nieces of his were huddled on the bank weeping, two soaking wet and bundled in blankets. Matthew had seen everyone but his precious daughter. Where was Amanda? Where was his baby? Buffeted by strangers he staggered onto the slippery ice. *"Amanda! Amanda!"* He screamed over the clamor, again and again.

"*Please, God, save my child.*" His hands raked through his hair, he spun around madly. *"I know I've been awful, but please don't punish my baby. I'll change, I promise…"*

A shout came from nearby, people were pointing and waving

their arms. "The boy! Someone take the boy!" Matthew quickly recognized Ewan being carried onto the shore and he began to run, stumbling just as he reached his son, pulling him into his arms, pushing the dripping hair from the child's face. "Are you all right?"

Before the boy could respond others called out. "It's giving way here!" Suddenly people were running past him and back up the snowbanks. The men lying on their stomachs, tossing out ropes to people, freezing now themselves and exhausted, scrambled backward.

Matthew passed his hand over Ewan's face, kissed his forehead, and sobbed when the boy wrapped his arms around his neck. The child was shivering from the cold water, but alive.

"Give him to us." Holding a blanket out, a stranger reached down for Ewan. The child began to panic then, he screamed, fighting against hands that were trying to take him away. He only burrowed deeper into Matthew's arms.

"Your mother's coming for you, Ewan. You'll be safe now." Matthew had spotted Bridget running along the path, struggling through the crowd. Then there was a horrible cracking sound, more ice beginning to give. "Let go, son. This man will take you to your mother," he whispered into Ewan's ear. "His mother is coming. Take the lad…"

"No!" cried Ewan, pointing back to the water. Matthew had no time for this, he needed to find his daughter. He struggled up the incline slowly to hand the boy over. "No!" Ewan was hysterical, twisting in his arms.

"Whatever is the matter?"

"*My Papa! My Papa! There!*"

Matthew spun around. "Where, Ewan? Where is he?" And then he saw the child in the water – still and limp as death, her blonde hair covering her face, her heavy cloak soaking. Some brave soul was in that freezing lake holding her up, even while their own head kept disappearing under the icy waters.

Amanda Rose.

He immediately shoved the boy at the nearest person and jumped in, the shock of the cold nearly stopping his heart. People were yelling to him but he couldn't concentrate on what they were saying, all he could see was his daughter's tiny face, her lips pale and blue… and, then she was gone. *No!* He screamed, struggling to swim in his heavy coat and boots. When he was finally near he grabbed for her blindly, wildly splashing his arms, gasping for air. Nothing. He dove under the water but it was too dark. All he saw were the vague outlines of a half dozen other wildly thrashing people – until…

Suddenly there she was, her golden hair floating around her. He pulled her to him and immediately broke the water surface, gasping for air. "Baby girl," he croaked, "baby girl, open your eyes for your Papa! Please!" One second, two seconds, three… the eyelash flutter was brief but wonderful – her eyes blinked a few times and she coughed out water. She was alive.

Then Matthew saw another form struggling beneath the water so he reached down and grabbed that man's collar, hoisting him above the surface, the fellow sputtering and coughing. It was the man who had risked his life to save Amanda's, the man who had been holding her up, keeping her alive.

It was Alex Durand.

"I've got you, Alex," Matthew rasped out, wrapping his arm around Alex's waist. Holding them both in his arms he then began searching for help, for something or someone to grab onto. Several men called out, passing a rope to each other and waving to him. *Thank the Lord.*

"… my boy…?" Alex could barely speak.

"Yes, he's safe," Matthew barely managed as well, his own lips now trembling in the cold. "Can you hold onto my neck while I secure us?" He somehow had grabbed the rope tossed out by the men huddled near the ice's edge. They shouted for him to hurry as he tied it around his waist, then they began to pull them in.

"Your daughter…?"

"Alive." Matthew trembled, not from the cold now. "You saved her, by God. Alex, you saved my child. She looks nearly frozen, but she's alive."

"Thank God," whispered Alex, just before he passed out.

After a few minutes, or a few hours – Matthew could hardly tell – he found himself on a bench, his hands clasped between his knees as if in prayer, his family scurrying around him, everyone talking at once. His brother, Luke, crouched down before him.

"Did you say something, Matt? Do you want another blanket?"

"No. No, Luke. Give them to the others."

"Are you all right?" Luke grabbed Matthew's hands and rubbed them. "How are your hands?"

"They sting."

Luke nodded. "Good, that means circulation is returning." Still, Matthew was so still, so calm… so out of character. "What is it? What's bothering you?"

"I don't know how he was able to do it, you know. How did he do it?" Matthew shook his head as a cup of hot tea was passed to him. "Do you know if Durand is all right? Has anyone seen him? Has anyone seen Ewan? What happened when we came ashore – I remember nothing."

"Well, we were told you both collapsed and then these men came running up to carry you off. It was one of Uncle Wills neighbors who saw it all and found us; but I have no idea where Alex was brought, or Ewan. All I can tell you is one of Papa's footmen heard that a carriage has brought Alex and Ewan both to Anne Marie and Jamie's house. I haven't the slightest whose carriage it was, though. Not one of ours. Father sent the footman off again for his personal physicians to hurry over there. I'm certain a doctor will soon be in attendance."

Harry joined Luke and placed his hand on Matthew's shoulder. "Matt, I don't want you to worry about anything except getting yourself and your little one back to father's. Are you able to walk?" Matthew heard the emotion in his brother's voice and clasped his hand.

"Yes, certainly. Don't worry so for me, just see that my child is cared for, please Harry."

"The carriages are waiting everyone, let us get ourselves home." Darcy's sedate, calm, measured words were followed immediately by Fitzwilliam's rough shout, "Move! Now!"

Matthew began to stand, his body responding slowly, his mind a fuzzy mess. "Wait! Clarissa!" He looked around frantically. "Where is Clarissa? Has anyone seen my wife?"

"Seen and *heard*." Luke barked out a laugh. "Your wife rivals father at shouting orders. As of this moment she has secured the warmest, most comfortable carriage for you and Amanda, has had hot bricks stolen from other carriages, and is waiting for you there now, holding your daughter in her lap. I would get a move on, if I were you. That woman is a force of nature and she wants you carried to her if necessary. We tried to explain how big and heavy you are, and how impossible carrying you would be, but she just shouted all the louder."

Matthew shook his head. "I will never understand women."

Luke and Harry both helped Matthew to his feet and all three began to walk. "I would never say this to another soul – however, she's actually been quite wonderful," Luke said, his amazement evident. "Who could have guessed?"

CHAPTER TWENTY-NINE

JAMIE DURAND CLOSED THE DOOR gently to his brother's room, turning to the woman sitting in the chair. "Are they asleep?"

"Yes," whispered Bridget. Her husband and son lay side by side in the big canopied bed, Alex soundly sleeping while his boy snored softly, curled into his father's side.

"I just saw the last of the doctors out, thought you could use a respite after such a long day, perhaps rest a little yourself? There's an adjoining bedroom to this where our children always sleep their first year."

"Thank you, Jamie, but there's no need. Your servants have provided me with a chaise and blankets to use in here, if that's all right?"

"Of course. Whatever you wish."

"I cannot thank you enough for allowing us to stay in your home. It makes me feel so much safer."

"Nonsense. Alex is my brother. Our home is yours." He sat beside her, took her hand. "I've sent a footman over to Claridges' to collect your things. You'll be with us as long as you wish.

"That sounds wonderful." She gave his hand a squeeze. "I've never seen so many physicians at once. They were all amazed Alex is doing so well, weren't they? They said… they said…" Unable to continue, she buried her face in her hands.

Jamie gathered her up in his arms, brushing away his own tears. "Hush, now, lass. No souls were lost today by some miracle. Our own Ewan and Alex, Amanda Rose and Matthew, alive and recovering. We have much for which to be thankful to our Lord."

"We could have easily lost him, Jamie. How could he survive in that cold water, how did he save that little girl?"

"You're daft, lassie. My brother Alex was always strong as an ox and a grand swimmer, one leg or two. As for the cold water, we're Scots! Our bath water is colder than that. Now stop your weeping and wipe your nose. They'll all survive. That's what counts." He retrieved his handkerchief from his coat pocket and handed it to her.

"You're right, I know." She blew her nose enthusiastically then mopped away her tears.

"Ach. Well, don't you dare try and give that back to me now," he grumbled, making her laugh – and cry – even more.

There was a knock at the door and Anne Marie entered the room.

"Are they asleep?"

"Yes," came the whispered answer from both Jamie and Bridget.

"Well, that is a mercy with all the traffic in and out of this room today."

"Are the children in bed?"

"Yes, finally. I am exhausted. Roberta was the first to try my patience, as always. She wanted to come in here and sleep on the floor in case Ewan needed anything during the night. Then Deborah began to cry because she feared the floorboards were going to crack and give way, and then Steven insisted he'd like to become an ice pond attendant in the future, thought it all looked very exciting. When I told him that would be over my dead body, he actually appeared to mull it over."

"Where was Nanny Bochs during all this?"

"Yes, about Nanny Bochs. I have some good news and some bad news for you."

"Shall we start with the good?"

"I have eliminated a household expense."

"Good heavens, what have you done?"

"Don't you give me that look, James. The physicians began questioning her about her procedures with regards to the care of the children, their health in general. It was quite eye-opening. Apparently, Bochs dislikes being questioned and simply left." Anne Marie stared everywhere but at Jamie.

"No. No. You see, I've lived with you too long. She didn't just walk off, did she, Anne Marie?"

"Well, she certainly did after I shoved her out the door."

"You sacked her."

"With the bottom of my boot, yes. Jamie, the woman believes in giving the children Opium Treatment for a bad chest; in fact, I suspect she's used that vile concoction to keep them quiet at times. And, since Uncle Fitz's friend, Sir Giles, has serious concerns about the use of Opium for adults, let alone children, he pointedly expressed his opinion to her. Well, the woman flew into a terrible rage, began assaulting that most distinguished of physicians! And, you should have heard her – for a moment I believed she was speaking in tongues! The look on Sir Giles face! Actually, it was very funny… never mind about that. Where was I – oh, yes, I almost went searching for one of your firearms to save him."

"It is fortunate then that I hide them. No, you did exactly the right thing, pet. However, this is becoming ridiculous; that was our fifth nanny since… well, since you left us, Bridget. You set a very high standard, you know."

"I am so sorry for all of this."

"Nothing is your fault, Bridget. In fact, the doctors had a very good idea. They suggested a nanny with medical training might be best, and I agree. Mr. Stevens even said he would look into it for us and perhaps he can recommend a woman. Now, tell us what happened today. How did you manage?" Anne Marie sat beside Bridget while Jamie brought over another chair for himself. "How are you doing, my dear?"

"Much better than this morning. Thank you for everything you've done."

"We should never have left you three off at the park with no way of returning, but we really did think we'd be back in time. The Admiralty assured us our report would only take a few minutes and it ended up lasting nearly two hours. I don't understand why you weren't cared for by our families. You were with them when we left, did you become separated?"

"Yes, I'm afraid I did." Bridget studied the handkerchief she twisted in her lap, feeling guilty as sin. "I don't know what happened, I just could not find them in the upheaval."

"And, however did you manage to return in Lady Linton's carriage of all things? I heard they were in Paris."

"Well, I was standing beside the bench where they had lain Alex, holding Ewan in my arms and watching the madness going on by the ice, when a woman I'd never seen before approached me, several servants in tow. Before I knew what was happening, she had secured enough blankets for Ewan and Alex, had someone start a small fire for heat, and then commandeered the carriage for our use. I shall never be able to thank her enough."

"Amazing. And you had never seen her before?" said Jamie. "I wonder who she was."

Bridget lowered her head. "As I said, I'd never met her before."

In the darkness later that night, Bridget watched the new snow sparkle in the moonlight outside her window. She remembered Matthew's tears as they sat on the bench early that fateful day, his heat and kisses and caressing hands… if he had asked her then to run away with him would she have gone, leaving her family and home? She hoped not, she prayed she had become stronger than that over the years.

Strange how such romantic desire felt insignificant compared to the moment she'd seen her husband carried from the chaotic, terrifying crowd. With her son wrapped in a thin blanket in her arms, she ran to them, screaming Alex's name.

"Is this 'un yours?"

"Yes! Yes! Oh, Alex! Is he all right? What happened?"

"What 'appened indeed! One leg and 'e saved a young girl's life is all. Now, where can we lay 'im down? We've other's in need of assistance."

Bridget motioned to a nearby bench pulling off her cloak to cover her husband. When the men turned to leave she panicked. "No, please! Could you start a fire for us, so I can warm him and the child? Please."

"Oy, miss, we don't got the time." The men motioned over two very young, very frightened looking stewards of the skating club standing nearby. "You there, come 'ere this, 'elp this woman, least ye can do after this fiasco. Build a small fire to warm 'em 'til authorities come round."

"Oh, thank you, thank you…" But before Bridget could ask

assistance from them in locating the families both men were gone, and when she turned back to instruct the young boys, they ran off as well.

Not knowing what to do next she called out for help, frantically attempted to stop passing strangers – but no one helped, no one stopped, she was just one of so many desperate people. With panic threatening to overwhelm she pushed it back for her son's sake, searched the blur of faces for someone she knew, one of the Darcy's, or a Fitzwilliam – but none were around… she'd need to begin searching them out, yet how could she leave her husband alone? Her boy shivered violently in her arms, closed his eyes, and seemed to drift away.

"No! Ewan," she begged. "Ewan, wake up for Mama, please, son, please!"

That was when she saw the woman walking directly towards her through the crowd, a tall, serene beauty, the turmoil surrounding her seeming to part like the Red Sea as she passed through. Regal, elegant, beautiful – and, even though a stranger, familiar somehow.

The woman stopped before her; looked her up and down. "Are you mad?"

"I beg your pardon?"

"Is this your husband? You must remove him to your lodgings immediately! His clothing is ice cold and wet, and why isn't there a fire to warm him? It will be no one's fault but your own if he develops a lung fever!"

Bridget wanted to burst into tears but kept her voice level, resting Ewan on her hip. "I do realize that, madam; however, I have no carriage here, and I cannot find my people and I dare not leave my husband's side. If you could help us, please. I am most desperate –"

The woman raised her hand for silence. "Isaiah 25:4 declares, 'For You have been a defense for the helpless, a defense for the needy in his distress, a refuge from the storm, a shade from the heat.'" She turned her head slightly to summon one of the servants following her. "Peters, you have the blankets I instructed you collect for the family?

Good. Leave them there and help Deavers remove this man's clothing, then assist her with the child. We shall wrap those blankets around them both. Branson, start a fire immediately, then search out more blankets for our own use.

"Amos."

Another servant stepped forward. "Yes, your ladyship."

"You shall go across the way and instruct Lady Linton's driver to bring her carriage around as quickly as possible." She turned to Bridget. "Since she's currently in Paris, I can assure you she'll not mind my procuring it's use. In fact, I shall explain to her how very much she didn't mind when I see her next."

Amos was still standing before her when she turned back to him. "Well? Why are you still here? Hurry on, you fool! Her home is that hideous white monstrosity across the way. No, not that monstrosity, the other one. When you return with the driver both you and he shall carry this gentleman to her carriage and transport him to the lodgings of Mr. James Durand. Amos! Where are you going? Whatever is the matter with you, I haven't finished. Tell the coachman to make certain there are hot bricks in the carriage and brandy."

"Thank you." Bridget's voice choked. "You are so very kind, madam. A saint!"

"I am hardly a saint, and any kindness you perceive in me irrelevant. I perform my Christian duty."

"Yes, madam. Of course."

"Give Peters those wet clothes. I shall have them cleaned and returned to you."

"Yes, madam." Bridget handed over Ewan's clothes and then wrapped the boy in the thick blankets, rubbing his arms and legs and back to warm him faster. It took a moment before she realized the woman was staring at them strangely.

Intently.

Grateful as she was, it was beginning to make her very nervous.

The woman finally spoke. "This is the boy."

"Yes. My son." Bridget kissed Ewan's forehead. "We nearly lost him today and he is still so cold. I cannot thank you enough for all of your assistance." She babbled on, hugging her son to her heart. "He kept falling asleep, and he never complains about anything really, and he… he's my only child."

The woman came closer, never taking her eyes from Ewan. "I had heard he looked very much like his father." Her frown was gone now, her voice sounding almost tender. "Such a lovely child."

"Do you know my husband, Sir Alex Durand?"

The woman stiffened, looked up slowly. Gone was the tender smile, the gentle words. She hesitated a moment then began to back away. "Yes, I am aware of your *husband*." Cold dislike had replaced the tender looks. "However, I was referring to the boy's *father*."

Bridget looked at the woman closely, shocked. Of course. She had seen sketches of Lady Clarissa Fitzwilliam in the society pages over the years, knew she was one of the most prominent and important fixtures of the British society. Elegant, poised, and still incredibly beautiful, even at forty years. She could see why Matthew had been dazzled by her in their youth. "Lady Fitzwilliam, please forgive me, I did not recognize you."

"It is of no consequence."

"Please, I know you have every right to hate me for asking you this; but, I've... I've been so worried about *him*. I must know..." Bridget had seen Matthew jump into the water as she ran from the breaking ice, Ewan in her arms. She had no right to ask this of his wife, it was bold and sinful. She didn't care, she had to know.

Even as Clarissa's eyes sparked she sounded calm. "Both my husband and my daughter are well. How kind of you to inquire. However, they too will be carefully watched to ensure a lung fever does not develop."

"Thank you for telling me." Bridget felt buffeted by waves of bitterness radiating from the woman, and with good cause. It was true she could never make amends to Matthew's wife for what they had done. God forgive her, it was also true she would never regret their sin either, and she could live with that. "We have both nearly lost a child today, I fear."

"Indeed." Clarissa arched her brow. "*And* a husband."

With that Lady Clarissa Fitzwilliam turned and strode regally back into the chaos, shouting demands and issuing instructions in her wake.

CHAPTER THIRTY

IT HAD BEEN MORE THAN two weeks since the disaster at the iced lake and Matthew was finally allowing himself an end to worry over his daughter's health. Amazingly, few skaters or onlookers that day had been seriously hurt, and Amanda was laughing again, even eager to return there with her cousin Roberta and the others. For once, however, her parents were in complete agreement – there would be no skating this winter, or until more regulation and oversite was provided for the park's skaters.

As for his hatred of all things Alex Durand, that had certainly been put to rest. What could he possibly say to the fellow to convey the enormity of a father's gratitude? Matthew had spent years detesting Durand for seducing the woman he loved; and, even when he had learned the truth, he'd fought against it, as if he was determined to hate no matter what.

Now he wanted nothing more than to sacrifice his own life in service to the man. He owed him everything. After all, Alex Durand had saved both his children – Amanda from an icy death, and Ewan from the stigma of being born bastard.

"Papa, you're squeezing my hand again."

"Pardon? Oh, I'm sorry, dearest." It was the middle of February, father and child in the family carriage on the way to personally thank his daughter's rescuer and beg forgiveness for Matthew's years of senseless acrimony. It was a sunny day, another tease of early Spring thaw.

"I don't really mind, Papa. I know when you have that sad look in your eyes you're thinking of the accident. I wish you could forget what happened. I'm all right, really I am."

He hugged her to him and kissed the top of her bonnet. "Of course you are, my darling, I just love you so very much. When I think of what could have been, it takes my breath away. You'll understand better when you have children of your own. There is nothing a father wouldn't do for his child, no sacrifice too great."

"Does that mean I can have another puppy?"

"Certainly not. Ah, here we are. Watch your step, dearest."

The door was opened by the ancient Durand butler, Timmons, summoned to London from Edinburgh years before, when Jamie and Anne Marie newly married. "A pleasant day to ye, Lord Fitzwilliam, Lady Amanda. Grand to see ye agin; however, Master Jamie and his wife are not in, and I canna say when they'll return. Y'see, they've gone to visit the Service Registries Office."

"You are not being replaced I hope."

"Oh nay, sir, but it's that kind of ye to be concerned. No, we've need of a new nanny for the wee bairns."

"Good heavens, yet another one escaped bondage? Nanny, I mean – not the children."

"Aye, sir. And, the 'Situations Vacant' items we've placed havna been fruitful."

"Word must be out you're skimping on the wages, increasing the floggings."

"Nay, wages are twenty pounds per annum – a verra grand sum t'be sure. And, we do offer the daily portion o'beer."

"I was being facetious, Timmons."

"Couldna tell b'me, sir. Ye know, we have a sayin' in Edinburgh. 'a nod's as guid as a wink tae a blind horse'."

"What does that mean exactly?""

"I havna a clue. As I was sayin' laird's bein' more selective now; usin' a more rigorous criterion as it were for the hirin'."

"No longer accepting penal colony returnees then?"

"Should I be laughin' agin, sir?"

"Not if you need to ask."

"Verra good."

"Well, I would love to stand and chin wag with you all day, Timmons: however, our desire today is to see Sir Alex. Is he accepting visitors?"

"Aye, I'm certain he shall for you and the wee lass, sir. But, if you will wait in the drawin' room I shall go upstairs and ask."

"Thank you."

Matthew and Amanda heard the thunder of running feet only moments before the door to the drawing room burst open and Roberta, Steven and Deborah came screaming into the room, followed closely by a laughing Ewan Durand pulling his mother along by her hand. The happy chatter and squeals of the children helped the two adults avoid eye contact – for a while.

Amanda cheered at the sight of Ewan and hugged him. "You look wonderful, Ewan. All recovered?"

"Stronger than ever. Look at my arm muscle here… well, it was there yesterday. You look splendid too. How are you feeling?"

"Very well. I do want to skate again, but…."

"Amanda." Her father's steady gaze quieted her.

"We can speak about it later," whispered Roberta and the three giggled.

While holding her hand Ewan urged his mother forward, then took hold of Matthew's hand. "Mummy, you know it was Lord Fitzwilliam who saved Papa from the water. We must thank him properly."

"Of course we shall, Ewan." Finally, she looked up into the eyes of the man she loved more than life itself. "Thank you, Lord Fitzwilliam. My life would be nothing without my husband or my child. Thank you."

"It was my honor, Lady Durand. However, it is your husband who is the true hero. I would have no reason to live if anything happened to this one. He saved my most precious gift." He stroked his daughter's hair then looked deep into Bridget's eyes. "You see, I know what you must be feeling." They stood in silence for a moment, lost in their shared memories, when Ewan stepped forward and hugged Matthew, surprising everyone.

"Thank you, sir. I was so afraid to lose my Papa."

Matthew was frozen for a moment, stunned, his heart breaking, realizing this might be the only time for the rest of his life that he could hold this son. He wrapped his arms around the boy tightly and kissed his head, his eyes misting over. "Do not ever forget, Ewan, I would do *anything* for you or your father, my boy. Anything," he whispered hoarsely.

"Everyone is being much too serious for me. Cousin!" Roberta threw her arm over Amanda's shoulder. "Doesn't your skin look splendid. Perhaps I should jump into an icy lake as well, Do you see this, I am getting spots."

"You eat chocolates all the time, Birdie; Auntie Kathy said that's why you're getting spots." Deborah took Amanda's other hand and began to pull her to the door. "Come and play sardines with us upstairs."

"Oh, yes!" clapped little Steven. "You shall never find me. Do you know, I hide in the nursery under the costumes." As he ran ahead the other children began to herd her noisily toward the door.

"Amanda, mummy is taking me to see Mr. Dickens, did I tell you? She wouldn't allow me to go before the accident, but she feels so badly that they weren't there that she's gotten us tickets! Would you like to come with us?"

"Really? Oh, yes." Amanda and Roberta's chatter could be heard from the hallway outside the door. "And guess what, Birdy – I may be getting a new puppy…" Soon the children's voices disappeared up the stairs.

Alone together, both Matthew and Bridget stood side by side and stared at the now closed door. The air was thick with tension. She moved to the window and looked out. "How is your brother Mark?"

"Much improved. Thank you for asking."

"I'm glad. I hear he may be engaged to be married."

"There appears to be a difference of opinion on that. He's decided they are better off as friends and she doesn't agree. Actually, he may leave for America soon, travel with Father Ted. I may even go with them.'

Certainly, a heart couldn't truly break, but Bridget's was crushed by that thought. "It will be nice for the two of you to have time together."

"Yes, I've missed him. I was told Anne Marie and Jamie will be having a family gathering next week, a celebration, since we've missed Twelfth Night. Your family shall be attending, I hope."

"Yes, I suppose we will." She moved pictures around on a table and straightened the cloth.

Another awkward moment of silence fell between them before Matthew finally spoke. Nervous, he cleared his throat first. "How is he truly, Bridget? Will he be all right?"

She turned. "Yes," she said gently. "And, thank you for caring, Matthew, thank you for your beautiful letter, for the flowers you sent over. There is no longer any danger of lung fever and he's able to leave the bed finally. Your father has sent over Mark's bath chair now that he no longer requires it, so Alex can move about more. He's become restless, always a good sign in a man."

Matthew nodded. "Absolutely true. His leg?"

She shook her head. "We're not certain if he'll ever be able to walk again."

"Damn," Matthew scrubbed a hand across his eyes in frustration. "He doesn't deserve any of this."

"No. He doesn't. Matthew, this must be the last time we see ever each other alone."

"Never say that, Bridget. I love you with all my heart."

He reached for her, but she backed away. "I will never betray my husband again, and I haven't the strength to fight you any longer. You see, I love Alex as much as I love you, but in a different way; my loyalty must remain with him. When he is strong enough to travel, I pray you will allow my family to return to Scotland. I promise you we will arrange for Ewan to visit you as often as you like, and you're always welcome at our home.

"Alex and I won't be returning to London, though. There shall be a special election for his seat in Parliament, he isn't strong enough for that now. And he loves the highlands so, the land revives him. Please allow us this much."

"All right." It was with both relief and regret that she saw understanding in his gaze. "I won't give you any more trouble about the boy, forgive me for that. And you're right about us. Sounds ridiculous, but I begged the Lord to save my daughter, vowed I would be a better man. Evidently, the shock of hearing my voice moved God into action, can't go back on that now." He reached out and swiped a tear from her cheek.

All she could do was nod her head, because, if she dared speak, she would scream to heaven how unfair life was, and how much she loved him.

Matthew pressed his handkerchief into her hand. "I want to speak with Alex, become acquainted with the man my son loves so dearly, whom you love. I want him to be my friend, I want him to be my brother."

Bridget nodded again and blew her nose.

"All right, lead the way, Lady Durand. I'm nervous as a schoolboy right now."

CHAPTER THIRTY-ONE

IT WAS IN A CAUTIOUSLY optimistic mood then, five weeks after the near disaster at the skating pond, that the Darcy and Fitzwilliam families gathered to finally celebrate Twelfth Night – or in this case, Thirty-Fifth Night – in appreciation for those beloved lives who had been in danger's path – Jamie, Anne Marie, Mark, Andrew, Amanda Rose, Ewan, Alex and Matthew – and survived. The family was a tad less naïve than they had been before, less apt to take each other for granted, and a great deal more appreciative of life.

Still, it *was* family, and it *was* a holiday. Always an eventual receipt for trouble…

They huddled around the crackling fire in Anne Marie's family parlor, enjoying its warm glow… some holding hands, some misty-eyed, some grinning like loons – possibly from selectively spiked Wassail.

"I say, Darcy, do you remember years ago – we were just pups then – when you fell through the ice? What a ghastly mess that was. It was a much, much larger lake than at the park if I remember correctly, may have been the ocean. You nearly drowned, but I saved you."

"Yet more evidence of your disturbed mentality, Fitz. It was a large fountain into which you *pushed* me then dragged me from, begging that I not call for my mother."

"That's what I meant. Heavens that was funny – only you could nearly drown in sixteen inches of water! Did I really push you in? What a little rotter I was. Say, wait a minute, you did tell your mother and I was sent up to bed without supper – a fate worse than death for a six-year-old boy. I hope you're proud of yourself, Darcy."

"You *pushed* me, Fitzwilliam. What about that do you find difficult to understand? Besides, I never did tell mother. We were screaming so loudly at each other that she heard the argument."

"Right. Right. I'd forgotten. Heavens but your mother had almost preternatural hearing. Like a bat. Wonderful memories though, what? Drama, intrigue, pirates, flirtations with the village girls, sneaking snakes into church, attempting the occasional parricide…"

"Grandfather Fitz, are you going to finish your piece of King Cake or not? I need to know if you have the bean or the clove." Little Henry was already sticking his finger into Fitz's second slice of cake, looking for the hidden pieces.

"You take the rest of this, Henry, and if you find the bean you can take my place as King, all right? I do believe Grandfather Darcy has already found the pea, which would make him your Queen."

Little Henry giggled at this, turning to Darcy for confirmation. Darcy took him in his lap and whispered, "I gave my piece to Grandmama," then kissed the child's head.

"Greetings everyone." Mark Fitzwilliam, walking now with the assistance of a cane, entered the room along with his longtime companion, Lady Lucille Armitage. "Greetings, everyone," she called out as well.

"Mark! Happy to see you've finally gotten him out of his rooms, Lucille." Fitzwilliam's smile barely disguised how intently he studied his son now. Children are always a worry to a parent, even at forty years old, and Mark was being especially uncommunicative these days. Fitz knew he had withdrawn emotionally the moment he learned of the nurse's death.

"Forgive us, Lord Fitzwilliam, our tardiness was entirely my fault. Mummy and father dropped me off at Mark's home with plenty of time, but then wanted to visit with him."

"No need to apologize to me, my dear. I only ever mean to aggravate my children, not others."

"Don't sell yourself short, Papa," grinned Luke. "You aggravate many more people than that."

Bunny Armitage accepted a seat before the fireplace next to Kathy, while Mark sat beside Alex, grabbing the man's hand to shake warmly. "How are you, Alex?"

"Much improved, or so I'm told. Thank you so much for the use of your Bath chair."

"Nonsense. Glad it helps. And the family?'

"Very well, although Bridget is home with a cold. Personally, I believe she's just exhausted from worry and wanted a rest."

"Understandable. Well, tell her hello for me, if you would."

"That's kind of you Mark, I shall. Wonderful to see you up and walking."

"Yes, thank you. Able to get about more and more; however, the doctors want me to rest my leg whenever possible. Very soon I shall toss this stick into the Thames. Terrible nuisance – *oof!* What the devil?" The littlest ones had charged their Uncle Mark, all wanting to sit on his lap, all chattering at once.

"Be still, the lot of you, and allow me to visit with my family. Now, Steven, come over to this side, on your left. No, your other left. What in the world is on your head?" Anne Marie's six-year-old wore Andrew Fitzwilliam's magnificent bicorne hat, dark blue and trimmed in wide gold braid. Since it engulfed his entire head the child kept banging into objects while on his way to his favorite uncle.

"Where are you, Unca' Mark?"

"Over here, sweetheart," laughed Mark when the boy fell into his arms.

"Have I missed your Twelfth Night play?"

"No, we only just finished our tea in the nursery when everyone began to arrive, and we've been having cake. If you don't want yours, I'll eat it for you. I don't mind."

"Yes, of course you should. I don't want to spoil my appetite for later."

"Why would having cake spoil your appetite? It never spoils mine."

"I know. I've seen you eat." Mark turned to say something to Bunny, noticing she had moved her chair a bit farther away from the children. It wasn't that she disliked them so much, she just would rather not be around them, a feeling Mark could not share – he loved children, and most especially his nieces and nephews. He supposed they should speak again about her refusal to accept his decision not to marry, remain as they were; but there was no rush, really.

"Well, when is your wedding to be this time?" The sudden sound of throats clearing made Kathy look about. "What have I said now? I thought they were engaged. I swear no one tells me anything in this family."

"Nothing is decided as of yet, Kathy." Mark's eyes bored into his sister. "After all, I shall be leaving for America in a few weeks."

"Why on earth would you be going to America now?"

"I thought I would help Ted with his move, if that is all right with you."

"No need for that tone, dear brother. I merely meant that you've already resized mummy's ring for Bunny, you have been keeping company for three years at least.You will be forty-years old within days, Mark.What is the problem?"

"Kathy." Her husband George hissed at her to be quiet.

Bunny sipped her cup of tea and smiled at her friend. "We have a few differences that will need to be settled first."

"Really?" The Mary's both said in unison. "That is very interesting!" declared Mary Margaret. "Just what are they?" inquired Mary Elizabeth.

Andrew adjusted his officer's frock coat, brushed imaginary lint from his epaulettes, and mumbled, "This is exactly why I live on a ship and go to sea."

"What is that supposed to mean?" Kathy narrowed her gaze on her younger brother.

"Nothing, nothing."

Bunny clinked her spoon on her cup for attention. "Kathy, the problem is Mark is still very unsettled by his memories from the hospital. I tell him they will fade with time."

Mark clenched his jaw.

"He was beaten and left for dead. I daresay that would be difficult to forget for anyone." Matthew kept his tone civil – this was the new Matthew, think before tossing furniture about. He knew Bunny well, liked her; however, the woman was too addle-brained for his brother, and much too self-centered.

"You would think so. Oddly enough that no longer seems to bother him. It is his care at the hospital that bedevils him."

Mary Margaret nodded vigorously. "I daresay it probably was the awful food they served him. He was incredibly incontinent when he first arrived home. Such a mess…"

Mark moaned softly and shifted in his seat. He hated being center of attention. Besides, his own sisters seemed especially adept in humiliating him. "I can tell you one thing, it is good to be back in my own home, away from all the 'assistance' I was subjected to here."

Fitzwilliam puffed on his pipe. "That apartment you live in is not a home – there's no heart there without a wife. It's a wardrobe in which to store your clothes."

Emboldened now, Bunny continued. "I tell him that all the time. The truth is he seems fixated on some dead woman."

"Lucille! I really prefer to discuss this in private."

"Our problem is that we don't discuss it at all, Mark. You refuse to speak with me about her. Besides –"

"Ahem. I hate to interrupt." Deliberately interrupting, Darcy moved to stand behind Mark, placing his hand on the man's shoulder. "However, we must be nearly ready for the performance, am I right, Alice? Time is getting away from us if the children are to have dinner and be put to bed by eight."

"Absolutely right, Father." Alice stood, clapped her hands. "Children, follow me, please. The older ones have been upstairs rehearsing with Father Ted and Mama, so I'll take the little ones with me now, get them into costume. Everyone else, your presence is requested in the Durand theater room in fifteen minutes."

CHAPTER THIRTY-TWO

"AUNTIE ALICE." ANNE MARIE'S EIGHT-YEAR-OLD daughter, Deborah, could hear the family laughing and talking as they took their seats. With the poise of an already accomplished actress, she was on her mark and eager to introduce the players. "Are Grandmama and the Grandpas seated?"

"Yes, sweetheart."

"Good. How is my hair?"

"Beautiful."

"All right, I am ready to begin."

At a nod from his wife Harry Durand began 'Greensleeves' on his violin, the lamps were dimmed, and a sparkling curtain, strung across the stage in the children's playroom, was pulled back to a burst of wild applause and whistles. On the stage stood several giggling Medieval townspeople, including a butcher and a baker, a blacksmith and a flower seller.

Anne Marie and Jamie Durand's children, Deborah and her brother Steven – dressed as a simple farmer and his wife – stepped forward holding hands.

Deborah inhaled. "Well, hello to everyone, Grandpa Fitz, Grandpa Wills, Grandmama Eliza, Uncle Harry, Auntie Anne, Uncle..."

Sitting in the back of the room, Clarissa huffed. "She's not naming the entire family, surely. I thought this was to be just a silly play Alice wrote, not Beowulf."

"Sh!" Alice glared daggers at her cousin's wife before turning back to her little niece, whispering, "Proceed, Deborah."

"Shall I? All right, thank you, Auntie Alice. Well. Hello, Grandpa

Fitz, Grandpa Wills and Grandmama Eliza, Uncle Harry, Auntie Anne, Uncle..." After another soft moan from the back Deborah decided to cut to the chase, "... and, everyone else." Then, as Deborah bowed from the waist, a wildly enthusiastic Steven pulled his thumb from his mouth to do the same, causing his fake mustache to fall off.

"Wait a moment, Debbie." After nearly toppling over the edge of the stage retrieving it, he proudly held the offending piece aloft and shouted at the top of his lungs, "I am six years old and I can print my name."

Thunderous applause followed.

He pressed the mustache onto his chin and bowed.

Deborah shook her head. "Auntie Alice, I cannot be expected to perform under these conditions."

"Steven, be very quiet while your sister speaks her lines. Go ahead, Deborah," whispered Alice. "Remember to speak loudly and distinctly."

Deborah sighed. "Thank you, Auntie Alice, All right. Where was I? Oh, yes. Hello Grandpa Fitz, Grandpa Wills and Grandma Eliza... and everyone else. Well, we're going to do a mummy play – I mean a mummers play – about, well, you know, Saint George and the Dragoon."

"Not *Dragoon*, silly. Dragon," whispered twelve-year-old Innkeeper, Mary Anne. "Remember rehearsal?" She was standing to the right of Deborah and pretending to wash an empty window pane.

"Are you certain? I thought it was Dragoon... sorry. Mary Anne says I mean dragon. All right then. Well. Hello, Grandpa Fitz, Grandpa Wills and Grandma Eliza..."

"I don't believe you need to start at the very beginning each time, dear. Just continue on from where you ended." Alice bit her lip to keep from laughing.

"If you think that's best. How do you do, everyone. As you will see, the beautiful princess Sabra is being held by the dragon and her Papa asks Saint George to kill the dragoon I mean dragon before he kills Sabra – the dragon means to kill her, not Saint George – because there are no more pretty ladies in the kingdom any longer if he does, so... " she gasped in a quick breath, "Saint George comes in and battles the bad knights and then one of them dies but the doctor cures her – I mean him – and then Saint George kills the dragon. The rest of us are the townspeople... you know... such as bakers and candle makers. I guess that's about all of it."

Sarah, the ten-year old blacksmith, her face smudged with charcoal, called out to her cousin from the front of her imaginary smithy. "Do not forget to introduce us all by name, Debs."

"No, no, no, no, no..." muttered Clarissa.

Annoyed with the constant interruptions to her otherwise flawless performance, Deborah set her hands on her hips. "Wouldn't that be rather silly, we all know each other." She brushed the hair back from her face. Her eyes were now adjusted to the darkness and she finally saw her Grandma Eliza. "Grandmama, you're wearing the hair ribbons I gave you for Christmas! You look so pretty!"

"Thank you, my darling. But do go on with the play and introduce the characters."

Deborah nodded. "If you like, but I'm pretty certain you know everyone. Let me see, Benedict is going to be Sabra's father, the King, Louisa and Sarah are going to be the Princess's attendants and Birdy will be the Princess because she already had the costume – but, she looks *really* pretty... and, Amanda Rose and Ewan are going to be soldiers and they have swords and they kill Henry but then James is the doctor – he looks silly in his hat, wait until you see – and, well, he cures Henry... and, Wills will be Saint George because he's the oldest and the suit of armor from Somerton Hall fits him perfectly. Anything else?"

"Here." Four-year-old Henry Darcy, Kathy and George's youngest, waved his hand urgently. "I have to wee."

"You're the baker. You can't wee!"

"I can too!" His hand now clutched between his legs Henry began to search frantically for his mother. Kathy came rushing forward, picked up her son and disappeared out the door.

"Won't be a but a moment. Seems he's already begun..."

Clarissa groaned once again.

Well, the tragic tale went off beautifully from that point onward. The King lamented his daughter's impending fate and the townspeople stomped around waving their arms and shaking their fists at the dragon – a large, green figure cut from wood with stiff red and orange scarves attached to his mouth as if they were flames. When the evil knights, Ewan Durand and Amanda Rose Fitzwilliam, arrived on stage to do battle everyone booed. Dressed identically, they wore matching black caps, tunics and tights, long gloves and carried wooden swords – they even wore matching black mustaches.

Both children dutifully hacked away at the much larger Saint George while Will Darcy tried not to laugh or tumble over in the ancient suit of armor he wore. Ewan and Amanda were laughing so hard by the end that they leaned against each other for support. In fact, by this time everyone was laughing and cheering the battle on.

Almost everyone, that is.

Clarissa had not approved of the children's theatrical going ahead during the country's period of mourning, so she decided her look should be appropriately severe. Besides, she was bored silly and found it difficult to pay attention. After checking the mantel clock for the fourth time she stifled a yawn, then glanced at the pandemonium on stage, only really paying attention when her daughter appeared. How typically revolting for the Fitzwilliam family to have the girl dressed as a boy, and with that disgusting mustache. Then Ewan appeared beside her daughter. She froze.

Good God! They were identical.

Her precious daughter and that bastard boy, so alike in their costumes and fake mustaches they could be twins – their eyes, the color of their hair, their smiles… right down to the dimples in their chins! This was unbearable. Even their mannerisms were alike. *This is deliberate, I'll warrant. This family takes great delight in shaming me, laughing at me behind my back.* Angrily she studied the others, ready to catch any eye wink or derisive expression. *Pretending not to notice are they? Well, this is not* my *shame.*

In reality, however, the only ones watching the play who appeared to be in any way surprised were the servants. It began with a cough, a throat clearing, then whispers behind hidden hands, giggles. One pretty young thing was even emboldened enough to catch Clarissa's eye and smirk.

"How dare you?" Furious, Clarissa jumped to her feet. "Get out – all of you," she shouted.

Matthew caught her wrist. "Have you lost your senses; sit down. You're making a spectacle of yourself."

"You bastard!" She slapped him hard across the face. "Get your hands off me, you're disgusting. You think I care a whit about this repulsive family of yours?" The play by now had stopped, the room frozen in shock, the children frightened, everyone watching in silence. Amanda's eyes filled with tears, she began to move forward.

Matthew slowly rose from his seat, his hand still holding her wrist. Although his voice sounded calm, his gaze held white hot fury. "Clarissa, apologize to my family or leave."

"Apologize? You allow that whore's son…" No one heard what followed because the room erupted with outrage. She was still screaming back and forth with her sisters-in-law when Matthew pulled her out the door.

"Do not say one more word, Clarissa," he warned as he propelled her down the stairs.

"Why? What will you do? You think I fear you, Matthew? I could chew you up and spit you out before the first blow!" He shoved her into the downstairs library and locked the doors behind them.

"This cannot go on Clarissa! You've become unhinged!"

"Unhinged you say! You realize, do you not, that your bastard son will now be the talk of the city, your shame on the lips of all of our friends! Did you hear those servants? They were whispering and laughing, your favorite little tart even smirked at me. By morning every household in London will have heard of this and spread the word. I shall be a laughingstock. How could you do this to me?! I refuse to remain in this family another day."

"Very glad to hear it. Leave."

"Be assured that I will. Do you believe for one moment I will allow myself to be portrayed as condoning this… this… acceptance of your mistress and your bastard son? Never! I will make it clear to all how I was completely innocent, duped by my philandering husband; and, I shall make certain she and her child are publicly shunned, don't think I won't. I shan't be branded by this scandal, Matthew! I do have a certain standing in society, you know."

He lit his cigar calmly. "Have a care, Clarissa. Think before you utter one word that could hurt *my son*."

"Or, what? You are already considered a libertine, a hotheaded, arrogant, opinionated brute; just the sort of man about whom people love to gossip."

"That may be so; however, if you say one word against my son, you will be finished."

"Ha! And how would you accomplish that?"

"Money. The dearest thing to your heart, dearer than God himself. I simply will block your funds. You will have no money, Clarissa. Think about that and close your mouth. Remember, your father gave me complete autonomy over your inheritance. Do you understand me?"

"You wouldn't dare."

"Think again."

"My friends would champion me!"

"Then they had better support you as well."

"You evil man. Now I know why you became so distant from me, so cold. You wanted a divorce so you could be with *her* – but, she's married now, isn't she. Not even your family could weather two divorces without damage. I suppose that is what this is all leading up to, your annual request to end this marriage."

"Yes. I simply want to live again." They stared hard at each other, a bridge had been crossed now and there was no turning back.

Without a word Clarissa turned to a nearby mirror to smooth her disheveled appearance. "You've messed my hair, you beast."

"Look at me, please. Can we end this marriage, finally?" Despite the animosity between them, saying the words out loud was painful, to both of them. They had been young once, in love, immortal. There had been joy then.

Clarissa's eyes moistened and she eventually nodded. "I agree, I've had enough of you." Matthew turned to leave and she tried her last card. "Amanda shall remain with me, of course."

He laughed out loud. "Not bloody likely."

"A child belongs with her mother; the courts all agree. Society demands it."

"We are at an impasse then, my darling. Either we divorce on my terms, in that we share custody of our daughter – and, I shall continue to oversee your funds, the better to keep you silent – or, I shall hand all your inheritance over to the National Society for

Women's Suffrage and cut off all your credit. I've already made the inquiries."

"What! That group of revolutionaries! You know how fervently we have been campaigning against them! You wouldn't dare!"

"I need only contact Lydia Becker and an article about your incredibly startling yet generous donation to the '*cause*' will be featured in the Women's Suffrage Journal. Do you know, I believe with that your father actually will finally turn over in his grave."

CHAPTER THIRTY-THREE

THE PLAY HAD COME TO a complete stop with Clarissa's outburst, everyone stunned into silence. It took seconds for Henry to begin wailing, the child terrified of the tension in the room, then Deborah began to cry and then the others. Tears running down her cheeks Amanda looked from one angry face to another, humiliated and frightened by her parents' behavior. She began to run from the stage when she collided with Roberta and falling off the platform with a crash.

Kathy scooped up the still screaming Henry as Anne Marie reached her sobbing daughter, Deborah, and then both hurried to Roberta to make certain she wasn't hurt. Elizabeth already had Amanda cradled in her arms. "Are you all right, sweetheart?" The little girl panicked when Elizabeth touched the blood dripping down the side of her face.

"I'm bleeding?" she whispered in a shaky voice.

"There, there, dear. You'll be fine. Luke," Lizzy called out, calmly. "Could you send a servant upstairs to fetch the new nanny, I believe you said that she's had training as a nurse? Excellent. Please hurry."

He ran to the door and called for a footman while the rest began crowding in around the little girl, all talking at once, some telling Lizzy to have Amanda lie down, others saying no she should sit up, others insisted she staunch the bleeding by holding a towel on the wound, a comment which was met with a 'certainly not, bleeding should be encouraged to clean to wound...'

"Please everyone," Darcy kept exclaiming to no avail, "let us all remain calm. Step back, give the child some room. Fitzwilliam, will you stop cursing."

"Excuse me... excuse me... move damn it..." Using his cane to slap ankles in his path, Mark reached his niece's side in moments. He was sick with concern, the child as dear to him as if she were his own. "Let me see her, Aunt Eliza." He struggled to sit beside them on the floor, taking a handkerchief from his pocket and pressing it to his niece's bleeding forehead. Damn his brother and that fool wife of his, always fighting, always thinking of themselves first, never considering that it was the girl who suffered most. "You may have a lovely black eye tomorrow, Amanda."

She gulped. "Really?" He grinned at her faint glimmer of interest. "Do you really think so?"

"I would be surprised if you did not. The boys will be green with envy."

Bunny hovered behind him. "Mark? Mark, please be careful; you have a bit of blood now on your sleeve," she bent to whisper in his ear. "Remember we're expected at the opera later."

"That's not a concern of mine at the moment, Bunny." Mark was tired of attempting to understand this woman. Her values would never be his; and, he would end up disappointing them both if this relationship continued.

"The nanny is here," shouted the Mary's in unison. "Come in, come in!"

The family began haranguing the poor young woman the moment she entered the room until she turned to them and raised her hand for silence. "Enough! Be good enough to stop speaking and step back. This child needs quiet and calm, and she alone deserves my full attention. Is that clear to everyone?"

She was so confident, so self-possessed, so poised that for the first time in memory... everyone obeyed. Even Fitzwilliam ceased cursing to see who dared speak so imperiously to his family, then stopped to look more closely at her. How odd. Wherever had he seen that face before?

Crouching beside the child the nanny smiled and gently took the girl's hand. "Hello, little one. Can you tell me what has happened here?" Suddenly shy, Amanda shook her head then buried her face in her uncle's chest.

"That's all right, sweetheart." Mark kissed her forehead. "The children were in the midst of their play…"

When he looked up Mark's brain suddenly seized. He was staring into silver eyes that haunted his dreams, the lips he still felt, the face as familiar to him as his own. It was his angel, his heart and soul, the love he had waited a lifetime for, his very own Inappropriate Clarke.

"Bloody hell!" he snapped. "You're supposed to be dead!"

CHAPTER THIRTY-FOUR

MOMENTS BEFORE MARTHA HAD BEEN resting in her lovely little room, still unsure whether this position had been a wise one to accept.

On the plus side, although she was newly employed with this family, she sensed the mistress was a decent sort and certainly grateful to have Martha there, a refreshing change from having been refused a nursing position at all the charity hospitals and clinics.

However, on the negative, there was yesterday when she had seen Mark Fitzwilliam for the first time from her third-floor window! Heartbreaking. He'd been riding with a woman in a carriage, laughing with his brothers riding alongside on horseback, their resemblance to each other very apparent. He looked wonderful and, best of all, on the mend, thank the Lord. From now on she would be able to see him from afar, but never speak with him again.

In addition, there was a real danger of being discovered. Earl Fitzwilliam hadn't pursued his complaint against her because he believed her dead. Working for a member of his family might expose her presence to him at some point – although that was unlikely. Servants were ghosts in a home, not meant to be seen by gentry.

If he did see and remember her, though, she would surely be sacked. Again. And then where would she find employment? Mr. Bridges had continued spreading his lies, ruining her reputation. There was no future for her now in the career she loved, but in service she could at least have a roof over her head.

Pity. Before she married her late husband, a soldier whose father had been poor cleric, she would have been this illustrious family's equal, a child of great privilege with servants and luxury herself, her father commander of British troops in India. Oh well. No use dwelling on what might have been. The sensible thing was to remember what was. *But, oh, how the mighty are fallen.* A woman had to eat. It was a habit of which she had grown quite fond.

So… if she absolutely had to be in service, at least she was with a family who seemed *uncommonly* grateful for her presence.

And… they were very kind. And very wealthy. And very generous.

And… the children were exceptionally bright. Martha was needed here, and inevitably she would be busy in future as governess as well.

And… most important of all, *they were related to him.* She had not believed her good fortune to have been recommended here by a physician with whom she'd worked. The one bright light was Mark Fitzwilliam. She would be in his world, even if never in his sight, and it warmed her to know a little of his blood ran in the children she would nurture. He would never be aware how close she was, though; nor how dear he was to her. She would live for the times she could see him from afar; not in the same room, of course, but from the top of the stairs, from the shadows.

With his new wife.

She wanted to vomit.

If Papa weren't already dead, seeing me humbled like this would kill him.

The clock on her mantel chimed and she checked her pinned watch for the correct time. In an hour she would have the children's meal to oversee next door in the nursery, she'd be listening to their giggly stories, supervise a few games, and then to bed. Martha was happy to be busy tonight; it would keep her mind off the fact that *He* and his fiancé were just downstairs from her, possibly announcing their wedding plans at that exact moment, the family celebrating and happy. She'd need a bucket nearby.

There was a hard rap on the door.

She hoped the children weren't early, the table setting was far from ready. "Come in."

"You're to come quick, miss. Been an accident durin' children's play and oh miss there's blood everywhere I think child mebbe dead but they sent Tommy for doctor so mebbe she isn't."

"Calm yourself and speak slowly." Martha dropped the book she'd been staring blankly at and hurried past the young maid. "You said there'd been an accident. Is the child still in the playroom," she asked, tying up her shoes.

"Yes, miss."

"Very good. There is a large black bag in the back closet, please bring it down to me immediately." With that Martha hurried out the door, forgetting entirely what was likely awaiting her...

"I don't understand this." Mark sounded both stunned *and* annoyed. When Martha gazed into his blue eyes she nearly swallowed her tongue. "I was told you were dead."

"Perhaps that report was premature," she muttered. Oh, she could stare at him for hours.

"Pardon me." Elizabeth tugged on the nanny's uniform sleeve for attention. "Can you see to the child, please?"

"Sorry, madam." Martha gently stroked the arm of the beautiful little girl clutching his coat. "Is this your daughter, sir?"

What did she say? What the shite was going on here? "No. No, Amanda is my brother's daughter."

"May I see where she is injured, please?" He was still unyielding, staring intently at her, seemingly irritated by her presence. "If you do remember me, sir, then you must remember I am also a nurse," she said softly.

"Of course I do. Amanda, dear, look up." This wouldn't do, he could hardly breathe. Although never truly accepting the news of her death, not in his soul at any rate, not in his heart, he'd never imagined to ever see the woman again! And, here she was within his own family.

A shriek from the maid entering just then made an already tense situation worse. Fitzwilliam stomped forward. "Whatever is the matter with you? Get a hold of yourself. It's just blood, girl, not snakes." Fitzwilliam snatched the satchel from her and handed it to Martha directly, whispering, "And you! After this, *Mrs. Kelly,* you and I are going to speak."

"All in good time, sir. First, I must tend to the child. Please stand back."

Her reprimand astonished him. "Well, I say..." Fitzwilliam huffed indignantly, his fists resting on his hips.

"Excuse me, please. There is so much blood. Do you believe the wound is serious?" Alice asked softly. Martha replied while retrieving items from her bag.

"Head wounds generally bleed a good deal, and almost always look worse than they really are, which I suspect is the case here. Amanda, please don't be frightened of me. I need to clean away the mess in your hair, so we can have a look at your cut, after which we will see what else is to be done. All right?" The little girl nodded but was still trembling, still snuggled closely to her uncle for courage.

"Where is Matthew?" grumbled Fitzwilliam.

Father Ted leaned forward. "Well. There's a good deal of shrieking going on downstairs," he offered. "I am fairly certain it's them."

"Well go down and tell them to get up here!"

"Me? Alone? You must be mad."

"Oh, for heaven's sake! Would someone please go with him?" After a moment Andrew nodded and the brothers slipped out of the room.

Gently blotting the blood from the girl's face and hair, Martha turned to Lizzy. "Is her mother near? I believe that would be a comfort to her."

"Never met Clarissa, have you?" As soon as Luke spoke the words his father slapped the back of his head, a not so subtle warning to be quiet. "Ow! You can't strike me, father, I'm thirty-six years old!"

"Sorry. My hand slipped."

"Shush!" Lizzy gave them both a hard stare, then all watched in silence as Martha tended to the child.

"Grandpa Will?" Deborah whispered loudly. "Is our Amanda going to die?"

"Oh, darling. Of course not, my love." Darcy rubbed her shoulder. "She'll be good as new before you know it."

"I certainly hope so."

"You love her a great deal, don't you?"

"Of course I do. Besides, she borrowed my dolly carriage and I've no idea what she's done with it. She better not have broken it!"

Darcy turned to his eldest grandson. "Will, take her somewhere."

"Yes, sir." Swooping her up onto his shoulder Will then clapped his hands for the other children. "All right my little band of heathens, shall we go have sweets and allow our Amanda some quiet?"

Bored to tears now the children rallied at the thought of more food and began filing from the room, Stephen urging them all to hurry. "As long as Amanda isn't going to die soon, may we have more King cake?"

Darcy then turned to the adults, encouraging them to leave as well. It was like herding blind cats. "Please everyone. We should proceed downstairs and wait for the physician to arrive."

"Darcy has the right of it. Everyone out. Send the leech up the moment he arrives, Darcy."

"Do it yourself, Fitzwilliam. You're coming downstairs as well."

"This is my granddaughter! I am not leaving. You leave."

"Honestly," Alice grumbled. "I cannot believe how you two argue like an old married couple." She and Anne Marie had snuck back into the room and were huddling together on the side, quietly watching Martha, occasionally offering her their expert medical opinions.

"You see, Amanda, it wasn't that bad," Kathy called out from the hallway. She, Harry, and George were also slipping back into the room.

"George! I thought I requested everyone wait downstairs."

"Can't I'm afraid. There's a very unpleasant exchange going on down there. Screaming. Crying. A vase was thrown. Shots may have been fired. It's all rather awkward."

Kathy tiptoed past Darcy then crouched down beside her niece. "Darling Amanda, you look as pretty as ever." She took the child's hand and kissed it. "Now, will someone tell me exactly what happened? I looked away from the stage when, well… I heard a thud and the children began screaming."

"I have no idea," said George. "I looked away as well."

"No one saw anything," added Harry. "Like you we were all watching Matthew and Clarissa."

"I did." Sitting on his father's lap in the shadows, Ewan's small voice broke the silence.

Alex kissed his son's head. "Tell them what happened, lad; and, speak up so they can all hear."

Ewan nervously twisted the lapel of his father's coat. "Amanda's mother began shouting at the servants about our laughing on stage. It was all *my* fault. I didn't mean to be disrespectful, I just found it *so* funny, both of us with mustaches. I'm very sorry."

"You've done nothing wrong, son. Tell them the rest."

"Yes, Papa. Well, Henry began to cry at all the shouting, so Birdy ran to comfort him, but Amanda was crying too and she was running after her parents. They both ran into each other very hard – knocked the wind from Birdy and Amanda just disappeared off the stage. Will she be all right?"

Martha smiled and nodded, satisfied that the injury was less severe than she had initially believed, although the child would need stitches. "Yes, she'll be fine. However, the doctor will be here soon to check on her wound, so we'd best get her up to bed. The children were all to sleep in the nursery tonight, but I should prefer Amanda sleep in my room where I can keep my eye on her. Does that sound all right with you, Amanda?"

"Yes. Thank you." She looked around for her grandfather. "Grandpa Fitz."

"Yes, my darling."

"Will you tell Mama and Papa where I am. I don't want them to worry about me."

"Certainly, my love." Fitzwilliam's smile was strained, *directly after I kill them both.* "Whatever you wish." He pressed his lips to her forehead. "Believe me, I'll be speaking with them."

Martha gathered the bloody cloths, handing them over to the maid. "Shall I carry you, Amanda; or, would you prefer to remain with your uncle?"

"Uncle Mark, if that's all right. Are you able to carry me, Uncle Mark?" Having been through so much these past weeks, the poor dear wasn't taking any chances with strangers.

"Naturally," Mark said, then wondered just how he would do that without the use of his cane.

"Nonsense, you can barely walk yourself. What if you reinjure yourself?" Fitzwilliam huffed, "I'll do it."

Mary Margaret pressed him back. "Father, not with your bad heart. Beth and I can assist. Will that be all right with you, Amanda? I do believe we are her favorite relatives anyway, are we not Mary

Elizabeth?"

"Indeed we are, Mary Margaret, I have heard us say that to her very often."

Amanda giggled, her tears nearly dry. "Yes, please."

Luke and George came forward then to help Mark stand, the child still in his arms, her head bandaged. "Mary Margaret, Mary Elizabeth, if you could each tickle one of her feet..." As he hoped Amanda squealed and began to laugh out loud. With his sisters at his sides supporting both him and their niece, the foursome lurched forward, looking rather comical as they made their way from the room, Mark occasionally stumbling on purpose to get another squeal from Amanda, and a reprimand from his sisters.

"Mark." Bunny, exasperated by this point, was reaching for his arm. "Mark. Look at you. We are obligated to attend the opera this evening – remember? Those acquaintances of ours went to great lengths to secure the box near to the Royal family tier. You cannot go looking like this. Perhaps you can borrow a fresh shirt from Mr. Durand? Mark? Mark!"

Elizabeth gracefully diverted her attention. "You have plenty of time, dear. Not to worry. Why don't we give them a moment to settle the child. Come, sit with me and tell me all about this lovely dress."

CHAPTER THIRTY-FIVE

SHE HURRIED TO HER ROOM, last door down the long corridor, ran to her bed and pulled back the covers. Martha looked about quickly, emotions in turmoil. *He's coming to my room. Mark is coming into my room*! She spun around, searching for anything in view that could be embarrassing to her, grabbing a stocking and a frayed corset to be mended.

She spied the book she'd dropped when summoned and replaced it on her nightstand. The title jumped off the page. '*Disease, Death and Medication, Before and After Smallpox*'. Martha groaned. *Not that, anything but that – I must have another book somewhere in here, something more feminine. Ah, here; what is this? 'Clinical Memoirs on Abdominal Tumours and Intumescence'. Good heavens, I am a boring person*. Then she saw the one she wanted, *Jane Eyre,* and pulled it from the box of books she'd brought with her. *An unlikely tale of a lowly governess and the wounded nobleman,* not that she was trying to imply anything. Hopefully there wasn't a mad wife hidden somewhere in his house, although after meeting his family it wouldn't surprise her. It was a silly book anyway, not one she would normally read; however, she wanted him to see her as female, not just the woman who had nursed him.

There. Now, everything looked neat as a pin – somewhat unusual for her but he needn't know that. When she lit another lamp in a darkened corner, she spied something else… a pair of lace trimmed cotton drawers laying across a chair, and she dove for them just as Mark and his sisters entered, carrying his niece.

He looked at her oddly, then raised an eyebrow.

"What?" Blushing to her hairline she leaned back and stuffed the undergarment into the chair cushion.

"Shall I settle her in this bed?"

"Oh, of course, yes. Here allow me to help you."

Mark set the girl down and Martha began untying her boots and fixing the pillows.

As she worked, he watched her, astonished that his prayers had been answered. She was actually here – she was real, she was alive and not lost to him, and they were in her room, in his beloved angel's feminine, delicate room. Lovely. Just as she was. The only thing off putting was the insipid Bronte book on her night table. *The things women read...*

"If you'll stay with Amanda until the doctor arrives, Mark, I think Beth and I should go down and see to Papa. He was looking a little flushed with all the excitement."

"Of course – by the way, please send up a footman with my cane, if you would."

The Mary's kissed their niece good night, then their brother, after which they were off, chattering away.

Then all was silence.

"This is a charming room," he volunteered finally.

"Thank you. It's very small."

"But the view is absolutely beautiful."

Amanda, who had been keeping her eyes closed against the pain, opened one. *What's this?* Something in his tone of voice had the child looking from her uncle to the pretty nanny, then back again. It seemed as if they'd forgotten all about her. Interesting. Not only was the lady pretty, *but* she was also blushing – her cheeks red as cherries against her pale skin – with Uncle Mark staring at her as if she was a box of candies.

"Well, um, do you know where the child's things are for over-night?" Martha spoke directly to the wall behind Mark, but he didn't answer. He just kept staring.

"Mama didn't bring anything for me to wear. She didn't wish me to stay." Finally, Uncle Mark and the pretty nanny seemed to remember she was in the room.

"What did you say, dear?"

"Uncle Mark, I said that Mama didn't allow me to bring anything for overnight. She was planning on my returning home. I don't feel very well though, my head hurts, and I'd rather sleep here with the others."

Martha felt the child's forehead. "It's just as well you remain, we have no idea when the doctor will arrive, and I cannot allow you to leave without being seen by him. I am certain Miss Roberta will have a nightdress that would fit. Give me a moment to find one." Without another word she slipped silently from the room.

"Uncle Mark, you won't leave me, will you? You'll stay until Papa comes to kiss me good night? Papa always kisses me good night. He will tonight, won't he?"

"Of course, and I will be here as long as you wish."

"Good. Have I made Mama and Papa very angry?"

He sighed. "Child, whatever disagreement is between your mother and father it has nothing to do with you. They both love you very much. You know that."

The little girl nodded and smiled, her eyes beginning to grow heavy. "Do you know, I think Miss Martha likes you, Uncle Mark. Isn't she *absolutely beautiful?"*

"Behave yourself, young lady." He cleared his throat. "But, as long as you brought the subject up, why do you think that?"

"She has wonderful eyes, and a very pretty mouth, and her hair is shiny, and –"

"Not that. I mean, why do you think she likes me?"

"Women just know these things, Uncle Mark." Yawning widely, she drifted off to sleep even as she spoke.

"Good lord."

A few moments later Martha returned to the room. "Here I am. I've found a very nice gown for you. Oh."

Mark put a finger up to his lips. "Too late. I believe she's fallen asleep."

"Poor dear. Well, I still will need to remove her costume before the doctor arrives. Hopefully, she'll sleep through."

Mark turned away for a moment as Martha undressed his niece, slipped the nightdress on her, then pulled up the covers. "There, we'll let her sleep until the doctor arrives." When he looked back Martha was very busy not paying attention to him, dimming the lamp, tucking in the covers, fidgeting with the nightstand, the water glass, the small dish of candies, untucking the covers again; all the while not noticing Mark had come around the bed and was now standing behind her.

"I remember everything now, you know," he whispered, and she gasped. "The four days, the Christmas tree, the wonderful talks. You saved my life from that lunatic doctor."

She spun about. Mark was so close she could feel his warm breath on her face. "Nonsense, I was merely doing my job. Excuse me, sir." Turning sideways she squeezed past him on her way to the other side of the bed.

What in bloody hell? Mark crossed his arms over his chest. He wouldn't allow her to freeze him out like this. He needed answers. He remembered a warm, compassionate, loving woman – not a piece of ice – and he'd be damned if she'd treat him otherwise.

"You fed me! You wiped my chin and we laughed."

"A nurse has many duties, sir. Nourishment, wound care, administration of medicine, cleanliness..."

"You sang to me."

"Are you certain? Cruelty is not normally in my nature, sir."

"Yes, well, you kissed me well enough! Nearly swallowed my tongue!"

"I did not! Besides, you kissed me first!"

Mark grinned. "All right! Now I know I've the right woman."

"Hush! The child."

He lowered his voice again. "Admit it. *We* kissed. Nearly melted the sheet between us. And, if the damn doctor hadn't arrived that day we'd have done more!"

"No. You... you misremember." Her voice was fading, not so crisp now, not so composed. "You were delirious, that's all."

"Really. It was merely the drugs?"

She nodded without looking up, repositioning the already perfect blanket and counterpane.

"There is only one way to be absolutely certain, though, isn't there?"

"Really? And, what would that be?"

Mark came toward her until she was backed against the wall, touched her cheek with the back of his hand. "Just as I remember; skin so soft, so perfect. You have the *most* beautiful eyes too. I've never seen eyes that color, like blue silver. With your black lashes they just mesmerize. And your mouth…" He ran his thumb over her bottom lip. "My God, a mouth like this is why men lose their senses."

Martha blinked rapidly, forgetting to breathe, not hearing a word. She had gone brain dead the moment he touched her. When he slowly covered her mouth with his, pulled her into his arms, she offered no resistance. Her own arms slid instantly, eagerly, possessively, around his waist, around his back, the kiss deepened. Tongues danced.

"You do such wickedly amazing things to my body, woman," he whispered before he wrapped her in his arms again and lost all reason.

"Calm yourself, Matthew. I believe they've brought Amanda to the nanny's room."

With the sound of Ted's voice Mark emerged from his erotic haze, he then heard people running down the hall. "Damnation," he growled as they pulled apart, just a breath of space between them. She was trembling. They were both trembling.

He stepped away just before the door burst open.

Clarissa hurried in first, already shouting at Mark. "How dare you bring my daughter into a servant's room. I insist she be brought immediately to a more suitable location." Matthew went directly to his daughter's bedside. "Amanda?" His voice was gruff with concern. He heard a soft, baby snore. "What is that sound she's making? Why doesn't she answer me? What's happened to her head? Someone bring her clothes to me immediately!" He began to pull back the covers. "I'm taking her home."

"You'll do nothing of the kind!" Martha's firm command, along with a strong yank on his arm, stopped him. "I will not permit this child to be moved until she's been seen by a physician."

"What did you say?" Matthew couldn't believe the cheek.

"I think you understood perfectly me well. The child shall not be bothered until she's been seen by the physician. After he examines her, *he* will decide if she's to be moved or not. Now, drop that bedsheet, sir, you are wrinkling the linen! Thank you."

"And just who in bloody hell are you?"

"That is enough. Keep a civil tongue in your mouth, Matt."

Mark's warning stare surprised his brother, but not half as much as when Mark stepped between the two, as if to protect the impudent servant.

"Wait. What are you doing?" Martha huffed and shoved, attempting to shoulder her way around Mark... but to no avail. He was too big. It was like moving a mountain.

"Have you lost your senses? Who is she?"

Although she was not visible standing behind Mark, her voice was loud and clear. And loud. "I am a trained nurse, sir, charged with the health and wellbeing of this nursery, *that is* who I am! And, until I hear otherwise from my employers, I will remain so! Now I will thank you all to leave my room. This is very upsetting to my patient." Another soft snore filled the silence.

Furious but confused, Matthew fully intended to tell her off, but instead pressed his lips closed. *Bloody hell.*

"You looked the exact same way when Mama would reprimand us for rude behavior," Mark commented, and Matthew began to chuckle.

Clarissa exploded.

"I cannot believe this! Are you going to allow a *servant* to speak to you in that manner? If you were in my employ, young woman, I should take a whip to you."

"Madam, reduced as my circumstances may have become, I still have some standards. There could be no incentive in the world that would compel me to be in your employ. It is clear your governess placed too great an emphasis on superficial physical appearance, and not enough on common courtesy."

"Well! I have never before been so rudely treated. Matthew, don't just stand there! Say something!"

"The moment I hear say her say something untrue I shall be certain to give her a piece of my mind."

"Completely useless, as usual." Clarissa turned back toward – well – Martha's general vicinity, irritated that she couldn't see the wench behind Mark's back. Instead, she jabbed her finger in the air to emphasize each and every word. "And you, I shall see you are sacked!"

"Sacked? You can't sack me, I'm your husband's brother."

"You know perfectly well to whom I speak! Oh, this family is driving me mad!"

"What are you shouting about, Clarissa?" Anne Marie had heard the rumpus down the hall and now hurried inside, the family physician in her wake. "We're receiving complaints from nearby villages."

"I demand you sack this person immediately!"

"Certainly not. He's one of my dearest relations, you know that."

"Not Mark!" Clarissa screamed. "The woman he apparently feels compelled to protect. She's standing behind him!"

"Oh, I see. I was beginning to think you'd lost your mind completely."

"Well, if I haven't by now it wouldn't be for your family's lack of trying!"

"That is just silly, Clarissa, we're a perfectly pleasant family; and, I certainly shall not sack a servant just because you became confused. Do you have any idea how difficult it is to find a qualified nanny, let alone a trained nurse, to care for one's children in one's home? It is practically unheard of. Why, she's even finer than Bridget was. Oh. Wait. Please don't anyone tell Bridget I said that."

"Mark, there you are." Lucille Armitage appeared in the doorway behind the physician. "Hello, everyone. What in the world are we all doing in this tiny room?"

Marked slapped a hand to his forehead. "Oh, damn me – the opera. I'd completely forgotten. Under the circumstances, Lucille, I don't believe…"

"Oh no you don't." She squeezed around the doctor, Father Ted, Anne Marie, Matthew, Clarissa and grabbed Mark's arm, surprised by the pretty young nurse standing behind him. "Oh. How do you do. Excuse me. Mark, you promised Lord Prescott and Lord Llewellyn that you would attend tonight." She turned to the group behind her. "I don't believe it unfitting if one begins to emerge from our great national mourning, do you? Besides, it is a depressing opera. No one attending will actually be enjoying themselves."

"Excuse me," in the jostling for better positions the doctor had been pushed further and further to the back by the others. "I say, might I be allowed to examine my patient, please? I would like to be home by nine o'clock at the latest."

"Oh yes, of course." Anne Marie pulled the man forward to the child's bedside where Martha remained hidden behind Mark, holding Amanda's hand. "Sir Avery, this is our nanny, Clarke. Mark, move your foot. She is a former nurse. And, your other foot as well, Mark."

"Mrs. Clarke? Yes, I remember you from St. Anthony's. Trained with Nightingale, did you not? Exemplary professionals. Very good. Now, let us see to the child. Are you sleeping, little girl?"

Amanda waved her hand around the room, indicating all the inhabitants. "You cannot be serious."

As the physician examined Amanda, Mark touched Father Ted's arm. "Where is Papa?"

"Downstairs. His face was flushed, so Uncle Wills insisted he rest. Poor old Wills is physically holding him down and suffering the worse abuse for it."

"*Mark!*" Bunny stomped her foot. "Lord Prescott is going out of his way to impress you; the least you could do is be impressed!"

"All right, all right, I'm coming." By now Jamie and Harry had arrived and were standing outside in the hallway with the Mary's. They waved a greeting to Mark.

"Dear lord, is there anywhere in this house a man can have a bit of privacy without the entire family assembling as well?"

"Haven't found it yet," grumbled Andrew, peeking around the door frame.

Mark raked a hand through his hair bringing into his sight the blood on his sleeve. "Good lord. Jamie, do you have a clean evening shirt for me to change into, perhaps a neck scarf as well?"

"Of course, Mark. Come with me.

At the door, he turned for one more look at Martha, his mind set. She was everything he'd wanted in a woman without ever knowing, without ever hoping. Now that she was found he'd not lose her again. "Matthew! Matthew, I'm speaking to you!"

"What is it?"

"Make certain Mrs. Clarke is treated with the utmost respect."

CHAPTER THIRTY-SIX

"FITZ, WAKE UP."

"What!" Fitzwilliam jerked up into a sitting position, very nearly rolling off his comfy chaise and onto the floor before he caught himself; looked about. "Oh. It's only you. You scared the drool right down my chin. Hand me a cloth, would you? What are you doing here?"

Darcy pulled a handkerchief from his coat and handed it over, watching his friend carefully, looking for any telltale signs of lingering illness. As far as he could see, though, the old fellow was again healthy as a horse. "I was in the neighborhood."

"So, on a whim, you decided to scare the shite out of me at eight in the evening?"

"There was a time when we would just be heading out the door at eight in the evening, eager for a night of depravity."

"When were you ever depraved, Darcy? As far as I remember you were merely elegantly wicked once or twice."

"I had my moments. You should be in bed, instead of cramped on this old thing." Darcy lowered himself slowly as he spoke, his knees aching from the cold.

"I dislike the direction of your comments. Sorry, rosebud, but you hold no attraction for me."

"'The lady doth protest too much'."

Fitz grunted. "You realize I was in the midst of a wonderful dream involving smoking cigars, drinking brandy, and enjoying a table filled with hot buttered breads, minced pies, roasted goose, smoked hams, venison, puddings, cakes, rich sauces, sweets…"

"No vegetables?"

"No, I said it was wonderful. Best of all there were no children around nagging me about my excesses."

"It's a wonder you have the courage to go on with life, considering the hell you live through every day."

Fitzwilliam finally gave way and began to chuckle. "All right, all right. Just why are you here?"

"This is very serious. I promised Beth and Meg I would discreetly discover if something is bothering you. They're at the house with Kathy and Lizzy, all the women worried to death because Meg said she heard you weeping last night. Truthfully, tell me, Richard, and be brave – was your Madeira improperly chilled?"

"Bosh!" Fitzwilliam pushed up from the settee in search of his pipe. "My daughters should mind their own affairs. Honestly, women these days seem to have completely forgotten that they are the weaker sex. Meg and Beth would do better to find husbands than bother me incessantly."

"That they are still unmarried is your own fault."

"Me? Why am I to blame for everything?"

"They are independently wealthy thanks to your investing for them over the years, have dozens of clever, interesting friends, are welcomed in the finest circles. They want for nothing. They have no need of husbands."

"I should be shot." Fitzwilliam finished packing his pipe and sat. "Bloody hell, Darcy, they *are women*! They should want *children*."

"Why? They have you."

"Perhaps you're right for once." Fitzwilliam puffed on his pipe. "I have been too good to them, I see it now. The daily whippings should *never* have ceased."

"Now, tell me what has you so low, keeping in mind I've known you for over sixty years, Fitz, and you cannot fool me."

"Where do I begin?" Fitzwilliam hesitated, poured them both a glass of whiskey. "I suppose I occasionally dwell on my old memories."

"That's it?"

"Well, pardon me if it I'm not at death's door. Surely memories pester you at night as they do me. Some are wonderful. Some terrifying. Either way I find myself pacing occasionally, unable to rest. You must know what I mean."

"Not at all. I sleep like a log."

"You really know how to annoy a person, don't you?"

"I have my moments. Continue."

"All right. I suppose I may slip into a sort of melancholia some days, miss my children racing through the house, watching them grow and discovering the wonder in the world around them. And the laughter. I dearly miss all the laughter, and the squabbles, and the family gatherings. Do you recollect my explaining to the boys how babies are made, when all they really wanted to know was where their step-brother Harry was born?"

"That fiasco," Darcy grinned. "George raced to speak to me straight away after that lecture of yours. Evidently you left off the naughty parts. Very confusing to him, and when I explained the true details he was horrified, put him off females for a full year."

"Really? I thought I gave a marvelous presentation, even provided a diagram of the female reproductive system using a stick to draw on the ground. Of course, Amanda did say I'd somehow gotten one or two points of the female anatomy backwards. Quite embarrassing." Fitz leaned his head back and smiled, puffed on his pipe. "I was always suspicious that was the real reason Ted entered the priesthood."

"Poor children. What we've done to them. Anything else bothering you?"

Fitz sighed and turned away.

"Oh, spit it out for heaven's sake."

"I miss her, are you satisfied! More and more every day. Damn, it's horrible that she's gone, I actually hate her at times for leaving me. I miss making love to my wife, I miss our fights, our laughter, our friendship. I miss that oneness a couple creates together. I'm only half a person without her." He swiped at a threatening tear. "Damn life to hell. I thought we'd have so much more time together, you see. That is why I hate that bed. Sometimes I can feel her still beside me, can feel her breath on my cheek, her hand in mine. When I turn and she's not there, it devastates me."

"Understandable."

"Glad you approve of my misery."

"What else?"

"Bloody St. Timothy's bum, Darcy. You're like a damn dog with a bone. Well, all right, *if you must know*, I have also begun having nightmares again of my army days, the battles, the butchery, the troops running wild, the looting, raping, the horror and terror, arms and legs everywhere, dead friends. Good God. The screams of wounded horses…"

"Enough. Sorry I asked. Well, the girls begged me to speak with you, so now we can tell them I have."

"Why do women put such importance into *feelings*?"

"Damned if I know."

"Are we done, then; because, all that talking has given me an appetite."

"Fine by me, I already told your butler to send a tray up for us. Gratified you can still scrape together a bit of hunger."

"I may be feeling a bit low, Darcy, not dead."

"That's my little soldier." Darcy took out his own pipe and began to pack it from Fitzwilliam's tobacco pouch. "Is it true about Father Ted? I thought he would be here at least through spring. What's happened?"

"And yet he continues to depress me. Yes, Darcy, Father Ted is leaving earlier than expected. Seems he is to set off for America within a few weeks. At least the children have relatives there on his mother's side of the family, uncles, a few cousins, a native or two among the Algonquins. Amanda's grandmother was from the Abenaki people, I believe." Fitzwilliam abruptly tapped out his pipe with so much vigor he nearly broke the stem. "America is so far. Darcy, I fear at my age I'll never see my son again."

"Don't dramatize," Darcy sighed. Truth was, he dreaded to see the boy leave as badly as Fitzwilliam did; and, America was an immense and often dangerous country. "Could he not refuse?"

"He could, I suppose. Truth is he actually seems eager to go. I always promised Amanda and the children we would return for a visit, but we never did. My fault entirely, I hate ships. Completely selfish, as usual, thought only of myself, but she rarely complained. She gave up so much for me, for the children, was so patient, so kind."

"But, when she did complain?"

"It was at the top of her lungs."

Darcy patted his friend's arm in commiseration just as the servants arrived with trays of food, dishes, tablecloths, the table set up for them before the fireplace. Wine was poured. The men ate for a while in peaceful silence.

But not for long. "Darcy?"

"Yes, Fitz."

"When did you learn about the boy?"

Darcy did not feign surprise at the sudden change in subject. He wiped his mouth and nodded, pouring them both another brandy. "The first day they visited us, just before the holidays began, Amanda and Alex had traveled down from Scotland specifically because Alex was so worried about his brother. I saw the resemblance then. He is the image of you at that age."

"Remarkably good-looking lad."

Darcy rolled his eyes. "What about you? Were you surprised when Ewan and Amanda appeared on that stage together?"

"No. I had believed the woman *enceinte* when she married Durand and ran off; suspected who the father was all these years – but, to actually see the boy!" He swiped away at tears again brimming in his eyes. "Weeping like a damn woman. I am becoming a doddering old fool, Darcy."

"What do you mean 'becoming'?"

"Oh, shut up."

More peaceful silence followed as dishes were removed and sweets were brought forward. A servant opened a box of cigars for Darcy, which he carefully looked over, studied, sniffed...

"Only one Darcy. Those are very dear."

Darcy gave his cousin an icy cold stare. "What?" Fitzwilliam had the grace to look embarrassed, but not much. "All right, all right, take another if you must. Just let me jot this down."

"You skinflint. Now, tell me, was Matthew serious last evening, is he really going through with the divorce do you think?"

"Yes. I tried speaking with him this morning but he's so desperate to be free of Clarissa he'll hear none of it; can't say as I blame him really."

"Fitzwilliam."

"I know, I know."

"I realize Clarissa is a horror, but to dissolve a marriage? There are times I don't understand the world, it moves so quickly now. Sir Cresswell's Court has managed to change the interpretation of matrimony from a sacrament to a contract."

"Spoken like an old fob, Darcy."

"Well, I suppose I am. They'll seek a private, sealed bill, hopefully?"

"Yes. However – listen to this – my brilliant son is allowing her to file under the grounds of cruelty, can you believe it? He wants to prevent her from bringing a charge of adultery into the filing."

"What? No, I don't like that at all."

"I've told him as much – but, children never listen to reason." Fitz pushed his plate away. "Now I've lost my appetite."

"Convenient since you've finished all the food. Have another brandy. How is Mark?"

"Splendid – undertaking a great deal of exercising suddenly, regaining his mobility. He's like a man possessed. Have you heard of Donald Walker?"

"He owns a place near the docks, instructs people in their homes in physical training."

"Very good. Well, he has been attempting to perform his rehabilitation work at Mark's apartment, but there's so little room there. So, I have arranged with Gustav Ernst, an orthopedic machinist based in London, to install one of his portable gymnasiums at my home so Mark can be ensured a full recovery."

"Plus, you'll be able to see him more often."

"Parents of recalcitrant adult children are forced to be devious at times."

"Actually, I was wondering more about that nurse last evening. I sensed… something. Were you able to speak with her?"

"Interesting, that. She was the woman I was hoping to have sacked from the hospital, until I found out she'd passed away."

"I beg your pardon?"

"It's a long, odd story." Fitzwilliam's eyes sparkled. "Apparently, however, he's now changed his mind about leaving for America with Ted, thank God. Also, I was taken to the side by our Mark and instructed to leave her be, that this was none of my concern and if I so much as squint my eyes at her he'll tell my daughters about the secret stash of brandy I have hidden in the false bottom of my dresser."

"They already know about that."

"True. What none of them know is I have another false bottom."

"Not from this angle. Looks damn solid to me. Absolutely immense."

"Shut up, Darcy."

CHAPTER THIRTY-SEVEN

ANNE MARIE HEARD A VISITOR being welcomed at her door by the family butler and, when she recognized the voice, hurried into the hall. "Mark! Hardly see you for years while you travel around the world, and now we can't seem to rid ourselves of you."

"Gracious as always, cousin." Both laughing, they kissed on the cheek.

"My heavens, you're walking very fine these days. More like a cat, less like a racoon."

"Thank you, I think. Have you interesting visitors or is it safe to enter?"

She took his arm. "No one remotely interesting. It's only my sister and your sisters. We're in the..."

"How nice for you all. I thought I'd visit with the children, if you don't mind. Make certain there is no residual trauma from our family festival of fun."

"Not that we don't adore your visits, Mark, but the children really are perfectly fine. As I told you last week, and the week before that, you needn't worry so over them."

"Well... I... have gifts for them. Yes, that's it. I have gifts."

"Are you certain?"

"Yes, of course I'm certain."

"You don't seem to be. Anyway, you cannot go up right now, they're having lessons. Geography. Or drawing. Or reading. Should be finished within quarter of an hour. First come to the conservatory and say hello. We're having tea and playing with paints."

"Who is?"

Could his head injury be flaring up? Perhaps his hearing affected? Kathy had mentioned how she'd needed to shout instructions to him while she'd nursed him, otherwise he completely ignored her. "Kathy and Alice are mud wrestling in the nude out in the garden. The neighbors are furious, say they're ruining the rhododendrons."

"Don't believe it will rain. No."

"Are you all right, Mark?"

"Absolutely. I've already told you I feel much better, even begun riding again. The doctors – wait. What did you say about Kathy and Alice?

"Nothing. Come into the back parlor and visit. We are gossiping at a fever pitch – some of it may even be true. In fact, I hear from my cook's second cousin's great aunt's daughter who works for Uncle Fitz that you and Lucille are no longer speaking. Heard you had a huge row and that she slapped you so hard she injured her hand - which, of course, serves her right. Come and tell us all about it."

"That was weeks ago. It was entirely my fault. I'll explain later."

"You will explain now, come along! We want details. You may visit with the children a little later, perhaps before their naps with Nanny Clarke. Do you know I think she's traveled nearly as extensively as you have, Mark. She's wonderful, feel ridiculous calling her a nanny. She is nurse, teacher, governess, all in one very pretty, very capable little package. And, did you know her father was General Sir Charles James Napier of India?"

"Yes, I had heard. Is that the correct time, Anne?" Mark compared his pocket watch with the immense, Bavarian grandfather clock ticking loudly in the hall.

"Yes, I suppose."

"Damn me, we haven't much time."

"We haven't much time for what?"

"Nothing."

"Mm-hmm. I don't believe you're at all well, Mark. Anyway, I have lovely gossip about Martha's father, Sir Charles. Would you like to hear it?"

"Not particularly."

"Well, Uncle Fitz knew him as well, said he ended a bankrupt, drank himself silly. I think your grandfather wanted Uncle F to court Martha's mother, many years ago. She's remarried some dreadful man. The wife, not Martha. Martha is widowed, you know; married beneath herself, or so I surmise, and Sir Charles and his wife tossed her out. How could anyone do that to their own child? Do you like my hair? Had it all cut off and Jamie hates it, wants me to wear a turban to bed. I said to him, I said, do you have any idea how long it will take me to grow all that hair back? I said, you'd better become accustomed to my hair short for a long while or you can just sleep in your own room. Anyway, they should be finishing up any moment. I mean the geography lesson, not Sir Charles and his wife. He's dead. The children love your visits, Mark, they really do. You should have children of your own, you know. Mark, what do you think of this painting? Mary Margaret gave it to Jamie for his birthday, insists we hang it here in the main hall, but I keep telling her how hideous it is… Mark, did you hear me? Mark?"

Anne Marie spun around in a circle, but Mark was gone.

Shaking her head, she went to rejoin her sister and cousins. "You'll never guess what Mark just told me about that hideous Bunny Armitage."

Mary Elizabeth looked up, completely confused. "I thought we liked Bunny."

"Unca Mark!" Little Steven snatched a paper from the table and ran as fast as his little legs could move. "Unca Mark, look! I drew a map of America for Uncle Father Ted! Did you know is going to America? Pick me up, please!"

"You are a bossy little fellow, aren't you? Hello, Deborah. Oh, I do like your dress."

The little girl had also run to greet him and was now pulling him further into the room. "Thank you. Miss Martha did my hair. I want to cut my hair like Mama's, but Papa said no. Did you bring us something today?"

"Yes, I did but–" He stopped mid-sentence when he saw her. "Mrs. Clarke."

"Mr. Fitzwilliam." She smiled shyly at him and curtsied.

"Why do you always stare at Miss Martha like that, Uncle Mark?" Deborah patted a chair for him. "You make her stammer.

She showed me how to check my heartbeat, she's a nurse. I want to be a doctor someday, and she and I will help all the poor people when I grow up. Sit with us – we are just finishing learning about Boston, Maine. I want to go there someday. Will you take me?"

"Me too!"

"Yes, I shall take both of you to Boston, *Massachusetts* one day, and we may include Miss Clarke as well."

"That will be very jolly. Did you bring me anything?" Steven peeked into a cloth bag Mark had set on the table. "Did you? Ooh, Debby, he did. I see something."

"I can see no grass will ever grow under your feet." He set Steven down, pulled an ornate whimsical little box from the bag then brought the boy back in with a hug. "This is for you."

"I love it! Thank you. I've always wanted one."

"Did you really?"

"Yes!... What is it?"

"This is a cricket box, all the way from China. You keep a cricket in here for good luck, but only for a few days. Then you set it free."

"May I catch one now?"

"Not until the spring, Steven. Then we'll look for one together." He turned to Deborah watching in fascination. "I haven't a cricket box for you, sweet."

"Oh, not to mind, Uncle Mark. I can listen to Steven's cricket sing, can't I?"

"No! He's my cricket," pouted Steven and then immediately felt badly for shouting. "I'm sorry, Debby, I didn't mean that. Here, you can have my cricket box, just don't be sad."

"That was kind of you, Steven, you do the family proud; however, I have a different gift for Deborah." Mark reached into his bag and brought out a small, carefully wrapped package.

"What *is* that?" Deborah asked, her eyes wide as Mark peeled back the tissue.

"Is she a princess?" whispered Steven, standing on tiptoe to see.

"This is a *Jumeau bebe* doll from France. It is rather delicate, so you must be gentle with her."

"I know." Deborah nodded then laid it carefully on their work table and stepped back, clasping her hands together in sheer joy. "She's beautiful, Uncle Mark. Thank you! She's even more beautiful than the doll from Spain you brought last week, and even more beautiful than the scarf from Brussels."

"And I love my music box and my soldiers." Steven wrapped his arms around Mark's neck. "I do hope you come back again next week."

"You like me that much, do you?"

"Oh, yes." Steven nodded. "You always bring us something wonderful."

As the children chatted excitedly over their gifts Martha finished moving the small desks and chairs back against the wall. "All right, little ones, no more school work for today; shall we put away our books in their proper places now? Perhaps we'll start learning about China and France tomorrow. Would you like that?"

Both children nodded vigorously. "Could we learn about Swisaland too?"

"Switzerland, Steven; and, yes. We can talk about Switzerland if you like."

"Good. Then Unca Mark can bring us chocolates!"

While the children stored their books and papers away Mark stepped back and reached for Martha's hand, whispering, "I must speak with you."

"Not here. Not now," Martha shook her head and chewed her bottom lip, watching the children to see if they heard. The truth was there was nothing Martha wanted more than to be alone with Mark again. They had been meeting as often as possible, both inside the schoolroom or outside in the park, but for only an hour each time so as not to raise suspicions. There was never enough time with him, the rushed conversations, the confidences spilling back and forth, the limitless tenderness for each other. The loving. He was relentless in his pursuit, and she was a more than willing participant. It had all begun in earnest weeks before…

On her very first afternoon free from her duties at the Durand household Martha visited her husband's grave. She had not been there in a long while, not since she'd used the last of her small inheritance to return his body from the battlefields of Crimea. Now she sat quietly on a stone bench in the old churchyard, lost in memories, good and bad. Finally, she spoke.

"Sorry it's taken me so long to visit. At first it hurt too badly that I'd lost you; and, of course, I was also a *bit* put out with you for deliberately charging into that cavalry stampede, attempting to save your friends, all drunk as lords. I was more than put out, actually; I was furious! I thought you very selfish, Thomas Clarke, never considering I would be left alone after abandoning everything to marry you – my family, my home, stranded millions of miles away from my country! I…"

She stopped and took a deep breath. "Dear me. Apparently, it still rankles. Sorry. I hate to admit this, but Papa may have been right after all – perhaps we were too young to marry when we did. Of course, we believed we were very grown up and mature at the time, capable of anything. I suppose too that I thought it would be exciting to travel to another part of the world and you were so very handsome in your uniform. In the end you gave your life for your friends, a true hero. Even if they were all idiots." She huffed a lock of hair from her forehead.

"But it has been difficult for me. I've been all alone, lonely enough to want to die some days; and well, the thing is… I've met someone very special. Tom, I have fallen deeply in love. Sorry. Anyway, you may be pleased to learn it is also absolute hell. Yet another incredibly impetuous emotion on my part; still, the heart goes wherever it wants. He's brave, handsome, noble, funny, brilliant. You have no idea how much I hate him." She dabbed her watering eyes with her handkerchief.

"The brute kissed me last night! And, oh my goodness, I melted into a sort of pudding at his feet before reality came crashing down around me. It appears Mark Fitzwilliam belongs to another woman, left with her to go to the opera – I hate the opera – and I stood there like a fool, all sweaty and with my heart pumping wildly. He just walked out, the cad. Why must he be so adorable? Well, he treated me no better than I deserved, a common servant being seduced by the master. Yes, dear, I do realize I'm being overly dramatic.

"If I'd only met him when I was in society, remember? When I was the daughter of General Sir Charles Napier. Of course, I never could have, since I was in India and he was here. Still…"

"Mrs. Clarke?"

A few feet in front of Martha stood the very man of whom she spoke. She stared dumbly at him for the longest time. Perhaps he was a dream. A sick, vile, wonderful dream.

"Mrs. Clarke, I hope you won't think me too bold – however, I followed you here today, when you left my cousin Anne's house. Actually, that makes me sound rather disturbed, doesn't it?"

"How long have you been standing there?" she squeaked.

"Not very long. I wanted to give you privacy. I could see you were speaking to… whomever is in that grave – in fact, it seemed you'd never stop speaking. May I ask who that is?" He had heard enough to know already that it was her late husband, felt the bile of jealousy rise up his throat for a dead man. Good God, he was losing his grip on reality because of this woman. Mark fiddled with his gloves, shifted his weight from one foot to another, nearly dropped his cane, cleared his throat.

She stood proudly. "Not that it is any of your concern, but this is my late husband, Thomas Elvin Clarke. He was a Lieutenant with the rank of Captain. I'd ask him to stand, however…"

Mark stifled a laugh; didn't seem appropriate, somehow.

"… that commission cost him both his life and his last fifteen hundred pounds. He thought that would impress my father. The purchase I mean. It did not. He was killed during the Crimean War. I learned to be a nurse there. After he died, I brought him back with me to be buried near his home – how silly of me, of course it was afterward, I would not have attempted that before – I mean – well, here he is. Are you satisfied?"

"It's nothing to me with whom you speak; however, I noticed he wasn't saying much back."

"He was always very shy. You probably believe it's silly to be speaking to a grave."

"No. On the contrary. My father speaks to my mother all the time. He also has his meals at her resting place during good weather where he argues with her, tells her naughty limericks. Sings. Must for torture for the poor woman. However, I don't find it silly at all. He adored her. He still does. Do you still *adore* Lieutenant Clarke?"

Her legs wobbly, she sat again, looking embarrassed, nervous, uncomfortable. "Adore? No. I will always love Tommy. However, in the end I still am upset that he didn't protect met. He knew I wasn't properly prepared for camp life, I was too young to marry, pampered. He never told me what to expect because he feared I wouldn't go with him."

"Why did you?"

"My father was very strict, my mother unfeeling. They fought a good deal over his gambling and drinking. And, of course, I was curious about life. I wanted to be thought a woman. Most importantly, Tommy had lovely hair." She smiled sadly. "In reality I was a silly, spoiled little girl."

"Yes. Sounds as if you were. Are you done here now? May *we* speak?"

Who could have guessed the man she adored could be so abrupt? And why did she find that bizarrely endearing? "Very well. What do you wish to discuss?"

"You know perfectly well." Mark loosened his suddenly too tight cravat. "There's nothing to it but for me to just say it outright. You'll find I'm a very forthright person. Always speak my mind. You ask anyone, especially my sisters. They're always telling me I'm too blunt for my own good. Well?"

"Well, what? You haven't said anything yet."

"You're in love with me."

"I am not!"

"You were just saying so, to *Tommy.*"

"I thought you were giving me privacy!"

"I lied!"

"Of all the ridiculous, arrogant things. Love you? I hardly know you."

"Nevertheless, you kissed me very thoroughly last evening."

"*You* kissed *me!*" Why *did* he keep pointing this embarrassing fact out to her! "Stand aside, I'm leaving."

"You don't deny you love me because you cannot. I just heard you tell your dead husband that you were madly in love – which must have been devastating to the poor fellow."

"Again, you told me you heard nothing!"

"Stop shouting. I heard enough."

"You – you took advantage of me yesterday. It was unfair – you're a family member and I am a servant. Decent men do not try and seduce servants."

"I didn't need to try very hard though, did I? And what of the hospital? You were not a servant then. No. You were a nurse and I your helpless patient. You could say it was you taking advantage of me."

Martha was shaking now with humiliated fury. "I could barely walk by your bed without you pulling at me," she hissed.

"Aha, so you do remember! And, you loved it! Admit it."

"Of all the egotistical men in the world, you must be their king!"

"You kissed me as if your life would end if you did not. Admit it."

She meant to grab her reticule and stomp away, but only ended up turning in circles in search of it. "To say such things! *And in front of my husband!*" Suddenly she burst into tears. "Why are you doing this to me? Why are you torturing me?"

"Who better to torture than the woman I love?"

The sudden shock stopped her tears. "Hmm?"

"I love you, Martha, as deeply as you claim to love me, and much more. In fact, I *adore* you. I always have, and I always will."

She blew her nose, never taking her gaze from his.

"Kissing you makes my heart race, my blood boil, my entire life worth the living of it! There, I've said it. I've never met any other woman that made me feel like this; and, believe you me I have made a very good sampling on four continents."

"You were doing so well until then," she sighed. Her heart would break if he were lying, if he walked away from her again.

"Yes, well, that's neither here nor there. You're wonderful and beautiful and kind and brave, and I'll not lose you again, damn it! Have I made myself clear?"

She melted. "You think I'm beautiful?"

"I'll never understand women. Of all your qualities that's the least important to me and the only one you seem to have heard. Yes, you're exquisite. Your face has the delicacy of a Delacroix, or a Manet. Your figure would seduce the Pope. Your voice is deep and sweet, like a dozen violins..."

Her knees were buckling...

"Your hair is golden rays of molten sunlight, your eyes a glorious summer blue – are you feeling all right?"

"No. I'm chilled suddenly. And very, very warm. Perhaps I have a fever."

He knelt on one knee before her, taking her hands in his. "Martha, we barely know each other, and yet here we are, loving each other completely. It is so illogical as to be comical, similar to one of those farces by Moliere or ..."

"You were much quieter at the hospital."

"I was in a coma."

She pulled her hands from his. "Please stop being charming for one minute. You left with another woman last evening. Are you engaged to her?"

"Bunny? Goodness, no. I have told her several times that we really don't suit each other, but we've been known as a couple, off and on for a few years, and we had obligations to others that she asked me to honor, so she'd not be embarrassed in front of her friends. Last evening was the end." He rubbed his cheek. "Believe me. Besides, she's decided to marry her cousin, Paul. She'll be a countess then… I suppose you wish I was in a coma again with all my jammering."

Taking his hand again she held it between her own. "No." Oh, his hand felt beautifully warm. "I love hearing you speak, love everything about you in fact; what I imagined you would be like seems to pale beside who you truly are." She caressed his cheek and smiled. "I've never believed in love at first sight before this."

"Must run in my family. My father fell in love with my mother at first sight. Yes. They were at a ball and she was being harassed by some randy soldiers when my father stepped up to rescue her. He said the moment she looked up at him with her huge brown eyes he was finished, said he saw their children in her eyes."

"Oh! That is the most romantic thing I've ever heard."

"Really? When they would tell us children that story we'd all make gagging sounds."

"There is nothing worse than children. And what do you think now?"

"I like children. I'd like several of my own."

"No. I mean about love at first sight."

"I am all for it. Shall we leave now? My carriage is waiting at the gate with hot bricks inside – very warm – and, woman, I dearly need you alone to myself for a while."

"Was that Mark's voice I heard in the entry hall?" When Kathy Fitzwilliam glanced up to speak her cousin noticed she had paint on her nose, chin, cheek and four fingers.

"Yes. This is the third week in a row he's visited, brought some gifts for the children. What on earth have you done to yourself?"

"Why? What's the matter?" Kathy turned when the others began to laugh.

"She was swatting at a fly," answered Mary Beth. "On her face. With her brush."

"I was not!" Kathy flicked the paint from her brush at her younger sister. "It was Alice. *She* claimed there was a fly there and began to attack me, and then I tried to grab the brush from her hand. It's all true. I am afraid Alice is insane and should have been committed years ago."

"Perhaps it was a mole with wings." Alice flicked paint from her brush at Kathy's shoes.

"Vengeful brat."

"Would you hooligans stop flinging paint around. I am running out of tarps."

Kathy chuckled as she wiped her shoe. "Remember the olden days when we painted little tea cups and small tables. We were all so much more ladylike then."

"Where is he?" Mary Margaret was the only truly talented painter in the family, so her concentration rarely left the canvas, except to worry about her brothers and father. And the weather. And age spots. And Greeks.

"Where is whom, dear?"

"Mark. Didn't you just say he'd arrived?"

"Oh, him. He's gone upstairs. He always goes upstairs first. I must say he's looking exceptionally handsome these days, don't you think? One could never guess he'd gone through such an ordeal."

"They'll make a beautiful couple. I hope they have children."

"Who, dear?"

Kathy rolled her eyes. "Bunny and Mark, silly. Such a handsome couple."

Her sisters and cousins stared at her in surprise. "Hadn't you heard?" Alice attempted to wipe paint from Kathy's chin but only spread it further. "Oh dear; well, now that's a mess."

"Give me that rag! What gossip haven't I heard this time?"

"Mark and Bunny aren't seeing each other any longer. It's been weeks."

"Pardon? Don't be ridiculous. Of course they are still seeing each other. They're to be married." As she spoke, the other women shook their heads no.

"I heard from my maid's son's wife – she's Bunny's seamstress – that she's become engaged to her second cousin, Lord Paul. Bunny, that is, not the seamstress."

"Well, bloody hell, why am I always the last to hear things?"

"Kathy, watch your language."

"Forgive my perfectly understandable pique, Anne Marie. Might I enquire when this all took place?"

Mary Margaret sighed with exasperation. "Over the last few weeks – where have you been, Kathy? You know they both kept putting off the engagement; it was obvious to everyone they were looking for better matches over the years. Mark wanted a love match and Bunny wanted a title."

"They'd better speed up the wedding if she wants that," added Mary Elizabeth. "I hear Lord Paul has one foot in the grave already. He's older than Papa."

"Don't be silly, Beth. No one's older than Papa. Be that as it may, Mark Fitzwilliam is a better man than any title. Well, you know what I mean. She's a fool." Kathy's eyes narrowed on her cousin. "And why may I ask does *our* Marcus bring *your* children toys, and not *mine?*"

"Or mine," interjected Alice, stirring the pot. "She must be keeping something from us."

Anne Marie picked up her knitting. "My children are adorable."

"What are mine, frogs?" Alice challenged. "Remind me to trip her when she next passes by," Alice huffed; but Kathy wasn't listening to her cousin. She was sitting back in her chair, staring at the open doorway as little Steven and little Deborah tip-toed past heading toward the servants' stairway and the kitchens below.

"Anne Marie? Was anyone else upstairs with the children when Mark went up?"

"Yes, of course. Nanny Clarke. I really must stop calling her that. She's so much more – a governess, a nurse, and a nanny all rolled into one. And, she comes from a wonderful family. Her father was Lord… something or other, I forget again. My memory is getting dreadful. Very important somewhere, I believe; I cannot tell you the relief I feel having finally found someone to replace Bridget, after all these years! Bridget was very good with Roberta and

Roberta loved her – still does. I could hand my child over to her with not a moment's hesitation. Until, you know, Matthew…"

Mary Margaret and Mary Beth both put a finger up to their lips for silence while Alice and Kathy cleared their throats, casting meaningful glances to Anne Marie concerning a servant setting up tea in a corner of the room.

"Yes. You're right. Well, you all know what I've been through since then, one woman after the other. Either they were too brutal, or too lax, or they stole something, or they drank, or they were acrobats of some sort. It has been terrible. I am so relieved; so relieved to finally find someone who is able to nurse and teach, who was raised as a lady, who… Kathy, did no one ever tell you it was rude to laugh when people are speaking? Unless, they've said something terribly funny, and I don't believe I've said anything even remotely funny for at least five years. Well, what is it?"

"You have visitors."

When Anne Marie turned around she saw Steven and Deborah standing behind her in the doorway, making faces at all their aunts. "What on earth are you two doing down here? Why aren't you upstairs at your lessons?"

"Mrs. Clarke ended class early."

"Really? Well, she must have had a very good reason. I seem to remember, however, that after class you are both to take a nap. Why aren't you sleeping?"

"Unca Mark said we didn't need a nap today. He said that we could go downstairs to the kitchen and cook would have special cakes for us that he sent around the back, but then Mrs. Davies said she hasn't time to prepare them now and that we should come back in a little while. Can we go outside and play until a little while is over?"

"No. Well, certainly not without Mrs. Clarke. Where is she?"

"She's upstairs with Uncle Mark." Deborah covered her mouth and giggled. "They're kissing," she whispered through her fingers.

Even though each of the ladies' jaws dropped open no sound emerged, until suddenly, they exploded with excitement.

All except Anne Marie. "What did you say?"

Playing with the fringe on his mother's chair, Henry wrinkled his nose. "She *said*, Unca Mark and Mrs. Clarke are *kissing*."

"Deborah, Henry, you must be mistaken. Perhaps Mrs. Clarke

had something in her eye." A sense of *deja vu* laughed in her face.

"No. I don't think so, Mama." Deborah fussed with the bow in her hair, shook her head thoughtfully. "Perhaps she had something stuck in her mouth, though."

"What about my clothes, my books." Mark was pulling Martha down the stairs behind him. She'd only had time enough to grab her cloak, bonnet and gloves.

"You won't be needing either for the next month or so if I have anything to say about it." He swung her into his arms and looked down both hallways for the butler, Timmons. "Good God. You must have weights sewn into your cloak."

"Mark put me down."

"No. Where is that butler? Stop squirming. Martha, I cannot put you down, you move too slowly and I really don't want to face my female relations at this moment, especially Anne Marie. Ah, there you are Timmons."

"Och, Master Mark, what's this? Has our Mrs. Clarke injured her wee foot?"

Mark turned his back to the man. "In the pocket-book attached to my trousers are two letters. One is our Special License…"

"Mark! What are you saying? I thought we agreed to wait."

"I am saying that I am an academic, a scientist, a mathematician, and the least spontaneous person I know. Look at what you've done to me. You've forced me visit a family friend and obtain permission for us to marry immediately. After all, I must make an honest woman of you now."

"Mark! Hush! *I* forced you, of all the… wait, who is this family friend?"

"The Archbishop of Canterbury. Did you find them, Timmons?"

"Aye, sir."

"Excellent. Remove them both, please. The note is for your mistress. Make certain you hand it to her *after* we've left, not before. You can give me the Special License. We'll be using that in a few moments."

"Och, this is verra unfortunate, Master Mark. The laird spent a good deal of time findin' this lassie for the wee bairns. What'll they do now?"

"It's all in that letter, and I have… there she is now. Answer the door Timmons. Quickly. My betrothed is becoming very heavy."

"You could always put me down."

"Not on your life."

Timmons opened the door to a plump little woman with a bright smile. "Can I help ye, madam?"

"Yes, hello, A Mr. Mark Fitzwilliam sent for me. I am here for the position of nanny – *Good heavens*!" Behind the butler Martha and Mark were involved in a passionate kiss. "Oh, I say! This does look like a jolly place to work. Yes indeed."

Martha broke away from the kiss at the sound of that voice. "Annie Kelly! What on earth are you doing here?"

The gregarious nurse looked equally shocked to see that the recipient of all that passion was none other than prim, proper, Martha Clarke.

"What am I doing here! What are you doing here, other than the obvious?"

"I work here. I am employed by the Durand family as the nanny."

"Really, so am I! Wait a moment. Isn't that your Bob Cratchit?"

"Yes, it is."

"Hello, Bob! Well! As I live and breathe, things are looking better and better. Does he work here as well?"

Mark hefted Martha higher in his arms. "All right, that does it – my arms are breaking. Miss Kelly, enjoy your new life. Your wages will be doubled if you prove satisfactory to my cousin after three months. Now, if you will excuse us, we are very late for a wedding."

"Your ladyship."

Anne Marie looked up from her children, shock and confusion still written on her face. "Yes. Yes, Timmons."

"I've a note for ye… and I think y'should know there is a lassie waitin' in the library. A Miss Annie Kelly. She tells me that she's our new nanny, hired by none other than Master Mark himself, verra generous – a personal trait t'be greatly admired."

"No. No. This can't be happening. He wouldn't do that, would he?" In answer, her sister and cousins stared back at her, not daring to laugh again. Anne Marie jumped to her feet. "No. No. No.

I could not have lost *another* nanny to *another* bloody Fitzwilliam brother. I'll just have a word with 'Master Mark' right now, give that brigand a piece of my mind! Where is he, Timmons? Pity he is no longer reliant on that cane of his, then I could kick it right out from under him!"

"Ach, miss."

She closed her eyes. "I don't like the sound of that."

"Truth is they left several minutes ago. He carried Mrs. Clarke out the door and right into his waitin' carriage, both o'them laughin' and soundin' verra gay and happy. He said they were gettin' married by Special License."

Stunned speechless, Anne plopped back into her chair.

Timmons' eyes twinkled with delight. "He also said to tell ye all good-bye for now, they'll be in touch with ye when the deed is done… oh, and he added that you'd better keep your eye on pretty Miss Kelly. Ye ken, he has other brothers."

EPILOGUE

1877

THE FIFTEEN YEARS SINCE THE marriage of Martha Clarke and Mark Fitzwilliam in the early months of 1862 saw many changes in the Darcy and Fitzwilliam households, the swiftness of time bringing joys, triumphs, disappointments, sickness, and, inevitably, the passing of loved ones.

Alex Durand succumbed peacefully in his sleep in 1865 at the family home in Scotland, where he and his wife had returned to live out their remaining days happily together, with Ewan leaving for Harrow just before his twelfth birthday.

And, true to his word, Matthew Fitzwilliam left the Durand family in peace, traveling to America – with his brothers, Father Ted and Luke – where he remained until his return directly to Scotland in 1866. With the blessing of their son, Ewan, and Matthew's daughter, Amanda, Bridget and Matthew finally wed in 1867, their children serving as their witnesses.

Sadly, the cholera epidemic of 1867 brought about the sudden death of Mary Elizabeth Fitzwilliam. The family was devastated, of course; her sister, Mary Margaret, found herself lost in a world without her twin. She became quieter and sadder over the years, staying to herself more and more.

In 1868 Mark Fitzwilliam proudly assisted with the design of the new St. Pancras Station in London, called the Cathedral of Railways, and later with the design of The Albert Hall in 1971.

In 1869 Kathy and George's two sons, Benedict and James Darcy, students together at Oxford University, participated on the team that beat Harvard University in the first International Boat Race. The family, every one of them, were there to cheer them on.

In 1870, a few years after his graduation from Oxford, Fitzwilliam Darcy the second, first grandchild of Fitzwilliam Darcy and Richard Fitzwilliam, passed his written exam and was promoted to Lieutenant in the Royal Navy. He had followed the path of his uncle, Admiral Andrew Fitzwilliam, but only after two years of aimlessly traveling around the continent with a group of very wealthy young men with nothing to do and no plans. His parents and grandparents were against the entire idea of his joining the Navy, making the idea just that much more desirable.

So, the grandchildren of Fitzwilliam Darcy and Richard Fitzwilliam were now taking their places in a new world. Amanda Rose Fitzwilliam and Roberta Durand had their first season in society together in 1871, both deemed to be diamonds of the first water, lovely beyond compare and great catches. They received dozens of marriage proposals, refusing them all, deciding to attend University together instead. Although women were not allowed to graduate, they could attend lectures, take examinations, and achieve honors in those examinations.

The independent young women felt perfectly safe attending Oxford, even if they were greatly outnumbered by the young men (a situation Roberta dearly loved) since they had a good many male cousins attending at the same time – including Ewan Durand – all keeping a protective eye on them (a situation Roberta dearly despised.) Romances followed until marriages began.

It was not until the winter of 1877 that the inevitable happened…

It was a bright, cool, autumn morning that saw Fitzwilliam and Elizabeth Darcy resting in their London home. Within days they would be leaving for Pemberley, their estate in Derbyshire, the social season in London now over. They would probably not be returning to London the following Spring, they agreed. After all, they were getting on in years, both in their seventies now.

"William, have Georgianna and her husband decided if they'll be joining us for Christmas this year?"

"I seriously doubt they can."

"Really? That's disappointing. Have you noticed we see her and her family less and less the older we all grow? Now they're living in some far-off country with odd cultures, speaking languages we can never understand?"

"Georgianna is in Ireland, Lizzy."

"As I said."

"Beverly writes me that granddaughter Louisa's confinement is soon. They'll want to be home for that."

"How swiftly the days pass. Imagine, a great-grandchild for Georgianna and Beverly – and from little Louisa. I still think of her as being twelve years old."

"Scottish law allows a girl to marry at twelve years of age and a boy at fourteen, without any requirement for parental consent."

"You can be annoyingly informative at times, William. Oh, I so dislike Christmas without Georgianna though. At least Jane and Charles will be with us, and my sister, Mary, of course. The Gardiners' children as well." Her aunt and uncle had passed on years before; however, their children were still close.

"And Lydia," mumbled Darcy. "There is always Lydia."

Lizzy's embroidering slowed. "I'd forgotten that."

"Have you spoken with Fitz? Is he packed and ready to travel?"

"No. I thought you had. Has Richard been acting oddly these past months?"

"Odder than usual?

"William, you know what I mean."

Darcy lowered his paper. "You're right, of course. Mary Elizabeth's death still haunts him I suppose. A parent should never outlive their child."

"And he's very forgetful lately, his mind wanders to the past."

"I was shouting at him about that just the other day."

"You shouldn't shout at him. It won't improve his disposition."

"I was shouting at him because he is deaf as a brick. Do you ever come upon him just mumbling to himself?"

"Yes," she laughed. "Last week he told me he was arguing with Amanda, still rather cross with her for dying on him."

"I mentioned something to the boys about this. He usually only listens to Harry though. I am please Luke and his wife will be returning home soon from America, along with Father Ted. Fitz misses them."

Just then there was a scratch at the door and a servant entered. "Excuse me, sir. There is a message from Somerton Place." He handed Darcy a sealed note which he opened immediately, his brow furrowing.

"What is it, William? What's happened?"

"It's from Fitz. He says something has come up and we should go on our own to Pemberley without him, that he'll meet us there next week. What in the world is bothering him now?"

"You don't suppose he's ill, do you?"

"Fitz? Hardly. He just loves to dramatize everything, always calling attention to himself…"

"William, you will stop speaking like that about Richard! He's dearer to you than a brother would be. You love him, and he you."

"Of course, I am quite fond of him, Lizzy. Next to you and the children he's the dearest part of my heart. I don't remember a moment of my life without him. Doesn't mean he hasn't spent a good deal of our lives driving me insane, though. Oh, I suppose I should scurry over there and see what his problem is this time."

"I'll go with you," Elizabeth began to look around her chair for her slippers.

"No, no need for you to go out in the cold. It may be nothing. You know how he gets into these moods of his. I'll send for you if it's anything serious."

"Listen to me, Mr. Darcy, Richard is just as much a brother to me as he is to you. Besides, I have an odd feeling about this."

He didn't want to tell her the last line on the message had said, "Thank you for everything, William. Say good-bye to Elizabeth for me. Tell her I'll always love her." With Lizzy's heart paining her in recent days, and the fact she'd just recovered from a chest cold, he preferred her to remain. Only heaven knew what Fitz had done, or what they'd find, the old fellow's mind wandered more than Darcy cared to acknowledge. Recently he'd found him alone and confused, roaming through the rooms of his old home, calling for his children.

"Elizabeth, I forbid it! If there is anything at all seriously wrong, I'll send for you. I won't have you traipsing around London in the rain, half dressed."

Pointedly ignoring her husband of many years, Lizzy called for her maid. "Carson, please come in here and help me find something warm to wear."

Within the hour they had reached Fitzwilliam's odd old mansion to the north of London and Darcy handed his and Lizzy's cloaks off to the Fitzwilliam butler. "Everything all right, here, Niles?" he asked.

"Yes, Mr. Darcy. Very quiet."

"I see. Where is his holiness?"

Lizzy pinched her husband's arm.

"His lordship retired early this evening, sir. If you would like to wait in the family drawing room, I'll have one of the footmen tell the master you're here."

"No, need for that; I'll go up and see him myself. Lizzy, if I ask you to wait here, will you?"

"That depends. Niles, did his lordship retire with a bottle"

"Just the one, do you mean, ma'am?"

"That's what I feared. You go on up, William. Let me know how he is, and Niles, would you please tell Miss Margaret I'm in the library?"

"Very good, madam."

"What are you doing here? I asked you not to come."

He looked pale as a ghost to Darcy, and oddly small, dwarfed among the several huge pillows propping him up in his immense bed, a bottle of expensive brandy in one hand, a large apple tart in the other. On the table besides him was Fitz's old pipe, lit and resting in its usual stand.

"What the hell do you think you're doing?"

"I'm Princess Odette in Swan Lake. What does it look like I'm doing? I'm having some apple tarts. Haven't had one in months – had to wrestle them away from my cook – at least I think she was my cook. Anyway, the old dear put up quite a fight. Good thing she has only one leg."

"You know that is not what I mean. The physicians warned you last week you simply must stop drinking and smoking. Your heart is fragile."

"My heart is finally ticking off, and it's about time too." He finished off the tart and licked his fingers. "Cooks' apple tarts are superb. Don't ever tell Amanda I said that." He swigged at the bottle of brandy, grabbed his pipe, closed his eyes with a contented sigh.

"You're a damn old fool! There is nothing for it but to send for the children. Perhaps they'll have better luck knocking some sense into you."

"I better drink faster then."

"Fitz."

"What, Darcy? How do you plan on spending your last days on earth? Contemplating the appropriate drainage system for Pemberley, or enjoying what makes you happy?"

"Drainage does make me happy, Fitz. Nothing like a well-set plot of pipes to make me weepy and dreamy eyed."

"For heaven's sake, sit down," Fitzwilliam chuckled. "Bring that chair over to the bedside and have a drink with me."

"Only if you promise it will be your last, because drinking at ten in the morning gives me stomach ache."

"I'm not going to die just so you can have a pain free bowel movement, Darcy. I love you like a brother, but I do have standards."

As Darcy settled a chair beside the bed, he fought back his tears. Fitzwilliam was leaving the world the same way as he had entered – a hellion. "You're in pain again, I see."

"No, I'm not. Why on earth do you think that?"

"You're rubbing your arm under the covers. When did they begin this time?"

"Last evening. Fremont promised me one more attack and I'd be done for, so I am holding him to his word." He passed the bottle to Darcy and closed his eyes. "You'll watch over my children for me, of course. You were always a more sensible father than I. Not as much fun, of course; but, more sensible."

Darcy grabbed the bottle, his hand shaking a bit, and noticed a gleam of sweat covering Fitzwilliam's face. *He must be in worse pain than usual. God Damn Fool!* Fitzwilliam, his eyes still closed, interrupted Darcy's thoughts. "Do you think it's true, that we go on after life, that we join our loved ones?"

So that was it, he was rushing to see his Amanda. Darcy huffed and looked away. "Well, if anyone could trick Almighty God into both of those things, you're the man who could do it. You could charm the dew off the roses."

"Or the fat off of King George."

"Or the bloomers off of Lady Deveroix."

"That was a vicious rumor. She never wore bloomers."

As the old friends burst into laughter, they began to reminisce, good memories, and bad. They had spent a lifetime together, had both fought and defended each other. Darcy and Fitzwilliam, a gentleman and an officer, until the end… and, now, Darcy's heart was breaking. "Fitz, you're looking awfully pale. Let me have Niles send for Fremont." He reached for the bell pull, but Fitz stopped him.

"Damn it, just sit with me for a while, we've time enough for fussing doctors. I say, Darcy, do you remember when you first introduced me to Elizabeth, at Aunt Catherine's house that Easter so long ago?"

Darcy sat again and smiled. "Of course I do."

"You were such a proud fool. Desperately in love with the woman and bungling it badly, doing everything possible to sabotage things."

"You were no help."

"I was half in love with her myself. You kept sending me over to Reverend Collins cottage to plead your case, and instead I tried to charm her for myself."

"And very nearly succeeded. Good thing you were still a second son back then, believing you needed to marry an heiress instead of the poor little bluestocking daughter of an addlepated country squire."

"Good for both of us in the end."

"It's been a wonderful life, that's for certain."

"I would not have missed it for the world." Fitzwilliam closed his eyes and smiled. "Oh bother. Kathy, stop hovering! Why is she standing over there, staring at me?"

Darcy frowned, looking around the room as if someone were there he'd forgotten. "What in heavens name are you saying? Kathy isn't here."

"I should know my own daughter, dammit. She's right..." Staring into the darkest corner of the room Fitzwilliam suddenly tensed. Tears flooded his eyes, ran down his cheeks. His hand came up slowly, reaching for something. Someone.

The end came quickly then. His entire body seemed to convulse, he clutched at his chest, there was a single gasp for air, a groan…

And it was over. Fitzwilliam was dead.

EPILOGUE
PART DEUX

WHAT IN HELL WAS GOING on here? Where was he? All around him was darkness with a pinpoint at the end, so he moved toward it, the light beckoning, growing larger with each step, the glow warming. He wasn't frightened, although he should have been. He hated darkness, ever since he was a child when his brother locked him in a cupboard where he sat, terrified, for hours and hours.

And then he saw himself. He was young again, his entire life flashing past, childhood, parents, aunts, uncles, his days at university with Darcy, his days in the army in Copenhagen under the mentorship of Wellington, battle after battle up through the Iberian peninsula and that goddamn bastard, Napoleon, may he rot in hell, the nightmare of Waterloo, then his wife, his babies, his…

"Richard."

He stopped, listened. That voice.

"Richard, open your eyes."

Wary of what was happening, he opened them slowly, seeing the familiar table beside his bed with his pipe, still in its stand, the green wallpaper, the velvet bed curtains, the pillows… and then, lastly, the old man lying there, blank eyes staring at nothing. Lifeless. *Bloody hell. Is that me*? "Well, I'll be damned."

"Richard."

"Amanda?"

Feeling a gentle touch on his arm he turned around slowly.

"Hello, my darling."

"Dear God." And there she was before him, as young and beautiful as the day he'd first seen her chasing her bonnet across St. James Square, the wind tossing and twirling until he caught it, handed it back to her (the hem of her dress fluttering enough to give a tantalizing glimpse of ankle as she ran back to the carriage of her awful mother-in-law). She turned around then to smile at him – that warm, loving smile haunting his dreams still – to thank him.

"Amanda," he whispered gruffly, barely hearing his own voice. He fought back a sob. "Well, where in bloody hell have you been, woman?"

"At your side, Colonel; and, don't take that tone with me."

"I shall take any tone I like. At my side, you say? When?" His gaze devoured every inch of her, but he didn't move, terrified to reach out, frightened to touch. Could this be a dying man's illusion?

"Every moment of every day, every day of every week, every week of every month, every month of every year."

Bloody hell, he groaned. Who cared if he was hallucinating! Pulling her into his arms he felt the softness of her, breathed in the scent of her hair, touched her skin. "If this is a final dream before I die, so be it. God be praised for such mercy." He cradled her face in his hands. "Amanda," his words cut off as he kissed her with all the passion of twenty years without, twenty years of solitude. "Are you really here?"

"Yes, Richard. Where else would I be, but with you?"

"Thank God." He pressed his forehead to hers. "Bloody hell, it's been a while. If I never have before, may I say that I love you. I always have, and it seems I always will."

"I know. And, I love you, always have and always will." She rested her cheek on his chest and sighed with happiness. "Oh, there are so many of our loved ones waiting to greet you. Aunt Catherine is especially eager."

"We're headed for hell then, are we?"

Laughing she threw her arms around his neck. "Oh, Richard, I've missed you!" He dearly loved her laughter. "Bethic is waiting too, along with the three boys we lost in childbirth. They're so happy to have you returned to them… Oh, Richard, look – poor

Darcy."

"Pardon?" Fitzwilliam turned around to see his closest and dearest friend, his cousin, his brother, sobbing over the empty body left behind. "Darcy, no!" Fitz shouted. "It is all right. I'm here!"

"He can't hear you, Richard."

"Nonsense, of course he can. Darcy, pay attention!" Amanda was correct, of course. There was no response – they were in different worlds. "I've never seen him this upset before, he's always the strong one. This is awful."

"Yes, it is. He loves you a great deal."

"Well, I cannot have him like this. He helped me stay sane when you passed. He's the finest, the truest person in the entire world. *Darcy! Speak to me, you bloody moron!"*

He tried to grab this cousin's arm but felt nothing, his hand going through thin air.

"Damnation. Do something, Amanda!"

"There's nothing to be done, Richard. He has a wonderful wife who loves him, children and grandchildren who adore him. He's led a beautiful life."

"That's true, however… "

"There is no 'however' Richard. Life is only for the living, we have no say here."

"What of our children? I cannot abide the thought that they would be upset like this at my leaving."

"You do try a woman's patience, Richard. If you were so worried about the children, why did you constantly disobey the doctor's orders? Did you believe yourself invincible? No, you were totally selfish and thinking only of your pleasures. I know you rarely took the medicines he prescribed."

"Well, thank you very much. I'll have you know, Amanda, after your passing I cared little whether I lived or died! That's true love!"

"Horse feathers."

"Pardon me? I had no life on earth without you, no reason to live."

"Nonsense. You traveled, you enjoyed the attentions of *several* much younger women, you attended the opera, the theatre, the museums. You had an adoring family that rushed about for the sole purpose of making you happy, you had satisfying work to do in Parliament. You had friends that admired and respected you.

You ate and drank whatever you wanted. Explain to me again how dearly you suffered."

"It was not the same, and you know that perfectly well. You make me sound like a self-indulgent child."

"Of course not, darling, but you were *alive*. There was nothing else for you to do, but *live*. I know full well how much you love me; however, you needn't have felt so very guilty about surviving me."

"So, you are telling me the children won't care a fig if I die? Rather disappointing."

"Richard, they'll be devasted. They all love you. Of course, they want you to be with them forever. This will absolutely break their hearts."

"I should bloody well hope so! But, damn me, Amanda, I really did miss you."

"I know, dearest, I know. Well, we are together again, and this time forever – or, until one chooses to return… Oops. Never mind about that, I'll explain later. As for the children, they love you to distraction; they will honor you for the rest of their lives and never forget you. We both will be remembered with tremendous love, through our children and generations to come."

"All right, all right, don't over sell it." Fitzwilliam turned at the sound of Darcy opening the door and frantically calling for the butler. "Poor fellow. He's been my rock for so long, my conscience, my brother. My friend. I hate that I'm hurting him like this."

"He'll be with us soon, dear, and Lizzy shortly after. This is life, Richard; and, strangely enough death plays a large part. We are all presented with experiences, challenges, good and bad, that test our mettle, our character, our faith, our integrity. Darcy is an exemplary man. His descendants will call him blessed." She kissed her husband's cheek then took his hands in hers.

"Listen to me, Richard, *for once.* For all your bluster about wanting the children to miss you, you will not wish to be here when they arrive. I remember watching you and the children in mourning. It was very difficult."

For a moment Fitzwilliam studied his old friend. "You're right of course – do you never tire of being right?"

"Haven't so far. Now, it is time for you to say goodbye."

"Give me a moment with him."

"Of course, take as long as you want."

Fitzwilliam sat on the bed, faced his old friend, and smiled sadly. "Well, I suppose this is it then, brat. For a while. I'm going to worry for you, no matter what Amanda says. You work much too hard for an old man – Lizzy is right about that. You'll need to learn to hand over more and more to George and not be such a stickler. He's a brilliant lad. You know he's wanted to introduce new methods at Pemberley, new ways; however, he would never force your hand. He loves you too much. We all do.

"And, you must admit you can be a right pain in the arse at times, lording over everything, expecting – no, demanding – that others perform up to your meticulous expectations. Georgie *will*. He's got the goods, he'll deliver." Fitzwilliam sighed, there was so much still to say, a lifetime of unspoken emotions. Perhaps women had the right of it, bring everything out in the open, have it done with.

"I never told you this, but it was I who crashed your father's library window when I was ten and you were eight. You received quite a tanning for that. I should have spoken up, but truthfully wild horses couldn't have gotten me back into that house, Uncle George was so livid.

"Well, the truth of it is you drove me mad some days, with your perfect wardrobe, your perfect family, your perfect life, your good looks. I admit it was a relief to see *you* in trouble for once. I mean, look at you! You've never even had the decency to age properly, or gain weight; badly done, especially around me. I always come off a bit wanting in comparison." Fitz looked over at Amanda and saw her roll her eyes, shake her head. *Tell him*, she mouthed.

"All right, all right. Now, here is the tricky bit to say. I have never really got around to telling you… how dearly I love you. There. I do, you know. You have been my brother, not my cousin, for my entire life, my best friend, my boon companion, my brilliant business partner, my confessor, my nightmare. *My conscience*."

Fitzwilliam attempted one last time to place a hand on his cousin's back and Darcy must have sensed something happening because he suddenly tensed, looked up and over his shoulder. And, even though there were tears in his eyes, he smiled.

He knew.

"Finally! Damnation, took you long enough, brat. That's it then, I suppose. Good bye, Will. Take care of yourself; and, watch over my children as long as you can, please."

Slowly Fitz stood, backing away until he reached Amanda's side. She tucked her hand under his arm. "Well done."

"May we go now? Don't believe I can take much more of this." Amanda nodded, and they turned into the bright light that was opening before them. Suddenly, Fitzwilliam began to laugh, he stopped and turned around.

"One more thing, Darcy. I hear that we'll be together again soon! God in heaven, what fun we'll have. In the meantime. though, fair warning, keep your guard up, brat, because… *I'll be back.*"

Pride and Prejudice
By Jane Austen

Darcy and Fitzwilliam, Book One
The Pride and Prejudice Family Saga

Sons and Daughters, Book Two
The Pride and Prejudice Family Saga

Wives and Lovers, Book Three
The Pride and Prejudice Family Saga

Saints and Sinners, Book Four
The Pride and Prejudice Family Saga

By Karen V. Wasylowski

All books can be read stand-alone or as a series
Available in both ebook and print form on...
Amazon, Nook, And other sites

Made in the USA
Las Vegas, NV
23 March 2021

19989406R00173